# THE FREEDOM IN CAPTIVITY



USA TODAY BESTSELLING AUTHOR

## M.L. PHILPITT

The Freedom in Captivity (Fractured Ever Afters #4)
Copyright © 2023 by M.L. Philpitt

ISBN: 978-1-990611-21-6



Warning: This book contains mature content. Reader discretion is advised.

Cover Designer: Cat Imb, TRC Designs
Editing and Proofreading: Rebecca Barney, Fairest Reviews Editing Services
Formatting: M.L. Philpitt

# AUTHOR'S NOTE

The Freedom in Captivity is book 4 of The Fractured Ever Afters series. While his can be read as a standalone, there is an overarching plot which starts in The Hunt in Elusion.

This book takes us a bit backwards in the timeline and begins with the events occurring at the end of The Craving in Slumber, and then occurs concurrently over The Beauty in Scars. There is mentions of BIS' events to act as markers. It then carries past BIS. This was necessary for Flynn and Rozelyn's story.

This book has content some people may find triggering. You can read the content warning list on the last page.

This book uses Canadian spelling. This means words will have U's in them, "re", or double LL's. (colour vs color, centre vs center, signalling vs signaling, etc.) These are not typos.

# PLAYLIST

"Heaven Was Full (I'm Headed Straight to Hell)" by TX2
"Not Strong Enough" by Apocalyptica & Brent Smith
"Numb" by Linkin Park
"rapunzel" by emlyn
"Dial Tone" by Catch Your Breath
"Head Above Water" by April Lavigne
"Dangerous State of Mind" by Chri$tian Gate$
"Shame on Me" by Catch Your Breath
"Let It Go" by Chandler Spirit & Lo Spirit
"Drinking with Cupid" by VOILÀ
"Creeping in My Soul" by Cryoshell
"Still Worth Fighting For" by My Darkest Days
"Another Life" by Motionless In White
"Nightmare" by From Ashes to New
"Middle of the Night" by Loveless
"Save Yourself" by My Darkest Days
"The Death of Peace of Mind" by Bad Omens
"Let Me Leave" by Currents

“I See the Light” by Mandy Moore & Zachary Levi
“Will This Be The End” by Self Deception
“No Longer Broken” by ALPHAMEGA

*For those seeking freedom*

# 1

## FLYNN

Life.

Death.

Two cycles that provide balance. Life and death are constant. Life comes and goes, death arrives and remains, and this is a part of being alive. It's predictable, and for that reason, comforting to me.

In some ways, life *is* death. To be alive means to feel pain. To endure the cruel sting of life's struggles over and over, and it's been like that since the moment I turned five-years-old and watched my mother leave through our run-down apartment's front door, never returning. She deserted me for her own selfish purposes of no longer wanting to be a parent. I was left to my father's vindictiveness and neglect.

Death as a whole is a relief. To dish it out and release the rage that's been building inside me since childhood is easing for my chaotic mind. Then knowing, eventually, Death and I will meet is relieving on its own. One day, life and the misery accompanying it will end. I will be free.

It's been a few weeks since the Corsettis have given me

someone to kill, and I miss the gratification of the act. I almost had one women in my basement, Della, who had tricked Nico, my underboss, but he ended up taking charge of her punishment, eventually even making her his wife. My presence the day he found and dragged her back here was to make a point of what she could have had instead.

Which is why when Nico messages, checking to see if I'm around the mansion or not, I know he's about to remove my boredom in the best way possible.

> **NICO**
>
> I have someone for you. I'll update you on what I need from her soon.

Her. I smile. Women react so differently to torture, but the differences are intriguing.

I exit my bedroom in the soldiers' wing of the Corsetti mansion and head down the hall, toward the basement, to await Nico. Given the time of day, most of the Corsettis are gone, allowing for complete silence as I tread through the ornate hallways that always have me feeling uncomfortable and out of place.

Silence is pleasant. It quiets my mind, subduing its frazzled thoughts and the chaotic way it thinks and analyzes, which can be tiresome.

As I reach and open the basement door, cool air from below greets my entry. Every step I take invigorates me, knowing what my day is about to become, and by the time I reach the bottom, I'm even smiling. A grin my captive will soon fear.

The basement is completely different from the rest of the mansion. It's the darkness within the beauty. Everything beautiful in the world always has a shadow beneath it. Nothing is *just* attractive.

A weapon might look clean and shiny, but it's deadly.

The Corsetti family may appear to be an elite group, but they're criminals.

A woman might look sexy, but she's a devil in disguise.

This lavish mansion is no different: its sprawling grounds, massive multi-floored complex, high, arched ceilings, and antique décor might seem impressive, but beneath it all, there's a shadow of obscurity.

This right here is that very shadow. The basement. A place countering the brightness upstairs, with only a single low hanging light dangling over the chair bolted to the ground in the centre of the room. That metal chair has seen more death than a graveyard. The blood stains on the floor don't get scrubbed away because they're a promise for the basement's next visitor. They say, *this is how it'll end for you.*

Each drop of blood staining the cement is a personal trophy. Every single one represents what *I* did.

Against the far wall, beyond the chair, there's a metal table holding a few of my favourite weapons, kept clean for their next victim. I check them over, recalling each recent kill. A few unable to pay their debts back, so they lose their lives. Those kills were clean and straightforward. Another thought it okay to pocket cash from one of the casinos. So he lost his hands. My fingers brush over the small machete that assisted with that.

At the end of the row, I pick one of my favourite knives. The handle is a smooth wood, the blade three inches long and polished to ensure the blood never rusts the metal. I slip it into the side of my boot before heading to the far corner of the room, toward the rope hanging from a hook for binding options.

When the door opens, I smile again, knowing my boredom will soon be gone.

*Time to play.*

Within seconds, Rosen, Nico's captain, appears first, a small body cradled in his massive arms. Her wrists are strapped together by a zip tie in front of her, and a dirty cloth bag covers her head, which is slumped to the side, meaning she's likely knocked out. A waterfall of blonde hair falls over Rosen's arms. Like, an *insane* amount of hair, a shade so pale, it reminds me of someone I once knew.

"Really took no precautions with this one," I comment appreciatively.

Rosen lets out a grunt, his eyes stormier than I've ever seen them. My own emotions might be trapped beneath barbed wire, but I've become attuned to reading others, and for all Rosen's professionalism, I've never seen him like *this*. The fire behind his gaze could be considered scary for some.

Nico Corsetti enters next, barely sparing me a nod before he erects himself in the centre of the room, arms crossed while Rosen drops the woman to the chair. With a knife, Rosen slices through the zip ties and twists her arms behind the chair. I hand him rope and he methodically fastens her wrists.

In the time he's taken to bind her, Rafael Corsetti and their older, and before recent events, long-lost brother, Hawke, has also come down. Hawke leans against the wooden post that connects the staircase to the building, his arms crossed, his stance similar to both his brothers. One wouldn't know, looking at the three of them, that Hawke grew up away from them.

Rafael slaps his hand on my shoulder as he comes up beside me. "Make this one hurt, Flynn. She's a De Falco."

Another one. It's been made common knowledge through the soldier lines that Stefano De Falco has been causing issues for Nico and his family. His most recent plan was to use Della, his stepdaughter, to lure Nico to his death, but based on the wedding ring that now decorates her left hand, De Falco's objective didn't go as planned. But if the woman in the chair is another De Falco, it makes me wonder how many he has in his reservoir to use.

"What'd she do?" Not that it makes much of a difference. If Nico commands death, she receives death, but I ask out of curiosity.

"Drugged Aurora," Rosen replies sharply. "She's in the fucking hospital because of this bitch."

This scrap of a woman *hurt* a Corsetti? My responding snarl is menacing, the need for everyone down here to go away growing with every passing second so I can deliver retribution for the family who've only ever done right by me. Enzo and Caterina Corsetti, parents to three of the four men present, became what mine never bothered to be: caring and supportive about my well-being.

Aurora Corsetti is their daughter, and while I've yet to meet her, I know who she is. Existing with Corsetti as her surname means she owns my loyalty and I'd die for her. She's recently returned to the family after Enzo and Caterina had sent her away as a child in fear for her life after Hawke was kidnapped, tortured, and raped.

That happened a couple years before Caterina found me.

After Rosen finishes tying the woman's ankles to the chair, he stands, glaring down at her. His anger seems stronger than normal, and I reflect on the tone of his words earlier, realization coming to me in a snap. Rosen was charged with protecting Aurora, but his grave expression tells me his protection detail has gone further than it should have. Paired with the dark spots beneath his eyes, the raggedness of his clothing, which I think is —*was*—a tux at one time, and the mess of his hair, he's exhausted. His movements are rough and jerky, uncontrolled and unlike the disciplined soldier I know.

Rosen's in love with Aurora.

Love is a strange emotion, but it's one even I've felt. Once.

It was fleeting and false, exactly like the girl who had enticed those feelings. But I've also witnessed the expression on Enzo's face every time he gazes at his wife like the sun begins and sets with her.

I don't bother with the family politics, but whispers claim Aurora is engaged to the underboss of an American a crime family. Whatever plays out there clearly has no part in Rosen's thirst for revenge.

"Remove the bag," Nico commands.

From behind the chair, I rip the bag off her head, drop it to the floor, and immediately head for the wall to the right for a better view. From my boot, I pull out the knife, mindlessly picking at the blade for something to keep my hands busy until I'm granted the permission I'm craving. But based on Rosen's expression, it's clear he wants the first hit, and I'll have to wait a bit longer.

His attention diverts toward the table at the back of the room, studying over the weapons there. I wonder how far Rosen will take his own revenge; how apparent he's about to make his true feelings known.

Against the wall, I'm able to see the woman's face and my grip barely remains on the knife. Hell, my grip on fucking *reality* scarcely remains.

An angel's face.

*My* angel's face.

Chunks of light, blonde hair fall over her face, covering the small, upturned nose, full cheeks, and light blue-green eyes that always hid a deeper pain, one she was hesitant to share.

Beneath my feet, the cement floor breaks apart, a crack connecting her to me. Like an energy compelling us to be near one another, even after all this time.

I shove off the wall, wanting to stand upright before I fall over—ironic, yes. But the confusion wracking my body needs to end before it drags me down completely, losing all stability.

The woman tied to the chair, a De Falco apparently, is a face that continues to haunt me to this day.

She's the only person to have made me feel *anything*. The reason Caterina found me semi-living when she discovered me hiding out behind dumpster. The reason I understand the fleeting emotion called love.

And one of the reasons I've lived my life covered in hate, the emotion that closely follows the briefest exchange of love.

Once upon a time, I would have died for this woman.

Before Rozelyn was a De Falco, she was *mine*. My friend. My sanity. The bright light that shone through our life of darkness.

I bathed in that goodness, fell in love with her very being, made promises I vowed to keep. Promises she made in return but didn't stand by.

Early on, I learned to look out for myself and myself alone. She was the *only* one to ever make me consider otherwise. To make me want to care for someone else. Even when my own emotional bruises were aching, she was my priority. Kissing away her pain made my own tolerable.

The saying that there's a thin line between love and hate is fucking true. My love for her transformed into hate in the same breath she told me goodbye.

# 2

## ROZELYN

**L**ife sucks.

It's packed full of darkness, even when we don't, or can't, admit it to ourselves. A darkness that begins early in life, and with every passing year, devours more and more of our being. It winds our body, seeps into our bones, and consumes our organs, our heart, and our soul, until the best means to survive is not to feel. To turn it off and only go through the motions.

"Turning it off" looks different for each person. For me, it's being the daughter—stepdaughter technically—to Dad. The one he thinks he needs. Being rude to my other stepsisters, Della and Ariella, when they came into our lives. Pretending to be happy for my own blood-related half-sister, Yasmine, simply so the darkness avoids consuming her. To accept Dad's various means of training, all while knowing I'm the second daughter. The one he doesn't care for.

Not like he does Yasmine.

In some ways, compared to what he did to Della and Ariella, my situation is worse.

8

Turning my emotions off meant not feeling. Bring cruel to who I had to be, only thawing when I was alone in my room and was allowed to, before switching it off again and going out to survive another day.

It wasn't always like this. When Mom was alive, life was better, even if that was fleeting too. Until I uncovered the truth of our lives. That was when the darkness made its presence known, using me as a host in the week leading up to Mom's death. Consuming me entirely on the day of her funeral, when the clouds were gloomy, when the mood was sombre, and when I held my weeping sister. I realize now, the environment was forewarning me of what would come. Mom's death signalled the start and end of so much change and chaos.

Of me. Of the life I was familiar with. Of the family I assumed I had.

What *is* family? I wish I knew because in my experience, family removed my individuality. In this life, in the life Dad pretended to build, family was created through blood or marriage relations. Being directly related didn't give a free pass to safety. Just gave us people to use and allowed people to use us.

But when it really mattered most, family was the first to turn their backs on us.

Dad left me in Montreal, so he and Yasmine could escape to British Columbia where the family he actually cares about is, while I took the fall for his actions. But it worked in my favour because while he believes he's in control, the first time he lifted a hand to me was the moment he secured his downfall. I've simply been following along, waiting for a moment to strike.

This moment.

I needed to get the Corsettis' attention and Aurora Corsetti gave me the perfect opening.

The moment Mom died, Dad told me everything. About

who he truly is, why he's in Montreal—every last detail. He did it to bring me into the fold, to train me to continue his work, to assist and become his own private assassin while he plotted and planned for the right time to execute years of work.

But at that point, it was too late. The abuse one occurrence too many. The ongoing reminder that I'm secondary in Dad's eyes, and always have been.

So when the dirty cloth bag is ripped off my head and the stagnant cool air washes over me, I keep my head lulled to the side, feigning sleep as I consider what loyalty and family truly means to me.

In my father's perspective, loyalty is transient. But for me, it can be a lifeline if loyal to the correct person.

Yasmine's fidelity is unwavering. She and I forged a bond, constructed by our father's cruelty toward me. She never asked for any of this hell, and is as innocent as they come, bred into a family with wickedness already immersed into its other members. The one flash of light among it all, and the fragment I still try to preserve.

I've *always* protected her. I'm loyal to her. She's why I followed Dad's insane plans. It's why, at the end of this, she and I will walk away alive and our father will not.

A sharp slap to the face jolts me from my thoughts, but I lock my muscles from revealing I'm awake. Other than slapping me, I want to know how far they'll take the torture from this starting point. They won't kill me because they need me, and as long as I protect my father's whereabouts, I'm valuable.

Another slap, this one harder, and I roll my chin, moving feeling back into it as I slowly blink open my eyes, revealing I'm awake. The hits will likely worsen the longer I fake being asleep, and I'd rather not experience too much pain yet.

"There she is." A cold voice growls. I recognize it instantly as Aurora's bodyguard, from the few times I snuck away from the garden after she left to listen to their conversation. "Wake up, bitch."

I'd expect no other name or treatment, and it's about to get worse.

Peeling open my eyes, I immediately take in my surroundings, starting with the people around me. Aurora's bodyguard looms in front of me. Two feet behind him, Nico, the Corsetti family's underboss and Aurora's older brother, stands poised, glaring. Beside him, I recognize Rafael Corsetti, standing in a similar position to his brother. I've spent the last two years studying every soul inside this mansion, starting with these brothers and their parents. Leaning against a post at the bottom of the steps is another guy, this one's appearance so different, but intriguing. Gothic almost. Bold eyes pin me, but they look less angry than the Corsettis'.

Against the wall to my right is the final person, and another one I don't recognize. His stance is entirely different than the four other men, pressing against the wall like it's holding him up. Rather than hate, his deep gaze seems curious. In some ways, he's more intent than the others, and there's a lulling sensation tugging at my senses. For a second, he makes me forget where I am and what's happening.

His eyes seem...*familiar*. Somehow. Somehow, because of the little features I make out, he's not recognizable.

I move my gaze from him to the rest of the room. A basement. Dim lighting. I'm tied to a chair, the rope digging into my wrists from where they're looped behind me, pulling my shoulders tight. I imagine it won't be long before my arms go numb. My legs are also bound.

Rosen moves behind me and snatches something off the metal table. Metal against metal, and I presume a knife. If they think they'll scare me with weapons, they're wrong. Dad's training was...rough. For this very purpose.

"We should get started," Rosen murmurs, as he returns to the front of me, a four-inch knife in his hand.

He leans over me, getting closer than I'm comfortable with, and grabs a small handful of my hair, using it to tip my neck back. I don't fight because I won't win and fighting his grip will only hurt me.

"You're going to answer some fucking questions for us, bitch."

*And here we go.* I plaster on my best lazy grin, hiking my brow. "And if I don't? You won't kill me because you want information about my father, and whether I hand it over or not doesn't change the status of my life. You won't get rid of the only person who could potentially provide those answers."

They think they have cards to play. I'll show them I already know their hand.

"That's where the knife comes in."

He lowers his hand, placing the sharp blade right at the base of my neck. His teeth bared, the muscles in his arm twitching with force. I'm thankful for his fraction of self-control because I'm certain his bosses wouldn't appreciate me dying yet.

"Why did you drug Aurora?"

*For this reason.* But there's a time and place for the truth, and right now isn't it.

My bottom lip slips over my top, a fake pout. "Aw, did I do that?"

"Why?" he repeats.

When I don't respond, his control lessens a fraction, and the sharp tip digs in slightly. Not enough to cause pain, but more of a sting. I am certain he's drawn blood.

"You could have killed her."

There wasn't enough Fentanyl in the pills to kill her. Just put her down for a bit. I need the Corsettis' help, which means killing one of theirs is bad business.

"One Corsetti down," I tell him though. "That doesn't sound like such a bad thing."

In a flash, so quick I barely catch it, he releases my hair at the same time the blade slides away from my neck. Without his hold, I'm able to move my head again, only to catch a flash of his action in the precise second blinding pain consumes me.

I deserve this. I know that.

I scream as my mind struggles to make sense of the agony. Through heavy, panting breaths, I find the source, spotting the knife sticking out from my thigh, red seeping through my jeans.

"Rosen," Nico snaps in a warning tone. If he says more, his words are lost amidst the pain, blood rushing from my thighs to my ears, dizziness making everything light. White spots take over my vision and my head falls to the side. This time, not feigning sleep, but unable to remain upright.

Rosen's voice cuts through the throbbing, which only increases as he presses his palm to the blade, pushing it deeper into my body. My jaw clamps shut, my teeth digging sharply into my tongue as I resist screaming again—a near impossible feat.

I won't give them that power. All men have ever done is control me, my body, my discomfort. *They* won't be allowed to.

"Answer me or I will pull this out and we can watch as you bleed to death. Then it'll really hurt."

With heaving breaths, as I fight to remain awake, and a cold glare, I grit a piece of the truth between clamped teeth, "For this. To be—here."

Somewhere in the distance, I hear a snap and Nico commands something in a low tone. The only word I catch is "doctor," which tells me I'm winning before they even know it. A doctor will bandage me up and prevent my quick death, and there's only one reason for that.

Rosen pays his boss no attention, his brows dipping slightly as he demands, "What does that mean?"

I don't answer because somewhere in the darkness, a figure moves. Nico comes up behind his soldier and grasps the back of Rosen's arms, propelling him away from me. Low, through the thick ache, I catch, "You're done. Before you kill the girl, you're finished."

There's a small scuffle I don't catch because my eyes are shutting again, sleep swallowing me whole. More conversation follows but I don't hear it all, the blood in my ears whistling so loudly now.

"...take over from here."

*Ah, so there's someone new in charge of my punishment. Lucky me.*

I should have expected that. Even my father has an enforcer. *Had* an enforcer before Nico stabbed him to death while escaping.

The four other men move toward the staircase and the final thing I notice before sleep takes me completely is the other larger man striding closer. The one with beautiful brown eyes and a captivating gaze that reminds me of someone else.

Someone who, for a short while, made the bad shit in life seem more manageable.

# 3
## FLYNN

"Stay until Dr. Shappo is finished, and then come find me," Nico instructs, before following his brothers and Rosen up the stairs and from the basement.

"Got it."

When the door shuts behind them, I move toward the centre of the room, toward the girl I knew. She's a woman now.

A girl I look back on and believe I dreamt her up half the time. That my shattered, lost brain, going through life frazzled and unfocused, managed to see clearly for a short time.

She went by a different name then, but knowing who she is, it's obvious Stefano De Falco enrolled her into school under a fake name.

I stand over her, looking down at the face I used to stare at all day. She looks like a fucking doll. Full lips and hair that goes on for days. I once wanted to get lost in it, always fascinated with how silky it felt between my fingers. Certainly something my tarnished younger self shouldn't have been allowed to touch.

Even the sight of her now dulls the chaos in my head. She

always had that skill, and I'm annoyed how eleven years later, she still does.

With my thumb, I brush it against her bottom lip. She's as soft as I recall. Kissing her was once my favourite thing. Her skin, I'd touch as long as she allowed me. I never got enough of her.

Now, I wonder how easily it scars.

And then I think about the reason I'll be marking her up.

Clearly, this life stole the girl I cared for. Or maybe I never really knew her. Evil controls her actions, and it did then too, I'm sure. The same as it does for me now.

Rozelyn isn't the girl I remember. The girl with pain in her eyes and a smile to distract as she cared for me in ways no one else ever has. After my mother abandoned me, so did my father in all the ways that mattered. The emotional, physical, and mental abuse was so much, it felt like I was drowning most of the time. School became my reprieve from home, even if I despised the institution almost as much as being at home. Until meeting her, no one wanted me.

But she did.

Or she had for a while. She told me she did, which I learned later, was all a lie.

She's her father's daughter. My enemy. She *hurt* a Corsetti. To hurt someone of Enzo and Caterina's bloodline is to hurt me.

Eleven years have passed since she told me goodbye. Since her lies came tumbling down around her. Therefore, who she was to me can't matter any longer. When she told me goodbye, she earned my loathing. And after recent actions, she's proven to me, it's all she deserves.

Yanking my hand away from her lips, I glance at the knife jammed into her thigh, placed there by Rosen because *she* harmed someone he cares for. If I remove it, she'll bleed to death, and this will be over. She'll return to being a memory of my past.

Judging by the lack of acknowledgement earlier, she doesn't recognize me. I should be pissed, but this could work to my advantage. Maybe a reminder of who I am will shatter her carefully erected walls and I'll break her from the inside.

Before I'm interrupted by the doctor, who's bound to arrive soon, there's one final thing I have to check, to ensure that I'm not imagining this girl to be who I want her to be, regardless of the shared first name and fucking identical appearance. A final confirmation.

I walk behind her, crouching by her tied hands, uncurling one to inspect her palm.

It's there. A small, white scar. Placed there as a promise to one another when we were different people with different goals and life outlooks.

Holding her hand, I uncurl my right one, finding the duplicate scar in the centre of my palm.

When the door opens again, I release Rozelyn with a jerk and move to the far side of the room to give Dr. Shappo, the Corsettis' private doctor, the space to work.

The grey-haired man inspects the blade sticking out from her thigh as he approaches. He frowns and finds me standing behind her. "Already?"

"Wasn't me," I reply gruffly. "Rosen's pissed at her for harming Aurora."

"Nico said to bandage her up," he explains, dropping his small leather bag by Rozelyn's feet. He stands out amongst the grimness of the basement, dressed in a pristine white-collared shirt and pressed slacks. The last time something white came down here and remained white when it left was...never.

"She's not allowed to die yet."

"You staying?" He checks as he unzips his bag and first takes out a square black cloth, which he stretches out on his other side.

"In case she wakes up, yeah."

He shrugs as he gets to work, first removing bandages, cloths, and tools from his bag and resting it on the black cloth by his side, revealing its purpose—keeping the medical supplies away from the disease-riddled ground. Once he slips on plastic gloves, he slices into her jeans, opening his work area and carefully grasps the knife's handle and begins sliding it from her body, a squelching noise filling the room. She gasps, her body jerking, but not quite waking up through the pain.

"Can you hold her still?"

From behind her, I press my hands into her shoulders, using my weight to keep her sleeping body down as he finishes removing the blade and covers it with a cloth, which instantly gets soaked with her blood.

He curses, but his expression remains neutral as he quickly works to hold the injury steady, and somehow, opens a large bandage and retrieves a wad of gauze.

"It looks worse than it is," he states. "Despite the size of the blade, Rosen missed anything vital. It'll heal in about a week. Will probably hurt but I doubt it'll even cause a limp."

Knowing Rosen, he likely was careful on purpose, aware of the precise spot to stab and where it'd be fatal.

Dr. Shappo finishes cleaning the area and wrapping the wound. "I'll have to come down tomorrow to replace the bandages. Possibly sooner. Unless your aim is for her to get an infection."

"Talk to Nico." I shrug, uncaring how they handle this injury. If doc comes back tomorrow, the leg wound likely won't be her only one.

Once he's gone, I double-check her ties, ensuring if she wakes up, she'll be going nowhere and then I exit the basement too, heading right for Nico's office. He's alone and is talking on the phone, but my quick knock on the open door has him hanging up.

"Flynn, good." His phone makes a loud thump as he tosses it to the side of his desk as I approach, stopping halfway between the door and the desk. "You can sit," he offers, though we both know I won't.

"Thanks." I don't move.

"Rozelyn De Falco used her real name on the community garden's volunteer form where she intended to get close to my sister. Whatever her reasoning for it, one thing's certain: she wanted to be found. I want to know why exactly."

I nod once. "She said it was to get in here."

"Exactly," his mouth flattens, "I want to know the importance of her getting captured. Clearly, there's a larger plan at play. After that, figure out where her father is. What he's hiding. What they're planning." He shoves to his feet, as though the aggravation finally gets to him, but instead of walking anywhere, he only turns and stares out the window behind him. "There's a big piece of this we're missing, and I need to know what before this family takes any more hits."

"I'll get it out of her," I tell him with confidence that I certainly don't feel.

When was the last time a prisoner made me second-guess my own abilities?

Never.

I should admit it to Nico, tell them all about my previous connection to her. Hiding this fact feels like a betrayal. Like, I *should* be admitting my knowledge of Rozelyn and her past—and *our* past, but then he'll question me, and I don't want to let him, or his family down.

"Sir—" But as fast as I start, I stop.

Nico turns. "Yeah?"

"Never mind." I step back, signalling I have nothing more to add. "I'll go back down there now."

He waves me away with an exhausted look of an underboss carrying too much on him. "Find me the second you know anything."

Once I leave Nico, I have new vigour coursing through me. This will be revenge, not only for the Corsettis, but for me too.

Rozelyn'll realize that after all this time of her holding my heart in her tight, little grasp, she's now in mine.

Mine to torture.

Mine to play with.

*Mine.*

I find her still passed out in the chair. It could be hours before she wakes. I check over her bandage, checking for any leakage, but it seems like the doc has done good work.

Touching her seems to rouse her, since her eyes flutter open, searching through the basement's lighting. I pull back, placing my face right above hers, studying everything I once treasured.

That mouth when she'd smile upon seeing me.

Those eyes that would brighten when she spotted me in the busy school hallways.

The slight curve of her nose which she always hated, but I believed it added to her charm.

The column of her neck that would move beneath my palm. For as much as she might have looked like a doll, she revelled in being taken roughly.

She moans and rolls her head, blinking again as she tries to focus. Her lips part, a slight huff releasing, as though trying to speak. When she finally does, she snatches away so much of my control with her single word.

"Flynn..."

She recognizes me? I whirl backwards, turning away, my hands scrubbing over my face.

This is precisely what I wanted but not for her to figure it out herself. I wanted to be the one to tear up her reality. An unfamiliar sensation washes over me, and I can't identify it.

Not pain. Pain is being punched in the face by my father.

Not hurt. Hurt is watching the girl I care for leave school one day and never return.

Not desire. Desire is fucking someone in ways so animalistic, the interaction ends with my scent imprinted on her.

Uncertainty. A foreign concept. Do I want her to recognize me?

*I do.* For multiple reasons, I want her to identify me.

I do because when she realizes the person she turned her back on is the one now controlling her life, she'll see another mistake. As much as she might look like the girl I once cared for, she's not.

She mumbles something else I don't make out before her eyes shut again. I'm eager for her to wake and to determine which version I get. In her sleep, her mind has obviously pieced together what's in front of her, but sometimes the conscious and the unconscious don't always mingle.

In her last few seconds, I catch her statement before she passes out again, this time, for good.

"The boy with the pretty brown eyes I..."

# 4
## ROZELYN

I once read that when we're stressed, our mind takes us to the last place we felt the safest. Whether it's when we're asleep or wide awake, our brain makes the journey.

Mine returns to a place it hasn't been in years, to high school. To my brief one-year stint in a public school, which was my attempt to distance myself from my parents, from mafia life, and from Yasmine. Dad was hesitant, but Mom, despite her family's unwanted advice suggesting otherwise, was all for it. She'd do anything for me, even allowing me to pretend to be a regular teenager, knowing one day, the family's pressures would land on my shoulders, and like her, I'd be useful in other ways— for marriage.

In that single year, I found something else. Some*one* else. Someone who I wouldn't have thought could affect my life so completely. But he became who I searched for the moment our driver dropped me off at the front doors each day. The person who needed someone as well, even when he didn't admit it. A loner by preference, but a loser, according to others. But he had scars. Scars he didn't enjoy sharing, but I became the lucky person who managed to get to see them.

After that year, after I was taken from him, I moved on because I had to. I knew he did too. We were a brief blip in one another's misery. It took many months to stop seeking him out everywhere I went, even when I knew I'd never find him amongst the lavish parties, high-end restaurants, or expensive shops.

Despite the memories, the wound in my thigh forces me awake before dragging me beneath the blackness again. Somewhere within it, I see them—his eyes.

Only his eyes. His face a blur of years gone by, of my brain aging the teenager I once knew into the age he should now be— twenty-nine.

This time, the dark eyes pull me from sleep again, but as I straighten my neck, rolling the kink from it, I find the figure standing a few feet away, partly shadowed by where the glow from the lightbulb can't reach, his eyes staring unblinkingly through the darkness.

*No...* That can't be. His eyes *can't* be the same as the ones I'm remembering. This is my mind playing tricks. Taking something I'd been envisioning and shoving it overtop reality is cruel. As if I'm not in enough pain as it is.

"Staying awake this time?"

His voice is deep, sexy, and if the situation was different, I'd appreciate it. The kind of voice I'd enjoy growling in my ear as he fucks me roughly. But it's not one I recognize.

"Does it matter?" I aim for venom, but I'm still sleep-laden and not sure it comes out in the way it should.

"You're no fun to me half-dead."

"Yet, I assume by the time you're finished with me, that's exactly what I'll be."

The darkness moves, his shoulder lifting in a shrug, trying

to downplay the truth within my statement. "Maybe you should have thought of that before poisoning Aurora Corsetti."

I scoff, pretending to not care, even knowing I'm digging my own grave with every action. "You're loyal to your boss, right? To this family?"

The shadow remains silent.

"That's what I thought. So why shouldn't I be loyal to my own family? That's all we can do in this life to stay alive."

False. Loyalty to ourselves is the best method of remaining alive. Everyone else is collateral. Dad taught me that.

The soldier still doesn't respond, but those penetrating eyes hold firm in their stare, making me second-guess everything in my head. I must still be asleep...no?

"Come into the light."

He scoffs, and instead, leans away, crossing his arms.

"I'm serious. I want to see the man who holds my life in the palm of his hand."

"In time. There's no giving without gaining something in return."

*Oh, boy, it's gonna be a dandy time down here.* Now, I'm even second-guessing my plan to hold out the truth for a few days.

If they're going to battle my father and an entire secret society, then they can't do it by storming in, half-cocked. I'll tell them the truth in due time. Enough time has to pass so Dad believes I haven't cracked during my first day of imprisonment, giving him a chance to amass who he needs to and return to Montreal. Here, they fight on Corsetti turf, and Dad has a better chance of losing.

"What do you want?"

"Truths. Where's your father? Why did you poison Aurora?"

"I already told the other guy that." My attention falls on my thigh. "You know, before he stabbed me."

"What did you mean by it?"

That's an element of the truth I can't explain yet, so I repeat, "I needed in here, so I got myself here. You think it's by accident your men found me? Would you all have been so welcoming had I strode right up to the front door and demanded to chat?"

The shadow is silent, as though he's thinking over the alternatives. "That's why you were stupid enough to use your full name on the volunteer documents." It's a statement.

"Precisely."

"Why'd you need in here?"

"That's not how the game works. I gave you an answer, told you why I poisoned her. Now, show me who you are. I deserve to see my captor."

"Your captors are the Corsetti family," he shoots back right away, an edge to his tone. "But the one with your fragile life in his palm is *me*."

Something about that statement makes my heart pound harder, but not in fear. If he is indeed the same brown eyes I'm secretly hoping for, then yes, yes, I do want my life held by him. Even now, after all this time, because I have a shot in remaining alive if it is.

"Does it matter who I am?" he asks.

"Yes."

"You're very persistent."

*Because I need to know.*

"Why *is* that?" he continues. "I wonder if you think I'm someone you know."

*Holy. Fuck. He just confirmed it then. Kinda.*

"Maybe I want to match the sexy voice to a face, so I have something to imagine when I'm passed out from blood loss, starvation, or exhaustion—whichever you choose to inflict on me."

He huffs, which almost sounds like laughter. "You have the same attitude as you had eleven years ago."

*Oh my god. So it's true.* After all this time, Flynn Rhodes is here. In front of me.

*He's not Flynn though,* my brain cuts in. He can't be because Flynn wouldn't sit idly by while I was tied to a chair with my life threatened.

The same second my lips manage to form a word—a single word—his name, he steps forward and out of the shadows.

He's different. His face seems sharper, his body larger and more filled out, dressed in dark cargo pants and a leather jacket. His brown hair longer, shaggier, strands falling around his face like he needs a haircut. His eyes might be what I remember, but the disdain in them is new. He stares at me like I'm dirt beneath his shoe, his lips pulled in a sneer. There's a scar above his lips, which wasn't there in high school. Tattoos creep up from beneath his shirt's collar, up the side of his neck, and over the back of his hands.

He bends, lowering to my height as he studies my face. He's only a foot away in distance but we've never felt further apart.

"Flynn," I breathe, my heart quickly catching up to its new reality. To the fact that after all this time, he's *here*. That the single year I was allowed to be a regular teenager wasn't some far-fetched dream.

"Rozelyn."

The same purr. The same dangerous tone that always caused my pussy to clench in desire. The same soft growl used right before he slammed inside me.

"H-how?"

"Life's funny like that, isn't it?" He straightens, walking behind me.

I turn my head, trying to follow him, but the tight hold of the rope means I can only twist so far. "You're with the Corsettis."

He doesn't respond. I hear nothing, and he's just out of my periphery. Unable to have any warning before he fists strands of my hair and roughly yanks. Pain flits over my scalp and my neck muscles don't have the chance to fight as my head is jerked backwards. He's leaning over me, his teeth bared, something sharp and cold brushing the skin of my neck.

A knife.

"I am a Corsetti, yes. And you're a De Falco. Certainly not the name you were using in high school. Either way, that makes you my enemy."

I can see why he believes that, given everything my father's done. Given what *I* did to their princess, but it was my attempt to remain safe. I'm not on my father's side, or Flynn's. Only mine.

"I'm not your enemy," I tell him, being careful not to swallow too hard and scrape my throat against the blade. "Believe me, Flynn."

The knife and Flynn disappear in an instant, my hair released so I'm able to sit straight again. Only for his menacing form to be in front of me, leaning close, the blade returned to the base of my throat.

Instead of resting it there, a sharp sting immediately follows, and the difference in temperature tells me I'm bleeding. He brushes his thumb over the sting, making it dissipate for the briefest second.

But then he pulls back to show me the dot of red on his thumb, his gaze never releasing mine as he says, "You want me to believe you, *mon soleil*."

*Ooh.* That hurts. That nickname. He started referring to me with that, and it became everything to me. *My sun* its translation. *His* sun. He claimed I was the spot of light in the darkness of his life.

"I have no reason to. You've told me so many lies, so what makes this different? This," he shifts his finger, the light catching on the shine of my blood, "is to prove who we were all those years ago means fucking *nothing*."

He brings his thumb to his mouth and swipes it on his tongue, licking my blood from his skin. Flames ignite in his depths, excited by the taste.

Why was that so hot? Why is my traitorous mind going there?

"How did you come to work for the Corsettis?"

"Doesn't matter."

"What does then?"

"Your life," he replies, his tone lighter than the words deserve. "My past is not important to your present or future. Who I am—who we once were, was a long time ago. So before you think to use it against me..."

His hands dart up, coming around the front of my neck, and he squeezes so tightly, he strikes a gasp from me. His fingers crush my neck, cutting off my air supply. My body jerks in response, my head fighting to be free of his unyielding hold. My arms, while still tied behind me, struggle to be free.

"...remember," he continues, "that isn't who we are now. You may have once been a distraction, but you were one year of my life. The Corsettis have been many. I *am* them. They own my loyalty because they deserve it, and fuckin' pussy I once spent months buried inside does not change a damn thing. *You* don't matter anymore." He leans closer, baring his teeth. "So don't think batting your eyelashes will change how this'll go down."

He's a predator now, and I'm his prey. The boy I knew manifested into something darker and more dangerous. Despite every instinct telling me to stay away, I find myself wanting to know this new version.

"Eleven years changes shit," I summarize. "We're *both* different, so instead of assuming I'd seduce my way to freedom, maybe consider that my goals don't include having sex with a killer."

Despite my attitude, he only smiles. Malicious, but almost genuine, like he enjoyed my comment. The kind of smile I can picture on his face right before he takes someone's life. A killer's smile.

"You forget, I know what you enjoy." His tone drops low, every word measured and capturing my heartbeat. "The force. The chase. The fight. You revelled in being my little slut, no matter who was around. So, tell me, Rozelyn, does fucking a 'killer,' as you put it, really sound that bad to you?"

**M**y hand is around her neck, her skin already cut from my knives. She's a fucking wet dream come to life and my traitorous dick is getting hard just looking at her.

Rozelyn jerks to the side again, trying to escape my tight hold. She doesn't understand that there is no escape. This basement is where her life will end, and the sooner she provides answers, the quicker we can head for the finish line.

"Fuck you," she hisses. "Besides, pretty sure your bosses will have something to say if they find you with your dick buried inside the prisoner."

Maybe. They would find the torture methods a bit different than my usual techniques. But also, maybe not. After all, even the Corsettis have their own inclinations. Rafael owns a sex club and I've spotted Nico sprinting after Della across the property late at night. Everyone has preferences, and my dark, depraved ones are no different.

I chuckle darkly. "You think anyone would know? I'm your only source of company for the rest of your life. The moment

Nico deposited you down here, he was finished with you. You only have one further use for us."

"Telling you where my father is," she fills in. "What if I don't know his exact whereabouts?"

"Then I'd say you're a fuckin' liar. You have to know. Where were you escaping to when Nico's men caught you?"

"Why should I tell you, when, as you said, it's my bargaining chip?"

Believing the information she has will save her pathetic life? I slide my knife to the front of her neck again, poking at her collarbone.

"There is no bargaining. No deals. Just torture." I drag the knife over her pale skin, dipping toward the curve of her breasts. "It's amazing what torture does to the mind, Rozelyn. The way the body screams and fights for relief, for life, all while trying to retain breath. To be awake and focused on the present because the moment you succumb to the darkness, you won't ever wake again."

The sharpened blade pushes into the top of her shirt and with little effort, it begins its tear. I grasp the base of her shirt, holding it firm, my eyes not moving away from hers as I slice her shirt in half, the edges falling to the side to reveal a lacy, black bra that makes my dick twitch. She doesn't blink even as I'm stripping her.

With a firm set mouth, she says, "What if I told you I *will* admit everything, once a few of my demands are met. But not now. In a few days."

*What the fuck is she goin' on about?*

"I'd say you were lying again."

With her chest now exposed, I draw circles with my knife over her breasts. Light enough not to nick her but a threat nonetheless. It dips close to the edge of her bra, only an inch from her nipple.

"I-if I'm not lying?"

Interesting. The subtle hitch of her breath, the stutter in her voice, is enough to prove the effect I'm having. Maybe she won't be so challenging to break after all.

"You'll say anything to live. But I have bigger plans for you, so until you talk, I won't stop."

Her attention drops from me to the knife, and she leans back in the chair, aiming to arch away from it. She can't make it far, and I easily follow, my knife lingering in the valley between her breasts.

"Careful," I warn in a tone implying I don't care if she heeds it or not. "Breathe too hard and you might lose your bra too."

"I'm sure that's your goal," she grits with venom. "Torture, is it then?"

"Yes," I answer easily. "A woman's screams are..." I pause, seeking the best word. "Delectable." Rozelyn's screams will be life-changing. Eleven years of emotion will be released into every injury. "Women are different than men. Break them too fast, they die. They require more paced torture. Daily reminders of what's happening to them."

The knife continues its trajectory, over her stomach, which she tries to cave in, but that's not my endgame so I continue. Over her waistband and stopping with it pointed right at the spot where her pants cover her cunt.

"Torturing a woman is a mental game, and I won't show mercy. We'll be down here for quite a few days unless you want to speak now and end this." I stop, waiting for her to take the offer, but she remains firm in her glare. Shrugging, I add, "So, I wish you luck. May the best person win, but I'll warn you now, I never lose."

Knife in hand, I step away from her, listening as she takes in a gulp of air. I revert into the shadows, taking a seat on the bottom step. Normally, I'd leave a prisoner alone for a few hours, allowing their injuries to become sore and infected between rounds. Someone would be stationed at the top of the stairs on the next-to-impossible chance they tried to escape. But with Rozelyn, I won't leave. I don't *want* to leave.

A truth that causes my stomach to flip with old emotions. Maybe part of the mental torture will be having to see me every day, knowing I claimed control over her life. The constant reminder that our old bond means nothing anymore. One year is *nothing* compared to the life the Corsettis gave me.

Shortly after Rozelyn left, I dropped out of high school. I was only attending because I was legally forced to, but her sudden absence in my life had me questioning its purpose. Attending class became worth it to see her smile. But once she left, she took the meaning with her. Why would I return home to be smacked around, when she wouldn't be able to heal me the next day?

The same day she said goodbye, I wandered the city, reflecting on everything her and I ever spoke about, dissecting her final words. That night, I only went home for a bag of supplies, but never again.

Never returned to that place, or to school, and my father clearly never bothered to report me missing. Dropped-out and lived on the streets, hiding in alleys at night, stealing food when necessary.

It was months later when Lorenzo and Caterina Corsetti found me camped between two buildings, one of which happened to be a club they owned. Hiding behind a dumpster, counting the money I had snatched from a pedestrian earlier that day, Caterina spotted me.

*"Holy fuck, you're just a kid," she breathes, her knowing eyes scanning me, right down to the clothing that needs a wash. "What are you doing out here?"*

*I don't answer.*

*"Enzo, get over here." She pulls at the man standing beside her before approaching me slowly, her rich heels striking against the dirty alleyway.*

*I shy away, tucking my money into my pocket as I push to my feet. From my boot, I snatch my pocket knife, lifting it to eye height in warning for them to stay away.*

*"Wrong choice." The man shoves his wife aside, a gun immediately in his hand, directed right at me.*

*I falter, leaning into the brick at my back. They block the entrance, and the alley's a dead-end, which means there's no escape. A knife against a gun won't win. Given his mass and healthy demeanour, compared to my half-starved, weakened state, I won't win in a hand-to-hand fight either.*

*The woman nudges his arm out of the way, forcing the gun toward the ground. "Enzo," she chastises, "he's a kid. He's scared."*

*"He threatened you."*

*"To keep himself safe." Turning to me, she takes another step forward, her hands held up, palms out in a submissive signal. "We won't hurt you. Can you tell me your name?"*

"So what then?" Rozelyn's voice cuts through the memory, bringing me back to the present.

It's okay though because it was yet another reminder of my reality. Rozelyn's absence drove me to the streets, but Caterina saved me. It started with revealing my name, and then them getting me assistance. A place to stay that night, some food, a shower, and new clothing.

And then an offer. I still don't know why. Why me, a random kid from the streets. All Caterina has ever admitted was she saw something in me that day. They gave me a home, a new purpose in life, and I never looked back, even when they forced me to get my GED, ensuring I at least had my high school education under me.

"You're going to stay down here?" Rozelyn asks snidely.

"There's nowhere I'd rather be. Watching you fall apart sounds pretty fucking appealing."

"Fuck you. It'll be a long few days then because I told you, I have my own plans, and they include shutting my mouth for the time being. It's for your boss's own good."

Her words make no sense. She's always spoken in riddles. Always used words that implied she had a richer education than she ever let on. Like she had come from another life, but never mentioned details. Always avoided my questions when I knew there was something more to her.

"What's that mean?"

She doesn't respond, but honestly, I don't really care.

With a deep sigh, I stretch my legs out in front of me and lean against the brick wall. It's gonna be a long night.

Rozelyn never could handle silence for long, and apparently that habit remains all these years later. "Are you seriously going to keep me chained in this chair?"

Staring through the room toward her, I wonder how much of me she can make out. "Yep."

She grunts. "Getting out of this damn chair would be great. Ever get stabbed in the leg and forced to be upright before? If you haven't, it fucking *sucks*. Find me a bed."

So demanding. De Falco certainly trained her to take no shit.

I laugh humourlessly. "Why would I do that?"

"Because if you want me strong for your torture, I need proper rest."

She's right, but she's still not getting it. "Suffer."

"Asshole."

I am, but now, I want to show her just how much of one I can be. Lifting to my feet, I say nothing to her as I stomp up the wooden steps and into the hallway again, the mansion's warmth so different from the frigid temperatures of the cement basement.

It takes me a minute before I'm returning to her, a fleece blanket and pillow tucked beneath my arms. The moment she spots the stuff, her expression lights up in the same way I used to appreciate, but she quickly folds her lips together, trying to hold back her excitement.

I toss the items by her feet where both land on the dirty ground. Then I return to my spot at the base of the staircase.

"Got you a bed."

She gapes at me, scoffing. "Getting me a bed involves allowing me to get *into* the bed, dick."

"Oh, my little captive," I purr, each word inviting in its own way, "you name-call, I'll show you how much I deserve that name. Now you can spend days staring at something you want but is just out of reach."

Her jaw clenches and not even a beat later, she mutters, "I have to piss."

"Suffer." I recline back against the staircase, staring at her through the dim lighting. This time, she can curse me all she wants, but I'd like to see how long it takes before her bodily needs become too much for her.

# 6

## ROZELYN

**H**ours pass. Maybe. It's difficult to tell because the lack of windows down here gives me nothing to go on. And Flynn, who remains stoic at the bottom of the stairs, seemingly staring at nothing, is no help either.

In those hours, I try to ignore the gentle throbbing in my bladder that increases with the passing time. I despise my body for its natural needs and ignoring it only goes so far. I squirm in my seat, hoping a new angle will take away the pressure on my bladder, but it doesn't.

My mind drifts through every topic as a distractor but centres mainly on my sister. The hug she gave me before getting into the vehicle with Dad to escape the city. The way she clung to me when I reassured her I'd be fine.

And I *will* be. We both will, after I finish this.

"I still need to go," I finally admit with a grumble. "And before you tell me to suffer again, just know, I am."

"Good," he shoots back right away, immediately coming out of his silence. "I'll get you a bucket then."

He lifts to his feet and ascends a step before I stop him with an, "Are you fucking serious right now?"

Flynn pauses, glancing past the wooden post connecting the staircase to the ceiling until finding me, his brows lifting. "Why would you think I'm not? You're not getting out of here for anything."

Because basic fucking human decency says a bucket isn't the most humane method.

"Where the hell do you think I'd escape to? Even if I tried, I'm sure this place is crawling with people who'd love to shoot me."

"So you see then, maybe the bucket is for your protection." He shoots me a cocky grin. "Soldiers aside, consider who else is up there. I believe your ex-stepsisters would love to get a hit or two in."

Della and Ariella. How had I forgotten about them? Dad knows Della ended up on Nico's side, but I never considered what happened to Ariella after their marriage. I guess it's not surprising Ariella's moved into the Corsetti mansion.

I was always such a bitch to them. When their entire family came into my life, I hated them simply for trying to replace Mom. Mom was irreplaceable, yet Dad was doing exactly that, which made no sense considering the love he claimed to have for her.

We were all destroyed by the loss of Mom, but Dad especially. I later learned that he might have married Mom as part of his grand plan, but he genuinely fell in love with her. Losing her reminded Dad of his entire purpose for being in Montreal and he didn't handle this reminder well. He became different...more erratic. In ways, nicer at first, but then crueller. He came down harder on me. His frustrations got heavier, and so did the abuse.

But when everything with Hawke Corsetti had gone down and the man I was supposed to be eventually engaged to—a fact

I learned *after*—fled the city, Dad's entire plan came crashing down around him. If he was crazy before, the loss of the union to the eldest Corsetti made him deranged.

From there, all of his actions got out of hand. That was when he began bringing me into the fold, and when he inserted himself into the Lambert woman's life and wooed her children. Although Dad's emotions were fake, hers weren't, and I despised seeing them fawn over each other. Then came Della and Ariella, who moved into rooms in the same wing as Yasmine and me.

So yeah, I was a bitch. I hated everything Dad was doing and was powerless to stop it. Watching three innocent people fall for his bullshit angered me—*for them*. But my heart was tormented by the fact that she took the name of stepmother when I barely could go a length of time without thinking about Mom.

I was a conflicted mess, forced to exist on the outside. My entire life had purpose—*his* purpose, and I loathed it.

When Della and Ariella lost their mother, I was silently sympathetic, having gone through an identical loss myself, but by this point, I shut my emotions off. The darkness had far consumed me, and it was easier *not* to feel. To let Dad play his games, knowing the Lambert sisters would be used in ways I couldn't stop. Fighting him, fighting the war for their benefit, was useless, so I shut down. Acted nasty because it was easier to pretend than to be the friend who'd later stab them in the back.

"I know what I did, and I won't apologize," I finally admit with a shrug.

Flynn narrows his eyes, calculatingly scanning me. "You're so much of a bitch, you don't have any empathy?"

"You want me to be empathetic toward the people keeping me captive? If you're worried about my safety upstairs, don't bother. I can handle them."

"If you 'handle them,' as you state, be aware Nico won't stand for shit."

I scoff. "Clearly. We arguing about this further or are you going to let me use the bathroom?"

He looks thoughtful for a moment, his lips pursed, before shrugging one shoulder lazily and turning back toward me. "Your funeral."

*Wait, that worked?*

Biting my lip, I hide my excitement to not only have some fresh air from upstairs, but the knowledge that with very little argument, I won.

Flynn walks behind the chair, his size casting a large, dark shadow over me. His musky scent yanks me to another time. A past only existing in my memories.

The ropes fall away from my wrists, and I immediately bring them to my front, twisting and rolling, stretching to return movement to them. I think I even moan, the pleasure of having full control of my limbs returned.

"Isn't it sad to be happy over something so simple?" Flynn rumbles, his heavy steps coming around to the front to undo the bindings on my legs. "Imagine what you'd sound like if I actually gave you something worth moaning about."

"You tell me," I shoot back. "You're the one kneeling."

His movements get jerkier, and I smirk, knowing I've affected him in some way. The moment my legs are also free though, his hands clasp them, replacing the rope that was recently tying them. Keeping me still, he leans closer, his face aligning with mine, his nostrils flaring with his impatient, irritated breathing.

"Careful what you say. I remember you enjoying being on your knees. Still the fantastic cock-sucking whore you used to be?"

Everything inside me wants to glance away, but I won't give

him that satisfaction. The term brandishes my heart, the pain striking me from the fact that it's *Flynn* saying these things. The boy I knew would cut off his hand before insulting me in such a way outside the bedroom. His degradation used to only ever be in the moment.

"Wouldn't you like to know." I tilt my head, aiming for a cocky guise to mask the churning sensation in my stomach.

"Not even in my nightmares." Pushing to his feet, he takes me with him, his hand a heavy belt around my upper arm as he drags me away from the chair but not toward the stairs. Pain flits through my leg as I use it for the first time since being stabbed. It doesn't hurt as much as I expected though. A throb rather than pure agony.

"So, you *are* still dreaming of me then."

He glowers before reaching for a pile of chains on the floor. The rings aren't thick, maybe half a finger's width, but it doesn't stop me from trying to free myself from his grip because I sense I won't enjoy what's next.

"What the hell is wrong with you, Flynn?"

Again, no response. He picks up the chains and tosses one roughly over my shoulder. The sudden weight hits a muscle at just the wrong angle, making me flinch, but he pays little attention as he reaches around me, bringing the chain around my neck once, twice, before releasing my arm, the end of the chain in his free palm.

It's not tight around my throat, but heavy, nonetheless, digging into my shoulders. I reach up, tucking my hands around the edge before I'm strangled.

"Relax," he mutters gruffly. "It's looped in a way you won't choke."

"Until you jerk on that." I nod my head toward the end he's holding.

Without warning, his muscle flexes and he yanks on the

chain. I prepare for it to tighten but as he stated, the chain doesn't. Opening one eye at a time, I curse his cocky smirk. At one point in my life, I enjoyed that smirk. Now I can't fucking stand it.

He turns toward the stairs, tugging on my chain until I have no choice but to follow, walking me like a damned dog.

"Is this necessary? Not like I can run anywhere."

"Won't take chances," he answers when we near the top of the wooden steps. "How do I know what you'll do? Desperation drives people to make stupid decisions."

"Why would I work my way into this place and then try to escape the first instance?"

Leaning over me, from where he stands two stairs above me, he growls. "Tell me why I should believe anything you say. You claim to have some master plan, but it makes no sense when it's your father who set you up."

"He left me here for those reasons," I admit, giving him a bit of what I can; nothing he'll be able to use quite yet. "But I took charge of how this is going down, so everything after his initial order is of my own decision, including getting captured."

His eyes narrow. "What does that mean?"

I turn my head away, feigning indifference. "It means I've spoken enough for the time being."

With a final huff, he grants my lungs a welcoming burst of fresh air as he opens the basement door, stepping into the carpeted hallway. I follow behind, without him needing to pull on the chain, enveloping myself into the Corsetti richness.

*Wow.* If I thought I grew up well, the Seven did not set Dad up in any way comparable to this luxury. This isn't a mansion. It's a fucking castle.

Flynn immediately strides down a connected hallway, not pausing to wait for me to catch up as his gait quickens. I speed up too, ensuring he doesn't reach the end of the chain.

"Where are we going?"

Of course, he doesn't answer. He silently leads me toward another hallway, but before taking the turn, my eyes complete a final sweep of the high, vaulted ceilings, the ornate décor on the walls.

Somewhere within this place is Della and Ariella. Somewhere else, a room full of Corsettis. Yet, as we stride through the hallways, we see no one. Mentally, I calculate the days passing Aurora's drugging. The weed gummies were laced with enough Fentanyl to keep her down for a few days, but nothing long term, so it's possible she still hasn't awoken and they're all at the hospital.

"Where is everyone?"

Again, no response.

Flynn leads me down a hallway with a dozen doors, passing many of them until stopping in front of one almost at the end. He slides out a key from his pocket and when the door unlocks, it hits me.

He's brought me to his room.

Flynn steps aside and, taking my arm, shoves me through the open doorway, immediately following. So close, his back brushes mine as he nudges me through the space before slamming the door shut. He flicks on a light and bathes the small space in colour.

A bed is pushed to the far side. A single table beside it with a lamp and a phone's charging cable. There's no décor, and everything is orderly. His dresser drawers are shut, no clothes hanging out. Across from the bed, there's another small doorway, and I catch the sight of white tile, a pedestal sink, and a toilet.

I breathe the room in. It's entirely Flynn. The same scent I spent months burying myself in. I used to enjoy hugging him, smashing my face into his shirt to inhale the musk of his natural scent.

He drops the chain unceremoniously and it thumps to the back of my legs, hitting a muscle at a precise angle that makes me hiss in pain. I reach behind me, bringing the end into my hold.

"Use the bathroom," he demands, stationing himself against his door as a guard. His hands press together in front of him: a stance he's obviously familiar with.

"Your room." I peek behind me, meeting his dark, watchful eyes, which give nothing away. "Why are we in your room?"

"So you can piss."

"But *your* room." Not one of the many bathrooms I'm sure this place is outfitted with. I feel there's a purpose, a deeper meaning, to bringing me to his space.

I wander through, pretending to head for the bathroom, but angling myself toward his bed. It's made, the comforter pulled taut. Like the rest of this place, it's clean and orderly.

"Don't like decorations, huh?"

Heavy steps come up behind me. His hands clamp my arms and roughly, he spins me, shoving me toward the bathroom. "Five seconds, Rozelyn. You have five fucking seconds to enter that bathroom, or we leave, and you hold your bladder until tomorrow."

He doesn't fight when I jerk my shoulders from his hold, sneering as I obey him because I have zero doubt he's bluffing.

Going pee is awkward, which almost ends up being impossible with the chain around my neck. It requires positioning the leash, for lack of a better term, to the side, heavy and chaffing against my skin. I take my time, enjoying my bit of freedom before he re-ties me to the chair inside the stagnant basement.

Once I finish, I return to the main part of the room but pass him and head for his bed instead of the doorway. I perch on the edge of it first, and then push myself to the centre. It's soft, and

I don't remember the last time I was in a normal bed. The night before Dad rushed us out of our home, maybe.

Flynn watches me from the doorway, his jaw taut, his hands forming fists by his sides. I'm sure he's imagining every way possible to kill me but until then, I fall backwards, almost moaning aloud at being able to lie horizontal.

I shut my eyes at the exact second I hear his steps move from the door. They approach, paced, one in front of the other, until the chain is tugged on so roughly, I'm lurched upright with a squeak.

Angry, stormy eyes collide with mine. The fist by his side now clutching the chain like a lifeline.

There's more than anger in his eyes though, and for all his claims, I find the past.

People don't come into my space.

Out of respect for me and care for their own life, they don't. It's my place, my stuff, *mine*.

Bringing her here was a mistake, but it was the easiest way to contain her. Given the small space, she won't be able to try anything.

Rozelyn's tenaciousness used to make me smile, but this time, I fume. When my little captive heads for my bed instead of the door, I almost stop her right then, but curiosity to see what she'll do keeps me still. The moment she sat on the edge was the moment she made a fucking mistake. Contrary to our previous conversation, she'll do anything to get ahead, including dredging our shared past into the present.

I'll let her play the game for a bit. She'll think she's in control, only to have me yank the chains and force her back into her rightful place.

*Tell Nico*, my inner voice suggests. In all those hours of sitting downstairs with her, it's the decision my mind continued to return to. Hiding the truth feels like a betrayal to the family I owe everything to, and I don't want to do that. Be that. Or worse, if Rozelyn opens her mouth and announces that fact, I'll be the one to take the fall. Telling the Corsettis will mean no matter what level she drags her game to, they'll ensure I don't lose.

The moment she falls backwards onto my bed, I'm right there, grabbing the end of her leash and wrenching her upright until she's sitting again. I stand between her legs, towering over her, bending as I angle her face up. Now I despise looping the chain in a way it won't strangle her.

The bitch deserves to be strangled to death.

"What the fuck do you think you're doin'?" I ask, keeping my words paced, so she feels the complete effect of each one.

Her lips curl up, a seductress's practiced smirk. "Sitting, Flynn."

"In my bed."

"Observant."

I growl, my irritation for her creating sharp spikes around my nerves. Done with this and needing her back downstairs and away from my room—*my room*, my safe space—I back up, taking her with me. Her feet dig into the floor, her hands into my chest, trying to get me to stop.

"Flynn, wait. Can't we just talk?"

Talk? She wants to fucking *talk*? If her goal was to get me to stop pulling on the chain, she's succeeded in this at least. "Talk," I repeat. "The only reason you should be talking is to start handing over answers."

She tugs against the chain again, still trying to gain control of it. "You don't think it's odd that after over a decade, we've found our way back to one another?"

Here it is. The seduction I've been expecting. She'll aim to dredge up old emotions and use them against me. Unfortunately for her, I shoved all those away long ago. The guy she broke is no longer who I am.

Her right hand releases the chain and somehow, I know what she's about to do even before she does it. She holds it up, palm toward me, the small, white starburst scar gaining my entire focus.

"This was a constant reminder of you, Flynn."

"Sorry to be such a burden." My own right palm heats, like talking about our twin scars is demanding my attention.

"No," she counters with a gentle shake of her head. Her expression softens and she reminds me of the girl I first met on a bench by the smoke pit. "That's not it at all. Sometimes, I thought that year was a dream, but this scar proves otherwise. It always grounded me when things got shitty because I'd think of you at first."

"At first."

Her gaze falters and her arm slowly lowers again, as does her frown. I think it's regret I'm witnessing. "It's been eleven years," she finally whispers. "That's a long time, Flynn. We'd both moved on from necessity."

Necessity is correct. I had to survive, and then this organization found me, and I was reborn away from hell.

"But I'd still think back to the moment we did this. The promise we made to one another."

*Sitting against the brick wall of the school, Rozelyn leisurely drags her nails up and down my arm, her head on my shoulder. There are very few things in life I've found enjoyable, but her touch always calms the monster in my head. The erratic thoughts that make it difficult to focus sometimes.*

*"I never want to leave you, Flynn. I want us to always find our way back to one another."*

*"We will," I promise. "You're inside me. I'll always find you."*

*"Can we seal that promise?" She lifts her head, twisting to better face me.*

*"What, like in blood?"*

*With my joke, there's no amusement on her face. Instead, she reaches beside her and picks up a fragmented rock from the edge of the school and brings it between us.*

*She's insane, but this is why I love her. I hold out my palm toward her.*

Fuck. I scrub my hands over my face, striding away from her entirely, giving her my back. She can't witness this—witness as the long-buried memory resurfaces. I'd forgotten about it. Well, not *forgotten* about it necessarily but certainly shoved it into the many boxes I placed anything to do with her in.

"Flynn." Then she's there, her small hand touching my back, and I react as the brief hold she has on my arm clenches around my heart too.

She owned that organ once but not anymore.

I spin and not bothering with the chain, my hand forms a vise around her neck. I walk her backwards to the nearest wall, beside the bathroom's entrance. She gasps as her back hits the it but doesn't fight my hold, even as a thumb and finger squeeze either side of her neck.

"Give up, Rozelyn."

"We made a promise, Flynn." Her gaze darts to my hand. "Somehow, it came true. We found each other again. It's fate that the family my father has been targeting is the very one you're working for."

The reminder isn't doing her any favours and I seethe. "You didn't tell me who you were back then, so how I see it, the girl I made the promise to doesn't even exist."

"I'm the same person."

"You've been saying this whole time, you're not. Neither of us are. The scars on our palms were the actions of stupid teenage hormones. Give up trying to find my heart, Rozelyn, because I don't have one."

I drop my hand but don't move away. And she doesn't fight me. Both of us breathing heavily, staring at one another. Her eyes flicker with sadness and regret, and I have no idea what she sees in mine. Ideally, nothing, even as traces of the past invade my mind. Memories I stopped focusing on.

Every kiss.

Every touch.

Every laugh.

The first time we had sex.

Every other time we had sex.

The experimenting.

The awakening of both our desires.

I can't help myself. Can't fucking help my eyes from studying her. Grazing the tops of her breasts. Ripped jeans and a bra is all I've left her in and my dick twitches in my pants. My jaw tightens, trying to breathe through the lust.

Rozelyn back then was beautiful. Rozelyn now is sexy. She's a wet dream come to life and seeing her like this, riled up, clothing ripped, a chain around her neck, minutes from being tied to a chair again excites me. Old desires are reborn.

But it changes nothing. Lust is secondary to loyalty. This bitch decided to play with fire, and since she's so interested in the game, I'll have to burn her.

I back away.

She reaches for me.

Final mistake on her part.

Keeping her eyes captive, I grab the end of the chain and lift it high above her head, locking her into place. She gasps, one hand clawing at the metal, the other me, but she has nothing to worry about. I'm holding the leash in a way she won't be without breath. In a quick movement, I also bind her wrists together in my free hand.

Leaning closer, I grit, "Give up, Rozelyn. Whatever goal you walked into this room with, lose it right fuckin' now. I'm not playing."

Rozelyn's desires have always run deep and despite the near-death hold I have her in, her pupils expand. Her breath hikes. Fear. Lust. The two mingle so closely within her—always have —that it's impossible to differentiate between them.

Her eyelids hood, her breaths come out in sharp pants. Her back arches, her breasts right there. If I thought earlier she was a wet dream come to life, no, this is fucking paradise.

Hell concealed within paradise.

"You're pissed," she breathes. "This is revenge for you."

*It's everything.*

"Yes." There's no point in arguing the fact. "Now do you get it? This cocky thing you're doing, trying to dredge up memories, it won't work."

For the final time, I shove away from her, releasing her wrists but pulling on the chain in one swift movement. We're getting out of here before I do something every fibre of my being will regret.

"That's not what I'm doing," she counters when I get my bedroom door opened. "I meant what I said earlier, about our scars. I think it's interesting how what we once promised actually came true."

I shut my eyes, the memory filtering through again. She won't destroy me like this.

"Keep talking, Rozelyn, and I'll gut you. I'm getting *very* sick of your voice right now." I drag her into the hallway with me and shut the door.

"You can't yet," she states in a haughty tone as I start down the hallway, toward the basement.

"Test me." This entire interaction made one fact clear: I need to admit to Nico who Rozelyn is to me. "If you forget," I whirl to face her, so she can see the lack of humour in my expression, "I told you, torturing women is a mental game, and *mon soleil,* we're just starting."

*Fuck.*

*Wait. No.* For the second time today that nickname slips out too easily and I try to claw it back in, but it's out. In the air, both of us having heard it. The way her lips twitch with the hint of a smile, her bright eyes getting even more lively, tells me she's amused by my slip-up.

"Understand?" I turn around again and give her my back to hide the regret, uncaring if she answers my latest question or not.

In some ways, Rozelyn fucking won that round. Whatever she set out to do in my room, she succeeded. She found a buried emotion, had me address the love I once held for her. Mentioned old promises that I spent months living by, searching for her, even when I hated her.

That might have been evidence of old dreams and nightmares, but it was also a reminder. *She's* a reminder.

Of everything she once was to me.

And everything she stole.

The fact she tried to use my emotions to get her way proves one thing though; she also still has these feelings, which means, it'll be easy to twist the game around on her. I'll confuse her senses. Be the good guy she remembers and wants me still to be before ripping that reality away. I'll blur her mind, break her heart, and crack her so wide open, she'll give me what I need.

We make it back to the basement, and instead of tying her to the chair, I give her the first piece of kindness. I loop the chain through a metal pole in the corner, which gives her about three feet of walking room.

"Generous." She's sarcastic, of course.

"Be grateful. Most would be put right back on the chair." But most would also be losing limbs right now.

When she's secured, I head toward the staircase, not breaking my stride until she speaks. "Wait. You're leaving?" A spike of panic. Good.

"No point in hanging around with you if you're not going to talk."

"You're not very good at torturing, are you? Makes me think of the boy I once knew."

I ignore the jab because she's missing the point.

"I don't have to be down here to torture you."

Then I exit the basement altogether, leaving Rozelyn in complete darkness when I flick off the light on my way out. See how she enjoys that. As I stride away from the door, I pull out my phone to respond to the text I received earlier when Rozelyn was using the bathroom.

NICO

Update?

ME

Done for the night. Where are you?

NICO

Greenhouse.

I head in Nico's direction, past the various other rooms in the hallway—the library I've never set foot in, a lounge, and even a game room—until reaching the glass door right at the end. Before I moved into the mansion, Enzo had the greenhouse constructed for Caterina.

An itchiness slithers up my arms as I step from the house and into the warm space. I hate it down here. It's so...perfect. So rich. I've never enjoyed being in this part of the house whatsoever. Normal people don't have small greenhouses built just 'cause or an entire room made to sit, talk, and drink. Caterina encouraged me to use the library frequently, to expand my literary knowledge, but it's probably one of the only directives I've always denied. I much prefer the desolateness of the basement or the aloneness of my room.

I enter the greenhouse slowly, completing a customary sweep. Nico's perched on the edge of the stone water fountain in the centre with Della beside him. Her hand is clenched between the two of his, and a flash of once finding Caterina and Lorenzo sitting in that exact position bombards my mind. It's scary how much Nico is beginning to become his father.

That day, I had gone searching for Caterina, wanting the gentle peace she always managed to source for me, when I found them together. I didn't stick around because the obviousness of their love caused my gut to churn. It was only a year after my time with Rozelyn and witnessing their love for one another, not masked because they believed they were completely alone, made me realize how I still wasn't over Rozelyn at the time.

This time, when seeing Nico and Della in an identical position, their love apparent, I don't have the same churning. My underboss has found his happiness, and I can only hope his sticks around and doesn't become comparable to a cold death, like what mine with Rozelyn had become.

"Flynn." Nico stands, rebuttoning his jacket when he spots me. Della follows him up, shooting a small smile at me. Our interactions have been limited and I tip my head respectfully to the organization's next queen. "Thanks for coming."

"Sir."

"How's Rozelyn now that a complete day has passed?"

"She's..." I search for the correct word. "Erratic. Shows no fear, which makes me wonder all the shit De Falco taught her."

At the mention of her stepfather, Della looks away, taking her bottom lip between her teeth. She nibbles it for a moment, distress curling the lines of her face.

"I'm not surprised," Nico says with a sigh. "Did she elaborate on why she wanted in here?"

I shake my head. "She claims she's planning on telling us eventually but not yet."

Nico's brows furrow and he inches to the side of the greenhouse, his attention sliding to the dark outdoors. "Unacceptable. She doesn't make the rules here."

"Working on that."

Della speaks up. "Is she stalling? Giving Stefano time to build up an army and attack? We know he likely fled the city, so maybe he's gathering forces. Hm." She looks to her husband and back, a hidden conversation passing between them before she finds me again. "I want to visit her."

"No." The answer is immediate, second to the realization I've denied my underboss's wife.

But Nico's lips pull into a smirk, suggesting we share the same thoughts, and I didn't piss him off.

"She's not safe, Mrs. Corsetti," I explain, forcing my tone softer than the situation calls for.

"Della. Please don't be so formal." She waves her hand in the air and counters with, "She's my stepsister. She's nasty, but poisoning Aurora seems a bit out of character, even for her."

"No one's denying it, *petite souris*. Both Rozelyn and Aurora confirmed what happened. I'm sorry because I know you don't want to accept it."

"I get that," she stands straighter, "but that's not my point. What she did was stupid, but I knew her. *Lived* with her. We both lost our mothers, were both under Stefano's influence... You think that doesn't have an effect? She might be confused between what's right and wrong. She's..." Della sighs, her shoulders decompressing as though with all her points made, she's lost the energy to continue, "traumatized or something. I don't know."

Emotions have always been difficult for me to make sense of. To comprehend how a person can hate someone so much and yet have empathy for them. But it's clear Della's showing her kindness by wanting to search within Rozelyn's dead, black heart.

"I'm leaving this up to you, Flynn," Nico states suddenly, his sharp gaze coming back to me. "Can it be safe for Della to visit?"

I search his expression, seeking anything indicative of which direction he wants this conversation to go, but find nothing. He remains stoic.

"I'll make it safe enough," I finally respond. "If you really want to see her, Della, and you're allowing it," I glance at Nico, "then it happens. But in a few days. Right now, I'm leaving her be."

"That's the best method?" Nico questions, his voice hardening. "We need answers quickly, Flynn."

"I understand, sir, but I know her type." Hell, I know *her*. "Leaving her alone to stew in her thoughts. Whatever she's hiding will be all she thinks about until it drives her crazy."

This is it. Do it. This is the time to admit our past to him. I'd already decided to do this, and it takes opening my mouth three different times for the truth to finally be spoken aloud. Guilt or maybe regret makes this difficult. So far, only Rozelyn and I have been privy to the truth, but now, it'll be shared. Shame that I have this past. That of all women who've become our enemy, it's *her*.

"Sir," I continue before he has a chance to reply to my previous explanation, "I need to admit something to you. I *know* her from my past. She wasn't a De Falco when I met her.

Or, at least, it's not what she called herself. We were in high school, and it was months before your parents took me in. She was a new student, and we became..." The next word scrapes up my throat, the admittance rough to hear. The recognition of what once was. "Friends."

Nico's poker face has always been one of the best, but for once, his shock isn't hidden. At his side, Della's mouth falls into an O before her brows furrow and she glances away to the side. If she's trying to figure out a timeline, she won't. When Della entered the De Falcos' lives, I was long out of Rozelyn's.

"You didn't say anything," Nico states after a complete ten seconds. Enough time for my nerves to tighten, for my instincts to rise, for the blade strapped to my thigh to become tempting, if I need to defend myself against the guy I've trained alongside of.

"I am now."

Nico meets my challenging stare with a slight incline of his chin.

"Until yesterday, I didn't know who she was. When I met her, she told me her name was Bray. Guess it's what she was enrolled into my school under, probably to hide her real identity. I knew her for that one year and then she told me goodbye, and I never saw her again. When you brought her in, despite the same first name, I didn't think they were one and the same. The moment Rosen removed the bag over her head, I put everything together. I'm telling you so you know I'm not hiding shit from you, sir. I do not care about her. She's your enemy, therefore she's mine as well. *Unisciti a leale. Muori leale.*" Join loyal. Die loyal—the Corsetti motto. "I'm a Corsetti soldier. She's a De Falco. That's all there is to it."

At the end of my tirade, Nico's only response is a tip of his head, a sign of acceptance, and a single question: "Can you do this, Flynn? Can I have faith in you torturing the truth from her or will you get caught up in old feelings?"

"What old feelings?" I counter. "She hurt me then; she's hurting me now. The bitch pays and that's all there is to it."

"Very well. Unless you have more to add, you're dismissed. Thank you, Flynn."

Without saying goodbye to either of them, I return inside, heading straight to my room where I crawl into bed without showering or changing. I lie right where she was hours before and ignore how her scent already faintly clings to the room.

I ignore the past.

No more games. I won't get caught up in her.

# 8

## ROZELYN

**B**eing the new girl sucks, and that's how I've found myself sitting outside alone during lunchtime, waiting impatiently for the bell to ring. At least being in class will give me something to do.

Three days into public school and I'm still trying to figure out why I begged my parents to let me come here. Public school kids are assholes. I left private school friends for this?

The September breeze passes over me. Warm from the leftover summer temperatures still lingering, but chilly nonetheless as fall creeps up. I cross my arms, curling my shoulders inward. I have a sweater in my locker but didn't think to grab it before coming out here.

Cars pass the school and from my perch on the wooden bench, I've been counting their colours as they drive by. So far, in the past ten minutes, there's been three red cars, eight black ones, two white, and a blue.

This is what my life has become, apparently. Sitting alone, counting cars while I ignore the rowdy crowd, not even twenty feet away from me, where they hang by the smoke pit. It's on the edge *of school property, where the staff allow students to smoke, while not being too near the building.*

*I suppose I've nearly encroached on their territory. But out here, I can avoid the unwanted, curious stares of people inside.*

*Still, this is a bit of freedom from the binds Mom and Dad force me to wear. Mom, for being from a prominent mafia family, and Dad, for creating us to be one, both putting a lot of pressure on me.*

*My gaze dives from the next car driving by—a silver one—to the dark mark on my wrist. Sometimes Dad uses too much pressure. He was drunk two nights ago and I'm not sure why he was upset.*

*When feet crunch over the fallen leaves, I cover the bruise with my free hand and curl them both onto my lap as I prepare my best fuck-off expression to whoever's checking out the new kid before they deem me not good enough.*

*Everyone took one look at me, at my designer jeans, the Louis Vuitton purse, and fresh highlights, and quickly assumed I'm not worthy of the lower-class school I insisted on attending.*

*The guy approaching is fucking huge. His unwelcoming expression mirrors mine, yet he continues, his gait slow and measured as though giving me the opportunity to run.*

*Smoke billows from the most kissable lips I've ever seen on a guy as he lowers the cigarette from his mouth. I've never believed such a gross act could look sexy, but this guy succeeds in making it so.*

*Intense dark eyes study me. They flick over my form, my face, down to where I'm holding my wrist. They're compelling...beautiful. Entrapping to the point I don't want to run away. Not when I need to hear the voice accompanying those eyes.*

*Without waiting for permission, he drops onto the bench beside me with a thud. His legs spread wide, his back reclines, and worse, he props his arm against the bench, his hand inches from my hair.*

*Um. I scoot over an inch, glaring at the small space between us because he takes up so much of the bench. The stranger's lips curl around the cigarette in his mouth, but he doesn't comment on me trying to expand the distance between us.*

*If this is some fucked-up claim on the bench and he thinks he can scare me off, that's not happening. His sheer size and hulking personality, even when I haven't spoken to him, indicates someone who could easily be a psycho, but I live with one of those, so he can't be worse.*

*"Hey, new girl."*

*His voice has a deep drawl to it. A voice I've only ever heard in movies and didn't know existed. A sexy growl.*

*"You know of me?"*

*"Well, considering we share two classes."*

*What? I would remember this guy but don't recall seeing him anywhere over the three days.*

*"Math and English," he continues, though I never asked. "You sit in the front in English, and in the middle of the farthest row in math. I'm at the back for both."*

*Of course he is.*

*"Good for you."*

*Again, his lips twitch, fighting a smile as he sucks a final deep inhale of his smoke, flicks it to the ground at his feet, and jams his shoe—Converse showing obvious signs of wear and tear—into it, twisting it into the dirt beneath our feet. My nose wrinkles in disgust and I don't bother hiding it.*

*"Something wrong, princess?"*

*"I'm not a princess."*

*"You look like one."*

*Compared to his ripped jeans, baggy, faded black shirt, and even baggier grey sweater, all of which look like they've seen better days, sure. Probably.*

*"Doesn't make me one." No matter how much Mom tries.*

*"Whatever, princess."*

*"That's not my name," I snap, my hands curling around the edges of the bench.*

*In a flash, his lazy slouch is gone, and he sits up, leaning closer. The hand by my head slips off the back of the bench, but I don't think it's an accident when he curls a finger around my hair, tugging lightly to draw my attention.*

*"Then what's your name? Because I'm seconds away from calling you Rapunzel because your insane amount of hair."*

*"Original." I roll my eyes, hiding the fact that, despite the waist-long hair Mom continues to insist I should cut, no one's called me that.*

*"Name," he demands, a growl to his tone that makes my grip around the wood even tighter.*

*I'm insane for responding to this stranger. The scary, hot stranger with gross habits, but he's so far the only one who hasn't stuck his nose up at me.*

*"Rozelyn."*

*"Better." He grins, releasing my hair and leaning back again, adopting the identical, lazy position as earlier. "I'm Flynn."*

*Flynn. Not a name I'd think to put to him, but I like it.*

*"People here are dicks, huh?" he comments after a few moments of comfortable silence.*

You're not. Yet. Until I figure out why you're being nice. *"Yeah," I agree, shrugging.*

*He jerks his head to the large building behind us. "Ignore them. They get threatened by new meat. We all know you're better than them."*

*Such a blatant statement. "What?"*

*He studies the deep blue of my jeans, following my legs to my black flats. "Look at you, Rozelyn. You obviously have a story, and it's one that doesn't align with theirs, but don't let it bother you. Be better than them because it means you have a fuckin' shot in this shitty life and they're jealous."*

*Bitterness tightens his words at the end, but I don't question him on it, not wanting to pry. Even though, somehow, he's read my entire situation perfectly. Not that I think I'm better than anyone, but I do have a shot in life, due to my family's circumstances.*

*"Yet, you're talking to me."*

*He turns his head, those addictive light brown eyes finding mine. "Because I don't care about having a shot, so I'm not jealous. If you haven't noticed," he gestures to the smoking pit where a dozen other students still mingle, chatting with one another, "I don't really like people. I get the sense, you don't either, so I appreciate that about you."*

*"Except I'm people."*

*His lips purse and he studies a passing moving truck, which turns down the next road, into the nearby neighbourhood. When it's gone from sight, he finally answers, "Are you? People are assholes and I've spent three days watching you, to know you're not."*

*My face heats. My fingers slip from the bench's edging and seek for something else to grasp onto that isn't my emotions quickly escaping my tightly wound form. He speaks so...so brashly. It's refreshing and a welcome difference from Mom and Dad's carefully structured statements.*

*"Maybe I haven't gotten the chance to be an asshole yet."*

*"Then let me give you that chance and we'll see who's right."*

*Did he just...? He grins and shoves to his feet, his hand held out toward me. An offer of friendship, I believe. If I take it, I have a person here. A connection. To deny him would prove I am an asshole, that I am the "people" he speaks of.*

*I take his hand.*

His touch brandishes my skin, ignites a flame around my neck, inches from the base of the chain he's left on me. The chain digs into my shoulders, and I'm sure there's a bruise now, but a simple swipe of his fingers feel so fucking good, I'm on the verge of admitting how pleasurable it is with a moan. How it takes away the weight of the chain.

Wait. Chain? What happened to the bench we were sitting on?

My eyes fly open. The basement is dark, but even so, the outline of his figure is so bright, those very eyes I was just dreaming about slicing through the dimness. He studies me like he can read me, and I hope not, or else he'd know that somewhere amongst the pain in my thigh, the sleepiness, my lack of energy, and the bleakness of being here, my mind travelled back to the first time I found peace.

Meeting Flynn.

"Wake up."

I jerk my head to the side. Or, as far as the chain will allow me to go.

"What?" Speaking makes my throat even more dry. It's only been a day without water, and I know from my father's inhumane practice, the body can go for multiple days. Forcing my throat to work only worsens it.

Silently, Flynn reaches behind him and returns with a plastic cup, which he shoves at my lips. He tips it and I eagerly drink, cursing how it's nowhere near enough. Considering Flynn hasn't turned on a light, I get the sense, he won't be remaining. Which means no bathroom breaks, which means being dehydrated is safer.

When the cup moves away, something round and cool lands

on my lips. I part them, not even caring what he shoves between them.

"Chew."

I do, biting through the round object, tasting the familiar flavours of a green grape. Wow, fruit. Healthy food. He must really be trying to keep me alive. He feeds me grape after grape and I try to count them, but hunger wins out, and I'm too focused on chewing than counting.

When I finish, his shadow moves away. His steps are heavy up the stairs and the door slamming shut behind him seems louder than usual.

I'm alone again, but it's okay. Gives my brain a chance to return to a happier time.

~

Flynn returns later that evening—I think it's evening. He doesn't make a sound as he unclasps my chain and walks me up the stairs and out into the mansion's comforting warmth. The light seems brighter, painfully so, after sitting in the dark for so many hours.

He interrupted another trip down memory lane. A few trips, actually. The first one occurred on the same day we met, when I had gone home at the end of the day and Mom asked me her usual question about how school was.

Every day prior, I shrugged her off and disappeared into my bedroom.

That day: *"It was good."*

*"You're smiling." She watches me stride down the hallway and into the kitchen, where I pour myself a glass of orange juice. "After three days, has it gotten better?"*

*Facing the fridge, I hide my grin. Meeting Flynn has made the idea of returning tomorrow more pleasant. "Yes. I think I have a friend." A term to appease Mom, but I doubt Flynn would refer to me as such after one day.*

*After lunch, we went to math class together, and I felt his eyes penetrating my back the entire class. Between periods, he trailed behind me to my locker but didn't stop to talk. Waggled his brows, grinned, and disappeared toward the gym. At the end of the day, he stopped by my locker, this time to say, "Don't let them scare you off because I'd miss your smile. See you tomorrow, Rozelyn."*

*"That's great, honey." Mom comes up behind me and wraps her arms around my waist in a welcoming hug. "I knew it'd get better."*

I hadn't known at the time, that hug would be numbered. That only months after our conversation, she'd die.

"Walk faster," Flynn commands.

His voice seems faraway. Or is it me who's faraway? Like I'm not completely here anymore. It's only been a day, so I shouldn't be losing myself already. This doesn't make sense.

Or has it been more than a day?

No. Earlier when he fed me, he said he'd return to let me use the bathroom. Therefore, we're still within the same time bubble.

"Speed up," he demands.

*I can't*, I want to tell him. I'm weak. My leg is throbbing from the wound. My energy feels depleted. The setting sun pouring through window panes blinds me more than it should, my eyes so unused to the daylight rather than the darkness.

My body is betraying me.

*I'll tell you*, I want to call out. My mouth forms the words but can't push them from my lips. To end this now, I'll tell the Corsettis everything. When they descend on him, Dad will know I'm a traitor. He'll know I fucked up, and when he fights back and wins, I'll be the one who ultimately dies, making all my effort for nothing.

Anything to end this.

Flynn was correct. Mental torture is worse than physical. I'll take any stab wound over this. It's making no sense for me to be this weak already.

"Flynn—" This is it. Where I'll tell him.

"Shut it."

We reach his bedroom at the same time and he lets the chain go, silently commanding me forward. I stare at the bed as I pass it. It takes every nerve to stride into the bathroom after being taunted by the indent left from his body.

And then to leave it when I've finished, when the shower mocks me with the idea of being clean, when splashing water on my face from the sink does little to remove the too prominent sweat and dirt.

I don't have the energy to fight him as I return to the main part of his room. I don't even look at him, to see if he's curious why I'm obeying so readily as he marches me out of his bedroom and immediately back to the basement.

I don't realize the temperature difference until I'm seated on the dirty, blood-stained, stone ground, still only wearing cut, ripped jeans and my bra. My shirt is lost somewhere in the darkness, dead alongside the pillow and sleeping bag he mocks me with that remain out of reach.

He loops the chain around the post and then the rope around my wrists and leaves me to my darkness again.

So.

Much.

Darkness.

~

On and on it goes.

Another day, and then another...and another.

They're blending together. Flynn's visits seem almost like clockwork twice a day. Predictable to use that as passing time.

But nonetheless, I'm losing my grasp on time. My exhausted mind slipping further and further away.

If Dad could see me now, he'd disown me. This doesn't feel any different than when he'd do the same thing to me, to "teach" me. He'd urge Yasmine out of the house, so she couldn't question why I disappeared, and then he'd shove me into the basement, hooked to a chain, abandoned for days without food and water.

The first time was the worst. When I didn't know what he was doing, and he didn't fully explain.

*Two soldiers tie my wrists and ankles to the chair, but I jerk and kick with every muscle I have to fight them. Even as they move away, baring the path for Dad to see me, I let him really see me. To gaze at the fear, the tears pouring from my eyes, mingling with the confusion I feel.*

*"Dad, what the hell is this? What are you doing?"*

*"Trust me, one day, you'll thank me for this training." He spins on his heels and heads up the stairs, disregarding the fact he's left his own daughter tied to a chair.*

*"Dad!" I yell after his retreating back. "Dad, no! Dad... Dad...!" They all go unheard though, including my final plea: a name I haven't called him in many years. A whispered appeal to the man who raised me before the two soldiers also leave, and all the lights shut off. "Daddy."*

Three days later, I was freed. My body weak, exhausted, starved, and dehydrated. I felt dirty. More so, I felt hatred. A deep-seated loathing, no praise would fix, even when my father tried to compliment my "strength."

Every time after that got easier, because I stopped kidding myself. If the hits didn't already show me the kind of man he is, that did.

So what's so different about being held captive by the Corsettis that's making this worse?

# 9

## FLYNN

The camera feed is up on my phone, which is propped against the wall parallel to my bed as I recline against the pillows. There are few surveillance cameras installed inside the mansion, but the two in the basement are for this very reason. Chained up or not, prisoners shouldn't be alone without eyes on them.

Three days have passed in which I've had limited contact with Rozelyn. I feed her once a day, in the morning, and bring her up for a bathroom break in the evening. Every visit, I'm seeing more of her fight gone. Less attitude and more submission. When she's docile, she doesn't speak, but she also only stares at the ground as we walk and follows my commands without question.

When I bring her food, Dr. Shappo accompanies me to change out her bandage. Guess the wound isn't as deep as it initially looked and it's been healing well, considering the limited time that's passed.

I barely speak to her as well, until yesterday when I started praising her for listening. Faking sympathy that I wish she'd

70

answer the questions to save herself. I pretend to be on her side, that my feelings for her creep up even when my actions show otherwise. If she's the girl I remember, a little kindness goes a long way.

Then I'll break her.

Or she'll break me.

I'm fucking agitated and just thinking about it has me shifting in bed. Every time I see her, every time she stops fighting, her submission feels *wrong*. Once, it used to be everything to me because the fight was half the battle. The half-assed, fake struggle she'd put on only for me to win.

But those were games. In the matter of life and death—of *her* survival or downfall—I want more from her. It's there, buried beneath days of isolation.

Conflicting emotions certainly. Rozelyn's broken demeanour makes my job simpler, but I despise the sensation, the clench of my heart, every time it seems like she's given up. It took me until this morning to realize exactly why her mood changes bother me so much.

If there's one thing that certainly has remained the same all these years later, it's her reaction to sorrow.

The first time she showed up to school seeming upset was when I realized how much the rich, mysterious girl who appeared in my life meant to me. When her lowered eyes and hunched shoulders shielded her from other people, I wouldn't allow the same with me. I wanted to protect her.

It's the identical lost gaze, hunched shoulders, and no drive that she has now. Witnessing her this week forces me into the past. To the moments I'd kiss away her distress and hope that, eventually, she'd trust me enough to open up to me.

Movement in the feed brings my attention back to the screen. She shifts, readjusting her legs to draw them up against her chest. Her head lowers into her knees and her stare at the ground doesn't break.

I watch her stare at seemingly nothing until exhaustion starts to drag my eyelids down, and eventually, I lie down entirely, watching the phone screen until sleep takes me.

Since Rozelyn's return to my life, sleep has become troubling. It's when my eyes are shut that my mind opens and relives the cruellest memories.

*She's coming around the corner, heading for the girls' changing room. Her footsteps get closer, and I brace for the lunge.*

*She enjoys the surprise. The roughness.*

*The moment I see a flash of the pink blouse I know her to be wearing, I move, shoving off the wall. In a blink, I have her in my arms, pushing us through the door to the girls' changing room, my back first to take the brunt of the door.*

*When the door shuts behind us, I press her front to it and I flip the lock to ensure we won't be interrupted.*

*"Flynn—"*

*"Shh." Grabbing the straps of her backpack, I wrench it to the ground and then reach for the edge of her dress. I fucking love the dresses she always wears. Makes her seem like she cares about this shithole of a school more than anyone else here. There's something about Rozelyn that's never made sense to me. Not since the very first day I found her seated on a bench near the smoke pit.*

*Knowing what my girl enjoys, I slip my hand beneath her dress, and then beneath the edge of her panties. Her head falls back as I stroke over her clit until she's wet. There's already something different about this instance though, as usually, Rozelyn enjoys pretending to fight me.*

*She's wet but I don't enter her, instead checking, "You okay?"*

*"Perfect," she whispers, an unusual edge to her tone.*

*"Do you want to stop?" She has a word to stop me, but this seems like a moment she wouldn't recall to use it.*

*"No, god, please don't. I need you, Flynn."*

*Rozelyn's smart as fuck, so maybe it's something with one of her classes. Maybe it's something else entirely, but her wetness has made me hard and her reassurance of her feelings manages to push through my own concern. I undo my jeans and palm myself.*

*Then I shift her panties aside because she enjoys remaining dressed for this. Makes it feel more rushed and hurried, more in line with her fantasies, and if I'm honest, I enjoy it too. She'll leave here today with her panties wet and the ache of my cock between her thighs.*

*From my wallet, I take out a condom, sheathe myself and lift her thigh to the side. I line my cock to her core and enter with a shared moan that, no doubt, others could hear from the other side.*

*There's not much to my name. I barely even call the bedroom I rest my head in each night as mine.*

*But Rozelyn Bray is mine.*

*And it's moments like this that prove to the world around us, she owns me too.*

*Being close to graduation, we've been together for months. I often question if it's possible to know someone's a soulmate after a short while, but I knew it early on with her. Rozelyn buried herself in my heart from her initial smile, and we've shared many firsts over these months. Many promises, and many hopes.*

*Her back arches, pushing her ass into me. I grasp her wrists in one hand and lift them above our heads, rendering her immoveable—an action often necessary in our play, even if she isn't fighting this time.*

*"It's been too long." I growl in her ear. Three days since I've been inside her, to be exact. "I'm starved for you."*

*She makes a noise in the back of her throat. "I'll always remember us like this, Flynn."*

*Odd words but my orgasm is sneaking up quickly, so I don't have time to question her. I drop one of my hands to her clit and strum the sensitive ball of nerves, urging her orgasm quicker, my own thrusts sparking an undeniable heat inside my body.*

*"Come for me."*

*She enjoys me talking her through her orgasms, and it's with a few other short statements, both praiseworthy and derogatory, she comes, her pussy milking me, her cry of pleasure tapering off into a low, dragged-out moan as she bites her bottom lip.*

*I drop her hands to take her neck instead, turning her head until I'm able to claim her mouth in a messy kiss. Not a gentle one, but a promising one. Her tongue tangles with mine and the moment her orgasm fully subsides, mine shoots off, my mind going blank for a moment. There's nothing on earth better than this.*

*When our orgasms pass, I bury my face in her long hair, breathing in the scent of flowers. Of everything good in my life. Of everything that makes returning to school every day fucking worth it.*

I wake with a jerk, escaping from the nightmare.

Nightmare. Certainly not a dream. Dreams end happy, but hours after that interaction, Rozelyn destroyed that happiness and bliss by telling me goodbye. Later looking back on that moment, her lack of fight during sex made more sense. She wasn't fighting because she was in her head about what was coming.

In my pants, my cock is rock fucking hard, the memory of her pussy invading my present reality.

The reality in which she no longer means anything to me.

*Fucking Christ.*

I swing my feet off the bed, rubbing a hand down my face, trying to rid my head of the thoughts. Of the horrible memories I've long tucked away. Rozelyn's very presence is making everything I'd shoved away resurface.

The time on my phone reads only three hours past when I dozed off.

*Fuck.*

Grabbing my phone, I open the camera app again, finding her in the same place as before. This time, she's managed to lie down, curled in a tight ball, her arm folded and acting as a pillow beneath her head. Then I hate her all over for new reasons. She's able to sleep down there while I'm struggling to pass out for longer than three hours in a comfortable bed, silence, and warmth.

Grumbling, I swipe away the app and stand, heading first to the bathroom, and then for fresh clothing before exiting my bedroom.

The mansion's hallways are dimmed but not dark; the lights are never switched off entirely. More often than not, someone's still awake in this place, and with the De Falco situation, lately, that's been Nico.

I don't seek him out though because it's a conversation I'd rather not have. I pass his office door, catching it open a few inches. Voices drift from inside. Maybe he's on the phone. Agitation walks me right to the mansion's large front doors and outside.

Summer's night air washes over me like a tepid bath. Nothing as hot as the daytime, but not the cool hints of fall that'll be on us in another month or so. All thoughts of Rozelyn are wiped away by the accompanying breeze as I drop onto the top stone step. The night sky is a deep blue, the stars twinkling in no apparent pattern, and the crescent moon above us bright and bold.

I scowl at the giant lit-up rock. Even fucking nature is taunting me.

To cool the irritation inside me, I'd fucking love a smoke right now, missing the way the nicotine always eased my nerves.

I quit after high school though. After she told me goodbye, every cigarette included a memory of her playful expressions of disgust, and they hurt. Quitting and experiencing the nicotine withdrawal was better than reliving those memories.

Countless times over the years, I've debated about taking the habit up again, but I never have. Something always seems to stop me before I can walk into the store to buy a new pack, which has been fucking annoying.

At the same time a bird squawks nearby, the large front doors behind me open, and someone steps out of the house. It's most likely Nico, having spotted me on the cameras, but then I note how the footsteps aren't as heavy.

Black heels enter my vision, peeking out from her usual pantsuit, which costs more money than what I have in my bank account. Regardless of the rich material, Caterina Corsetti lowers herself onto the step beside me, her arms wrapping around her knees.

Somehow, I know what she's about to say before she does. From the moment she found me between the two buildings, Caterina's heart has been undeniably large toward me.

With knowing eyes, she gazes at me. "Can't sleep?"

"You're here late," I state instead.

"Enzo's in with Nico," she explains, answering the earlier curiosity of who Nico was talking to. "Rafael found Maurice's daughter, but she's led to more questions than answers. They're debriefing on a few things." She pauses. "Between you and me, Enzo's readying to step down completely, but before he does, he wants to get Nico's plan of action. I think he feels like he's doing his due diligence by triple checking Nico's leadership."

Nico is a great leader. Much like his father in that, and in all my years working and training with Lorenzo, he's been unfailing. In recent months, all the soldiers have noticed that he's been allowing Nico more command and control, and while I'm used to Lorenzo's leadership, I also look forward to Nico's.

"Saw you walk by the office," Caterina continues. "Besides, if there was any soldier stalking the hallways at this time of night, it'd be you."

Caterina knows a lot about me. Over the years, it was easier to lower my walls with her. Maybe she found me at the right time, or maybe she just knows what to say. Either way, I'm comfortable with her.

"Can't sleep?" she repeats her earlier question.

"Nightmare."

Her lips press together and she glances away from me. She tucks her golden hair behind an ear, her gaze going toward her feet. She might know me, but I also recognize her behaviours, and she's biting something back.

"Just say it."

"Nico told us what you admitted. Rozelyn De Falco is *her*?"

Over the years with the Corsettis, I slowly opened up to Caterina about my childhood, and everything leading up to the day they found me, which included high school and my single year with Rozelyn. I never gave them a name though. First, last, none of it mattered. She left me; therefore, she didn't deserve to be named in my recounting.

"You loved her once."

"Love*d*," I emphasize the final letter. "Past tense being the key." My eyes cut to Caterina, a tenseness knotting my shoulders. "But yes, that's who Rozelyn was. I didn't know because she went by Rozelyn Bray back then."

"Flynn, I'm—"

"She was a lie. Everything back then was a fucking lie. I was a game to her. She told me as much when she broke up with me. Someone to amuse herself with as she partied in the slums, away from her princess life."

Caterina shifts, almost looking uncomfortable. She maintains the two feet of distance between us, an unspoken length she knows I feel okay with. "You don't know that for a fact. She might have—"

For the second time, I interrupt her, something others wouldn't dare do. "What—loved me in return?" I scoff, shaking my head, staring down the long road making up the Corsetti driveway. It's pitch black, the lights having been switched off for the night.

"Maybe," Caterina replies in a soft tone, which only sets my teeth on edge. "Look who her father is. We don't know what happened back then."

"You sound like Della. I don't really care to, to be honest."

"This isn't you, Flynn."

Ignoring her, I add, "She's Nico's problem. Once she reveals her secrets, he decides what to do with her. If he orders her death, I'll do it." *So why does the flash of her lifeless eyes gazing at me churn my stomach and send a murderous rage through my bones?* "If she gets to go free, then I'll turn my back to ensure I don't shoot her in hers when she goes."

Caterina makes a sound of disapproval in her throat, and finally murmurs, "I don't believe you'd do either of those things. Nico said you wouldn't be allowing your emotions to hinder your job."

"I'm not," I respond sharply. "The only emotion I feel toward her is hate."

After a full beat, when I think she won't further argue the case, she sighs. "Oh, Flynn, it's not that simple. The line between hate and love is thin. Look at what happened with me and Enzo. With Della and Nico."

Caterina was once engaged to be wed to a member of the Rossis, from the New York *Famiglia*. Lorenzo, for whatever reason, murdered her fiancé and stole Caterina for himself.

Eventually, I guess she realized she'd be happy with him, as the couple I've witnessed leading this organization is completely enamoured with one another. Della was once Stefano's step-daughter, sent here to trap Nico. She succeeded, only for him to escape, hunt her down, and then they found their own fucked-up happy ending together. Instead of death, she earned his forgiveness.

"This is different," I finally reply. "I *hate* Rozelyn. Besides, what happened was eleven years ago. Everything's changed, obviously. She isn't the innocent girl I knew. She's this family's enemy; therefore, she's mine. She harmed Aurora, and who knows who else she would have, if we didn't catch her." I lift my eyes to her so she sees the facts plainly on my face. *"Unisciti a leale. Muori leale* are words I live and die by."

"I know." Tentatively, she rests her hand on my arm and my first instinct is to flinch away. My second is to embrace her because Caterina's never harmed me. "But I also remember the boy I found hiding between buildings. People come into our lives and affect us in—"

"Exactly," I interrupt, finally jerking away from her touch. I slide to the farthest edge of the steps, pressing against the stone post. "You and Enzo came into my life, and I'd never turn my backs on you."

As if I hadn't spoken, she finishes her earlier line. "And affect us in ways we don't realize. Would you be out here at three in the morning, unable to sleep, if it wasn't for what's happening?"

There are very few instances where something surprises me, but that's twice this week now. First by Rozelyn's reappearance and second by Caterina's valid point.

"Precisely." She grins, like she's discovered the answers to the universe. Slapping her knees, she gets to her feet, walking backwards up the steps, apparently ending this conversation. "I remember the boy we found that day, Flynn. Don't lose the man you've become to this. Be honest if this is a struggle for you. Nico wouldn't hold it against you. No one will for being truthful about your feelings."

She disappears inside the house again and I don't look back, until the door shuts, to check she's gone. Once she is, I stand too, but head in the opposite direction, away from the mansion. Away from her words.

*"Don't lose the man you've become to this."*

Rozelyn once held a lot of power over me, but not now. Not when the Corsettis have earned my loyalty.

Every step away from the mansion, clears her from my thoughts enough that I can rationalize clearly. Like I'm leaving her bubble of influence. Rozelyn is in my head because I'm processing her return—that's it. My confused heart is making sense of the new emotions battling the old ones, but my present feelings *will* win.

They *have* to.

I need her out of my head.

I don't know if I've put into words the plan formulating in my head before a newfound urgency turns me away from the driveway and back into the house, where I head straight for the basement.

I hate her.

I fucking *hate* her. Everything she stands for. What she's doing to me—now and in the past.

I need to cleanse her from my head. To remind myself, I'm caught up in old emotions and that's it.

I hate her; don't love her, and I'll fucking prove it.

To myself. To her. To everyone.

# 10

## ROZELYN

In the dark basement, my mind flits to more memories. Whether asleep or awake, it finds peace in the past. A way to cling to my sanity as it returns to a better time.

All moments when Flynn was in my life the first time.

The months we grew close.

The first time he kissed me.

Every lie I fed him to protect him.

Every time he stole more of my heart.

The three-month anniversary of meeting Flynn, when he gave me my nickname.

And I gave him his.

A name bathed in light but buried amongst dead memories.

*Mom believes I've stayed behind after school to work on a group project, but based on the look she gave me, I think she knows I'm lying. Nonetheless, she agreed not to send a driver until later, which means, my excuse did exactly as it was meant to and gave me more time with Flynn.*

*It's November, and the ground is cold. Soon, snow will fall and winter will be upon us, so while we're still able to enjoy the outdoors, we are. Lying in the middle of the field behind the school, right in the centre of the race track.*

*Flynn is on his back, and I'm curled into his side, clutching his hoodie to ensure he doesn't go anywhere. His arm is around me, his hand cupping my hip while his other combs through my hair. It's downright relaxing, and despite the nip in the air, I'm able to focus only on his touch.*

*In theory, Flynn and I shouldn't work. Hell, when he introduced himself to me three months ago, I genuinely didn't believe we'd become friends, and then very quickly more, officially getting together on Halloween. It wasn't in the plan, and every single day when I arrive, I want to admit the truth of who I am and why he can never visit my house. The guilt of lying is hefty, then I see him, and knowing Dad, I can't risk Flynn's reaction. And a part of me fears what it'll be. What if he hates me for lying, or simply because of my family?*

*Like he's read my mind, he suddenly says, "You know, if you told me where you live, I'd visit. I'm sure I can climb into your house or something."*

*I'd love that. To have him there with me, to see him lying in my bed, to have him hold me, but Dad's an angry person, and seeing me with the very reason he didn't want me attending a public school, would set him off. It'd be Flynn at the most risk then.*

*There's a fresh bruise on my upper arm, the one his hand is nearby, but my thin jacket thankfully covers it. Dad was drunk last night, mumbling about something regarding the number seven that made no sense to me.*

*"You know why that's a bad idea."*

*"Actually, I don't." He's right; he doesn't because I refuse to tell him any details regarding my home life.*

*He drops the subject, ending the conversation with a kiss to my forehead that makes my toes curl. I love his kisses. They bring a* warmth to my body that even the bright afternoon sun overhead doesn't.

When he lowers his head again, instead of stroking my hair, he arches his arm over his eyes, mumbling, "It's bright. Clouds shifted, I think."

"Still nice to have sun while we can before the winter hell comes and takes over." A slight joke. The sun still comes out in winter, but it certainly doesn't feel warm at all. "I enjoy staring at the sun. It provides a feeling of life and reminds us that amongst the shadows of reality, there's still some good that emerges every day."

Flynn doesn't respond. His arm slowly lowers though and he turns his head to look at me. After a beat, he reaches for me, dragging my body over his. My legs go around his hips, my hands to the ground by his shoulders to keep me upright.

Light brown eyes flick over my face, my lips, my hair, studying everything. "Like you," he murmurs suddenly. "You're my sun, Rozelyn. Vivid, energizing, warm. You make me want to come to school each day, and I have no fuckin' idea how I've made it three years without you by my side. Your kindness is so bright. Your heart so fucking warm, like the sun. Mon soleil."

My throat is tight. No one's ever called me something so meaningful. Something that has the guilt gnawing at me again because I do not deserve such a kind nickname.

He does. Flynn, who's become my entire life. He might not be around at nighttime, but he's out there, waiting for me. And during the day, he's right here with me.

My moon to the sun.

"I might be your sun, but you're my moon, Flynn. Encompassing, serene, unfailing. Full, waning, or crescent, it represents change and that's exactly what you've been for me. You changed my life in all the best ways possible. My moon, Flynn. Ma lune."

Every emotion passing through his eyes promises forever,

*rather than a high school relationship. It says eternity. Lifetimes of the sun and moon orbiting one another.*

*How do I end this in a few months? When I graduate and Dad drags me back home and back into the organization's lifestyle. When Hawke Corsetti ran away from his family, he thankfully broke off our impending engagement, which means I'm free, but at what point will Dad search for a replacement?*

*Flynn grabs the back of my head and yanks me toward him, his kiss so consuming, I'd be fine if my life ended in this second, as long as his touch is the last sensation my body feels.*

*It's not our first kiss, but this one is packed with a new emotion, driven by our need for one another. The safety and love we find in each other's arms, away from our shitty lives.*

When a door slams shut, I wake from the dream. One so vivid, I could recall the sun's warmth as clearly as I felt it then. I'd never smiled so much as I did that day and it was a struggle to hide my constant grin when my driver came for me, in fear he'd mention it to Dad.

The overhead light snaps on at the same time Flynn appears in front of me, glaring down like a god of death, so opposite from the love etched on his teenage face from my memories. The differences are striking, but are a reminder that my reality isn't pleasant.

*"Ma lune."*

I don't know why I say it. When he slipped up yesterday and called me his sun, it gave me the opening to use his old nickname, but I hadn't. It doesn't change that as surreal as having him in my life again is, years have passed. We've orbited the sun eleven times; the moon's orbited over one-hundred-thirty times in the time we've been apart.

We're no longer each other's sun and moon.

I'm not giving him life, and he's no longer encompassing mine.

Flynn's jaw tightens and his body goes still. I could swear he stops breathing entirely until a burst of anger buried amidst his hatred comes free and storms forward, dropping to his knees in front of me. He grasps my chin roughly between two fingers and forces me to look at him.

I don't fight him. Not sure I'd be able to anymore. I'm exhausted, not sleeping more than an hour at a time, and starved. The lack of light has fucked up my internal cycle.

"What the fuck did you just say?"

"*Ma lune.* I dreamed of when I gave you that nickname, and you started calling me *mon soleil.*"

With a snarl, he releases me roughly and gets to his feet again. "You are everything opposite of my sun now."

"Telling me or yourself? It can't be morning already, which means you're visiting sooner than normal." A complete guess, but it feels like I haven't slept through the night. If my math is right, it's the middle of the night. "No?" I add with a challenge.

His eyes narrow and his jaw clamps somehow even tighter when he paces around the pole. He crouches again and I feel his soft fingers sweep my pulse as he undoes my chains.

This conversation certainly didn't earn my freedom, which means, he's about to find some other way to hurt me.

He hauls me to my feet, roughly jerking me around like I'm a doll. Suddenly, the rope around my hands is also gone, and he's lowering the blade that seemingly appeared from nowhere into his boot.

*Good to know where that is.*

"You seem a little wound up." Through a weakened state, my lips spread in a slow smirk.

"Would there be another reason I'm fuckin' awake at three in the morning and down here?" His grumble is lined with an annoyance that I can't help but be pleased at, even when he tugs me to the opposite end of the basement.

We pass the sleeping bag and pillow he dropped down here the first night, and I nearly beg him for it, except I won't give him that satisfaction.

"I had a nightmare," he adds.

"About me?" It's only right he's dreaming about me as well. It means the past is fucking with us both.

Flynn doesn't respond, which tells me I'm right. Keeping one grip on my upper arm, he reaches up for the attached chains looped around a metal pipe running across the ceiling. He pulls them down and moves me into position.

*No.* Hard limit. I'll play this torture game because this is what I signed up for, but I'm not hanging from my wrists for an unknown length of time.

I jerk away from his hold, only for his fingers to tighten, for his movements to be quick and methodical as he clamps a cuff around one wrist, locking it in place. With me stuck, he releases me entirely, knowing I can't run. It doesn't stop me from lifting my entire weight onto the chain, testing its restraint.

"Is this necessary?"

"Very much so." He reaches for my wrist, but I shy away from him, narrowing my eyes in a glare.

"I'd rather return to the pole."

He reaches for me again, but I bend out of the way, aware that at the end of this, he'll win, considering I have nowhere to go.

He moves like a snake, quickly, and suddenly, his body is pressing against mine, the chain around one wrist, meaning I have nowhere else to escape; I've reached my limit. He's a few inches taller than me, so he looks down, but I'm not focusing on his face. Rather, the sheer size of his body, his muscles, the arms that flex, the tattoos running up and down his arms. The lighting is dim down here, so I can't make out much of the black.

Without a word, his hand grasps my wrist and wraps his fingers around it, holding tightly. A finger presses against a specific nerve in my hand, I know all too well—*thanks, Dad.* I fight; he pinches; it hurts like hell.

Slowly, making his point, he brings my arm up and clamps the second cuff around it. With a final challenging glare that says, *I won,* he smirks and moves away.

"Asshole."

Stuck in the chains, my arms held above my head, I realize that chaining me to a pole and a chair were the better options. How long is he planning on keeping me like this? I give it an hour at most before my arms are numb. And that's not counting the stab wound in my leg that's been healing well, according to the friendly doctor who comes down here with Flynn each day. Standing on it isn't painful, but it's certainly *not* not painful.

Flynn takes two paces back to position himself directly in front of me, and any sign of annoyance or amusement from the struggle to get me chained is long gone. For the first time since being captured, fear weaves its way through my body, freezing my nerves and numbing my insides.

It's what's in his eyes that has me feeling like this. Not hate like before. Not annoyance.

Death.

Is that what this is? Am I out of time and Corsettis are finished with me? Mentally, I try to count the passing days. It hasn't been enough; if I say anything now, they'll attack, and I can't risk them potentially losing.

Not when I've made it this far.

"Flynn—"

"Shut up." He reaches down and retrieves the knife he used earlier to slice my bindings away.

*Fuck.* I've been lucky so far, but I think that's about to change.

I arch away, as far as the chains allow me to go, knowing how useless any of it is. Something about this says *more*. Like I'm about to get a true taste of the Corsetti enforcer.

"Flynn. Stop."

Ignoring me, he lunges, grasping the hair he once used to hold onto when he fucked me; the hair he'd stroke afterwards. This time, he twists it around his fist, using it to render me immobile. A gasp of pain soon follows. A whimper more than anything, and I hate conveying any sort of emotion toward his actions.

"Stop?" He growls, lowering his face until we're lined up. "You're asking me to *stop*? You know what I'd fuckin' love if you'd stop? Gettin' in my goddamned head!"

*What?*

"You wanna know why I'm down here at three in the morning? Because my fuckin' head can't get *you* out of it. And then I come down here and the first thing you say is—" He stops speaking, his mouth still parted, like he physically can't repeat the words. With a hurried jerk of his head, he continues, "It was a fuckin' decade ago. You lied to me then, and you're hiding shit now. I do not care about you anymore. I need you out of my mind so I can focus on my job."

There's so much of that I wish I reply to, instead of my stupid brain shutting down. My heart fluttering in my chest until the pain becomes unbearable.

But there's not an ounce of pleasure from his words. No matter the fact I'm in his head, clearly messing with his sleep, I can't find it. With the hate emanating from him in strong waves, it's impossible to find any joy in his misery.

But that's what this entire show is, I realize. Chaining my

arms above my head is simply his way of working through his rage.

"If you let me go, we can talk. I understand what I did to you then. How I upset you."

He scoffs. "Understand, huh? Yes, I can see the empathy rolling off you."

He brings the knife between us, dragging the sharp blade along my breasts, peeking out from my bra. The metal slides back and forth, blade side down. Any effort on his part and my skin will be sliced.

"This can end," he murmurs in a low, inviting tone. His eyes lower to my breasts, and while I wish I could say there's pleasure there, that there's a chance of his kindness, there isn't at all. Just a mild curiosity. "If only you start telling me what we need to know, Rozelyn. I'll undo the chains immediately. Then you'll get out of my life again and I won't have to deal with you."

"I will," I vow without giving him a timeline.

A short huff. "You won't because it's always been lies with you. Everything *about* you was a lie, right down to your name. Rozelyn Bray doesn't exist and never did."

I wanted her to be, but I think telling him that will make this worse.

"You made her real," I whisper instead, voice lowering to the soft tone of the girl he once knew. If he's dreaming of our past, maybe I simply need to become who I was then in order to keep my life.

When he trails the knife down between my breasts, my insides heat, igniting a flame only he can.

Like a sun.

It feels great. Like, really fucking *good*. Like the past. Like everything once pleasant in my life before it became fucked-up. And maybe it's because I'm fucked-up too, because I stop fighting against the tight hold he has on my hair. I remain still, tilting my head up until I can look him dead in the eye.

"My father chose the fake name to protect me, and now, I'm sure you can see why. I attended a public school. If word got out that I was there, I could have been in danger. Not telling you in the beginning was an obvious choice, but as we got closer, it became more about protecting you."

His face pinches like I physically pained him with my words. All I know is I did something because his hand loosens a fraction in my hair and even the knife slips down an inch, like his grip slackened.

Then he roughly shakes his head, and that hardness is back. "You're lying."

"What other reason would I use a fake name?" I challenge, but based on the manic look coating his normally deep gaze, I'm losing him. For a slight second, I wonder if he's even completely awake because he doesn't seem to understand logic.

He releases my hair suddenly and pain blooms over my scalp. When I think I've gotten through to him, his arm snakes my waist and I'm tugged firmly against his chest, my bare skin rubbing against the material of his plain shirt.

With a low sound, his knife presses against the base of my neck, and based on the abrupt sting, he dug it into my skin. Nothing painful enough that makes me flinch away, but something I'll likely be feeling later.

"Give me one fucking reason I shouldn't slice your neck this second and watch you bleed out. You'll say anything to creep into my head again, but the thing is, I need you *out* of it."

"You're not allowed to. The Corsettis won't let you."

"And if I don't care?" His gaze drops from my eyes to my lips and I instinctively lick mine. I used to enjoy his kisses more than anything in the world. He watches me intently, catching the dab of my tongue, but then his gaze lowers to the knife, to my neck, and presumably, the bead of blood.

"You do care. Because I'd be dead by now if you didn't."

He blinks slowly, his mouth curving in thought. "You think so?"

"Know so. You've been touting how much you hate me since the moment the bag was removed from my head. If you didn't care about their trust, you wouldn't follow their orders."

For a long moment, he doesn't move. Doesn't blink. And based on his chest against mine, doesn't breathe either. When he finally speaks, it's with a tone colder than I've ever heard from him.

"Your death will be worth it."

The knife drags down the side of my neck but doesn't cut me. For a second, I think I'm safe from actual harm and will only receive the mere threat of it, but then, he reaches my collarbone and slices there, and I cry out in pain.

"Stop," I whisper in the least threatening tone I can manage. "*Ma lune*, stop. Please." A feeble attempt to reach the guy I once knew but the rage taking over his expression is like nothing before. The guy I loved isn't there anymore; this deadly, cold version of the man long consuming him, ridding him of anything peaceful and logical.

The knife continues, and he slices right through the centre of my bra, cutting it away. The material falls to the side with gravity, baring my breasts to his hardened gaze. His throat moves and my stupid body reacts to his attention the same way it always has. My nipples bud, but I tell myself, it's from the cool basement temperatures.

The knife replaces his gaze, and the blade presses right above the areola of my right breast. I don't hold back my whimper this time. If he's pulling the revenge card, then he can hear exactly what he's doing.

"That hurt."

No response.

He stated coming down here, he wants me out of his head, and it's clear now, he's planning on doing exactly that—in whatever fucked-up way he can.

The knife leaves my body and for a moment, I think I've won. But then he clamps the blade between his teeth for free use of his hands, which dive right for the waistband of my jeans. I don't feel his fingers undoing the buttons; don't feel him touch the skin between my stomach and waist; don't feel anything but my stomach flipping at the sight of him biting down on the knife.

It's messed up. Flynn's always had a dangerous air to him from the moment I met him. When he walked over to me from the smoke pit, sucking on that gross addiction, he screamed like someone I'd be wise to avoid. Lucky for him and me, I returned home to the real-life monsters, so Flynn's demeanour was nothing up against the real thing.

But I'm seeing what I foresaw back then. Ten years later, tatted up, playing with guns and knives—*seeing* how comfortable he is with these weapons, considering the one clamped between his teeth—I hate to admit how it makes my core clench, my body heat with desires not felt in a long time.

When he yanks my jeans down my legs, I return to the moment. The cool air feels like a threat against my bare skin and he lifts each of my feet up, controlling my body as he rips the pants from me, leaving me in nothing but my panties and a cut up bra.

"Flynn. No." I lean away from him. "What are you doing?"

He removes the knife from his mouth to reply. "Making your life a bit shittier." He smiles, but there's not an ounce of kindness within his gaze. A serial killer's smile. "Reminding you how you no longer control me, Rozelyn, no matter what my mind seems to think. Fuck your lies and your deception and everything you did to me in high school."

He cuts away my panties and strips the ripped bra from me, leaving me completely bare to his inspection. His eyes sweeping from the cut on my collarbone, down to my breasts, and over my stomach. He pauses on the trimmed strip of hair between my legs.

I don't fight. Don't move, or arch away. But I *do* react. Nothing visible but my body wakes up. Not that I haven't fucked the occasional guy over the years—mainly soldiers and my father's staff for convenience—but no one's stared at me like Flynn is. Like Flynn always *has*.

Hunger. A voracious study of every inch of my body, right down to my toes with their black painted nails, now chipped from it being weeks since my last pedicure. My core clenches with every sweep and despite my life literally hanging in the balance, all thoughts of danger, of my why I'm here, of taking down Dad, of finding Yasmine, are gone and replaced by one thing—*him*. Nothing specific, but rather everything. The memory of his touch—his hands exploring my body, his tongue lapping between my legs. The memory of his emotions—his love, his care.

"Like what you see?" I finally manage to speak.

His response: a silent, mouthed, *Fuck.*

"Is this helping you clear your mind of me? I'd think it's having the opposite effect."

My near-taunt finally jerks him into action. Eyes narrowed, he presses his thumb right against the cut he made and drags it down my chest, presumably painting me with my blood.

"Beautiful," he murmurs, seemingly to himself.

*Why does this feel good?* My muscles go lax, my head tipping to the side to keep him in sight but losing the strength to remain upright. His psychotic actions shouldn't excite me the way they are.

Shouldn't make me want him, despite all the hell around us. Despite that a decade has passed and somehow, though we've found our way back to one another, we couldn't be more different. Existing on two different sides, enemies, each with our own goals.

He returns to my neck, pressing into the injury, only to bring his hand toward my left breast. He traces my nipple with his thumb, shifting the blood from my neck to my breast.

It's not the blood, or even his actions. It's his fucking touch because it returns me to another time. A better time.

It's pretty fucked up to be feeling *any* enjoyment in this moment, but I am. I'm losing myself to his touch, but maybe this is just my exhaustion emerging again. My brain isn't well enough to be making sense the way it should.

His head tilts and he steps toward me. I don't move. That makes his eyes narrow, as though he was seeking an argument from me. His finger leaves my breast and trails a single line down my stomach, and then lower.

"No fight?" he murmurs. "That's sad."

I find my voice to ask, "Is it?"

"You're supposed to fight back, Rozelyn. You're not supposed to make this easy. Make me want to hurt you. I need you out of my head."

He wants a fight, except I'm completely frozen after his latest words: *Make me want to hurt you. Want* to hurt me.

"You're enjoying this?" His eyes lift to mine, and for a moment, the hardness is gone. A flash of his old self seeps in, but as quick as I see it, it's gone.

If I say yes, I might entice his wrath. He'll believe I'm lying and will unleash more anger. But is denial what he wants to hear?

His hand drops away and he removes the final inch of space between us. He takes my neck again, angling me in a way convenient for him. "My nightmare," he starts in a low tone, "was about the final day I saw you. When I waited for you out in the hallway between classes and yanked you into the girls' changing room. It's not the first time we did something like that, and usually, you enjoyed making it a struggle, but that day you didn't." Devastation flashes in his eyes, making my stomach tighten, aware of what he's about to say even before he does. "I didn't get it then. Something was off, but I didn't question you. It made sense by the end of the day."

Amidst his speech, he touches me again. His free hand finds mine, his fingers pressing into the old, white scar in the centre of my palm. Our promise to one another.

"Living that again, seeing you now, looking like you're *sorry* about the past—" His fingers push into my hand harder, until it hurts, and I flinch away from him, as much as the chains allow. "This is all you've ever done, Rozelyn. From day fucking one, you've played me for your convenience. You're doing it now. For fucking once, show me your real emotions."

They are real.

They're as real now as they were back then, even if he doesn't believe it.

I *hated* that day, and eventually, had to tuck it away in my mind. Stopped reliving it, aware that it was a few months of my life, and the pain would fade. Even when, in the following months, it didn't feel as such. Months turned into years, and I was able to stick memories of Flynn right into the same compartment as the ones I keep about Mom—away from the surface. Away from *feeling* them.

He blames me for pretending the day I told him goodbye, but I faked most of that week. Mom was admitted into the hospital and doctors were throwing around words relating to death and final days, but still, I used school as an escape. Not school, but Flynn. I *needed* the distraction he provided. Even Mom told me to go, somehow just knowing.

Without the school being aware of my real name, they had no clue of the drama surrounding me and I kept it all inside. Went to classes in a daze, nothing the teachers saying even registering.

The day the doctors said would be Mom's final was the same one Dad yanked me from school. Yasmine was already on leave from her private school—my old one. And my time was up.

All morning, I feigned happiness. At least, I plastered a smile on my face to pretend, knowing that every minute ticking away on the clock was one closer to breaking up with Flynn. At eighteen, being forced to end a relationship that had given me life felt like literal death. I didn't eat that day, barely spoke. Felt like throwing up every hour on the hour, the constant and mounting stress becoming more unbearable, especially when Flynn would look at me with that scorching gaze of his.

Guilt. Love. Grief. It all mingled, and I wasn't managing any of it.

I *needed* Flynn more than air, and when he pulled me into the changing room, yeah, I didn't fight it. That would be our last time having sex, as it was between classes and the final period of the day was approaching. My final one there ever.

Once Flynn and I came down from our high, I almost admitted everything right then. The truth of who I was, to see if he could see past my lie, of Mom's illness, so I could finally release the grief I'd been clinging to and what it meant for us that day.

Scared of rejection, fearing his hatred, I didn't go through with it. I'd be breaking his heart one way or the other that day, but not telling him the truth meant protecting him. Flynn would march his way right up to the De Falco mansion and Dad would lose his shit. Flynn's life wasn't worth the price of my peace.

So I didn't.

Instead, we cleaned up from sex, returned to our lockers to get materials for our last class, which we shared. Once second semester came, we shared most classes. Sitting through History, constantly peeking between Flynn and the clock until the end-of-day bell rang and I stopped breathing.

Stopped feeling.

I allowed him to walk me to the front doors where Dad's driver was waiting outside with the car, our normal routine. Flynn wouldn't see it coming—and didn't.

Then I broke his heart.

Ruined mine in the process.

Two days later, Mom passed.

And everything changed after that.

Me included.

# 11

## FLYNN

**W**herever Rozelyn is, she's no longer with me. She's lost, staring over my shoulder. Emotions pass through her eyes, making them first tighten, then mist. The skin of her forehead ripples and smooths twice. Whatever's in her head, it's taking her away from the present.

Speaking might bring her back, so I say, "You wondered why I can't sleep. That's fuckin' why."

I'm holding her. My hand around her neck, my other by my side, having just been stroking against the scar on her palm. I hate that I'm touching her. I hate that she's naked—that *I've* made her naked.

I hate that she's in my head. I need her out of there, whether through death or fucking her out of it. Clearly, my mind and heart lost the battle to my dick, so I came down here with the intention of sating that part of me. Fucking her out of my system so then I could move past the cloud of despair she's constructed in my head.

She's always relieved the noises. For once, she's making

them louder. Not only louder, but she's *causing* them. Period. She's the root of many of them.

Fucking her won't only help me. It'll help prove to both her and the Corsettis that the past truly holds no meaning. That I *can* and *will* hurt her. That I hate her, and everything Nico and Enzo and Caterina are concerned about is useless. That my brain will realize she's unable to fuck with me.

That's why I'm down here anyway. With her naked body pressed against me, with her bare pussy right up against my jeans. One snap and I can have mine undone, my cock hard, and fucking her from my system.

Yet, I don't move.

I *can't* move.

*You can't hurt her this way.*

I can and I will though. Once upon a time, her pussy controlled me. Owned me. With her return, clearly my cock thinks it's still this way, but it's not. I'll prove that to myself.

The noise in my head is cluttered, staticky, but I push past all that and stroke the side of her thigh, feeling pure silk beneath my calloused fingertips. She's always been soft, and I used to love that about her. Must be all that expensive body cream she has—or had—access to.

When I saw her in class on her first day of school, nose lifted in the air like she was better than everyone else, and that long fucking hair of hers, it all reminded me of some movie princess. An elitist amongst the poor. But it was her eyes that really captured me. Opposite from her attitude, which I later found to be her means of self-defence, soft and welcoming. Scared. When I was finally able to touch her, I knew she wasn't like the other girls in school. Rozelyn paraded around with a richness, even when she tried to hide it, and I loved it about her. Going home to my own shithole didn't matter because I was already captivated by the girl beneath the mask. When I was allowed to touch her, I couldn't stop. Her skin was like a cloud. One that hid the sun behind the girl.

"Flynn," she whispers. Her teeth scrape her bottom lip as she watches me. Judging and waiting for what I'll do next—where my hand will go.

I wish even I knew.

Why am I hesitating?

*Fucking Christ, what is happening to me?*

When have I ever hesitated? Never. So I won't start now.

My fingers trail around her thigh, coming between us, stroking her mound. I tighten my hold around her neck, searching for fear in her eyes, but come up with nothing. That only annoys me further. She should absolutely fear me. The fact she isn't says she believes our past will save her. It won't—I *have* to prove this to her.

I lower my head into the curve of her neck, scraping my teeth over her pulse. Her steady beating pulse. If she was at all nervous, her heartbeat would reveal it, but she's not. I need to speed this pulse up.

"Is this a lie too, I wonder?" My teeth graze her skin again, indicating what I'm referring to. "Faking not being scared of me?"

"No." She tries to lift her head, pulling on my hold, but gets nowhere. "I don't fear you, Flynn. Not sure I'd ever be able to."

"Liar."

I bring two fingers down to her core, stroking over her heat, and my fucking cock jumps to life. This is good though. This is needed. I'll get hard, I'll fuck her, and this will be over. She'll be out of my head, my body sated and able to focus again.

"See," she challenges. "Would I be wet if I was lying?"

"Arousal can be faked."

No reply.

"What changed, Rozelyn? When in that fuckin' head of

yours did you decide to stop fighting me—fighting this—and decide this would be the way to remain alive? Think distracting me with your pussy will save you?"

Little does she know, it just—*No.* I shut down the stupid thought.

With a huff, I stroke her core one more time, watching her face as I sink a single finger halfway inside her. Her eyes flutter shut and that's it. She falls victim. She officially loses herself to not fighting. I once told her down here would involve a mental game and she turned the tables on me.

The chains holding her arms jangle, a low moan filling the room. She shouldn't be enjoying my downfall.

She's wet. She's taking my finger. With little preparation, I can have her on my cock.

My confused, rattled head can be satisfied by morning, allowing me to focus again.

"Flynn," she whispers in a low tone, no fight whatsoever. "Flynn, I told you we'd find our way back to one another. This is..."

*Wrong,* I mentally finish for her. This is *wrong.* There's wanting to hurt her, to rid my mind of her, and then there's this. I can't hurt her, but I also can't play into her games. Into *any* of these mind games. Hers, mine. Fuck.

I tug my finger from her slowly, exiting bliss, and her eyes reopen, her mouth parting in question. In disappointment, which annoys me further considering *I'm* the one unable to sleep because of her.

I release her like she's on fire, both of us panting. I push back two steps, needing to put distance between us.

*Why did I think this was a good idea?* My hands rub at my face. I'm exhausted. I should have gone back to bed after my stint outside. Should have gone anywhere but here, thinking being around her could ease my dick enough to let the rest of her go. From day one, she's been my fucking addiction and what's to say she won't suck me right back in?

"What the hell was that?"

*I wish I knew.*

"Do you want to fuck me or hurt me?"

*Both.*

She huffs, clearly annoyed with my stares instead of gaining answers. "Well, maybe you should figure that out first before you come here again."

"What's your game?" I finally ask.

"No game." She rattles the chains again, making a meaningful expression. "Bit stuck, if you haven't noticed."

"You know what you need to do to get out of here."

She shrugs a shoulder. "Not sure, Flynn. Kinda enjoying the feeling of being used and abused like I've been. Strung up when it's convenient for your own mental battles. That's what all this is about, isn't it?" Her brows lift. "You think touching me will ease whatever fuckery's going on inside your head, but ask yourself, how's that working out for you. As much as you try to, you can't erase our past."

I hate that she's right.

About me, about my purpose down here, about everything.

I move before I realize what I'm doing, my hands around her neck before I think it through. My thumbs pressing right beneath her chin on either side, sucking the breath from her lungs before she can make another snarky comment. I walk us backward, though there's nowhere for her to go, making it no farther than the three steps the length of the chain allows.

My mind is fuzzy again. My thoughts erratic. My reasoning and sense long gone. *She's* doing this—she's always done this. This reminds me of the days leading up the break-up, when she had me feeling fucking insane because she was different that week. I was so on edge that when my father made his typical comments, I didn't remain silent any longer. One swift punch to the face and I was finished with his ass—with the emotional and mental abuse that came along with living with him.

Breaths come heavy from my lungs. No air feels enough to clear the dense fog covering the sense buried deep inside my head.

"Did you even fucking love me back then or was everything you said a lie?"

Of all the things I was going to say to her, that wasn't one of them. It was nowhere near the top, but some-fucking-how, it's what made it between my lips. Perhaps, it's my need for her response. If it's a *no*, my brain can catch up to reality.

*But if it's a yes?*

I ease my hands around her neck so she can respond.

"The only thing I ever lied about was my last name. I did love you, Flynn, and leaving you was the last thing I wanted to do."

*Lies.* She still lies!

A red rage fills my vision and it takes every bit of willpower not to squeeze the life from her throat. "At least there's that," I manage, the replay of her words barely easing my torment. "I don't believe you, but at least there's that." A contradictory statement.

"I'm telling you the truth," she whispers, her voice lined with a pain that makes my own insides hurt.

Guilt. Motherfucking goddamn guilt. That can't happen. I shake my head, trying to clear it.

Everything about her has brought me heartbreak. Before this week, I was happy with my life here. Content. And now I'm fucking conflicted. *She* makes me conflicted about the present and my past and that alone makes me hate her.

"Maybe," I mutter, jerking away from her. "Whatever bullshit you spew now doesn't change anything, Rozelyn. You're a De Falco. I hate you."

I give her my back, ready to leave this basement and my mistakes behind—her included.

"Are those your feelings toward me or my last name?" she calls out, pausing my quickening exit.

"Are they different?" I ask, an edge to my tone.

"Yes. My last name is the woman my father forced me to become. That's what you'd hate. If you hate me, then it's the girl you knew back then."

The girl who gave me light only to cast me in the darkness again. The girl who made me *feel* something for fucking once, who woke me from my daze for a short while, who gave me a sense of what life is like. That is who I hate because that's the girl that promised me forever.

A normal breakup, I could have handled. After all, exactly as she said days ago, it was eleven-years-ago. We were idealistic eighteen-year-olds, even if, looking back, I could decipher the difference between dreams and the future. It's not that she ended us; it's *what* she said. How she left me.

Feelings I've long shoved away only to have dragged to the surface with her re-entry into my life. She's a constant reminder of the misery she forced me into before Caterina helped me dig myself out.

"I protected you by not telling you the truth, but that didn't mean I didn't love you. I might have broken your heart that day, but I ruined mine too. It hasn't beat normal since I said goodbye to you."

*Lies.*

I need to get out of here.

Turning my back, I avoid the physical representation of guilt—her stuck in chains, naked, forced to stand until I release her back to the ground. I can't look at her because then the unspoken thoughts in my head will formulate into sentences that I'd rather pretend don't exist.

I exit the basement and flick the light off as I pass, leaving her in complete darkness again.

While she's physically in darkness, I return to my metaphorical one.

~

If that visit was meant to keep the dreams away, it doesn't work.

I dream.

Nightmares of that final conversation.

Flashes of every interaction.

Every time I had her naked.

It's in those memories, old, buried facts slowly reveal themselves, granting me ammo to end her.

*Game on, Rozelyn. Game fucking on.*

# 12

## ROZELYN

Being stripped naked and chained to the ceiling puts one's life in perspective and raises questions.

The first of which: wondering how many days in total have passed. How much longer is it best to remain silent before admitting what the Corsettis want to know? How much longer will Flynn and I survive each other?

Because that's what this feels like. A combat for control. Of him and me fighting a battle that the Corsettis and my father aren't a part of. He gained a captive, but what he actually found was a piece of his past, one he clearly pushed away. Now I'm back, maybe reminding him of a different time, one he isn't interested in recalling.

Tipping my head, I look at the scar on my palm. Ask me a month ago, if my plan would have been to get in good with the Corsetti enforcer, and my answer would have been a no. But now, it feels like a chance. A chance I have no idea what I want to do with. If I could leave here with my life, a plan to get Yasmine to safety, my father in captivity, and a band-aid on mine and Flynn's past, then I've done more than I originally planned on.

*Yasmine.* Finally thinking her name after days down here, weeks without seeing her, is a hit to my heart. She's been firmly tucked into further parts of my mind because I know thinking about my younger sister will make my plan explode. I'll fuck up my own strategies for the sake of her safety, and right now, if I continue to play it right, she and I will both be freed from our father.

So for now, I shove Yasmine into the back of my mind again and shift on the balls of my feet. A numbing sensation coursing through my arms, already sore from being chained above my head.

I sigh. I should be more disgusted by Flynn's actions than I am, and maybe it's wrong to be rationalizing what he's done. I should be at least angry at him, but I'm not. That'd be a normal response; one expectant of someone in my position, but not one I'm apparently experiencing.

The animalistic look in Flynn's eyes should have been terrifying, especially backed by his actions. The knife, the cuts, his finger in my pussy. He never stated it, but I think he came down here with plans of more.

Is it wrong to say I wouldn't have stopped him either? Wouldn't have fought him. Would have happily re-experienced that part of him. My attraction to Flynn hasn't dissipated over the years, clearly.

He's accusing me of lying back then, and now; that my present actions aren't real, and I'd like to believe that. But they're not. They're realer than anything I've felt in a long time.

Love—that's a thing of the past.

But a connection...that still exists. He's feeling it too or else whatever fucked-up situation we just lived through wouldn't have happened.

Question is, which one of us will break first?

With another long sigh, I lean in one direction, resting my exhausted head on my arm, knowing it won't be long before I shift again. When my side goes numb and my arm gets sore from the weight pulling on it, I'll have to move.

Morning better come quickly.

~

I don't sleep. *Maybe* I doze off for minutes at a time, but that's it. My feet ache from being poised on cement all day. My thigh is burning again, and I wonder if they'd give me any pain meds. Apparently standing upright isn't preferred by the injury. Even my neck muscles, which I roll every couple minutes, are tender.

Yet, when the light turns on and Flynn's telltale boots come into sight, my body is vitalized again, enough that I can straighten and attempt to cling to a meager amount of dignity.

I wonder which version of him I'll be getting today. The wonder is only for a moment because when he comes into sight, it's with a dead gaze again. A mask. A sneer.

But when I spot a shirt hanging from his hand, I nearly cry.

He stops in front of me, his eyes flicking over my face. "You're a mess."

"Yes." My voice is hoarse from lack of water and usage in the hours passing since he left me. "That's what happens when my tormentor strips me, slices at my skin, and leaves me hanging by my wrists after days of darkness and limited visitations." Saying all this feels like I'm admitting my struggles. "I'm fucking weak, Flynn. But that's your goal." Then again, maybe he deserves to know exactly how I'm affected.

From his pocket, he digs out a key, and when he lifts it to

one of the cuffs, tears become a real possibility. The moment that wrist is freed and falls to my side, my entire body decompresses. Turns out, there are natural positions for the human body and that wasn't one of them.

Flynn undoes my other one, and this time, instead of just my arm falling to my side, my entire body does too. I land on my knees with a pained thump, exhaustion *really* hitting then. The cold, cement ground, probably disease-riddled too, has never seemed better than this instance. My shoulders slowly meld back into place and my head lowers, my body curling in on itself. Despite death hovering over me, the craving of sleep immediately creeps covers my vision, only banished when large, firm hands reach down and slip beneath my arms.

"No." It comes out as a pathetic mewl I hate myself for. There's admitting I'm in pain, and then there's showing it in such a way. But he's winning. "No," I repeat, head lolling as he lifts me up again, my feet dragging on the cement, all my weight on his hands.

"You don't look so good." His words don't have the usual hardness in them. I'd like to think it's pity, but it could be exhaustion making me delirious.

Yeah," I agree again. "That's what happens when you leave someone hanging all night."

"It was only three hours."

Only? It felt longer.

His arm goes around my waist, taking my entire weight, and my head falls into his chest, smelling clean soap, not caring that I shouldn't be seeking comfort from the very person who is causing me pain.

He lifts my chin, his eyes bouncing over my face. "Stay awake a bit longer, *mon soleil*. You have a day planned out and if you behave, I'll reward you."

*Mon soleil.* Was the nickname used on purpose? His way of trying to break me? How I feel now; he won't need to try for long.

But then the rest of his sentence registers and I have no idea what he'll demand of me, other than answers, but at this point, the reward might be worth it.

He says nothing more and drops his hand from my face, just holding me. With his touch, I allow the old emotions to surface. He's wearing a leather coat and it should be chilly against my bare skin, but the soft material feels comforting instead. *He* feels comforting.

He's always been that for me.

If there's one regret I'll never have in life, it's hiding out by the smoke pit that day.

Which prompts me to ask—more to mumble, "Do you still smoke?"

"No."

My breath stalls. Why do I feel that means something?

"The last day I smoked was the day you left."

*Oh.*

Before I have a chance to further probe, his arm unhooks from my waist, his hand from my head, and he abandons me, swaying as I reach for him again, a sound of denial creeping up my throat.

Sneering, he shies away and shoves the clothing in his hand at me. It's one of his shirts. "Cover yourself," he demands, still not facing me.

Almost as pleasant as his hold, the clothing warms my form, falling nearly to my knees, the sleeves to my elbows. His distinct scent permeates from the material.

Before enjoyment can settle in though, he's roughly yanking my wrist right back into the chain hanging from the ceiling. It's not clamped around my wrist yet and already, I feel the injuries and pain returning.

"No." I jerk from his hold, but his fingers tighten into a vise, pinching the bone. "Not again, Flynn. I *can't*." If I act desperate enough, maybe he'll grant me this.

Using sheer strength, he wins—not that there was much of a battle—and clasps both wrists above my head. He's hardly sparing me any attention, which means the man who was here a second ago, who was holding me, is once again gone, beneath the new enforcer.

It proves one thing though. The struggle he went through last night wasn't from his own sleepiness. The Flynn I knew and loved is still here, buried beneath deceit, duplicity, and hatred.

He moves behind me, out of view, his hand stroking the skin right where his shirt ends. It reminds me of when I'd borrow his hoodie in high school, and he commented how sexy I looked in it. I always wanted to take it home with me but feared Dad finding it.

With his face in the curve of my neck, I feel his next words imprinting into my skin. "You will because I know you, Rozelyn. You enjoy the pain. Makes you feel alive. Be good and I'll reward you."

Even when he's finished speaking, he doesn't move away, and as messed up as it is, I don't pull away either. He feels...nice. Comforting. Warm. Encompassing, like the moon.

"What do you need from me?"

"You have a visitor."

People. Someone other than Flynn is coming down here? Based on my quickening heartbeat, I don't think that's a good thing. Don't think I'll want this. With Flynn, I know what to expect, but anyone else...my leg can speak for what happens when other people torture me.

"Who?"

He moves away from me and retrieves his phone from his back pocket, his fingers flying over the screen before pocketing it again and moving toward the side.

I track him. "This is your shirt."

His sharp gaze slices through the basement's stench. "And?"

I shrug, feigning disinterest. "Nothing. Interesting choice of clothing."

The door opens, gaining my attention as a man enters the view first, followed by the distinct legs of women. They reach the bottom of the stairs, fanning out into a line, and my stomach drops.

I knew they were here, but somehow, it was easy to ignore that fact. Hell, Flynn and I even spoke about them the other day. They're realer being down here, ignoring them is no longer an option as I'm faced with my ex-stepsisters, Della and Ariella, and Nico Corsetti.

Nico approaches first, one arm angled around Della, which is ridiculous if he thinks I'll be able to attack anyone in my current predicament. He's dressed as he is every time I've seen him, in a suit, and in direct contrast to the leather jacket and dirty jeans Flynn's wearing. Despite Dad's insistence to play the mobster game, I never did enjoy a man in a suit.

At Nico's side, Della leans forward to see around the wall he's erected with his body. She's wearing makeup, her hair shiny and clean, and I'm instantly envious of the signs related to my old life. The feeling of clean hair compared to what I'm living with presently. The most noticeable fact is how much she looks like a queen by Nico's side. The future Corsetti leaders.

Funny how circumstances change so easily.

At her side, Ariella, who I haven't seen since the day Dad shipped her off to some medical centre somewhere in the city, deciding she'd no longer be useful to his plans. Knowing him, I expected him to rid himself of her completely, but in typical Dad fashion, he took the opportunity of Ariella being in the car crash too, to use her as leverage against Della.

That day, I had a few choice words for him but I instead walked away, hid in my room, and screamed into a pillow. Kept my emotions turned off, knowing the outcome if I showed any empathy toward the Lambert sisters' situation to Dad.

Unlike her sister, who's trying to step into the light, Ariella's content in the shadows. She's always reminded me of Yasmine. Both their personalities are of a quiet demeanour. In some ways, I suppose, Della and I also share similarities.

I roll my neck, looking at Flynn, finding enough energy to mask my face into a snarl and find my cocky tone again, pushing through the exhaustion. Nico and the rest don't get the pleasure of my weakness. Stupid really, considering Flynn's on their side, but it's...different. Even if I can't explain how.

"*They're* who you're scaring me with."

Flynn's mouth flattens, but he ignores the bait at the same time Della steps forward, pushing into Nico's arm.

"*I* asked to speak with you," she says.

"Why?" I keep my tone flat. "Think some sister bonding will loosen my lips?"

*Be a bitch. Hide the truth. Hide the emotions. Don't let anyone see how close they are to breaking me.*

"No," she denies, half-surprising me. "Came to see you. Talk to you. That's all."

She and I end up in a stare down, with Ariella watching her sister. I feel Flynn's sharp gaze on me, while Nico's attention flips back and forth.

"Alone."

I gain everyone's attention for that comment, but my focus shifts from Della to Nico, knowing he's the only one here with authority. Flynn might be holding my life, but it's Nico who pulls the trigger or not.

"I'll only speak to them alone."

Nico moves at the same time Flynn's at my back, one of his many blades jamming into my throat on the opposite side of the slice from last night. "Remember what I said about behaving? You don't make decisions."

I turn my head, right into the blade, uncaring as it presses into my skin. If I cut myself, then he loses the power to injure me. That was something Dad always taught me. Take the punishment so when it's granted later, it hurts less.

"Then I don't talk."

Della's soft voice rises from behind Nico. "Leave us alone. She's chained. She can't do anything."

Nico's blazing eyes find his wife's, shifting his wrath from me to her. Difference is, he'd happily stab Flynn's knife into my heart; his anger for Della comes from a place of love. For everything that happened, Della made a home here. Found love amongst these people. She literally led their underboss to his death and lied and betrayed them, and *still* found herself on the inside. Dad underplayed her abilities.

"Della—"

Ignoring her husband, she pointedly looks at Flynn. "Is there any chance of escape?"

"No," he answers in a regretful tone as though he wanted it to be a yes, so they'd have a reason to stay.

Della's winning smile shifts from Flynn to Nico. "See? Ariella and I will remain right here." She gestures to their feet. "No closer than this spot, I promise."

There's a silent argument between the couple that's almost tangible from over here, but whatever influence Della holds over Corsetti has him finally folding. "Fine. If you're not up in ten minutes, we're coming back."

He glances at Ariella first, as though looking for an argument in her passive expression, but finds none, and then jerks his head toward Flynn. Flynn's huff blows warm over my neck as his knife comes away from my skin. With a final meaningful glare toward me, he follows Nico to the staircase and exits the basement with his boss.

"That was magical," I muse. "Della, you really have Corsetti wrapped around your finger."

Already, she breaks her promise to him by pacing three steps closer, walking right over that invisible line she told Nico she'd stay behind. Ariella remains in the shadows though.

Della ignores the jab and asks, in that soft, perfect voice I've always hated her for out of pure jealousy, "Are you okay?"

Seriously? The chains jiggle when I move my exhausted limbs, reminding her of my current situation. "Do I look okay, Della?"

"You look like a woman who's made a few mistakes."

Her statement stuns me for a second and I end the rattling, before I shake the feeling off. If she's seeking truth and genuineness, she'll find none here. Not yet anyway. "I made no mistakes."

Pinching her lips, she whispers, "You drugged Aurora, Rozelyn. That's not you."

*You have no idea who I am.* "Yes, Aurora. Your sister-in-law. Congrats on your wedding, by the way."

"You were always a bitch, Rozelyn, but I didn't think you'd do something to harm another person."

She's right about that. I was a bitch because kindness only goes so far in this grim, depressing world.

"Yeah, well," I shrug, pursing my lips, considering how best to convey a façade of carelessness, "like I've told others, I did it for my own reasons."

"To gain our attention," she correctly states, crossing her

arms with a slight head tilt, like she's trying to figure me out. "Whatever Stefano commanded you to do, *I* can help you." She steps closer again, her brows dipping as she talks, emotion packing every word—hope. "Ask for anything and I can make it happen. You're wrapped up in his plots, Rozelyn, but it doesn't need to be this way."

Silence. She's pleading with me to speak—to ask for something that shows I'm redeemable in her eyes. Giving her that, though, opens the floodgates for more, which I'm not ready to do.

Della peeks back at Ariella, who hasn't moved from her spot. Then she looks to me again, her brows lower than before. "Where's Yasmine? If he's holding your sister over your head, I *do* know what that's like."

"She's fine." Maybe. She better be.

"So you're not doing this to protect her?"

*Not exactly.*

Della frowns and lowers her arms again. "But you're here and not her, which means you were his scapegoat. You're the distraction, while he escapes, right? That's what Stefano does, Rozelyn. He *uses.*"

*I'm aware more than you know.*

"If you're trying to appeal to me on a familial level, give up." I jerk my chin to the stairs, indicating she can leave now.

"I'm trying—" Her hands fist with the word, her annoyance building in ways witnessed before. By Corsetti's side, clearly she's found a bit of a backbone. When she restarts, it's with words more paced and thought out. "I'm trying to make you understand. We can be on the same side."

*We are on the same side, but it's not time for you to know that yet.*

When I don't take her bait, she sighs, her shoulders slumping. "Look, I wanted to come see you. We were stepsisters, after all. Deny it all you want, but we're family."

"We're *ex*-stepsisters," I emphasize, so she understands the difference. *Ex* holds less of a current connection.

"Ex," she murmurs her agreement. "Why were you such a bitch after we moved in? Was it because you thought my mother was taking the place of yours?"

Glancing past her to Ariella, I catch the slightest movement as the redhead finally comes into the light. Clearly, she's interested by this question.

"No," I grant them the truth, "not completely. Maybe at first, but it was more than that."

"And after the accident?" She asks it so bluntly, she misses the way Ariella flinches. Ariella, who was in that car too, and is now living as the only survivor from the incident. For Della, the accident is a horrendous fact, but Ariella's still directly affected by it, and for that, I feel sorry for her. Ariella never deserved to be the brunt of Dad's evilness.

The same way Yasmine could be at this moment.

"You were so cruel," Della continues. "Both you and Yasmine were, and I always found it odd. Considering you lost your mother too, we had that shared heartbreak. You know what it feels like to lose someone close to you."

*Because being mean to you made everything easier. The second I viewed you as a friend, as another sister, I'd tell you the truth. I wouldn't be able to protect us all, and Yasmine was my priority.*

"Maybe I'm simply a bitch, Della. Ever think about that?"

With a slow shake of her head, her eagerness falters to sadness as she leans away. Obviously, she was hoping for more from this interaction and I gave her nothing.

"So that's it?" she murmurs after a long moment of terse

silence. "You're going to continue being the villain. My question is, is doing so your father's plan or yours?"

I can't give an answer to that. Truth or lie, she's so close to the facts, it's terrifying to my self-control.

"Does it matter? It's not getting me out of these chains one way or the other."

She glances up to the pipe attached to the chains on the ceiling. "No, but you can end this. You're prolonging your own torture, and that's why I'm down here. Why I'm trying to make you realize, this can end. The moment I admitted the truth to Nico, he helped me. He'll do the same for you. He recognizes loyalty, Rozelyn. Have some for us, and we can help."

Loyalty doesn't matter to me. Survival does.

"Do you really care for your father that much that you'd risk your life for him? If anything, it should be the other way around. That he'd be keeping you safe."

*Should* being the key word in her final statement but Dad's never done anything for his family. Not Mom, Yasmine, and me, anyway. Everything's been for *them*.

Della is correct on every single count, though. Only one fact she's still missing.

Thankfully, the door opening at the top of the stairs ends this interaction. Within seconds, Nico rushes down the stairs and tugs Della back to his side, studying the distance between her and me, the spot she claimed she'd remain.

"Ten minutes is up."

Della nods, glancing from her husband to me, wearing that sad expression again, before gesturing for Ariella to ascend the stairs first.

At the bottom of the stairs, Ariella peeks back at me. Her lips open and I find myself leaning closer, waiting intently for sound to come from the mute woman, but then her brows furrow, she shakes her head, and quickly escapes, almost running up the stairs.

Della watches her sister go before glancing at me a final time. "Goodbye, Rozelyn. I'm sorry for what this life has done to both of us. From here on out, you could change it."

She leaves, and Nico follows behind her, not sparing me a glance.

I'm alone for a few minutes after they go, but my heart thumps to a new, chaotic beat.

Ariella appears from the basement first. She throws a tight smile my way and disappears down the hallway, not that I expected her to say anything. I've never heard the woman's voice, and I doubt I ever will. Quiet and shy—I can respect her desire for privacy, although I'm now wondering if there's more to her. I'm not exactly privy to every detail of Nico's private life, including that of his new sister-in-law.

The door opens shortly after, and Della and Nico appear. Della's eyes are downcast, her mouth curved in a frown. Fuck Rozelyn for hurting her feelings.

*This* is what I needed. A reminder that Rozelyn De Falco isn't a good person. She's our enemy and continues to harm this family. The family I've vowed to protect.

When Nico shuts the door behind them, Della shakes her head once and tells me in a dejected tone, "Nothing. She's hiding something. There's a feeling in my gut that she's not doing all this in loyalty to Stefano. Or maybe she is," her frown deepens, doubt making her eyes shift to the far corner of the hallway, "because why else would she agree? There's just...I don't know. What asshole sends his own daughter into the enemy's house?"

Nico rubs her back lightly and reminds, "He sent you."

Once again, I hide a possible fact from my boss. What Della's learned only reinforces where my own thoughts have been since last night. Where, in the depths of my head, memories resurfaced, which explains much of her behaviours back then—and some of her statements now.

If I'm right, it explains a lot. If I'm wrong, then I got Nico's hopes up for nothing. So until I know for certain, I remain quiet.

Della walks away looking more dejected than I've ever seen, and while Nico stares after her, he doesn't follow. When she turns a corner, he says, "My mother mentioned seeing you outside last night. Flynn, no disrespect if you can't do this. If emotions are hindering your actions, I won't fault you for that."

This is the very reason I need her out of my head. She's not only filling it and making me doubt myself; it's also becoming obvious to the Corsettis.

"I'm fine." I step by him and open the door to the basement again to end this conversation. "Last night, I needed the reminder of who really matters, and it's not her."

Before I can walk down the steps, he stops me with another question. "Is taking her to the bathroom in your room really the smartest idea, when there's ones in the common areas?"

Licking at my suddenly parched lips, I realize I have no concrete response for him. Nothing that logically makes sense. Hell, even I don't fully understand my own actions, but formulating some sort of half-assed response, I tell him, "It's smaller. The one down here has a window I'd have to ensure she doesn't escape from. Mine doesn't."

He grunts and turns, his expression telling me he doesn't quite believe my explanation, but he doesn't push for a different answer, so before he can, I shut the door and descend the wooden steps.

When I first came down, before Della's planned visit, to get Rozelyn dressed, her life seemed to be completely drained. Limp, looking lifeless, she stood with her body sagging and head lolling to the side. Exhaustion dominating her.

Until her stepsisters came down here. Like a switch, I watched her flick on, feigning attitude to get through the interaction without revealing what she thinks is weakness to others. She's letting me see it and I hate how that makes me feel.

I find her in a similar position this time too. Her head is resting against her chained arms, her eyes shut, but they slowly open as I tread across the cement. Her skin is paler, the dark marks beneath her eyes more noticeable.

The shirt she's wearing—mine—makes my chest burn with old emotions. It reminds me of when she'd wear my hoodies on the frosty, winter days when Montreal's icy temperatures made the school's ancient heater struggle. She shivered a lot in class, but I enjoyed that something of mine warmed her.

Reaching into my pocket, I grab the key that will free her from these chains and get to work on her first wrist.

"So you do keep your promises."

"Yes, because I'm not you. I don't make promises and then turn around and break them."

As I go for her other wrist, I catch sight of the scar in the centre of her palm, making this conversation even more bitter in my mouth. Talking about broken promises when the white mark is a visual representation of old vows made.

With both wrists free, her arms fall to her sides and she sways, catching her balance at the last second, right as I turn for the stairs.

"Follow. Or don't, and see how much I care."

She'll follow, even if it kills her because she'll want her reward for getting through the interaction with Della and Ariella.

"No chain around my neck this time?"

Amused, I smirk over my shoulder, noticing how she's barely started up the steps, even though I'm nearing the top by the door. "Given how you just hobbled across the room, I doubt you're able to fight."

It takes her a moment but finally, she meets me at the top of the stairs. Her stride doesn't break as she heads in the direction of my room, knowing that's where we're going even though I'd never told her so. She's limping, her pace slow. I wait by the basement door and watch her, knowing with her speed, it'll take only a moment before I catch up.

She's clearly in pain and it sets something off inside me. Something I *won't* title. *Won't* admit to myself. Something that reminds me of the old sensations I'd get when I saw the dark spots on her skin. Instead, I lie to myself and pretend to find enjoyment in the scene.

The lie bursts as soon as I try to convince myself of it and I'm by her side in a moment, my arms reaching around her body to scoop her up bridal-style. She doesn't fight, not that she has the strength to, and her head immediately goes to the curve of my neck.

*Fuck. Me.*

"You're carrying me."

"You were always smarter than I was."

"Funny. I assumed you'd be fine seeing me collapse."

*Me too.* I tell her instead, "I am, but I'd also like to get this over with sometime today."

She doesn't talk again as I enter my room, locking the door behind us, and march her straight past my bed, past the food I had brought in earlier, and right into the bathroom, depositing her on the shut toilet seat.

"Shower. Do what you need to. You have fifteen minutes. Don't think about drowning yourself to escape. I know CPR and *will* bring your ass back."

Then I back away and shut the door, granting her an ounce of privacy that she doesn't deserve. Why? Wish I fucking knew.

Just like I wish I understood what I'm even doing right now. These niceties are to play right along with her. Days of hell downstairs, only to grant her a reprieve. Show her we're not the villains she thinks we are. Loosen her lips.

When the shower switches on, I stupidly imagine her stripping my shirt off, the cuts I've left on her body red and apparent as she steps beneath the steaming water. Did she moan when the hot water hit her sore muscles? Is she appreciating what this moment means?

Staring at the ceiling, I invent an invisible grid on it and then count every square, simply to keep my mind busy as I wait for the fifteen minutes I've given her to pass. I almost hope she goes over the time limit, so I'll have a reason to release this electrifying energy igniting inside me.

The fifteen minutes come and I give her an extra moment.

And then another.

Still, no noise from beyond the door. No doubt, she's now being straight-up defiant. I swing to my feet, the hint of a smile taking over as I enter the bathroom and step over my shirt, which she's left in the middle of the floor.

She's bound to have heard me enter so I know with certainty, she's ignoring the single rule I've given her. No matter. I grasp the edge of the flimsy plastic shower curtain throw it to the side, the plastic loops scraping loudly against the metal pole.

Pain. Hate. The only emotions I've felt since Rozelyn told me goodbye.

Never fear.

But the icy sensation that passes over my heart, that makes my nerves rigid, and forces my feet to move is new. I don't like it. If it's fear, I don't ever want to feel it again.

Rozelyn is curled on the floor of the shower, the water washing over her back and thighs from where she's upright, slumped against the tiled wall. Her arms are limp around her, and that fucking insane amount of hair is drenched, darker against her pale skin.

Immediately, I shut off the water and reach for her, two fingers finding her pulse. Nerves unwind at the steady thump.

Breathing. She's alive, which means she's asleep. So exhausted, she's passed out.

Lifting her, she soaks my clothes and I grab the nearest towel from the rack and toss it over her form as I head back into my room. She deserves to be woken, dressed, and placed right back into the basement. At the very least, maybe I'll grant her access to that sleeping bag I've taunted her with before she truly breaks, both mentally and physically.

Instead, I do none of that. Shifting her to one arm, I pull the blankets of my bed back and rest her down, quickly patting her dry with the towel, spending a moment longer to wipe away the water drops speckled on her face.

She looks so different when she's asleep, and it hits me then, I've never been granted this part of her. I've seen the girl I fell for be miserable, happy, focused, and sated after we had sex. I've seen the woman, who reappeared as my enemy, be cocky, resolute, emotional, and even defeated. But not this. Asleep with her guard completely down.

Resting the towel to the side, I bring my hand to her face. Not quite touching at first, but hovering. Watching and waiting to see if she can feel me above her, but there's no sign of alertness in her steady breath or her shut eyes.

There's a single water drop sliding toward her eyes, abandoned by her hair, so I catch it with my thumb, stroking her skin as I do.

Rozelyn wet was always my favourite sight. There's something about how the water clung to her face that made me jealous of it.

*"You really need to quit smoking. It's raining. I can't go out there," she argues as my unyielding grip yanks her to the wet outdoors. The weather isn't harsh enough to make smoking impossible, simply a challenge that cupping a hand over the cigarette will fix.*

*Still, it drips all over her face, trickling down her cheeks and gathering on her dark lashes as I drag her to our bench. Our bench. I remove my coat and rest it on the wood, gesturing for her to sit while I wander a couple feet away to light up, keeping the cigarette away from her, as per our pattern. She's unfailing to join me outside for my smoke breaks, and despite the weather, I didn't want to see that pattern broken.*

*She sits gingerly, repositioning the coat in a way suitable to her needs, and then stares at me expectantly. The slow rain bounces off her form, a contrast to her narrowed, playful eyes and pinched mouth.*

*She's never looked more gorgeous.*

When the water drop I stole from her skin drips down my hand and disappears completely, it returns me to the present with a low gasp and a sudden force, propelling me away from her.

*Fucking Christ, no.* I refuse to have any positive flashbacks of us. The only ones my mind craves are the moments of misery. When it makes hating her easier and more natural. Not the ones where I knew how fucking utterly in love with her I was, even if I didn't say it at the time.

The memory was a rainy October afternoon, only days before Halloween. Probably one of our final rainfalls before the temperature got so cold, it'd turn the precipitation into snow. I loved that kind of weather and longed to see her outside with me in the rain. God, it didn't disappoint either. It was a month after we started hanging out, and it dawned then, that I was liking her more than simply as a chill girl to hang out with.

Rubbing my hand over my face, I release all those thoughts too, ridding my mind of them. Now, not only am I fucking reliving positive moments; I'm *rationalizing* them.

I won't lose myself to this. To the past. To her.

Grabbing the towel, I toss it into the corner of the room by my laundry basket and draw my comforter up overtop her. She makes her first noise, a breathy moan, and turns her head, snuggling deeper into my pillow.

A sight that makes my body heat with angry flames.

Because I hate her.

Because the sight of her in my bed makes the memories stronger. Makes old feelings more apparent.

The day she told me goodbye, it was raining.

It's ironic that I realized I liked her romantically on a rainy day, and then lost her on another.

If only it was *that* memory seeing her wet from the shower made resurface. *That* memory would drive me to get her away from my sanctuary. *That* memory makes me happy.

Even when, of all the moments between Rozelyn and me, it's my worst one yet.

But it makes me happy because it's a reminder.

A reminder of what love can do to one's heart.

# 14
## ROZELYN

For once, my ass isn't numb. My feet aren't arching from being forced to stand. My shoulders feel relaxed and unstretched.

No pain.

Just softness. A cloud.

I open my eyes, staring up at a white ceiling. No grimness of a basement ceiling. There's a dark comforter over me and a scent way too familiar. I'm naked but warmer than I've been in days.

I'm in a bed.

By my side, an arm brandishes mine. Flynn's skin briefly makes contact as he readjusts from where he's asleep, his head on the pillow beside me.

I'm in *Flynn's* bed.

With him sleeping, which is a sight I've never seen. All that hardness is gone from his expression, and he looks...peaceful. The comforter is resting on his hip, his body bare from the chest up. All his tattoos are on display, and he's *covered* in them, so I can't make out individual ones.

I study the room, first glancing in the direction of the last place I recall—the bathroom. I was in the shower. I remember turning it on, standing beneath the water and quickly washing my hair with his shampoo, a scent so contradictory to my normal one. It felt heavenly to not only wash away the grime but to feel genuine warmth for the first time in days. The heat penetrated my skin and heated me straight to my bones.

That's when the sleepiness started to increase. Remaining on my feet felt like an energy drain, but I wouldn't miss the gift of that shower for anything in the world. I don't recall sitting, or anything else.

Which means...I bring my attention back to Flynn, realization making me breathless. He carried me from the shower, likely once his fifteen-minute time limit passed. But instead of returning me to the basement, he tucked me into his bed.

And then went to sleep too.

Flynn's asleep.

And I'm unhindered by anything. Unbound and free to roam.

Slowly, inch by inch, I slide from the bed, resting one foot on the ground, and then the other, before straightening. Every minor movement, I glance back, to make sure he's still asleep.

And then...I don't know. I need to pee, and escape is pointless. After all, I still need the Corsettis but not being tied to a metal pole is a nice change. To pace his small room and stretch my legs, to feel my wrists unbound.

In the bathroom, I find his shirt from yesterday and toss it on. There's a comb on the back of the seat, which I use on my hair, now clean but still damp. The few minutes of self-care revitalizes me. Energizes me to continue Flynn's game.

He's still asleep when I return to the bedroom. In the far corner, I spot Flynn's pants and that's when it really hits. All the weapons he keeps on his body.

There's probably one in here.

*What's the purpose?* For the same reason I'm not escaping, I won't fight him. But maybe something to have on me, just in case.

*And hide it where?*

Despite the purely logical questions, I rifle through his jeans and find the switchblade he's so fond of. It's heavy, a deep, blue-coloured handle. With it in hand, I stand, thumb stroking over the button that'll open it.

In the next flash, my vision blurs. There's a large arm banding my waist. I'm staring at the wall, and then the ceiling, my body flat on the soft bed, his hands pinning each of my wrists down to the mattress. I'm stuck, his legs on either side of my thighs. Somewhere in that, he managed to grab the knife from my hand and laid it on my chest.

Instead of irritation, his tone is soft. Seductive. Meant to lull and it seemingly works, considering my insides clench with desire. "What the fuck was your plan?"

"I don't know," I respond honestly. "How long were you awake?"

"*Mon soleil*, I'm a light sleeper. Always have been. Felt the moment you started to inch off the bed."

That nickname again. He uses its so sparingly, I have to wonder if it's a mistake.

"You faked being asleep," I accuse with narrowed eyes.

His smirk is playful, and from our position, I could imagine him giving me it for another reason entirely. One much more pleasurable. "Wanted to see what you'd do. I'll admit, I'm a bit disappointed you didn't try to escape, but getting a weapon was a nice touch." He releases one of my wrists to pick up the knife, clicking the button that opens it, his gaze studying the blade with the same look one would give their lover. "What was your plan with this?"

"I have no clue," I answer, but it comes out breathy as the blade lowers to my chest. Still covered by his shirt, I don't feel it as he lightly traces the material, lifting himself off me with every inch.

"That's too bad," he murmurs. "I really wanted to see you fight, Rozelyn."

When he passes over my stomach, I still. "Why?" That's contradictory to everything happening.

"To find a bit of the girl I once knew in there. Submission isn't your style."

"Told you, I'm not the same. *We're* not the same."

"No," he agrees, dragging the blade over my hip. "We're not. And yet, I still can't get you out of my head. You've fucked me up. You're *fucking* things up."

He inches his shirt over my hip until my pussy is bared to him. His actions take me back to last night when he was hateful and vengeful and apparently trying to make a point that I think he failed in making, but there's a stark difference this time. He doesn't look irate. Doesn't look like he's ready to kill me.

He blames me for playing games, but I have to wonder if that's what this is.

"Why did you let me shower?"

Dark eyes flash to mine. "Because you wanted it."

The room falls silent, with only our breaths filling the space. Maybe what he said was purposeful on his part; maybe it was by accident, but there's a deeper fact buried within his words.

An emotion neither of us will name.

Add that to the fact he knew what I wanted even before I did. Obviously, I wanted a shower. A comfortable place to sleep. Not to live out my potential final days in a dank basement, but the moment Dad handed me those laced marijuana gummies to drug Aurora Corsetti with and when I didn't hide my identity by using my full name on the garden's volunteer list, I knew the outcome of my future. Things I wanted would no longer be a part of it.

Breaking our stare, Flynn trails the sharp blade in the space beneath my stomach. I suck in a breath, careful not to make it easier for him to cut me.

"Why am I in your bed?" I dare ask.

"Because you want to be."

Do I? I don't know what I want anymore, but he apparently does.

"That so?"

Flynn makes a noise of agreement in the back of his throat and he leans back on his knees, gaining use of his other arm again, which was propping him up. He's still crouched though, his face dangerously close to my pussy, where he drags the blade back and forth over my mound.

"Yeah," he finally speaks, bringing his free hand toward my core. A single finger swipes between my slit; he moves quickly and effortlessly, my desire for him making it easier. "Because how else do you explain this, *mon soleil*?"

In the light of his room, the tip of his index finger shines.

*Jesus.* I'm getting turned on by his knife—by *him*. By the perilous danger involved in being in this bed with him.

"And?" I challenge with a lift of my eyebrows. "I bet you you're getting hard by this too."

"Maybe. But I'm not the one pinned to a bed." With the same hand, he pushes between my legs, parting them slowly. I don't fight it and his gaze drops right to my core, a fresh wave of hunger filling his expression. "You're not arguing, Rozelyn. Not fighting. You're enjoying this, aren't you?"

I am. I shouldn't but I fucking am. With the blade, he traces down to my thighs, skirting over the most sensitive parts of me that have my teeth biting into my bottom lip.

"You are too," I counter, when my voice begins working

again. It's low, wanting. "You're in control here. If you don't want me to feel pleasure, maybe you should stop."

The look in his eyes reminds me of a better time. The playful viciousness as he drags the knife back up, lifting it a fraction so it breathes over my skin as he dances it along the hood of my clit.

"Maybe I don't want to because I adore the look in your eyes."

"Strange words from a man who despises me." He pauses, tensing. One wrong move and he could stab me in a place I doubt healing from will be quick—or even possible. Still, I continue talking, every form of danger provoking me. "That's why you visited last night, isn't it? You went on and on about getting me out of your mind, and you went down to prove it to me and to everyone else here." I jerk my chin in the direction of his door. "Your mind is filled with the past as much as mine is and you think by being cruel, you'll be able to forget it."

For a full minute, there's complete silence. A stillness from him.

Then finally, "Maybe I'm trying to make you hate me so I can remember how I feel about you."

"I told you why I lied, Flynn. I couldn't tell you who I was because you'd search for me."

"You give yourself a lot of credit," he shoots back, snarky, but the truth in my statement is in our past—in everything he's said to me since I was captured and brought here.

"Now you're lying."

"Maybe. Maybe not. Maybe it's not only what you did, but how you did it."

He speaks so low, so honest, I'm stunned for a moment. The pain's there in his gaze, reflecting against mine. Two soldiers in this war, unknowingly fighting on the same side but divided by enemy lines.

"You look completely helpless," he croons, moving the knife again. Whatever emotions he was just showing are gone now, switched off as his mental walls rebuild. It took a lot eleven years ago for me to break them down because he's so apt at keeping them rigid and letting no one on the other side.

When I finally broke through, it was equivalent to winning the greatest prize ever. But now, I'm back on the other side, with everyone else in the world. Shut out from this man's trust, and his heart.

*That's* what hurts the most.

"I am helpless," I whisper back. Helpless to move, not only from his hold on me but from my own desires. From the fact that *something* is keeping me chained to this bed.

"Are you? Or is this exactly what you were hoping for, Rozelyn? Trying to find the good within me? I can promise you, it doesn't exist."

*It does. But you've buried it.*

Two fingers stroke over my wet centre, and while his touch is so light, almost non-existent, I feel it throughout my entire body. The light that ignites within my heart as the moon over-shadows the sun.

"But you," he goes on, and I'm starting to think he's only talking to remind himself, "have no power here. Memories might exist in my head, but they're reminders of the pain you've caused."

"Flynn." A plea—for him to touch me further or to release me, I'm not sure.

With eyes enchanting mine, he teases my core until my legs spread wider and my hands fist the bedsheets. Hiding my desire is useless at this point when he can see and feel it for himself.

I don't stop him.

And dare I fucking urge him on? My feet press into the bed, and I rock my hips lightly, silently encouraging his touch, careful of the knife he keeps against my skin. He knows what I'm doing with a slight lift of his brows, a sexy, winning smirk.

"Flynn." This time, it's a plea for more.

His thumb circles my clit and explosions go off in my head. I bite down on the noise in my throat, waiting for him to break first—for him to fuck me with his fingers.

"Begging, Rozelyn. Begging to come, but not for your life. That's pathetic, no?"

Oh, it definitely is, and it's completely contradictory to every ounce of training Dad shoved me into, but neither of us foresaw it being *Flynn* who'd be with the Corsettis. I'd already lost before all the players were even on the board.

Flynn's lips curl into a sexy, evil grin, and with eyes still on mine, he places his index finger at my core and pushes it in to the first knuckle. All restraint—gone. I don't hide how good this feels. How he broke my own barriers.

How much I *missed* him. *Him.* Sex since high school has been lackluster, and I realize why.

It's like a part of me has always belonged to *ma lune* and it took me over a decade to comprehend this.

"Flynn..."

I'm so wet, he's able to easily get his entire finger inside me. His thumb still circles my clit on rotation and the finger he has inside me curls, finding that spot he and I both love. The place that makes fireworks go off inside me and my legs fall open wider, pressing to the bed, encouraging him deeper.

And then he crawls over me, his head right above mine. A slight adjustment and he's pumping his finger into me to the point of near pain, but I won't say anything. Won't end the bliss.

"Tell me what I need to know, Rozelyn."

Tell him what? He wants me to talk now. At a time where even my head can't formulate a proper thought?

His lips are only a few inches from mine, and fuck, I want to kiss him. After all these years, I want that part of him. Now, before he ends this moment and returns me to the basement, and I possibly lose the chance.

There's no ulterior motive, though I'm sure he'll think there is. Just my own unbridled need.

Releasing the blanket, I grab his face and pull him down to mine, lifting at the same time, until we clash. At first, he freezes. Beneath my hands, he's completely still, even the finger he has inside me, ending its torment.

When I move my mouth beneath his, encouraging him, I discover the Flynn Rhodes I once loved. He takes over the kiss, his hand looping around my throat to keep me pinned, his finger inside me picking up its torturous pace again. His tongue battles mine and in the silence of his bedroom, we share a moment similar to a cosmic supernova that leaves me panting and his cock hard: proof we both desire the same thing.

I feel the bubble inside me, the orgasm right on the edge, and it's like he does too because he shatters the kiss but doesn't move away. "Tell me what you know or you won't come."

"Now look..." I swallow against his palm, "...look who's using sex to get ahead."

Since I didn't meet his challenge, he gives me a final meaningful look and slides his finger from me. A plea for him to not end this almost bursts from me, but I won't let him defeat me in every possible way. Instead, I pant, my orgasm stolen from me as fast as it nearly hit.

He rears back, his gaze lingering on my lips, which feel puffy after that kiss. He brings his hand between us, showing me his finger, which is coated in the evidence of my betraying body.

And then he slips the digit in his mouth, sucking on it until his eyes brighten. Until, in a deadly tone, he says, "Neither of us can avoid this truth."

"You're an asshole, Flynn."

"You're a bitch who refuses to tell the truth, Rozelyn."

He reaches between us again and, without warning, sinks the same finger deep inside me before pulling out once more, his digit coated again.

"Need proof of what your body craves? Maybe it'll encourage you to open that fuckin' mouth of yours."

My lips do part—to argue. But he pushes the tip of his finger into my mouth with a single demand.

"Lick."

My tongue wraps the tip of his finger, tasting myself, eyes narrowing as he makes his useless point. Regardless, he pulls away with a self-satisfied smirk.

"Looking back, if there's one thing I missed most, it's that. Your taste. And how does one appease a craving? By having what they want."

He shuffles down the bed and retrieves the knife from where he dropped it earlier. I can't pinpoint when he stopped threatening me with it, too far gone in the sensations. He drags it along the inside of my left thigh, right where his fingers were. It passes over my centre and every muscle in my body tenses. He lightly circles my clit and that's when I stop breathing altogether.

"You're not gonna want to move for the next part."

Resting the blade on the hood of my pussy as some sort of barrier, he lowers his head, his tongue dragging over my centre and it feels like I'm having an out-of-body experience. Like I'm no longer *here* with Flynn.

His tongue begins at my core and ends with a flick of my clit before completing the circle again. By the third pass, the knife is a fact I no longer care about. He's not injuring me with it, so it's no real threat either. My entire focus is on his tongue and its unchoreographed dance. Up and down, he dips inside me for a second, but most of his focus is on that ball of nerves.

I don't bother biting down on my noises. In fact, I want to be loud. To scream. To reveal to the other soldiers how Flynn desires his captive.

My hips roll, trying to chase the sensation, but with the pleasure comes pain.

When I lift myself into the blade.

*Oh.*

"You're a dick."

"I am," he mumbles into my skin. "Move too much, that knife will cut."

"I don't care." I *don't* care as I arch again, this time expecting the sting. It's nothing overly painful; nothing more than I'm used to anyway. I feel my skin break, and I'm positive I'm bleeding, but his licks don't end.

The orgasm from earlier begins to return at the precise second Flynn lifts his head and robs me of it *again*. Then a different kind of explosion sets off inside me when he crawls up my body, his tongue sweeping over the spreading blood from the cut I created. He doesn't lick it per se, but paints the blood over my skin, his tongue like a paintbrush before lowering back to my centre and he's pushing that blood inside me.

This is everything wrong, and I'm sure, we're on the verge of giving me an infection, but I can't find the effort to care.

"I hate you because you told me I was enough for you."

I freeze, his admittance overtaking all bits of pleasure. But he returns to sucking my clit like he hasn't spoken.

I'll take his kindness, while he's offering, because he's likely seconds away from shoving me back downstairs and locking away the key when he comprehends what's happening.

My legs tighten, gripping his head to keep him in place. The knife digs in again, but pain is so far gone, it doesn't even register at this point. The heat builds, expands, my moan, the tease of what's about to hit and—

Flynn pulls away, tossing the knife to the side, and wipes his mouth with the back of his hand as he shifts into a kneeling position over me. For a third time, he's robbed me of my orgasm, changing my shameless moan to a frustrated growl.

"What the fuck?"

His mouth on me wasn't in kindness, or even desire. I was so wrong to think something had gotten patched up here. This entire time, it was some fucked-up revenge thing.

He lunges forward again and grasps my chin between two fingers, pinching painfully. His lips brush mine as he yells, "Tell me why you deserve to come, Rozelyn. You broke my fuckin' heart! You deserve nothing but pain."

And here it is. All his emotions hidden beneath his tough exterior emerge.

"You once vowed to me to never leave me. You *knew* how I felt about myself then. How I had *no one* in my life because I wasn't good enough. You told me I was, and I took that seriously. Months later, you're telling me goodbye. Fuckin' *why*?"

My breaths come out in heavy pants that he immediately swallows, taking my life into his body. The same he once vowed to me he always would. The first time he saw a bruise was only days after our first meeting on the bench. He spotted a dark spot on my wrist and asked in a casual way, *"Who the fuck did this to you, Rozelyn? Tell me, so I can ensure they never harm you again."* After only days of friendship, he took it upon himself to be my protector.

In the months following, as I got to know him, I hid more and more of the marks because while his care was everything, each one had him asking questions I couldn't answer. Denying his help, his love, even his fucking honour made me sick to my stomach.

I try to speak, but his rampage continues, the pain of this conversation hurts more than his pinch,

"I deserve to take *so* much from you. So much more than just a fuckin' orgasm."

In a blink, his mouth slashes against mine, his kiss heated and possessive. His tongue probes, claims, strokes, and drowns me. There's no more air to breathe; no more life to cling to—there's only him. He kisses me like I'm the air he needs, like a weapon he's wielding. It's chaotic and explosive, packed with a million emotions. Vicious hate, conflicted passion, with a punishing hold I don't want to be released from.

With a sudden jerk, he rears away, releasing my face with a snarl, as though wanting to punish me for him losing control.

The time to reveal my secrets isn't here yet, but I also never foresaw Flynn being with the Corsettis. The moment he emerged from the shadows on the first day, all my plans have been changing. Survival became of upmost importance, but he became a secondary one.

So why can't I tell him some of it?

"I'm sorry," I whisper, wincing when he flinches. I reach for him, sitting up, laying my hand on his smooth chest, right over his Corsetti mark. After I finish, I want his story too.

"Sorry?" His tone is flat—deadly. Emotionless.

"I wanted to tell you who I was all the fucking time, but my father would have lost his shit if he knew about you. And you now see why. He threatened you once and I couldn't allow it again."

His heart skips a beat beneath my palm.

"This is the truth, Flynn." The truth of our story at least. Of what I can tell him.

# 15
## FLYNN

L ies. More lies. All fucking lies.

That's all this woman knows how to do.

"This is the truth, Flynn."

*I doubt that.*

But I want to hear her out and listen to whatever tale she spins to get out of this mess. It's bound to be a good one. I push her hand away from my chest, unwilling to let her feel any part of me that could indicate how her story affects me. That it'll even affect me at all.

"Dad was protective, in weird ways. Yasmine, my sister, and I attended a private school our entire lives. Yasmine was fine with it, but after a while, I wanted out of there. Private schools are so...formal." Her expression pinches. "Hated it. Not entirely sure why since it's the life I grew up in but," she shrugs a shoulder, "I did. It felt fake and that wasn't me. So I begged my parents to let me attend public school and be like a regular teenager, despite my family constantly reminding me, we weren't typical. My mother was, as you probably know, the daughter of an Italian mafia don that my father somehow managed to gain a connection with. Her family was very old-school, and they hated her decision when she allowed me to drop from private to public education. Dad and her fought for days over it. But Mom," her tone turns wistful, her lips forming a barely-there smile, "wouldn't hear of it. She didn't care about anything other than my happiness. She enrolled me in the school of my choosing. She was a determined woman, and a great mother."

I've never had a good familial relationship; Lorenzo and Caterina would be the closest thing I have to parents, and listening to how she speaks of her mother makes me jealous I never had a positive relationship like that growing up. Someone who'd do anything for the person they love.

"I chose a school that was far from home, on the other side of the city. Partly so no one would recognize me, and partly because it represented the opposite of everything my family was."

My school. How different my past would have been if she chose to attend somewhere else.

"Dad was beside himself when I chose there of all places."

Because it was underfunded and not in a great neighbourhood.

"Three days in, I met you."

She blinks up at me, her smile soft and genuine as she recounts *our* history. Meanwhile, I'm not sure my internal organs recall their function, so I demand, "Skip this part. I was there. I know what happened." I care about the *why* and the *after*.

"After a few fantastic months with you, life changed. I could tell something was really bothering Dad. Something always seemed to be, actually." Her gaze lowers, finding the wall beside us as she talks through the next part. "He was...erratic. Very angry."

Which explains the bruises. Old hatred rises to the top again, which I quickly quell, shoving away the unwanted emotion.

"Life at home got worse when I started faking a lot of after-school projects and clubs in order to hang out with you for longer. Because every moment counted." She drags her sharp nails up my arm, but I shrug her off. "Then Mom got sick. Lung cancer." Her eyes lower, her entire countenance dropping. "She didn't even smoke. That was the cruellest part."

The early loss of De Falco's first wife is well-known to the Corsettis but having not known his daughter was *my* Rozelyn... The very one sitting in my bed, recounting her mother's death.

*Hate. Hate, hate, hate who you've become.* It's that chant that keeps my hands locked by my sides to resist from holding her as her mood plummets.

"There was nothing any doctor could do. We were waiting it out basically. It hit hard and fast, and school became my distraction. Mom wanted me to go. Dad obviously didn't, but I was able to forget about my family issues when I was with you." She looks up at me again, the base of her eyes red-rimmed. "For a few hours every day, I pretended to be fine. *You* made me fine.

"Then it got worse, and the doctors said she had mere days left." Rozelyn's lips press together, and her eyes squeeze shut. I count every second it takes before she reopens them—ten—and the pain has me ready to throw away every horrible thing I've thought about her, just to have her in my arms this one time.

"You seemed different that week too," I admit. "I didn't look close enough apparently."

She throws me another sad smile, one tinged with old regrets, before speaking again. The protective feeling grows with her next words: "Two days after our breakup, Mom passed."

I give her a moment to sort through her grief but then bring her back to a point she mentioned before her mother's loss.

"You continued coming to school when you were grieving. When you knew you'd only have days with her."

*"Ma lune."* The old nickname makes me jolt. "You were my everything, Flynn," she murmurs. "I was an idiot, maybe, but you consumed me. Being with you and pretending all was well gave me something to focus on or else I'd be a mess." Her tone immediately switches to bitterness when she continues, "Of course, not everyone understood that. Dad hated that I continued to go. The day I told you goodbye was less about Mom's upcoming death and more because of what he did.

"The day before, he brought me into his office and pulled out a folder. It was your school file. He had your name and home address. Your father's name. He knew your fucking grades. And then the pictures," she shudders, "so many photos." Her eyes flash to mine, naked and honest. "Of you, Flynn. Of *us*. Dad wanted to know why I was insistent to go to school that week. I kept telling him it was *for* her. She wanted me to be happy, and I was, but he didn't believe me. He had pictures of us kissing outside, of holding hands in the hallway. Of you entering your house. He knew who you were, and threatened that if I didn't withdraw from school and return to the life I was, as he put it, 'abandoning,' then he'd have you killed. He started using Mom to lay on the guilt, claiming I was turning away from her heritage. I didn't know what to do, other than to obey him. Everything was a mess. My sister...*me*. I was..." She trails off, lowering her eyes to my chest so she doesn't have to look me in the eye, but I can imagine the ending of her statement.

*I was scared.*

"I waited to the very end of the day because I was trying to cling to *us*. When the final bell rang, I felt sick. I had no choice but to leave you, and I know I said the nastiest things I could have." Her voice drops to a near-whisper, pain laced in every word. "I'm aware of what I did, and it was on purpose, so you wouldn't find a reason to look for me. I was terrified the promises we made to one another would drive you to comb Montreal for me. I'd die before letting my father harm you, so I did what I had to. In the months following, I learned who my father is, and everything he ever said to me made sense."

I freeze, replaying her words. Not the stuff about us, but the hint of her father, because as much as I cling to everything regarding her and me, that's not why she's in my life this time around.

*"Who my father is."*

*Who's your father, Rozelyn? What aren't you saying?*

"I'm sorry, Flynn," she finishes, her nails scraping up my bare thigh until reaching the edge of my shorts. "I-I...I hated it."

She's lying.

She was protecting me.

She's making it up.

She could have searched for me afterwards. A decade passing and no explanation.

She's *sorry*?

The two conflicting rationales battle in my head, one no closer to victory than the other.

I don't realize I'm breathing heavier, that my hands are forming fists by my sides, that the sight of Rozelyn in my bed gets hazy with my blurring vision until she murmurs my name.

Does it even matter though?

This might be some grand tale spun for her benefit.

Because even if it is true, why is she protecting him now? If what I remember, what she's hinted at in that story, is true, and she was abused by him, then why protect him? Why not hand over all his dirty secrets the moment she was captured?

It makes no sense, which is why her lying is the most logical.

She's making it up to fuck with my head more than she already has.

And why tell me *now*? At a time when it's most convenient for her.

My head thumps. My gaze is unfocused. I'm losing myself.

*She protected me.*

*No.* I shove the intrusive thought away. She wasn't protecting me because everything she just said was a lie; a well-practiced story she and Stefano weaved before her capture.

*Why are you back in my life? Have you returned to make me miserable?*

*I fucking hate you.*

I move before I realize what I'm doing. I place myself directly over her, my palms in the bed by her sides, our bodies lining up. In truth, I don't have a plan past this—whatever it is I'm doing.

I should shove her right back to the basement but the nagging voice in the back of my head questions her story. Of everything I know of this woman, lying is her second language. But what if...?

She watches me, her blue-green eyes flicking over my face. There's no fear though. Like this, she reminds me of the girl I once knew. Of the sad face that peered up at me as I approached from the smoke pit that day. She thinks she had her walls up, but I saw through them. She was hiding her sadness, her hope-fulness. It's what I see now.

When she told me goodbye—when she said what she had—she did so with a blank expression, without care. She could have at least faked an emotion then too.

*"You're not good enough—"*

I slam the memory to a close before it has a chance to fully form.

"You're sorry." I finally speak. "Sorry isn't cutting it, Rozelyn. Despite what you said, I searched for you, for days, sick with fear that there was something else happening. That something was going on and you were in danger."

Because despite the blank expression, the lovesick fool I was then was hopeful she was hiding something. So I looked and got nowhere.

I don't realize I'm still staring at her until she reaches up to touch my face. As fast as her skin brushes mine, I smack her away, pinning both her wrists to the bed at our side.

"Don't touch me."

"Kill me or kiss me, Flynn. Because you look confused over which to do."

*I am.*

With her beneath me, either is so fucking simple. Her life can be in my hands in mere seconds. Instead—

I kiss her.

Not gently. Not slowly. Not passionately.

Angry. Hateful. Punishing.

With all the rage coursing through my body, mingling with the sickening thought of actually harming her. Whether she's lying or telling the truth, something holds me back from causing her pain.

She doesn't push me away but accepts me.

*She's surviving.* She doesn't want me—probably never has. No one has, and she was certain to remind me of it.

Her tongue strokes against mine, tentative against my roughness, like she's reminding me yet again of the differences between us.

That pisses me off. I release her wrists, instead using the hand to bind her neck to the bed. Thumb and forefinger beneath her chin, I angle her face up.

"You claim you're sorry. You're gonna show me how fuckin' sorry you truly are."

"Flynn—"

I take her mouth again, and with that kiss, I steal her air. My fingers pinch her neck, even as every nerve inside me is demanding to release her.

But that long-buried voice in my head is growing fainter and fainter. In its place, the enforcer I've semi-kept in its cage since Rozelyn re-appeared. It's in my kiss, in the chokehold that I unleash every pent-up emotion that's had me in knots for the past few days.

She pulls back, breaking the kiss, and her hands come up to block my shoulders—to stop me. She's shaking her head, but a tinge of sadness darkens her gaze. "Flynn," she whispers in a tone so low I barely hear it, "stop. This isn't you. This is revenge, but it's not what you want."

*It is. I* know *what I want. I know this is it...I know it...*With every point, my argument fades until I'm left with a blank mind and an uncertainty of which to believe—her story today or my gut, demanding I recall the girl from years ago.

"You will say anything that you think will save you."

"Maybe." She cups my face and the blankness in my mind shatters. A million crystals fall away until I only see *her*. "Or maybe not. But that's irrelevant, isn't it? Whether you believe me or not is secondary to the fact that in this instance, you feel out of control. Believe me," she scoffs, "I know the feeling all too well. You'll do anything to reclaim control of me, of the situation, even of our past, and that's why you're confused. Your heart believes me, but your mind doesn't."

She's always been able to see inside me, to know what's in my head, but this time, it's like she fucking *sees* my soul. Can witness my black heart chipping away into pieces, which land at our feet in a messy pile, waiting for me to toss a match on it and light it in flames. To rid myself of the useless organ altogether.

Either way, my hand slides from her neck and props me up

again. A weakness courses through my muscles though, and only clenching them keeps me upright. *She's* making me weak.

Just like in the past.

The past she's lying about. Whether I believe her truly or not changes nothing of the circumstances, of what she did, and of who her father is.

Somewhere amid the silence, she decides to speak again. "I promise, I'm telling the truth. My father threatened your life, so I pulled away. You wanted to know what happened in the past and why I left. That was it."

She must be lying.

She must be...

She *must*.

She has to be because I can't accept otherwise. It'll mean all the hate I've clung onto over the years will have been for nothing and I won't survive that.

Rozelyn lifts her hand and places it right over my heart, over my Corsetti tattoo, which is the symbol of my vows. I live by them, and I'd die by them. I'll kill anyone who threatens the Corsettis and that's exactly what Rozelyn De Falco is doing. From the moment Caterina spotted me in the alley, this organization earned every part of me.

*Except a single piece of your heart that was never theirs to claim.*

Rozelyn De Falco is presently my enemy, and I will repeat that reminder until the past and present stop worrying about one another and it becomes the entire focus.

*But she's mon soleil.* She's a living nightmare hauled from the trenches of my dark history. The spot of light from that period.

I push myself off her and the bed, twisting for my dresser. From it, I grab a fresh shirt, which I slip on, and find my shoes quickly. I toss her a new shirt from my drawer as well and demand, still facing away from her, "Shower again. Wash the blood from your cunt. Dress. Then we're leaving."

Then I escape into the hallway, slamming the door shut behind me with a noise that travels far down the hall, not that I care. With a deep sigh that does nothing to ease me, I fall back against the door with a light *thud*, partly guarding it and partly using it to keep me upright.

Out here gives me a surge of fresh air, which I suck into my lungs.

Air that doesn't smell like Morning Glories or freshly fallen rain. Like Rozelyn.

Like my every mistake and my every desire.

# 16

## ROZELYN

The moment I enter Dad's dark office, he slams a file folder onto his desk. Although curious what's inside, all I'm thinking as I pace toward him is how depressing this room is. No wonder Dad's soul is so black—it matches the environment he immerses himself in.

Stopping just shy of the other side of his desk, I plaster a fake smile onto my face and wait for him to gesture toward the file. I've learned early on to never assume with him.

"Hi, Dad."

Dad isn't smiling back. His chin lifts as he reclines back in his desk chair. He's studying me, watching me in that weird way he does, like he's assessing me. After ten seconds—I count—he decides he's satisfied with whatever he's found, or didn't, and gestures toward the folder.

"Look inside."

With permission, I flip open the top flap and my stomach drops at what I'm seeing. There's no fake smile that will get me through this moment, and Dad knows it, I'm sure.

Pictures. Dozens of them.

*Of Flynn.*

*Walking downtown, his head low, hood up. But the picture's taken from the front so I know it's him.*

*Entering a tiny house, one the size of Dad's garage. The white siding is peeling, and the paint chipped. The once-red door has lost so much paint, the wood beneath is showing. There's a crack in the living room window, but Flynn's sticking a key into the door, so I presume this is the very house he despises going home to each night.*

*Of Flynn and me together. In class, the picture snapped from afar, zoomed to catch us through the windows. Outside, lying on the grass. Walking through the halls hand-in-hand. Me sitting on the bench while Flynn remains a few feet away, cigarette between his fingers.*

*Beneath the pictures are documents. School records. Details about him.*

*"Break that off or I break him, you little whore. Fucking some lowlife isn't what your mother hand in mind when she agreed to send you there. End whatever that,"* he waves his hand carelessly to the folder in my hand, *"is or I send men to Flynn Rhodes' house. Tomorrow, Rozelyn. Or he's dead."*

*End my relationship? He wants me to* break up *with the only person who heals the pain this family dredges me through.*

*"Dad. You can't—"*

*He slams his fist on his desk, cutting off my words. "I can and I fucking will. Your mother is on her deathbed, and I was curious why you were so insistent to keep going to school lately.* He's the *reason, I see."*

*I don't bother denying the truth. It'll only piss him off more.*

*"You're a fucking disgrace, Rozelyn. To me, to your mother, to your heritage. Spreading your legs like some whore for that good-for-nothing kid is shameful. All you're doing is abandoning your lineage and there's only one way this will end."*

*Dad can say what he wants about me; it's nothing I haven't heard before and learned to deal with. But putting down Flynn won't do. Not him, who's been everything to me. Who is more than Dad will ever be. Flynn's a decent human being and that's more than I can say about the other male in the room.*

*"Tomorrow," he repeats with a finality.*

*Every nerve inside me is screaming to fight this, to fight him, but I stare at the pictures again, feeling my heart slipping away second by second. I can't argue with him because Dad will do what he's threatening.*

*"Besides," he continues, his tone lighter now that he's won, "you're graduating very soon. What did you expect afterwards? To still be with him?"*

*I did. Or at least I pretended that was the plan when, really, I have no idea how I was managing that next step.*

*"Fine," I whisper because there's no other acceptable response. "But you don't know him." Contrary to all the information he's had dredged up. "Flynn won't let this go easily."*

*For the first time since I've walked in, Dad's flat expression breaks into something I pretend is care. It definitely isn't, but it's gentler than anything else. He sits forward, leaning on his desk.*

*"Then break his heart, Rozelyn. If you know him as well as you claim you do, then you'll know precisely what to say."*

*I do.*

*And that's the part that terrifies me.*

That day was the beginning of the end.

Not the end of me. Not even the end of Flynn and me because the scars on our palms said we'd find each other again.

The end of *him*. Of Dad's demise.

I already hated him for the abuse, but threatening Flynn hit me deeper and harder than his hands had ever. The next day, when Mom passed, it felt like the world made me its own personal punching bag. I was losing everyone I cared about in such a short amount of time and the only person left was Yasmine. I grew distant from everyone but her.

I'd been proficient in turning my emotions off already because I didn't want Mom to know what Dad was doing to me, but the day I told Flynn goodbye was the day I turned it *all* off. When protecting Yasmine was my entire purpose in life and nothing else mattered. Because it wasn't allowed to.

His heartbreak back then was discerning.

His recollection of it earlier was evident.

*"Tell me why you deserve to come, Rozelyn. You broke my fuckin' heart! You deserve nothing but pain."*

I still didn't end up coming because I ended up admitting what drove me away back then, all for him to get further from me. He doesn't believe me, but I don't blame him. Deep down, I think a part of him does, but it's a worry for another time. For now, thoughts of Flynn need to be sucked down the drain alongside the shower's water because he can't be my entire focus.

The water that feels so fucking *good*, it's nearly causing me to groan. Two showers back-to-back is not only a dream, but pure bliss.

With his soap, I wash away the blood, noting the slim, red line across my mound. I'm not bothered by it, even when I should be. In fact, I kind of appreciate it. I might have pushed into the blade, but it feels like a renewed version of the scar on our palms. Like in a fucked-up way, he's marked me. Even fucked-up, I even enjoy the thought.

When my hands wipe soap over my breasts, my nipples get hard with the thought of Flynn here in this shower too. It's been so long since I've seen all of him and crave knowing what he looks like now. When he's standing in my place, and I imagine him also washing blood from his skin after a long session doing his enforcer duties.

Dad had an enforcer too, until recently when Nico Corsetti murdered him in his escape. I'm not bothered at all by the loss. He was one of many creepy men working around the mansion, who paid me no attention under my father's orders.

But being aware of what the job entails and knowing Flynn —or at least the guy I used to know—is strange to think *that's* what he does. How many people has he killed, and how many of those were merciless? How much blood has gone down the drain at my feet?

A flash of the Flynn I've seen downstairs enters my vision. Heated and brutal, bent over a person begging for their life. Putting aside the gruesomeness though, my mind focuses only on *him*, reliving how he first acted with me. Vengeful and dominant, even a little bit psycho.

And still, my core clenches.

When my hands pass soap over my stomach, over my hips, my fingers linger right over where the cut is, remembering how I got it. What he was doing to me when I got wounded.

My eyes flutter shut, and I let myself go. My fingers slide between my legs, stroking right over my clit, imagining my fingers as his tongue. Remembering the heat he quickly built inside me and the way he so easily brought my body to the edge before pulling back and demanding answers.

This time won't be stopped, and I slip one finger inside myself.

In my mind, Flynn rises from between my legs and stands, grasping my hair in his unyielding hold. I used to love when he'd keep me still, using me like I was a toy for his pleasure. He was a kid then, and imagining the man now, I bet it's no longer a game for him.

Flynn fucking me would be an otherworldly experience.

*What is wrong with me?* Amidst the pleasure coming from my fingers, the question slips in. I'm a captive, kept until I reveal information about my father, and the future beyond that is unknown. Yet, here I am, thinking about Flynn in such a way when my life is still no less on the line than it was days ago.

Still, my fingers don't stop. My mind doesn't end its fantasizing.

"Flynn..." My fingers swipe over my clit before entering me again. I hadn't meant to speak aloud, but my body isn't in control anymore. Not even my mind, I think, as I release that too. "Flynn..."

"The fuck do you think you're doin'?"

That certainly wasn't in my head.

Cool air washes over my skin, replacing the water's heat. Flynn's standing at the edge of the shower, curtain gripped between his tight fist as his eyes drop to where my fingers are.

It's not only his fist that's tight, I notice. It's everything. It's his expression as his jaw ticks. The muscles in his arms cording.

"You took too long," is all I mutter.

Hunger passes over his expression, and he grits, "What the fuck, Rozelyn?"

My fingers don't stop pumping inside me, but they slow, in a teasing manner more for him than me. "You didn't finish me when you had the chance, so before I'm stuck in chains, figured I would."

"You deserve nothing less."

*Back on that, I see.* His battle over what I 'deserve.' Over if my story is real or fake.

Wherever his mind is, I shove away everything logical in my head that demands my survival. Everything that says I return to treating Flynn like my captor. After we leave his bedroom, something feels like it'll be over. As though leaving ends the progress I managed here today and I don't want that.

Stupid, dumb—pick a term. Maybe it's what I am. But I remove my fingers from my core and reach for him.

He shies away from my touch but doesn't back away from the shower entirely. Instead, he reaches by me and turns the knob until the shower water fades into nothing. I'm left panting, the room's cool air brushing every inch of me now.

Just when I think Flynn's going to demand I dress and we leave, he hauls me from the shower, one large hand splayed on each side of my hips. Before my next breath, my back is shoved against the wall, his body pressing into mine, and his mouth stealing any possibility of air.

My legs wind his waist, which frees his hands to explore. He skirts them up my thighs, my side, until reaching my core. His thumb swipes through, gathering my wetness with a low groan.

"What were you thinking about in the shower?"

"You."

He makes a noise in the back of his throat. "What was I doing to you?"

"Eating me out again, and then fucking me."

"Then let's make it a reality."

Without warning or preparation, he shoves two fingers inside my core, stretching me with a light moan. My head falls back against the wall, my legs tightening around his hips. He pumps his fingers slowly. Too slow. I won't come like this. I arch my back off the wall, silently commanding him faster.

"This can end now, Rozelyn, or it doesn't end at all."

He's offering me an out. A means to protect the precarious balance we've found ourselves in. Both of us wanting to connect with our past again, but neither of us willing to let go of our present realities.

"For now, nothing else matters," is my response and I hope he understands the underlying meaning. *For now, put the past aside.*

Based on the noise from his throat, he gets my words.

He pulls his fingers from me and while I want to protest, he cups my ass and backs us out of the bathroom and toward his bed. By the time my back touches the mattress, his mouth is fused to mine again, his hands cupping my breasts, fingers tugging roughly on my nipples to the point of pain.

He's not gentle but he is explosive. Flynn knows what I prefer.

I claw at his shoulders, yanking on his shirt and he pulls away only to tug it over his head, tossing it to the side before he's also reaching for his pants. Nothing's slow with Flynn, and it never has been. I'm no psychologist but I figured it out long ago. Flynn has so little positives in his life that he continuously grasps onto what is before he loses it.

He's lost me once. And this moment is just that—a moment.

A moment we will both make worth it before we lose it.

His eyes pin mine as he undoes his jeans and that's when I finally remember to breathe. When the realization hits that I get to see him—all of him—for the first time in over a decade. Hooking his fingers into his waistband, he pushes down his jeans.

*Well, that's new.*

Thankfully, he doesn't block my touch as I reach for him, my thumb stroking over the piece of silver in the tip of his cock. I rotate my thumb around it, slowly lifting my eyes to his, to ask my question.

I suppose more of a statement, given how my breathy words manage to get out. "This is new." My mouth is parched, the urge to feel that piercing in every way growing stronger by the second.

Eyes on him, I wrap my hand around his cock and stroke him. He doesn't stop me, merely stares down, watching me. His jaw is tense, but with every stroke of my hand, I shatter more and more of his resolve. Soon, his lips part the tiniest fraction, his breaths coming out a bit quicker than earlier.

"If not you, at least a part of you missed me."

For a moment, it looks like he's about to comment, but then his lips firmly slam shut, his eyes soon following. A long blink and finally he looks at me again, his expression somehow even more resolute than before.

"Can't help lust," he says gruffly, but I already know, it's not the first sentence that was in his head.

"Clearly."

I release his cock to shift to the end of the bed, placing my legs on either side of his. With one hand, I cup his base, and in a quick movement, I have my mouth on him, sucking him as deep as I can in one go, sliding my tongue against his underside and then sinking back down.

Flynn and I have *never* done gentle and I'm fucking happy that he isn't starting now. A hand tightly weaves between the strands of my hair, and he creates a handle from it, urging me deeper, moving slowly before I choke. His other hand comes up to my neck and he strokes it, groaning low.

"This is a sight I fuckin' missed."

I pull back, teasing his head with my tongue, fiddling with the ring. It only lasts for a second before he's shoving me back down his length, using my hair as his leverage. His need for control makes me want to hand him all of mine in a neat little bow.

"Ain't the time for teasing." He grunts, tightening his hand with his words, making a point. "Prove to me how sorry you are, Rozelyn. You always enjoyed sucking my cock. Show me exactly how much you've missed it."

# 17
## FLYNN

There's a point where rationality flies right out the fucking window.

The second I found Rozelyn masturbating in my shower, something flicked off in my brain. Or on—depends which way you look at it. Regardless, the fingers she had buried in her tight cunt became my solitary focus.

And my downfall.

I could very well be betraying the Corsettis in a way none of us fully understands. She might have fed me complete bullshit earlier for this exact reason: to break me. Or she was being truthful, and Stefano De Falco really did threaten me back then.

Whatever her reason for reaching for me, I had my own when I yanked her from the shower and pinned her to the wall. That no matter what I've denied, no matter how much I claim to hate her, I still want her. And maybe one time only. Maybe this is what I needed to do the other day—to fuck her once and rid my head of her—but I couldn't bring myself to hurt her when she wasn't willing.

Maybe her granting consent means I can do everything

good and bad to her I've been dreaming of since the moment she reappeared.

All I fucking know is I'm done thinking. About the past, the present, and the future. For now, I stop thinking. And just *feel*.

Her mouth is wet and warm and she's sucking me like a champ. I know for a damn fact I was her first back then, was the one who taught her to give oral and benefitted from it quite often. But the way her tongue drags along my underside, her teeth following behind to the point my balls draw up tighter, the threat of pain right there, tells me *mon soleil* practiced with other men and the urge to hunt every single one down and—

She gags, pushing back against the weight of my hand. I let up a fraction because I won't have her dying now of all times. Guess the thought of where and how she's been improving her skills had my hold on her getting heavier than I meant.

But as fucking fantastic as her mouth feels, I have better uses for her body. I won't be coming down her throat today. Tightening my grip on her hair again, I pull until the burn on her skull has her mouth unlatching from my skin and I tip her head back to better inspect her face.

She's breathing lightly, the edges of her eyes slightly watery. It's fucking sexy.

Keeping my hold on her, I bend her backward until her hand falls away from where it was still gripping me. I press an open-mouthed kiss to her lips, my tongue licking against hers, tasting myself on her, until she whimpers.

"Guess you are still the fantastic cock-sucking whore I remember." Cruel words, maybe, but they're a throwback to ones I said to her when she first got here.

The corners of her lips curl up because this girl's always embraced what I've thrown at her, and sometimes, even enjoyed it.

I reach between her legs, swiping a finger over her core, feeling how drenched she is. Soaking, and all without me touching her.

"No fight this time?"

"None," she responds breathily and shifts her knees farther to the side, silently encouraging more of my touch.

So I give it to her, pushing my finger inside, watching her face as she takes me. She's so wet, I immediately add a second one, curling them both until I find that button that makes her react. Makes her core clench, seeking more of the feeling.

"You're going to come like this, and then I'm going to fuck you so hard you won't stand for a week." *And then we're going to leave my room and this will be yet another memory of our past to never speak about again.*

"Yes." Her eyes slam shut, her focus completely on what I'm doing to her. Her lips press together, and her hips rock into my fingers.

"Eyes on me," I command, and surprisingly, she obeys right away. It's unlike Rozelyn to do so, but I'm pleased it's not a fight. "I want your eyes open when you come."

As though that was the command she needed, her insides tighten around my fingers, her body going stiff with the orgasm that wracks her body. Her head falls back, right into the hand I still have in her hair, so I release her, granting her some movement back. I trail that hand down her neck, between her breasts, stopping to cup each one as her heavy breaths slow and she eventually lifts her head again.

I pull my drenched fingers from her and take my time licking each one clean under her watchful gaze.

"Fuck," she whispers.

When I'm done, I tap her thigh and back away from the bed, giving her the space to follow my order. "On your back."

She moves but doesn't shift to lie down. Instead, she flips

on her hands and knees, lowers her front until her ass is all I see, and peeks at me from over her shoulder. "I'd prefer this."

Rozelyn's never been a complete submissive. Never more dominant than me certainly, but never one to obey every command. I appreciated that about her back then, but in the years following the breakup, when my needs grew too strong and I finally sought a woman out to fuck, I only ever found one who listened to me. Did as I commanded, touched when I allowed her to. I never wanted more; the thought of a stranger trying to take control sickened me.

But that's not what I'm feeling now, and the burn across my sternum tells me it's more than old desires resurfacing.

That's the worst fucking part of this.

I *should* flip her onto her back. Prove to her and to myself that her seeking control isn't allowed here...but I don't. Because I don't want to.

I'm finding myself pleased that no matter what life has thrown her way, there's still bits of the old her here. That De Falco's evilness hasn't made her into a complete puppet of his control.

When she wiggles her ass to regain my attention, it's precisely what happens. The bed's height puts her at the perfect angle for this position, and for me to see that drenched slit of hers, swollen and begging to be fucked.

"On your knees, my little slut, that's what you want?"

"Yes."

I step closer until my thighs are touching the bed and with a hand around each of her legs, I drag her toward the edge of the bed. Taking my cock in my hand, I drag it over her, using all her wetness as lubricant.

She continues to watch me, an excited gleam in her eyes. She pushes herself into me, but I don't listen to that silent order, instead taking my time with her.

With ending this.

Because once I finish fucking her, this is it. This ends. My sanity returns and I get back to my job before my boss and underboss have reasons to question my methods more than they already do.

So I drag it on for longer, stroking my cock over her core, paying special attention to tap my piercing against her sensitive clit. The piercing was done after a drunken dare with one of the other guys here, but I've never regretted it. For this purpose. For watching her back tighten, her hands curling around my comforter as she fights to hold back her reaction. Eventually, she breaks my gaze and her head falls forward.

The moment she looks away, I grant her what we both need. Angling myself at her pussy, I push inside her. Two inches first before I pull out halfway, and thrust back in. I repeat this a few times until I'm seated inside her, our shared groans filling my bedroom. A sound I'll now replay every night I'm in here.

"Oh my god," she pants.

I move my hips, pushing deeper inside her, feeling her core clench as I stretch her.

"Oh my god," she repeats. "Do not move."

I won't until I know what her hesitation is.

"Y-your piercing."

*Oh.* I smile. Not a good enough reason to stop then.

Gripping her hips with both hands, I slam into her again, and she moans, dropping her head onto my bed. The blanket muffles her next sound.

"Flynn...Flynn, I won't last."

Good. She doesn't deserve to witness my demise drag on longer than it should.

"You're pressing right at the—"

The rest of her sentence is cut off by another low cry as the orgasm clearly builds inside her, but I got what she was attempting to tell me. My piercing is stroking right against the spot that'll soon make her lose every ounce of control she believes she still has and I'll have her coming until she's a quivering mess to use at my disposal.

I pull back almost all the way and her breath catches. Almost like she knows what I'm about to do before I do it. With a hard thrust, I push all the way back inside her, bottoming out, and that's what does it for her.

Her core tightens in a way no words can accurately describe. Her cum drips between us and every muscle in her body tenses. She cries into the bed, but I reach for her hair, using it as a rope to tug her face away from the mattress.

"Let me hear you, *mon soleil*. If you're going to come on my cock, we're gonna make sure the world understands who owns your ass."

# 18

## ROZELYN

We've barely begun, and I will not survive another orgasm. *That* was powerful. That was better than even the ones he gave me in high school, but it's more obvious now than ever, the Flynn I knew then and the Flynn inside me now are vastly different men. And his piercing is only one damn aspect of it.

How can such a small piece of metal make me lose my mind? It was that fucking thing that broke me. The moment he was fully inside me, I knew he'd be my downfall. His cock stroked me at precisely the right angle; there would be no holding back, even if I wanted to try.

Eventually, my muscles unlock, and I release the blanket clenched in my grip. My breaths return, though shallow and paced, and I manage to glance over my shoulder, toward him. Big mistake. I swear I could come just from the sight of Flynn standing behind me.

His cocky grin isn't helping the case. "Well. Let's see how many times you can do that."

One before I'm mush. Two before I'm lifeless.

His fingers tighten around my hips, and he moves again. Maybe I hadn't given my body enough downtime, but the heat builds nearly immediately. His piercing knocks at the right spot inside me and the fluttery feeling in my stomach returns. The tingles that course up and down my arms, my legs, and right to my core, mingle with the heat, creating an explosion inside me.

I come again, and this time, I don't bother trying to bite down on my moan. How many people are in the rooms around Flynn's? Who can hear us? How much trouble will Flynn be in after this?

I'm breathing heavy again, but this time, I return to earth quicker.

From behind me, Flynn curses. "Fuck, Rozelyn. You're…" He never finishes, but I don't turn around. Don't act like I'm clinging to every syllable of that sentence, pleading for him to go on. "At least like this, *mon soleil*, I can pretend."

*Pretend you're not denying the truth to avoid accepting it?*

He moves again, but I will not survive a third orgasm in this position. Pushing my hands into the bed, I end up kneeling, Flynn still buried inside me, my back to his front. I reach an arm behind, wrapping around his neck as my head falls against his shoulder.

"What are you doing?"

"What does it look like?" Peeling open my eyes, I focus an amused expression toward him. "Helping."

He almost laughs; a breathy chuckle against the skin of my neck that coasts between my breasts. He shifts his hands until one is a band against my waist, keeping me tight to him, and his other binds my neck, locking me in place.

He moves and I soon learn how repositioning myself like this is a beautiful, wondrous mistake. The angle has changed slightly, but somehow better and worse. More sensitive and my head rolls against his shoulder.

"I won't last," I tell him. "Not again."

"You will," he demands. "Hold on so we can come together. I'll tell you when."

"I can't," I whine as another spark of heat flashes through my form. My nails dig into the back of his neck, seeking reprieve, but he doesn't stop me. He enjoys the pain as much as I do; both of us inflicting the other with our darkness.

"You will," he repeats.

When his hand shifts from my hip downwards, he passes right over my clit, which does not help my case at all. Clearly, he's testing me, and I'll be damned if I fail. He strums my sensitive nub, and it takes every fibre of focus for me not to come. For my eyes to squeeze shut and to ignore the feeling.

His thrusts quicken, his own breath becoming shallow. The hand he has around my neck slips down and his head drops to the curve of my neck. From the outside, our position looks almost tender.

He curses three times before he whispers into my skin, "Come with me, Rozelyn. Come *for* me."

He stiffens and my core clamps down with my orgasm, urging his own from him, and I'm very thankful for the birth control shot I'm on. My arm slips from his neck, but he quickly replaces it, hugging me to him as he groans into my neck, his teeth scraping over the sensitive skin.

*"Mon soleil."*

Slipped out through a murmur, through lips that nip my neck, imprinting that nickname into places deeper than my heart.

It buries into my soul.

Because every time he calls me that, he gains another piece of it.

*Ma lune.* I don't say it aloud though. Somehow, I get the sense he'll pull away entirely.

When he finishes and we both come down, neither of us move. Like we don't want this to end because when Flynn exits my body, that's exactly what will happen.

Flynn and I have always been two puzzle pieces. We just work, even when it makes no sense. Even when our sides seem like they won't fit together, they do. Like a puzzle though, one day someone deemed us too difficult to solve and we were separated.

Exactly like what Flynn decides now as he sighs low and releases me, pulling from my sated body. I fall forward and roll onto my back, examining the mess between my legs.

"Starting to believe me finally?" I ask as he turns for the bathroom. He returns with a towel and a scathing look. He doesn't clean me; only tosses the towel toward me.

"Wipe," he demands.

"Do I get another shower?" Three within twelve hours isn't so bad.

His eyes narrow, any sign of the Flynn who was holding me gone and clearly tucked behind his own protective walls. "Make it quick. I mean it, Rozelyn. Don't make me come looking for you."

Then he turns away and retrieves his own clothes from the floor. Clearly, he's back to ignoring me, placing distance between us. A reminder of the feelings he thinks he needs to have toward me.

I'm still smiling as I head for the shower again because I'm getting beneath his skin.

He might hate me, but this unexpected scenario in which our lives intersect again means one thing: neither of us can ignore the promises we once made to one another.

I stare at the scar on my palm.

～

The basement feels chillier than before, but I suppose it has to do with the fact I've been warm upstairs in his room all night. It's been a tease I hadn't expected, so now I'm back to ground zero with managing this place.

The moment I'm at the bottom of the stairs, I head toward the pole, assuming that's where I'll be tied up. He doesn't follow, instead lingering by the base of the stairs, his arms crossing as he drops into a lean on the wooden post connecting the staircase to the building.

He watches me watch him and just when I think he's about to say something, he jerks his head roughly, and then pushes off the post to turn for the stairs again.

My stomach lurches. After everything in the past twelve hours, he's leaving. He can't leave...I don't know why, but he *can't*.

"I turned it off." I say the first thing that comes to mind. It works, for he pauses at the base of the stairs and casts stormy, dark eyes onto me again. "My emotions. I was a bitch when I arrived here. I was a bitch to Della and Ariella for years. It's all I know how to do, Flynn. What I've been doing to protect myself. It's easier to not feel at all than feel guilt. The first time —" My words choke in my throat. "The first time was after I left you. When I went home and hid from Dad. If he saw how affected I was by his threat, I feared what he'd do, so I closed myself off. Only Yasmine and my bedroom ever saw me cry after that day."

He stares at me.

I stare at him.

Silence is palpable between us. Electrifying.

Tense.

He takes a step and it's in his single move away from me, my heart cracks.

Another step.

He pauses and glances toward me again. "Thank you for trying to protect me from your father, but I would have paid the price to be with you."

By the time his statement registers, he's gone and up the stairs. The light flicks off and the door slams shut. A distinct locking noise finds its way down to me.

And that's it.

# 19
## FLYNN

Nico was right. Caterina was right.

They were all fucking right, and that's the part I dislike the most.

I request two men to station themselves at the basement door since Rozelyn's not locked up. A nicety I still don't understand in myself, but I wouldn't put it past her to try to get out either way. The men have instructions to go down twice a day: in the morning to deliver food and in the evening for the bathroom. I tell them to take her to one of the bathrooms on the main floor.

Then I head directly outside and find my bike in the garage and use it to escape to the Corsetti-owned gym a few blocks away. An old warehouse converted into a gym, only for those within the organization to use.

Maybe here, I can work out this...this mounting feeling without murdering anyone.

The mounting feeling of loss.

Of grief, yet I don't completely understand what I'm even grieving.

172

I pull my bike into my usual spot by the metal door, noting the couple cars that are here. Nico's isn't, nor is Rafael's sports car, which makes sense considering he's on babysitting duty with Maurice Dupont's adult daughter.

Grabbing my duffel bag, I stride through the metal door, passing the front desk with a woman manning it. Nico employs few staff here, typically only ever one per shift to maintain the equipment and ensure no outsiders broach the private gym.

Not bothering to return the waves of a few of the guys here who spot me entering, I head to the left, toward the changing rooms to get into shorts and a sports t-shirt.

Grabbing a disposable water bottle from the fridge right outside the changing room, I head straight for the weight machines. Maybe if I exhaust myself enough, I won't be tempted to return to the basement.

Again, Rozelyn's derailed my plans. Nothing in the past twelve hours should have happened. And I'm no closer to ridding my mind of her. If anything, I continue to replay every moment of last night and this morning. Her breathy moans, the feel of her tight cunt squeezing my cock, the damn sight of my every desire come to life.

With every thought I have of Rozelyn, I add another level of weight to the dumbbell bar. It's heavier than I normally would go for, but maybe if I break my body, it'll be a suitable enough punishment worthy of my betrayal.

The moment I recline onto the bench and position my hands around the metal pole above my head, a shadow encompasses me.

"I don't need a spotter," I tell whoever believes he's about to be helpful.

"I know. But you do need some sense knocked into you."

Rosen.

I sit up, abandoning the bar, and swing my legs to one side

of the bench, finding Rosen leaning against the leg press machine close by. He's in shorts and a black tee, which is damp from his workout. I hadn't noticed him here when I arrived, or his car outside.

"Surprised you left Aurora's side long enough to come here." Their relationship created a lot of drama within the organization that I ignored, having no care about it. What Rosen's doing with the sister of our underboss is his business.

"Funny," he replies dryly. "I almost said the same thing about Rozelyn."

I shrug, feigning indifference. "She's guarded and isn't going anywhere."

His mouth curls in the corner, like a cat who got the milk. "We both know that's not what I mean. Aurora's out with her mother so I went back to my old room to get a few more items that I left behind from moving."

*And?*

"The walls are thin, Flynn."

*Fuck.* Shutting my eyes, I turn away from him. Rosen's the most loyal of us all—despite recent transgressions—so he'll head straight to Nico with this information. I won't deny my actions; I'll own my mistakes. Perhaps, it'll even be the sense I need knocked into me.

"Relax." His hand claps my shoulder, breaking my glare with the floor. "The moment you stationed two men to do your job, Nico already guessed something's up. He texted me asking to be on the lookout for you."

Lucky me walked right into where Rosen was.

"I didn't give up," I immediately counter, shoving to my feet to head elsewhere, away from him.

The treadmills are in the far corner and they're noisy enough I can block Rosen out. There's three and two are in use, but the guys conveniently find somewhere else to be when they see us approaching. Fuckers. It opens one for Rosen to also use.

I hop onto the nearest one and set it to a walk, quickly speeding the treadmill to a jog and then a run, falling into an ideal pace. Rosen waits and watches, moving right in front of my machine. He props his hands on the treadmill.

"You might not have given up, but you're running away from it. Literally." He nods to the machine, smirking, clearly amused with his own joke.

"Funny. You're not one to talk. The mafia princess."

He shrugs a shoulder. "Believe me, I tried to ignore the attraction. But we're not talking about me. We're talking about you. What you did, Flynn, it's okay."

My feet stumble, quickly righting themselves as I replay his latest words.

"You hate Rozelyn but now you're okay with this? *You're* the one who stabbed her. She drugged your girlfriend. You probably have one of the biggest reasons to dislike her."

"Oh, I don't care what happens to the bitch. Death would be generous, yes, but even Aurora's having her reservations about that. Della's been arguing with Nico about Rozelyn's future. Put all that aside though, it's *your* feelings, your past, getting entangled with her, and that's what I care about."

I level my stare with him, despite the rocking motion from my run. "Gonna tell Nico what you overheard?"

*Yes.* "No," he replies instead. "Not unless this becomes an issue." He slaps the machine once and steps back. "When Nico told you he understands, he meant it. He's lived what you are with his wife. Once, Nico was stuck believing he *had* to hate Della for her actions...and not hating her."

Ignoring him, I tap the speed button, quickening the machine's pace and forcing my legs to keep up with it. Nico's experience with Della was different. She lied to him for a good reason. Rozelyn's secret-keeping isn't the same.

I run even faster, escaping the duplicity living in my head. Lies. Truths. One's a fact and one isn't.

"Anyway," Rosen finishes, "if you need someone to talk to, you know where to find me."

"Yeah."

Talk. I don't need to talk.

*She* does. Rozelyn needs to reveal what she knows about her father so this can end.

~

After the gym, I don't return home.

I drive in a direction I haven't been in a long time. To a place in the city that I haven't returned to since I abandoned it.

My high school.

*Our* high school.

I park my bike right in front, dropping my feet to the cement to hold myself steady as I inspect the building. The siding's been updated to a new colour, now a light blue from the grey I remember it being. Like they're trying to modernize it, but the building itself won't ever change. The massive grass yard, the track far behind, a place Rozelyn and I spent a lot of time.

The very spot I recall thinking how she's made my life brighter. She was the light amidst the darkness. *Mon soleil.*

And she gave me her own nickname for me, with a meaning only we'd ever understand. I felt wanted with her.

It's the middle of summer so no one's around, being off for the hot months, and I inch my bike farther down the property line, heading for a large tree, the distinct garbage can, and dozens upon dozens of cigarette butts strewn around from the last time students were here.

The smoke pit isn't what has my attention. The bench a few feet away does.

*The* bench.

How different would my life be if I didn't approach Rozelyn that day. I was curious about the quiet, new girl. She was a confusing mystery, discreet and shy, but walked around in her expensive clothing with her nose held up like she was too good for the place. I hadn't understood at the time.

Immediately, I wanted to knock her down a few pegs and return her to reality, but then I spoke to her and she opened that fucking mouth of hers and stared at me with her round eyes, and I was a goner. Her attitude only increased my interest, and I couldn't help but be sucked into her vortex.

I recall the very first time I ever saw her, when she entered the math class her first morning there. Her hair, long enough to nearly reach her waist, was the first thing I was intrigued by. It hung free like a cape she used to protect herself from the probing stares, which only amplified when the teacher introduced her. I sat in the very back of the classroom, always bored in that class because math was my enemy. Every school subject was my enemy really.

Despite her hair, she met everyone's stares head-on, before stalking back to the desk indicated for her and then barely spared anyone a second glance. That was when the whispers began, and people started referring to her as the 'high-class bitch' in the days following.

From the outside, it looked to be true, but my classmates and I also didn't get along, so before I sided with their beliefs, I wanted to make my own. To determine if she was worthy of the title they gave her.

I shared two classes with her that semester, so for the next three days, I spent both watching her. She did attempt to talk with others as the new student anxiety began to lessen, but everyone already discounted her as being too good for them and no one paid her the attention she desired. That was the first time I felt truly empathetic for another person, since it was only the first impressions she made that drove them all away. No one cared to consider it was likely only first-day apprehensions preventing her from being friendly.

Regardless, their attitude never shattered hers, and that's what I became most curious about. It was obvious from her behaviour, her clothing, and the expensive black town car that dropped her off and picked her up from school each day, that she came from a world most could only dream about.

When I spoke to her, the second most compelling fact about her was that while she *was* high-class, her self-perception wasn't.

*"Something wrong, princess?"*

*"I'm not a princess."*

*"You look like one."*

*"Doesn't make me one."*

*"Whatever, princess."*

*"That's not my name."*

She did look like a princess. Someone I shouldn't have been worthy of gazing at, let alone touching. Kissing. Fucking. Clearly, her father thought so too.

If it wasn't her self-perception, it was her determination to embrace what everyone already believed her to be that won me over.

*"Maybe I haven't gotten the chance to be an asshole yet."*

*"Then let me give you that chance and we'll see who's right."*

She took my hand. Small compared to my large one. Soft compared to the roughness of mine. Manicured nails strikingly different than my stubby, chipped ones.

I claimed her then, even if she didn't realize it at the time.

If I never approached her on the bench, we never would have been friends, and then more. Maybe she would have eventually given up on the public school system and returned to her fancy, private school. I would have continued going through the motions and faking my way to a high school diploma, exactly how I'd been doing for years prior.

We wouldn't have lived through the heartache and wouldn't be in our current scenario. Rozelyn De Falco would be exactly what her name deems her as: De Falco's daughter. She'd be my prisoner and I'd have no prior knowledge or feelings toward her. I'd hate her because she's the organization's enemy and that's all there'd be to it.

But if I never met Rozelyn, I would never have given up on school that day. Doing so led me to escape home for good and survive on the streets. Which means Caterina and Lorenzo wouldn't have found me, and I wouldn't be here. I'd be someone else. Some*thing* else. Dead perhaps.

No matter the pain Rozelyn brought me that day, I wouldn't trade anything in the world for my current life.

A car driving by the high school snaps me from my thoughts. It's a cop's cruiser, which slows, the officer poking his head out of his rolled-down window to study me. I know what he sees. The jeans and leather jacket. The rumbling bike.

Nodding respectfully, I kick off the ground and speed away from the past.

# 20

## ROZELYN

Days pass but I don't know how many. I try to count the visits as I'm provided food and allowed out for the bathroom, but they seem to happen at different times, making tracking difficult.

Either way, it's not Flynn who comes down anymore. Instead, two other soldiers alternate, and they barely glance at me, and they don't speak to me other than to command me up the stairs and position a gun at my back as they walk me to a bathroom in the main hall, which makes me wonder why Flynn's always brought me to his from the very first instance.

I've asked about Flynn's whereabouts, but they pretend not to hear me. This is a daily activity now.

Other than during their visits, the basement's lights are kept off, but thankfully, I never return to that dark place I went to the last time I was alone for an extended length of time.

In the silence, my mind travels a lot. It relives everything Dad ever did to me. His malicious means of training me for this. His cruel ways of raising me to be his soldier rather than his daughter.

*"Fight him." Dad flicks his fingers to one of the soldiers he's brought to the training room. A mountain-sized man with biceps as wide as my head, height that towers two feet above me, and a menacing snarl that says he'd eat me for breakfast if given the chance.*

*"You're kidding me?" I look from Dad to the solider and back. At twenty-four, this isn't the first soldier he's had me train against, but no one like* this. *"I'll lose. More so, he'll break me."*

*"Attack," Dad commands. "Before he does."*

I didn't move for almost a week afterwards. His soldier took me down in less than a minute, bruising my back.

He never taught me enough to fight back against him. Or, somehow I was hardwired unable to do so. Maybe because I was already in the monster's web, and his training never exactly got me into the fighting shape it should have.

The single time I tried to block his incoming hit, I paid for the act of defiance.

The basement door opens and shuts again, taking me from the latest trip through my hellish memories. It feels like it's only been an hour since they brought me to the bathroom so I can't help but be dismayed that I've clearly lost an entire night. Time is slipping faster and faster away. Not sure if that's positive or not...

Through the darkness, I'm able to make out the shape of who comes down and it's not either of the men. It's also not someone new. I know his figure as well as I know my own.

He doesn't approach, so I don't move from the sleeping bag I've dragged to the centre of the room. Being unchained means having access to these luxuries he once teased me with.

I wait for him to speak, counting sixty seconds, and wonder if he's also waiting for me to begin. Uncomfortable silence, is it?

Eventually, he sits right at the base of the stairs, his back against the far wall so he's facing me. His legs stretch out in front of him, crossing at the ankles. That's all I'm able to make out though, and I wish he'd turn on the light so I can see his face. A long sigh follows, signalling the break in silence.

"Your last day of school was also mine. I dropped out after you left."

He's telling me about the past. Somehow, this feels like a win.

He hadn't said the exact words, but I feel I was the reason for him dropping out. He could have fucked his high school education because of the words I chose that day. I'm not sad for having saved him, even if I didn't go about it in the kindest way, but the domino effect my words caused was unplanned.

"I didn't want to return to a place where every room would remind me of you. I went home that day, packed a bag, and left while my father was still at work. From what I know, he never searched for me, and I never returned."

His father was a verbally and emotionally abusive asshole. I'm sure he would have been physically too, had Flynn not stood up for himself when he started getting bigger. In so many ways, Flynn and I share a similar past with shitty parents.

"I was hiding between two buildings when Caterina Corsetti spotted me. I don't know why the Corsettis chose me, but once Caterina realized I wasn't a threat, they offered me food. It was the first proper meal I had in a while. They took me to their private gym for a shower and Lorenzo gave me fresh clothes. After that, Caterina refused to let me go. They gave me a room in the mansion. Still not sure why," his voice lightens with a fondness that makes me jealous of the Corsettis, "but they took me in, accepted me into the fold. I started working out with Enzo—Lorenzo—and eventually he trained me to fight. Hand-to-hand combat at first, and then with weapons. I assumed they were helping me before sending me back out into the world, but as the months passed, I found myself not wanting to leave the life they had provided. Caterina insisted I get my GED, so I had my high school diploma. To this day, I haven't needed it, but I'm still thankful she cared enough to pressure me. After a few more months, I asked to be sworn in. Took the oaths and never looked back." He pauses. "In the beginning, you asked how I got here. That's how."

After what I assume is a few days without any contact from him, he's found his way back to me, presumably late at night based on my most recent bathroom trip. And the first thing he says is a story of his past. This means something. I think.

"I'm glad you found a home," I say truthfully. "How'd you make it to this role?"

"Over time," he responds right away. "I hung out a lot with their current enforcer at the time. Not sure why, but I appreciated his job. The others, as great as they were, stayed away from him. He once told me there's silence in his position, even amongst their enemies' screams, and that statement's always stuck with me. When their ex-enforcer retired, Enzo offered me the role. Said I was perfect for it. That was five years ago."

I glance at my palm, the scar—our promise. If he wasn't an enforcer, would our lives have even intersected? He could very well be off, working as the other soldiers are. Fate brought us together.

"What about Nico and Rafael? You're close in age. You would have trained with them. You guys close?"

"Yes and no. Yes, as in I feel comfortable with them. Almost as much as I do their parents. But I've always preferred to be alone, so I spent more time away from them than with them. Besides, by the time I was inducted, a lot of their own training was already finished. They were full-fledged members for a couple years."

"I'm glad," I tell him without explaining why. Even when he's distanced himself, he's still found people who enjoy his company and respect his boundaries. Somehow, these mobsters seem like genuine friends to him.

The next time he speaks, the question he poses is seemingly random, but I get the sense it isn't. Flynn obviously came down here with a purpose, and it wasn't to tell me his story; it was to get mine.

"The bruises you came to school with, they were from Stefano, weren't they?"

My thumb strokes over the spot on my left arm where Dad frequently used to grab me. His abuse was never around Mom, but once I saw a matching mark on her. She noticed that I spotted it, and both our injuries became the silent entrapment Dad forced onto us.

"Yes."

There's a shifting noise, but he doesn't stand. "Your father abused you. Are you honestly that loyal to him?"

*No.* I say nothing.

"Why would he hurt you?" Flynn asks after a moment of silence.

My shoulders lift in a shrug, although he likely can't see. "Why do abusers harm anyone? Dad was...angry. Always pissed off." Eventually I learned why he was so on edge most of my life. Still not an excuse, but an explanation. "He took his mood out on me sometimes."

"You never told me."

Is that hurt in his tone?

"I asked that one time and you shut me down."

*I did for the exact reason I never told you who I was. Dad would kill you.*

I wanted to. So many times, I wanted to tell him, only to see if Flynn would become my hero, but I learned early on in life, fantasies are simply that—dreams we convince ourselves to want. How many times did I beg the universe for Mom to live, or for Dad to stop hitting us? Neither of those wishes came true so telling him about the abuse would have just led to another letdown.

"You wouldn't have been able to save me. I often dreamed you could, but it was for your safety I didn't say anything."

"Did he ever rape you?" A blunt question but Flynn's never been exactly subtle.

"No. He'd only hit me. Sometimes I believe he tried to be in control of himself, but on tough days, he couldn't help himself."

Flynn growls. "Protecting him again? What fuckin' load of bullshit have you fed yourself?"

"I'm protecting myself."

A beat of silence, and then: "What does that mean?"

*How do I tell him the truth without giving away the details?*

"Dad's...bigger than you all realize."

"And?" he demands when I don't add to that statement.

Huffing, I explain, "Look, if you hunt him down now, you *will* lose. Trust me on that. There's one person who'll be dead at the end of this, and it won't be anyone with the surname Corsetti."

He remains silent again as he pieces my words together, searching for the underlying meaning.

"You're not loyal to him at all then, are you? When you said you were determined to get captured, it wasn't bullshit. You truly wanted inside here." There's marvel in his tone that almost makes me smile because, *finally*, he believes me.

"Nothing I've ever said to you since getting caught has been a lie, Flynn. *Nothing.*" The final word is emphasized because I hope he'll realize I'm also including anything about us within that statement.

Another scuffle and this time I spot the dark shape of his body lifting to his feet. His steps take him across the room and to my side, where he drops onto his knees on the ground beside me. With his nearness, I can finally make him out.

The grey shadows beneath his eyes, like he hasn't slept in days. The scruff on his face, which is darker and longer than normal. Lowered brows and a deep, frazzled gaze find me in the dark and he cups my face, touching me more tenderly than he has in a long time.

"Tell me everything, Rozelyn."

"How many days have passed since you captured me?"

"Eight," he answers right away. "Relevance?"

Dad insisted on driving, not flying, knowing air traffic can be too easily tracked. Enough days need to pass for him to arrive, amass his army, and then be on his way back. That's when the Corsettis can attack.

It'll take about three days to make the cross-country trip if they haven't stopped for long breaks. Which, with Dad's staff alternating as the driver, it's likely the case. He told me gathering forces in B.C. might take time for him to convince them, which means they could be on their way back by now, or days away from starting the trip. Based on what Dad told me and the reports he's gotten lately, he thinks they'll be hesitant to listen to him.

Then there's Yasmine. Dad's placing my sister right in their crosshairs. A sister who, by blood and DNA, is from there. They technically own her...which makes them my next enemy to battle.

"Soon."

I want to tell him now. I want this over and done with. There's a single fact that keeps my lips shut.

Fear.

If this doesn't work—if they lose...then I do too.

Flynn's thumbs dig into the underside of my chin, right at the start of my throat. "Rozelyn—"

I shove him away, physically fighting him for the first time. "No. Give up."

"Why the wait? Why the games?" He leans closer, positioning his hands on the ground beside me. He looks seconds away from touching me again.

"From the very first day, I've told you I'd admit everything. You chose not to listen to me and were determined to keep the torture games up."

"But why?" he repeats. "Your father owes us his life for everything he's done, so if you're not protecting him, what are you doing?"

*Remain silent. Don't break.*

*Don't tell him.*

The more I say, the more he'll probe.

I don't realize I'm breathing heavy again until he cups my face again, forcing me to look at him. It's his touch that opens the floodgates and I release the words, unable to pull them back in.

"I'm protecting *all* of you. Ensuring my own safety. I want this done as much as any of you, but trust me, you have *no idea* what you're up against, and I do."

"We can handle ourselves."

Of course, he'd think that. I shake my head, knowing he can feel the motion beneath his palm. "Maybe. Maybe not, but I don't want to take chances."

Flynn rips away from me with a grunt and he stands, backing toward the stairs. "Anything else?"

"Nope. Go run to your bosses now." I gave up a few facts and they'll devour them.

Within seconds, Flynn listens to me, and he's out of the basement, the door shutting behind him and leaving me alone again.

Nico responds to my text instantly and I find him in his office, Della perched on the edge of his desk. They're having what seems to be a heated conversation, based on the rising voices greeting me at the door. Whatever Della's shouting cuts off at my entry, and she huffs, leaping off the desk.

"Flynn, give us your opinion: moving Rozelyn to a proper bedroom will warm her up to us."

That's what they were arguing about? Based on Nico's grim expression as he stares daggers into his wife's back, it's clear who is and isn't for the idea.

"The basement is equipped for my needs and ensures she doesn't escape. My job within the confounds of a bedroom can be..." I search for the best term, "...messy."

"My point exactly," Nico grumbles, crossing his arms. "Add that to the fact that she's our enemy." He growls the final part at Della, who refuses to face him.

"I spoke with her." Her eyes dart between us, finally giving

Nico an ounce of attention. "The stepsister I knew and the woman down there," she points to the floor, indicating the basement somewhere below us, "is not the same person. Stefano corrupted her mind and if we give her a reason to work with us and prove to her we're not villains, then she'll be more amicable. Allowing her to shower and sleep in a regular bed and not on that disgusting, disease-coated ground is a bit of kindness to make our point." She faces Nico, her hands going to her hips. "Do you not remember I was once down there. Only for two days, but Rozelyn's been there for a *week*. It's bound to be fucking with her."

"That's the point," is the only response Nico gives. "*Petite souris*, there's a huge difference between you two. By the time you fucked me over, I was already obsessed with you. That's not the case with Rozelyn. She's the bad one here. We don't negotiate with prisoners."

Della huffs and turns her head toward me, completely ignoring her husband's final words. "And there's the argument, Flynn. Help."

Behind Della's back, Nico lifts a single brow, instructing me exactly how to respond. Not that I disagree with him either way. "It's a bad idea, Mrs. Corsetti. That's just...it's not how it goes. Prisoners don't get kindness."

She throws up her hands and a growl, one louder than I ever could imagine her making, releases. "You mafia men are all the same. No one ever considers that the lack of kindness is what's fucking this up."

"Della," Nico starts in a tone suggesting he's finished with this conversation, "you're trying to change methods that have worked for decades. Give up."

She rolls her eyes. "And yet, apparently it's my tenacity you love. Seems you only love it at certain times." With a final huff, one indicating she's about to give up, she says, "Fine. But consider offering her a room *after*. She can't remain down there forever."

I'd much prefer if she wasn't. Once Nico gets what he needs from her, if he could have her removed from below, that would be better for me.

Nico sighs, staring unimpressed at his wife. "Where in my life did I go wrong by not marrying a submissive woman? Fine. I will have her moved to a bedroom after we get what we need from her." With a heavy sigh, he shifts his attention to me. "Aurora was in here earlier after a heated conversation with Rosen. She wants to visit Rozelyn because once learning Della and Ariella were allowed down there, she's claiming I have no reason to deny her."

Considering Aurora was drugged by the woman in question, I can imagine why she'd want to face Rozelyn.

"I've agreed to her request," he continues. "Aurora's lurking somewhere in this place, waiting for us to give the green light for her to go down."

I tip my head to my underboss. "I'll ensure Rozelyn's kept away from your sister, sir."

"Thank you," he replies. "You also had news?"

"It was something she said. She wants him dead. 'There's one person who'll be dead at the end of this, and it won't be anyone with the surname Corsetti' were her final words."

Della spins, focusing on her husband, her hands gesturing animatedly. "*See*? Give her some leeway after that."

He ignores her completely. "Why?"

For the first time, I hesitate in telling my underboss the truth. While she never admitted it completely, I have a feeling it has to do with the abuse. Or maybe there's more to it, but it's somehow connected.

But that isn't my story to share.

So lying to him, I reply, "Not sure. She refused to say." That part's the truth.

"Hm." Nico shifts his gaze away to the far wall, his lips pinching. He grunts again and sits forward, reaching into one of his desk drawers. From it, he pulls out a file and tosses it onto the desk, indicating for me to approach as he flips open the top flap. "See if the name Haynes means anything to her. I have a theory."

I scan the document he's pointing to, catching a name more familiar to me.

"Maurice Dupont."

Nico nods. "Yeah. Rafael found Maurice's daughter. Turns out, neither she nor her father exist under real names. Maurice Dupont is an alias. The RCMP just dug up their real backgrounds." He flips the next page. "They traced the entire Haynes family to British Columbia. That's as far as we could get. Trail goes cold there. Whatever their backgrounds, they're buried."

"You think De Falco's connected?"

He leans back to look at me again. "That's my theory. But don't tell her all that. See what mentioning the name Haynes dredges up."

"Got it."

"Let Aurora down there first before she drives me nuts all night. Then speak with Rozelyn. Let me know what you find out in the morning."

As I turn away, Della's holler follows me out the office doors. "And then put her in a damn bedroom!"

Nico's heavy sigh is the final thing I hear before shutting the door. Still, I chuckle. I don't know much about Della, but it's apparent those two are so evenly matched, it'll do my underboss good to have her by his side. When he's made Boss, it'll be Della running the organization with him, carrying it into the next generation.

As I head back toward the basement, I text Rosen to bring Aurora there, and by the time I reach the door, they're already waiting. Rosen throws me a smirk as Aurora's energy can't keep her still.

Rosen throws me a tight smile. "She's impatient."

*Clearly.*

She throws a scathing look over her shoulder at him. "When someone you thought was a friend stabs you in the back, let me know how you feel."

Rozelyn certainly is good at hurting those closest to her.

I unlock the basement, flick on the light, and they follow me down. I don't have to check to know Rosen's behind me with Aurora entering last. His protectiveness would demand he enter into what could be a dangerous situation before her.

Rozelyn's seated in the sleeping bag in the centre of the basement, in the same spot I last left her in. I should chain her, to ensure Aurora's absolute safety, but based on the way she struggles to sit up, her wary gaze flicking over the three of us, she's no threat.

She looks like she's given up. Like the girl I know, the fighter has gone. She looks...tired. Like everything's pointing to the ending approaching.

Aurora and Rosen step deeper into the room, stopping a few feet away from Rozelyn. I move beside her, positioning myself at the ready to get between the women if I need to.

"Should have known," Rozelyn mutters, her voice hoarser than it was even an hour ago. "Should've known you'd be down here eventually." She's looking past me and at Aurora, who takes a single step forward before Rosen's tugging her back to his side, his own glare slicing daggers into my captive.

"She won't hurt me," Aurora murmurs, patting his hand in request to release her.

"She did once."

"You see me, right?" Rozelyn weakly gestures to herself, breaking up their argument. "Do I look like I'm fit enough to attack, even if I wanted to, which by the way, I don't."

Rosen loosens his hold on Aurora, who slowly takes a step nearer. And then another, her ex-bodyguard a constant shadow until Aurora stops at the edge of the sleeping bag and crouches down, one hand positioned on the cement ground to steady herself. Her manicured nails, light pink in colour, and the ring she's wearing on her pinky are a complete contrast to this basement.

Rosen's hand darts toward her. "Aurora, get up."

She throws a scathing look over her shoulder at him. One that makes my own balls shrivel and it's not even directed toward me. "I play in dirt for fun, Rosen. A dirty ground isn't much of a difference."

I doubt the community garden involves blood stains, but the mafia princess choosing to stand or sit isn't my concern. Ensuring Rozelyn remains still and doesn't try to attack is.

"Hi." Aurora directs her attention to Rozelyn. "Feels like a long time."

"How was the wedding?" is all Rozelyn asks. "Bet it ended with a good nap?"

Aurora flinches at the reminder, and Rosen looks seconds away from murdering Rozelyn. I inch closer to Rozelyn, for her protection.

"Obviously," Aurora replies dryly. "So getting close to me at the garden was all a set-up."

Rozelyn's tongue dampens her drying, cracking lips and she nods once. "My father's plan. He wanted the distraction while he escaped. You were freshly returned to the family and he knew you'd be more receptive than the others. He wanted to taunt you all." She glances up at me and then Rosen. "The notes outside your clubs were also from me on his orders."

Always on his orders.

Aurora's brows scrunch together. "You were the only person, outside this family, I thought I could have a genuine friendship with. I even hid your presence at the garden from him," she gestures to Rosen, "because I knew he and my brother would lock me in my room and not allow me near strangers. That's how much you meant to me."

"That's your mistake then."

My attention slides from Aurora's hurt expression to Rozelyn. This isn't at all the woman who was here an hour ago. Her walls are back up; her comments snarkier than they need to be. She's protecting herself again—for whatever reason, she's viewing Aurora as a threat.

For all her words, Rozelyn's eyes lower, seemingly looking through Aurora rather than at her. Rozelyn's many things, but she's becoming worse and worse at lying. Or she's simply giving up.

Aurora shakes her head slowly, the dip between her eyes deepening. "I don't believe you one bit, Roz. What you did wasn't because you wanted to."

Rozelyn flinches with the name she used at the community garden; the name Aurora knew her as. Her gaze lowers again until she's staring at Aurora's feet. I'm not the only one noticing Rozelyn's demeanour change because Rosen is continuously looking between me and the women.

"Believe what you want," she weakly shrugs, "but it's the truth. You should hate me, Aurora. After all, them sending you in here is a pathetic attempt." She glares at me. "Do you not recall the conversation we had less than an hour ago?"

"*I* wanted to speak with you," Aurora cuts in. "I wanted to know why you'd harm me if your father had already escaped."

"Did he?" Rozelyn asks in a taunting tone, indicating otherwise. "Or was he hiding in the city, right beneath your noses, putting everything in place before his escape? Including me. And now look," she scans the room, "you're all so focused on me, my father made his escape."

This isn't the truth. Not all of it. For whatever reason, Rozelyn's editing the facts. She followed her father's orders to help him—or be under the guise of helping him—but using her real name in the garden, getting captured willingly, it's a set-up. From her father's point-of-view, she's been caught. He has no idea she's had her own plan this entire time.

Unbeknownst to Aurora, who devours everything Rozelyn tells her, I think Rosen comes to the same conclusion based on the way his expression drops, the tenseness evaporating. He meets my eyes and mouths, *Double agent.*

"And yet, you used your real name to get in here because you and I both know your reasons go deeper than obeying your father." I wait until Rozelyn glances at me to silently remind her of our conversation earlier.

"Or talking about the possibility of there being one less Corsetti?" Rosen speaks up, bringing up his reason for stabbing her.

Aurora glances back and forth among the three of us, finally catching up that there's more happening around her than she realizes.

Rozelyn shrugs. "I had to make it look real. He slipped out of the city while you were hunting for me. Left me here because I was the distraction, but he had eyes on me still, so I couldn't walk right up to you. He'd know." She looks at Aurora to explain, "Getting close to you was an act, drugging you the outcome, as he requested."

"Did you even like me at all? Was *anything* we spoke about real?"

Rozelyn merely stares. And stares. The weight inside the room becomes tangible, electrifying as we all bide our breaths, waiting for her to shatter Aurora's heart.

Just when I'm about to reach for her, to shake her until she responds, she speaks. "I used you, Aurora. I lied to you about my identity, but everything I said to you was genuine. When you spoke about your stress regarding the engagement party and later the wedding, and the pressures of your family, the limited information about my own life I told you...it was all the truth."

Aurora pays her no visible attention. After a final stare, her lips fold together and she pushes to her feet, giving Rozelyn and me her back as she heads for the stairs, Rosen close behind.

Rozelyn shifts onto her knees, as though about to follow. Every inch she takes, I do too, magnetizing myself to her.

"Wait," she calls so softly, if the room wasn't silent, no one would hear her. "Aurora, wait, please. I don't deserve your forgiveness, but I *am* sorry. I hope you'll soon realize why I did what I had to do. You know Della. You've heard the things she did to survive. I'm no different, except she got away from my father, and I didn't. When we talked, or hung out with those kids, and I was on my knees digging through the dirt, pretending I had a clue how to garden...that was me. All me. My personality was never faked."

Like flicking a switch, Aurora's smooth expression crumbles and her responding breath is heavy. In a blink, she's rushing up the stairs, without providing a response, Rosen at her heels. When the door above slams shut, Rozelyn falls back to her ass and sits there, dejected, until I shatter her moment of peace.

I sympathize with Aurora. Everything she's dealing with, I did too once.

Moving in front of her, I study Rozelyn's face. The down-trodden expression. The flat eyes as she's still staring at the stair-case. I grab her chin, forcing her to look at me instead. Her cheeks look more sunken in than normal, and my gut twists.

"Hurting Aurora won't save you."

"Maybe I'm getting tired, Flynn," she whispers and doesn't try to fight my hold. "Tired of everything. Tired of waiting for the vengeance I want more than anything."

"*You're* the one keeping the truth hidden from us, so don't give me the bullshit of being tired."

Roughly releasing her, I create distance, stalking to the other side of the basement, my hands weaving into my hair. She fucking pisses me off. Worse because at the moment, I *want* to despise her with every fibre of my being, but seeing her now, miserable and beaten down, sparks another urge. The compulsion to take her from here and care for her.

"We're gonna play a game, *mon soleil*, and you're up first. Question one: tell me about the Haynes family."

# 22

## ROZELYN

**D**ad didn't reveal everything right away. More like when he deemed me useful for more than only a punching bag is when he disclosed the last bit, about the Haynes family.

*"One thing you need to learn, Rozelyn, is having the most people on your side is best. Many years ago, I received an interesting phone call from back home, with another assignment, secondary to the Corsettis. One of our own, Lawrence Haynes, fled, taking his four-year-old daughter with him."*

*"Okay?" Where's Dad going with this?*

*"That daughter is valuable because of who her mother is. They want the child back and to have him punished. He was easy to find, of course—"*

Is this where Dad steals the remainder of faith I have in him and tells me he murdered a child?

*"—but he's desperate, and desperate people make difficult decisions. Exactly like the one I made in that moment—"*

Oh, here's the admittance of child murder...

*"—The Corsetti assignment is taking longer than it should,*

*and they're getting impatient. Therefore, I saw an opening with Lawrence. We got his and his daughter's names changed after faking their deaths. Home believed I'd completed the assignment; meanwhile, I now had an inside man who owed his life to me in debt."*

*Except it's been years and nothing's come of having that benefit. Crossing my arms, I ask, "And how'd that work out for you?"*

*"One man wouldn't help me accomplish my goal, Rozelyn, but it's the little things that matter. The small attacks that unhinge a person. That's been what he's doing for me."*

For years, we never spoke of them again, and the Haynes duo didn't matter to me.

"Rozelyn." Flynn's throaty growl breaks through my thoughts, compelling my head to tilt, to find him in the dark basement.

Minutes after Aurora and her bodyguard left, he went on the attack.

There's no need though.

If they know about the Haynes, it's a matter of hours before they trace their origins. Then I'll no longer have leverage. Right now, I'm still useful.

Not sure what changed or why. Seeing Aurora feels like the rest of my life has been sucked out of me. The hurt in her eyes made my stomach physically knot. At the garden, I hid my pain, while she spoke about hers. Built those walls again, even as I found similarities between her and me. Both of us dragged through our families' situations, while also on the outside of it all.

For her, nearly being married off when she didn't want that future.

For me, being whatever assassin my father's made me out to be.

"The Haynes needed to hide. My dad helped him." A little bit of information to begin feeding his curiosity.

"Why would he do that?"

"Why does my dad do anything?"

*Why did he hit me so many times?*

*Why did he hurt Mom?*

*Why did he hurt Della and Ariella's mother too?*

*Why do anything?*

*Why be that loyal to an institution that is clearly using you?*

Why do I feel like I've given up? All my determination to ensure the Corsettis do it on my terms, do it *right*, to get his ass and drag him to the executioner table. To end the pain and suffering he's brought into my life...to Yasmine's. Mom's. My ex-stepsisters.

Gone.

This needs to end.

My mind is broken. That must be the reason for this sudden shift. Nothing else makes sense, but also, nothing else matters either.

And within my broken mind, like a movie playing on speed two-hundred, I relive every hit. Every bruise. Every raise of his hand. Every bellow.

"Because then he owned them. Don't ask for details because I have no idea who, but before he left, he told me he was having them dealt with. That's all I know, but I'll assume it was Dad's way of tying up loose ends. He had their deaths faked, and with him on the run, he couldn't risk Lawrence saying anything to the Corsettis."

"Thank you, Rozelyn." Spoken softer than I could have ever imagined him able to speak. Kind words, gentle tone, they're almost wrong coming from his lips.

Flynn approaches again and reaches for me. I lean closer, craving his touch. The way he'll stroke my cheek like I'm a doll, even when we both know I'm anything but delicate. Both of us, bound by our pasts.

His—a motherless past and a father who didn't give two shits about him. Neglected as a child, despised as a teenager.

Mine—living with Dad's frustrations. Knowing Mom took every hit. Always behind closed doors, away from the prying eyes of Yasmine and me. It was their attempt at shielding us from the grimness of their life. Until she was no longer here, and for all his hate, I learned then, despite marrying her for her family name, knowing it's one in many steps to get him noticed by the Corsettis, he truly loved Mom. I never understood why he abused someone he genuinely loved, but I'm sure Dad's not mentally stable, and doubt he ever was.

I believed after Mom's death, everything would be okay. Or, as well as 'okay' can be without her. I'd hoped Dad's mood would shift into only love for Yasmine and me since we're the living forms of his deceased wife.

Yasmine, sure. She was a product of their love, but my biological father was a nobody from before their marriage. Mom was shunned and forced to give me up when I was a baby. Stefano was all I knew as a father. He was Dad in every sense of the word, and for many years, I was dumb enough to believe I was also his daughter. Without Mom, all his hate shifted to me. When I fought back, it got worse. If he drank, it was even worse. He drank a lot, as news and calls from back home were piling up.

It was fine because it kept him away from Yasmine.

Perhaps that's why he told me the truth. I wonder how aware Mom was, but if he's replaced her with me, he needed a confidant. Although, I frequently believed it was his way of explaining every slap, every punch. He believed if he provided a reasoning for his troubles, it'd excuse his actions.

It never did. Nothing had.

But I wasn't silent the whole time. I didn't have a plan then. I didn't know how to end this or get away from him. With every hit, my hate for him festered. Itching inside my heart, seizing my body, firing through my veins.

Dad sealed his own death the moment he made me into one of his many soldiers, clamouring for his attention. Paid to assist him in his decades-long drive. At this point, I'm unsure if he even remembers why he's doing what he's doing. His obsession has long taken over. All the pieces he put into place stacked on top of one another, creating a confusing mess I'm not sure he can get out of.

Let alone recollect why it's so important for him to complete this task for *them*. Everything in his life—my life, Mom's, Yasmine's—has been in *their* name. That family is more important than the manufactured one he created here.

*We're* only here because of them. We're a façade. A deception. A smoke show for his purpose.

*"Mon soleil."*

Did I imagine that?

Pressure strokes over my cheek, and coolness follows.

"Rozelyn, you're crying."

Am I? Despite Dad's determination to make me cold and unaffected, the emotional effects cloud my heart.

What—who—broke me? Why now? Why after days of keeping the truth inside, determined to design this plan so Dad knows *I'm* the reason he's losing.

Was it Della's visit? The reminder of my past, of seeing Ariella there, representing my own sister? Della and I aren't any different, after all. Both losing our mothers, both the eldest of two daughters, both stuck on Stefano's designed path, all in the name of bettering him. Ariella and Yasmine share similarities too, besides being the youngest. Ariella's soft demeanor is so much like Yasmine's, I understand Della's entire determination to do right by my father, only to keep her safe.

Or was it Aurora's visit? The reminder of what I did for *him*. He's the one who put the hit on her. I was trapped because I was being watched. One wrong move, and I likely would have had a bullet in my skull.

Or, was it Flynn who destroyed me, the very way he vowed to? He was the safety net for me back then. The embrace to heal every bruise left by my father. The smile I saw in my dreams and the person who reminded me I was surviving. All for Dad to rob me of my stability when he commanded me away from Flynn.

Or was it the amount of time passing? Being down here did exactly what the Corsettis always planned for it to do—break me. My mind wandered so many times, it officially isn't a part of me any longer.

"Rozelyn," Flynn repeats, an echo in my mind. I loved that tone. *Love*—present tense. Flynn's always had this way of chipping away at pain in my head and making things clearer.

He used to tell me the same. That his world had been grey until I came into it. But then, I made it black when I left.

"Rozelyn!"

Pressure.

Pain.

Air.

Life.

His lips move against mine, his hands gripping the sides of my face as he holds me steady, even while I remain limp. Lifeless. There's a desperation in his actions to get me back. I doubt it'll work...

Until his tongue licks the seam of my lips, and I respond.

Until his tongue finds mine, and I respond.

Until I grip the bottom of his shirt and lift onto my knees, trying to get closer.

"You were gone," he mumbles against my lips, and for once, there's fear and concern in his tone. His thumbs stroke my cheeks as his hands move to cup my neck. His forehead drops onto mine with a tenderness I've never experienced from him, even in the past. "There you are."

"You say that like you were worried."

He doesn't respond, but it's in his lack of answering that he truly speaks. If he wasn't worried, he'd agree with me and deny the emotion. He doesn't.

Because he was worried.

"Just making sure you're not broken. Can't have that yet."

Words spoken to mask his true feelings—his care. An explanation accompanied by sneer and a callous tone, when he means everything opposite, but I get it. I'm still the enemy and he's the enforcer.

So before he pulls away, I lean forward and initiate the kiss. He's still against me, his lips firmer than moments ago, but he doesn't push me away. His fingers pinch the back of my neck, and I'd like to believe, it'd hurt anyone else, but he and I were made for one another's pain.

When I pull back, I'm ready for everything to change.

"I'm ready to tell you where my father is."

# 23
## FLYNN

Since it was well past midnight when Rozelyn agreed to admitting everything, and most of the family was asleep already, with Rafael off consoling Maurice's daughter after telling her some facts about her own history, Nico instructed me to wait until morning.

So I do, waking Rozelyn with my entry. Much to her obvious dismay, I retrieve the chains from the far corner.

She scowls, pushing into a sitting position inside the sleeping bag. Her hair is slightly erratic around her face, her eyes sleepy and blinking quickly to wake. For a second, I pause to watch her, before recalling why I'm down here in the first place.

"Are they necessary? Not like I'm gonna run away."

While I believe her, Nico would not. With us about to walk in front of every member of the immediate Corsetti family, a role must be played. A role in which the prisoner isn't allowed to be free.

Ignoring her comment, I drop the chain around her head and over her shoulders, but wrap it looser than last time. Once

205

secured, I grab her chin and angle her face toward me, searching for any signs of the shattered woman from last night.

She's still there, but the pain is hidden now, shadowed by a fierce determination. That's new, but I appreciate it.

Holding one end of the chain, I head for the staircase. She puts up no fight and trails along.

Once out of the basement, I first walk her to my bedroom to use the bathroom, a place she hasn't been in days, and I've been thankful for it. Over the days, her scent has faded, which means my room has become mine again.

"Do what you need to." I release the chain, watching as it hits the back of her leg.

She obeys and even shuts the door this time, but I don't make a point to comment. A few minutes later, the tap stops running and she emerges, her face damp. The dirt on her skin has been smudged over her cheeks, like she tried and failed at washing it off.

Yet, she somehow looks more beautiful than ever.

I grab hold of the chain again and lead her from my room. She walks beside me this time, instead of behind me, as I lead her toward Nico's office.

"Who's all going to be there?" she asks.

"The Corsettis."

"All of them?"

My eyes slide to her. "Second-guessing your decision?"

"Not at all. Simply curious."

At Nico's office, I pause, turning to face her. "You lie, you're dead. I won't save you from any one of them, Rozelyn." Her mouth opens, as if to comment, but I immediately switch to my next point. "Whatever made you finally fucking wake up and realize you're on the right side, keep reminding yourself of it."

She only glances at her wrists with a solemn expression. I assume she's recalling the bruises De Falco put on her as a teenager, and now I wonder, how many invisible injuries are still on her. Within her. Imprinted onto her soul, darkening it.

How much has she truly hidden from me? After today, I might never get to find out. Once we're finished here, Nico's already set aside a bedroom for her, as per Della's request—or demand, more like it. Inside, there's fresh clothing for her, which means she won't be stuck wearing my shirt any longer. There will be a bathroom she can clean up in, and this time, stay clean. Besides the items she'll need and the bed, everything else has been cleared from the room to ensure she doesn't fashion herself a weapon from anything. A guard has already been assigned, which means very soon, I'll be free from dealing with her.

My stomach lurches, my heart burns, and a shudder coasts through me, tensing my nerves with an emotion I refuse to name.

"Are we going to stand here all day?" Her voice cuts through my thoughts and she jerks her chin toward the office doors.

*Right.* Giving her my back, I open the doors without knocking, as per Nico's earlier instructions.

Inside, the room is lined with Corsettis. People I've known my entire life—most of them, anyway—and still, my skin crawls, my dislike for crowds creeping up again. Yet another reason, Lorenzo thought the enforcer job was most ideal. Means not working alongside others.

Against the wall to my right, Rosen stands with Aurora's hand in his. She leans against him as Rozelyn enters behind me, but looks away the moment their eyes clash. On Rosen's other side, Della's sister, Ariella, stands looking more stoic than I've ever seen her. Not that my interactions with the woman have been many.

Opposite of her demeanor is Della, standing beside Nico,

who's leaning against his desk, his arms crossed. Della's mask isn't in place at all, and at the sight of Rozelyn, she shifts.

Beside the desk on Nico's other side, Lorenzo and Caterina watch us enter impassively as well. They both meet my gaze for a brief second before focusing on the captive. Beside them and against the wall to my left, Rafael is holding onto a short, brunette woman. Having never seen her before, but knowing Rafael's current assignment, I assume this is Maurice Dupont's daughter.

Rozelyn and I stop in the centre of the room, her in front of me. The room's entire focus is on her—and on Nico, who shoves off his desk and meets us halfway. His gait is slow, a sly smile taking over. He's a man who's about to get the answers he's chasing and has every reason to be pleased.

Then he starts talking.

# 24
## ROZELYN

Certain things signal adjustment. In high school, it's a bell, alerting students to the periods changing. At a stoplight, it's the altering colours, instructing vehicle drivers how to behave.

For me, it's Nico Corsetti's slow pace from his desk to the centre of the room, a king in his own right. It's in that second, with his family surrounding him, his enforcer literally holding a chain around my neck, I wonder why Dad and his true family *ever* believed they'd be able to obtain Corsettis' power.

He's old money. A mob family. There's numerous, simpler means my father could have gone about this rather than the fuckery he devised.

Nico's grin signals he's about to start speaking. "You've decided now to talk. But the thing is, we've gotten the information needed from our sources. When learning who the Duponts really are, it only took a few hours before gaining their backgrounds. What city they're from. And I've pieced together why your father is so invested in the status of their life. Because where they're from, he is too, isn't he? So why do I need you?"

Now, that's interesting. Seems like Flynn lied to me and already know where the Haynes are from, which means they likely have Dad's location. Regardless, I doubt they have the biggest piece of the puzzle yet and that's my leverage.

*"Get in here."*

*Dad yanks me in by my wrist, which feels like it'll be ripped from the socket with any more force. He pulls me into his office and slams the door shut. Thankfully, he also releases me, but it doesn't stop the burning. I don't hold the skin because then he'll notice my pain and right now isn't the time to fight with him. Not with the crazed look in his eyes, his hair a mess from being tugged on it too many times. Frustration tightens his every step from me to his desk.*

*"Fuck!" he screams. "Fucking Della! That bitch flipped sides."*

Blinking from the memory, I focus on the man in front of me. Della may have once switched sides...but so have I.

I'm picking *me.*

"Maybe. But do you know why my father chose Montreal as his base? Why your soldier's life and death were so important to him? You claim to know what city they're from, but do you know what's there?"

*One, two, three...*He'll take the offer by my count of five, I bet, and when his jaw clenches, it's his silent admission he wants what I'm presenting.

A hand shoves into my back, knocking me forward, at the same time the chain around my neck wrenches me the opposite way, and I fall against the large, warm body behind me. Just the feel of him against me untenses one of the many knots in my shoulders. His familiar and electrifying scent only reminds me of another thing Dad took from me.

He growls in my ear. "Stop playing fucking games."

"You came in here wanting to disclose information, so get talking," Nico demands. He takes a single step toward me, getting much too close for what's comfortable. "You have two minutes to talk before I stick a gun to your head, and we decide breathing isn't in your future."

*Testy man.*

Flynn tugs on the chain again, though gentler this time, and I throw a quick glare his way. Now I see why he wanted me in these damn things.

"What do you know, so I can just fill in the gaps?"

"No," Nico responds. "Because then you'll edit the truth. All or nothing, Rozelyn. Tick tock."

*Fucker.* But this only works in my favour. I have a single thing I need from them before I agree to talking. The *only* thing in this world mattering more than Dad's death.

"You know better than anyone else, truth isn't free. I want to strike a deal."

Nico laughs once, humourlessly. "In case you haven't noticed, you're nowhere near being able to strike deals."

Ignoring him entirely, I demand, "My sister. Or you kill me, and you'll only have half the answers."

"The half that matters," he counters with a slight hike of a brow.

"Is it?" Plastering my own knowing smirk, I taunt him with a second of silence before gesturing to myself. "I have nothing left, Corsetti. In case *you* haven't noticed, I'm stuck. Captured. I know very well any one of you will stick a gun to my head and end me instantly."

Flynn grunts, in denial or hope, I'll never know.

"I have nothing left," I repeat. "Nothing but my humanity, which I plead to you with." Glancing at Della, who has slowly approached, I use her presence to make my point. "Clearly, you fell for my stepsister, despite her operating under my father's commands. Why? Because you thought her to be strong, admired her drive to protect her family, right?"

For a complete ten seconds, the room is completely silent.

With the silence as a barrier, I make my request: "All I want is my sister's safety."

Della takes another step, injecting herself into the conversation. Low, she asks, "Where's Yasmine?"

She's asked this before, downstairs in the basement when she came to visit me, but the response I gave was half-assed at best. An indication she's with our father, but Della is seeking for definitive details now because that's who she is. After today, if I know my ex-stepsister, she'll want to help Yasmine, which means handing over everything I know will only benefit us all in the end.

"With our father. *She's* his favourite. She's his only blood-related daughter, after all." And Dad was certain to remind me of it often. In other families, DNA doesn't always mean shit, but with him, it's everything. "Regardless, my deal is for her life. We're both products of our father's choices." I look from Della to Ariella, who's standing to my right by Aurora. To both my ex-stepsisters, I tell them, "We're *all* products of that life. We're *all* on the same side," emphasizing specific words to make my point. "You might have had it bad, Della. But I had it bad in other ways. Remember when you first came into our life, how kind he was to you? How much conditioning he forced upon you? Picture that, but for nearly one's entire life. Then come back to me and you'll be allowed to bitch."

*"You will be getting a new stepmother," Dad announces in the most offhanded way at dinner one night.*

*That's the second surprising action he's taken today. The first being the fact he joined Yasmine and me for dinner, except now I see why. It was to divulge this news.*

*"What?" Yasmine practically squeaks, dropping the steak knife in her hand.*

*"What?"* I echo. *"Is this why you've been gone most nights lately?"*

*Dad throws me a scathing look. "Yes. Don't worry, she's not replacing your mother. I don't love her. But she'll be good for the household. Comes with two daughters too, both around your ages."*

*Two new sisters is secondary to the importance behind his words. He doesn't love a woman he's marrying, so why is he going forward with it? Why now, only months after they met?*

That was before I knew any of the facts.

In my peripheral vision, I catch Nico sharing glances with his younger brother through my speech, and if I'm causing the underboss to falter, I've won.

Making his next question expectant: "What do you want?"

"When you go for him, keep her out of it. *I* was my father's soldier, not her. She's innocent. I want her safe."

Nico's jaw ticks again, but this time, it's less subtle. He peeks back to his father, then toward Della, the debate swirling through the room, keeping me on edge. I'm ready to fight his denial if I need to.

Yasmine has nothing to do with our father's actions. The day Dad said we needed to escape Montreal and head across the country, Yasmine was more concerned about messing up the progress on her Bachelor's degree than anything further. She was confused and I let her be right up until my final hug with her when I begged the universe that watching them drive off wouldn't be the final time seeing her.

"Fucking sake," Nico grumbles. "This agreement feels awfully familiar. Deal."

After a very long stare, in which I ensure he doesn't back out of the agreement he's just made, I accept it with a tip of my head.

It's in that second, I *feel* every hit again.

Every curse.

*"Fuck, Rozelyn, you have* no idea *the pressure." The slap that followed that one.*

*The time he slammed my hand onto his desk. I think he meant to hit it himself and forgot he was gripping me. No matter, since the agony was enough to make me shut down again.*

I've gotten very good at shutting down. Ignoring the physical aches as they got buried beneath the emotional pain.

*This is for you, Dad. For everything you've done. All the evil. All the—*

A final breath fills my lungs.

"White Rock, British Columbia."

I pause, letting it sink in. Everyone seems to share a look. Nico continues to glance to his brother, a silent conversation occurring between them until he nods once quickly, his gaze on the girl by Rafael's side.

I'm sure the documents they've dredged up on the Haynes point to B.C., but they have no idea what's really there.

Stefano De Falco, Boss of the opposing Montreal mob family—false.

Me, mafia daughter—only fifty percent on Mom's side.

We were both a persona Dad adopted. A guise. A character he played while working toward the larger picture

"There's an institution there," I continue when it seems like they're prepared for more. "An academy. You guys are the mafia. You might rule the crime, the underground dark spots of this place, but they control the *country.* They're inside every level of government. They manipulate everything you could ever imagine. They're huge."

*There. I said it. It's out.*

My breath remains steady and calm, opposite of the harshness I was preparing for as I officially betray Dad.

*"Honey, I need to tell you something. Something that will explain a lot."*

*I hate that tone and that name. It means whatever he's about to say won't be good.*

"I'm not..." he rolls his lips together, pausing to think over his statement, "...who you think I am. Or who your mother thought I was. I'm only in Montreal on orders."

*"Orders?" I repeat, my stomach dropping. Whatever Dad's attempting to tell me makes no sense.*

*"Across the country, there's a hidden society that runs things and I'm from there."*

"Name?" Nico demands, his voice harder than earlier, edged with anxiety I hadn't believed him capable of.

"The Seven. I'm telling you the truth when I say I know little about them, only that they exist. Only that they're seven leaders scattered around the country, and my father works beneath one of them." He's never told me which one either, or what each of them are in charge of.

"Why B.C. then if they're all over the country?"

I shrug one shoulder. As if I'm supposed to understand why a centuries-old institutional power chose that *one* city to be based out of. "Where do you think they're trained? Again, I don't know much about these details, but from what my father told me, there's an academy. It's where the richest of the rich kids all over the country attend university. It's where the kids of the Seven are raised, trained to one day take their fathers' spots. Fed under the umbrella of a degree, they're spoiled, rich... dangerous. Go through their own trials before taking their places hidden in society."

That's where Yasmine is presently. If there's one thing Dad better be doing, it's keeping her safe. Yasmine's bloodline links her back to Mom's Italian mob family, who wanted nothing to do with us after Dad created distance between her and them, but it also connects her to the Seven. While not descended from any of them, Dad's association puts her in their path.

"My father attended. Got close to one of the Seven. After graduation, he was given a single task: take down the crime lords in Montreal." I toss a meaningful stare toward the Corsetti Boss standing the farthest away.

Lorenzo Corsetti could make grown men shit themselves with his deadly guise as he approaches. I force my back straighter, my shoulders up, in order to look stronger despite the chain around my neck.

"If this place controls the country, what does us owning the province matter? As you've said, they're manipulating things higher up."

My head falls slightly to the side, aiming to seem nonchalant. "That's the thing. They're so tightly wound into the entire legal, political side of the country, they've let other things slip. And in that time, in the past few decades, their hold on Quebec's underground crime has gone unmanaged, leaving room for Corsettis to slip in."

I remain silent for a second, scanning the room, watching the varying degrees of shock.

"You really never wondered why it all went down how it did?" I smirk, amused at the level this is hitting them. "How my father is Boss of his family, but where's the rest of them?" My eyes drift over each Corsetti, making my point. "His father, his mother, siblings, cousins. He wed my mother for the connection to the Costa family because he needed that alliance for strength. The deal between Hawke and me for marriage—another ploy. He was all too eager to capitalize on my mother's request. Pretty sure she had no idea about the snake she got into bed with, but," I shrug again with half the amount of energy, "here we are. When she died, grief hit him hard, but worse—she was the *in* to you guys. *I* was his in. It's why he was sent here. The Seven knew it might be a multi-generational takedown, but in the end, they want to control you. My father was simply laying the groundwork for it to happen."

Caterina Corsetti steps closer, pausing beside her husband, a hand floating to cover her mouth, which has fallen open. "How did we not see any of that?"

*Because he was good. He made you see what he needed you to.*

"Because he flashed my mother's fancy family name in front of you. You were distracted by the alliance. When the engagement was broken off, you assumed he was upset for losing the union. It was more that he lost his link to you, and he was frustrated."

Della cuts in from the side, stepping in front of Nico to demand, "Is that why he married our mother?"

For a minute, I'm empathetic to the sisters because while the marriage was never a love-match for Dad, it might have been for their mother. The struggling woman working two jobs found herself enamoured with my father's riches and charm, which he flaunted the moment he conveniently entered her life. They were a quick fling, to wrap her up in a whirlwind romance filled with fake promises and pretty words because Dad was trying numerous ways to take down the Corsettis after my engagement fell through.

"Told you, we're all the same," I remind her of words I had said to her previously. "Pawns in my father's elaborate plan. Actually, no, because he too is a pawn in the Seven's plan. When I say they control everything, I mean *everything*. Yes, that's why, Della. His plan fell through with me, so he wed a woman with two teenage daughters. It wasn't random you two were chosen. Struggling family, no father in the picture, it was easy. He was able to be your mother's saviour, a father to you two. You'd fall for his charms. And then your mother died." Before more has a chance to spew from my lips, I manage to shut myself up.

Mom's death was a genuine illness and unavoidable, but the

accident happening on the very day their mother's driver was unavailable and she got a last-minute call, which took her away from the house was too convenient.

I've never known for certain, but the rough feeling in my stomach every time I think about it has me wondering. The single instance I asked him about it, he rolled his eyes and shoved—physically shoved—me out the door. He never said yes...but he never said no.

I might not make the most ideal choices and I've become proficient at hurting others, but there is no gain in watching two sisters grieve a mother. Not when I don't know for absolute certainty.

When the invisible band around my throat manages to unwind enough so I can speak again, I do. "After your mother's death, my father went to work on his plan. There was some deviation," I peek at Ariella, indicating my meaning, "but in the end, one of you managed to get in here under the belief he simply wanted Corsetti power."

"How do you know all this?" Lorenzo asks. "How do we know *you're* not lying?"

A reasonable question I shrug off, lips pursing. "You don't. That's up to you to figure out. I can't do everything for you." Focusing on Nico again, I add, "It gets better when two Haynes disappeared."

I look to my left, to the woman clenching Rafael Corsetti like her life depends on it. She pulls from his hold, walking right up to me and murmurs, "Me."

*You.* Who, by all my father's accounts, should no longer be alive.

"My father never shared the details of your past, but all I know is you're from there. B.C. I doubt you're one of the Seven or else they would have found you by now, but you were supposed to be in that life, one way or the other. Your father fled with you here and struck a deal with mine. That's how he ended up working for," I roll my head until my gaze is on Lorenzo again, and finish by speaking directly to him, "you. My father helped Lawrence Haynes get new identities for him and his daughter, provided he manage to get inducted here."

Silence. Complete and utter silence as everyone comprehends what I've told them. Nico looks seconds away from snapping; his need for control growing by the second. And his parents don't even seem like they're present.

Must suck to learn so much is a lie. They believed Dad's animosity was simply from a broken engagement, but it was more than that. It was lost progress. Then finding out one of their own men was an insider, assisting my father. Let alone the fact there's an organization larger than them.

"What was the point in sending me in?" Della asks. "If he already had someone on the inside."

Something else I originally asked too. "My dad was determined to do right by the Seven. Guarantees and insurance. He was setting up layers. Besides, Haynes was able to report back on the little details. You were able to get more *intimate* with the Corsettis. You think it was random the attacks on your clubs? Nothing's random in this world. You should know that."

"Anything else?" Nico snaps.

I shake my head, the chain rattling with my movements. "Only that I hope to see you keep your promise, Corsetti." I'll lose the only thing I have left if Yasmine is harmed during this.

*I'll find you, Yasmine, and we'll get the hell away from this chaotic life.*

Nico doesn't comment, simply shifts his attention toward Flynn, to whom he flicks his fingers at. "Get her out of here. Put her where we've discussed."

Is that not the basement? Am I finally free?

Flynn turns for the door and the chain around my neck

pulls, his leash commanding me to follow. After a quick sweep of all the pain in the room—all the pain my father's caused—I take the lead that Flynn gestures for me to.

But then I stop, and shockingly, Flynn doesn't react. Maybe he senses I'm about to say more. Maybe he can somehow read my expression, even when I don't fully understand what's in my head.

"When escaping the city, my father went back to B.C. He was driving there to get backup because he knows he's in over his head. If I said anything earlier, you'd go to him. Attack on the Seven's territory, and you'd all die. If he brings them here, and you fight on your territory, you'll have a better chance. That's why I waited. I want him gone as much as you all do, and I needed to ensure your plan works. So I made my own."

Dad *will* die after this. He will get what's coming to him, for all the pain he's caused. All the distaste he's brought to my life. He's done.

"Why would you want your father dead?" Della's voice spikes, not only with confusion but panic too.

My gaze lowers, the strength no longer there to look at any of them when I answer.

*Because he deserves it.*

*Because you were used as an assassin, but I was used as a punching bag.*

*Because I watched him love Mom, while questioning if he comprehended the meaning behind the emotion.*

*Because he loves the Seven more than his family.*

So many answers.

But I go with: "Because."

Then I turn and follow Flynn to the door.

I f someone told me the girl I found sulking on a bench, the one who became my sun on life's gloomy days, was a woman who was related to some elaborate secret society across the country, I would have believed they were high.

Rozelyn may have given the Corsettis their answers, but there's still a few I want. A few I *need*. But before I manage to get her out of Nico's office and into private so I can ask those very things, we're interrupted by Maurice's daughter, who lunges to our side, stopping with short pants.

Large dark eyes that somehow grow rounder with emotion focus on the blonde woman at my side. "Your father had mine killed, didn't he?"

For the first time since entering Nico's office, Rozelyn looks almost regretful. Her mouth curves into a frown. "I think so."

"But why?"

Rozelyn shrugs. "Insurance, if I had to guess. When he needed to escape and his plans didn't pan out how he wanted them to, you and your father were loose ends. Someone who'd been working beneath the Corsetti influence for decades and who knew everything. Your father left B.C. for a reason, and whatever it was, scared mine enough that he took him out."

*Damn.*

When the woman falters and Rafael is right there to catch her, I remove Rozelyn from the room entirely and start walking her toward the staircase and the bedroom assigned to her.

Rozelyn's speech signalled not only the ending of De Falco's life and the possible beginning of war, but the end of her and me. It was pure chance eleven years ago I fell for the woman who'd one day affect my future family's lives.

With my right hand, I make a fist, hiding that scar away. That promise had been kept. We made our way back to one another, but exactly like we'd both been saying since that day, neither of us are the kids we once were and this is where chapter two of our story ends.

It's now up to Nico and his parents to decide what to do with her. If they'll hold her to her father's crimes alongside him or release her into the wild, where she'll likely track down her sister and they'll live the remainder of their lives free from De Falco's treachery.

I'm silent as I stalk through the hallways, heading to the smaller guest wing. Rozelyn's also quiet with only the jangle of the chains filling the space. Her shoulders are bent inwards, her head lower than I've ever seen. I'd kill to know what's in her head, after revealing all that she had.

I've pieced together why she wants her father dead. For the abuse, there is no love between them any longer. Rozelyn's turned her back on him the same way he did to her many years prior.

We reach her new bedroom and I push open the door, stopping at the doorway to lift the chain from her shoulders and over her head, tossing it to the floor. Without her collar, she's free.

Ocean-like eyes flash to mine, the skin between her brows furrowing until I tip my head, indicating for her to enter the room. She does, her mouth pressing into a flatter line, and I trail her, scanning the space Nico had prepared.

The room has been emptied of everything except a single lamp on the bedside table, the deep purple bedspread covering the king-size bed, the dark curtains draping the window—much smaller than all the others on this floor, a fact I'm certain Nico considered—a fresh set of clothing on the bed, and the bathroom across from it. Everything else, all the extra furniture, has been removed.

"So telling the truth gets me a private room."

"Could have had this the moment you arrived if only you spoke sooner."

She spins, and the arc of her unbound hair, the momentary pass of glee in her expression yank me right into my head, into a memory of her doing the exact same thing.

*When her spin ends, her curtain of hair falls around her but she tips her head back, her tongue peeking out to grab onto a falling snowflake.*

*I despise snow with my every fibre but seeing Rozelyn in it makes that hate go away. Such a simple thing to see her smile like that earns my respect.*

*It's the first snowfall of the season and she was insistent to drag me outside to the field. I can never deny her anything, not if it makes her so happy. It's not a lot, only an inch of snow has fallen between arrival and lunch, creating a blanket over the field that the grass still pokes through in some places. But she was determined to be the first to walk through it and break the peace nature was constructing.*

*I stride over to her and take what I've come to care for more than anything else in the world between my hands and kiss her. Kiss the small dabs of cold against the warmth of her soft lips.*

*Watch as the falling flakes decorate her hair like a crown for a second before her body's heat melts them and creates small wet spots.*

It's Rozelyn's responding frown that returns me to the present because she didn't frown that day.

"Yeah. Well, you know why I didn't talk sooner."

"Yeah." *Because you were insuring your own safety.*

Everything I planned on asking her all falls away. Everything I wanted to say—gone. Nothing matters at this point because this is where our story ends. For good, this time. Our lives intersected once by chance, and this time, by battle, but there won't be a third. Once the Corsettis make their plan, her father will be hunted. Rozelyn will have no further use to them after he's gone, which means if they let her go, she'll run fast and far away from here. And me.

I turn for the door after retrieving the chains.

"Wait."

Her command stops me short, but I don't face her. Not sure I can.

Once, she walked away from me, but this time, it's I who'll make the first step.

"You're leaving?"

"As opposed to staying?"

Silence. But a heavy silence telling me she has more to say—unspoken answers to my questions.

A full ten seconds pass before she asks, "What's going to happen to me?" Her tone isn't soft or scared; that's not Rozelyn's style. Rather, confident. Assured. Curious.

"You'll stay here until Nico decides your fate."

"I'm assuming Nico will soon search for my father."

For that, I want to see her expression, but I ground myself with a steady breath. "Most likely. Regretting your choices?"

"Not at all," she whispers with a fierce determination. "It seems weird, you know."

"Which part?"

"All of it. You. Me. This. Us."

*Us.* I face her again.

Her hands are clasped in front of her, but there's a gentleness on her face I've never seen.

Peace.

"Soon, Dad might not be here any longer and I...I don't know." She turns her head, her curtain of matted hair blocking her face from me. "I feel like I should be more upset by the idea than I am."

This is the ideal opportunity to get out of here. When her emotions are frazzled and she's not arguing with me. And yet, I stride away from the doorway and toward her, not hesitating when I take her cheeks, one hand on either side of her jaw, and wrench her face up.

"Tell me everything he did to you, Rozelyn. Every fucking thing. I want all the facts you didn't give the Corsettis."

I *need* them.

Fuck the argument I just had with myself—and believed I'd won. That not knowing will be fine since our story ends shortly. Could I let her go without all the puzzle pieces together?

Because no matter who this woman is to me now, she *was* someone to me once. When we find De Falco, I'll make him pay for everything he did to Rozelyn. For the trauma he's caused, the shadows he's forced her to survive in.

She's limp in my hands, like a doll. Always strong, always wearing her mask to keep others out, yet always so willing for my touch. All mine.

The *only* thing that's ever been completely mine.

*"Mon soleil."*

Through her eyes, I see my nickname imbedding right into her heart.

"The hits started before Mom got sick. One day, when Mom and Yasmine were out shopping, he called me to his office. He'd finished a difficult phone call—his words. I was seventeen. Remember standing there, rocking on my feet, trying to figure out why he was bothering to tell me."

Probably only months before I'd met her. Seventeen. She was a child. My blood runs cold and I have to remind myself to cool the tenseness threatening to take over, before I hurt the woman whose face is between my hands.

"He ranted and raved. At one point, stood from his desk. The more he spoke, the more he yelled, and then he got erratic. Started throwing papers around. His lamp." Her eyes tighten. "I don't know if he meant to, but he threw it toward me. It hit the wall beside where I stood. To this day, there's a dent there. Dad got angry often, but usually not around me or Yasmine, so I was in complete shock. I remember feeling so cold, so numb," her voice drops to a whisper, her eyes no longer seeing me but rather looking through me, "and I just wanted to leave. I excused myself on the guise of homework, but he shoved the door shut and forced me to remain. Said he wasn't done talking."

Ice freezes every nerve in my body. The more she talks, the more body parts he'll lose.

"He continued yelling, and I kept trying to leave." Mist fills her eyes. "I barely remember what about; his words were so jumbled, mixed with the copious amount of alcohol I smelled wafting from him. When I tried again to escape, he grabbed onto my hand and squeezed so hard, I ended up feeling the pain for an entire week afterwards."

Three body parts gone.

"And then his hand swung. I wish I saw it coming."

Four body parts.

Five.

Six.

"I was in so much shock, trying to process what happened."

Seven.

"I don't think he realized his own actions either because he just stood there. After the longest minute of my life—I *still* relive that moment—I managed to get the door open and he didn't stop me."

Eight.

"I was shook but also not...because I'd noticed bruises on Mom's arms too. She never mentioned them and when I asked, she ignored me. But I understood in that moment."

Nine. This time, for her mother.

"That wasn't the only time," I state, my voice deeper, my throat feeling impossibly tight. There were marks on her shoulder once, her upper arm; I've seen others. De Falco didn't stop after the one time, accident or otherwise. The teenage rage I felt every time I found a bruise on her, every time she denied its existence or how she got it, that was child's play compared to the deadly rage coursing through me now, igniting a fresh wave of wrath.

My hands grip her face tighter, stealing the physical reminder that she's *here* with me. She's safe from him.

For eleven years, I haven't been able to breathe normal. Since the day she walked away from me.

But for the first time in years, I breathe.

Her.

Me.

"Ow." She flinches. "Flynn, you're hurting me."

I want to claim I don't care because her pain is to remind us both she's not with him any longer, but I do, and it takes a long, steadying breath before I release her face and instead, grip her hips, pulling her against me. She can feel the steady beat of my heart like this, can know how she's affecting me with her story, no matter the walls I've pretended to be building between us this entire time.

She tips her head up, our lips only an inch away. The angle causes her hair to brush along the back of my hand, a feeling I've missed over the years.

"That wasn't the only time," I prompt again through clenched teeth.

"No," she agrees. "But I won't relive every one."

"Not good enough, Rozelyn." I'm not asking her to relive her trauma, just to extinguish the flames burning inside me. The erratic noises in my head.

She shakes her head. "No, Flynn, but I'll say that after Mom died, it got worse, not better. Dad lost control after that. So much of his planning had begun to slip away. I believe his mind actually snapped, and that's not a joke. If it wouldn't have gotten me hurt, I would have recommended he go see a psychologist."

It's been eleven years since she walked away from me. Eleven years of abuse. "Eleven years of this," I voice my thoughts.

"Yes and no. Dad buckled down and went into planning mode. After Mom's death, even he went into mourning for a while. For a few months, he seemed to have lost focus. Direction. I felt for him then obviously but looking back now," she scoffs, "the grief, I think, is what did it. He felt his plan collapsing and all that quiet time was dangerous. Whatever insanity went through his head at the time eventually led him to Della's mother. I was so hurt to see Mom being replaced, but he claimed he didn't love her, which I suppose made it a bit better, even if I didn't understand. I didn't know anything about B.C. or the Seven or who he truly was at that time."

"The abuse during those months?" Not a complete question but thankfully, she gets it.

"A bit more infrequent," she says matter-of-factly. It's her shutting it down again. The violence is a shadow in her gaze; a dark fact she can't run from, not completely. "Occasional but maybe he was hiding his true monstrous self from Della's mother."

"This whole time you've been biding your time."

"I guess." One corner of her mouth lifts into a sad smile. "As years passed, Dad admitted his background, his job, his purpose of being in Montreal. It's shocking to hear shit like that, and then I was pissed. At *them*, at *him*. His entire marriage to Mom, the marriage deal between me and Hawke, our entire lives were fabricated as part of some elaborate scheme because *they* demanded this task of him. It was a giant test that drove him mad. Two decades later, I barely understand how they're still waiting for him to accomplish this. Makes you wonder what they're thinking."

It does, but I'm more focused on her story right now. Clinging to every single syllable as I plan De Falco's most painful death.

"When Della succeeded...and Dad failed, even when having Nico in hand, he realized how much he fucked up. When Della made the deal to get her and Ariella free, he tracked her out west. Once Nico found her, Dad demanded Yasmine and I pack what we could, and we hid out in the city, watching and waiting. He knew it was a matter of time before Della completely turned on him and led the Corsettis to our house."

Which is exactly what happened. I didn't go with them that day because Nico had me stay back and prepare the basement for our would-be captive if they managed to get De Falco.

"Then it kept going." She sighs, her body sagging even lower. "Dad realized with Lawrence Haynes still alive, he risked being exposed. He hired mercenaries to avoid using his own men to take them out. Dad also couldn't chance, once heading home, the Haynes' lives being tracked back to him because the moment he disobeyed the Seven's orders was also the day he betrayed his own people. Ironic, huh?" She smirks, a lightness once again entering her eyes. "Deceived them in order to obey another command from them. But that's my father. He's wound himself up in so many complicated plots and deceit that nothing makes sense anymore."

"Then he escaped to B.C." Leaving his own daughter as a scapegoat and I bet, didn't think twice about it. The Haynes were disposable to him, so were Della and her family, as well as Rozelyn.

Flickers of sadness travel through her eyes, but they're gone as quickly as they arrived. She coughs and straightens, feigning being okay.

I, meanwhile, am stuck. Stuck between thinking I need to leave and standing stonily in place, holding her, wanting to remain.

And then her next words make it worse. They don't ease the storm brewing inside me. The one whipping at my organs.

"I'm sorry for not looking for you, Flynn. I debated it often. So many times, I've wondered if you remained in the city or moved away. I feared what would happen if Dad learned I found you. Leaving you was for your safety and letting you remain in my past was too. Plus..." She trails off, biting her lip.

My heart pounds faster, my fingers digging into her hips, demanding she continue. "Plus what?"

"It was a high school fling. A few months of fun. A temporary connection which broke so easily, with only one goodbye."

Temporary. *She* was never temporary for me, even when I fucking wanted her to be.

Even with her right against my body, I step into her, forcing her to walk backwards. One, two, three steps she takes, and I match each one. We continue our dance until her back hits the wall closest to us, a slight gasp escaping her throat as she scans the area, noting how far we've gotten from the room's centre.

I release her hips to grab her wrists, lifting them overhead, arching her back into my chest. My mouth presses to hers, swallowing those breathy gasps, her gentle moans.

We absolutely shouldn't be doing this when I have a job and her future is unknown. It's fucked up, but this moment in time is *mine*.

I kiss her until she's panting, until I break away and her heavy pants fill the barely-there space between us, warming my face. When her eyes fill with lust and her lips are swollen with desire.

"Did that feel like we were a moment in time, *mon soleil*?"

"No," she answers mutely. "I never believed you were, Flynn, but I wished you could be, so it'd be easier. I hoped, for you, I was. For years, I convinced myself the emotions were one-sided and you'd long moved on, meanwhile I was clinging to the only brightness I'd known."

Both of us stuck in our own, private hells. Both of us letting go of a teenage relationship, convincing ourselves it was only that. Both of us clinging to that very relationship to fuel us.

Before releasing her wrists, I press my thumb against her right palm, right over the white scar. Then I reach for my shirt draping her form and pull it up and over her head, dropping it at our feet.

Her nipples strain against the change in temperature, and my mouth waters, the desire to lap them growing. I cup her breasts, one in each hand, and pinch her tight nubs.

"The moment I saw you in the basement, did anything imply we were ever temporary?"

"You hate me. You've said so many times."

"I hate what life did to you, to us. I hate you for what you said to me back then. I hated you because I thought I *had* to, to be loyal to the only people who've given me a family worth fighting for. I believed I was a game to you, but I didn't understand everything." I release her breasts to grip her face again, one hand at the back of her neck, the other beneath her chin, tipping her face to mine so she can feel my next words. "How can I hate someone who's been fighting alone this entire time and who's still come out on top, fuckin' stronger than ever?"

"I'm sorry," she whispers, though I don't know what for. I've never asked for an apology. I don't believe in regrets because every action a person chooses to make is made for a purpose. Whether good or bad, it was made, and there's only moving forward from it.

"Don't be. You're not the one who needs to apologize." I brush my lips over hers, feeling the moment her breath becomes rattled, her breathing fragmented. "If I hated you, I wouldn't have fucked you. If I hated you, I would have been able to hurt you—truly. Do you know how many times I'd gone down there with the intention to but couldn't bring myself to actually harm you?"

She doesn't respond with words, but rather, with an action. She lifts her hand and rests it right over my heart, over my Corsetti tattoo, put there alongside my oaths.

"I've been a shadow, Flynn. Forced to live in the backdrop of my father's plan. You were the only one to ever rid me of the pain. You made breathing easier. You gave me *life*. It took me a long time to stop thinking about you."

"Me too," I admit, my tone rough. "*Mon soleil*, you did something to me." I lift my hand, resting it over hers. "You made me feel wanted for fuckin' once."

"And you made me feel appreciated."

Both of us fucked-up in our own ways. Designed by our own traumas. Controlled by the shadows.

# 26

## ROZELYN

In the basement, we were in our own little world. It was a game neither of us were winning or losing. The torture, the pain, the provoking—it was life. For Flynn, he was on a high executing it while I revelled in receiving it. The world outside that room paused.

Telling the Corsettis about Dad, not only ends my captivity, the pain he's caused, the hell he's dragged my life through, but also *this*. Flynn and me.

The future is unknown. I'm not safe until Nico allows me to walk out the front doors. Even then, I have no idea where to go from here. Hunting down Yasmine and finding us safety where we can live happily will be my next goal. Flynn will return to his job, and the life he's constructed here.

Perhaps that's why I haven't pushed him away. Once Flynn walks out that bedroom door, I have no idea when, or if, I'll ever see him again. This could be it and I need a better goodbye than the first, disastrous one. This time, with all our cards laid out and not a mounting pile of lies between us.

With his eyes pinning mine, I pull my hand from beneath

his, away from his heart, and finger the bottom of his shirt before tugging it up his chest. He helps, tossing it toward mine.

I skirt my hands up his chest, my skin bright compared to the dark and numerous tattoos covering his body. I long to study every single one, to ask him the stories behind them, but we don't have that kind of time. Instead, I lift onto my toes, wrap my arms around his neck, and brush my lips against his, as an invitation.

That's all it takes before I'm in his arms, my legs winding his, only my panties and his jeans between us. There's not an inch of me that isn't on fire from touching his skin.

He cups my breasts again and breaks from my mouth, nipping his way down my neck, and my head falls back to allow him the space. My core clenches with every flick of his tongue, as though he's licking my pussy instead of my neck.

"Hold onto me," he commands.

I am, but I tighten my hold as he releases me to reach down and undo his own jeans. I can't see what he's doing, only feel as his pants get shoved down, and then I'm met with his hard length between us.

I rock my hips against him and with a low noise, he rips those away, dropping them also to our feet. With his hands freed again, he holds me under my ass again and drags his cock through my core.

"Always ready for a good, hard fuck, aren't you?"

My nails dig into his shoulders, commanding him to continue. "Only with you, *ma lune.*"

He stills, a beat of silence filling the air. Even my heart pauses its thumping, and I wonder how bad of a mistake I made until he tips his head again and takes me in another one of his breathless kisses that makes my head swim.

Then his cock enters me, just the tip, and I push my hips down, urging him deeper.

"Fuck me," I beg, my voice a tone even I don't recognize. "Hard, Flynn. Remind me of everything we are." *Imprint my body with your touch, so no matter what happens next, I'll never forget this.*

He pushes another inch inside and stretches me, enticing a pleasured whimper. My nails scrape his skin again, my hips rocking to take him deeper.

"You're not in charge, so give up. If you're not good, I'll have to tie you back up. Keep you on the edge until you remember who is."

Words. I grin because I know this man. "I dare you, Flynn. You don't enjoy complete submission, and you never have."

He pushes more of his cock inside me, making my point more apparent, but grips my chin between his thumb and fore-finger, brushing a bruising kiss to my lips, which feel swollen from his mouth.

"Careful now. It won't be about submission when I have you tied up like my little slut, ready for my use whenever and however I want. We both know you'd still be in control."

In another life, I'd dare him again, to make that a reality, but not in this one. Not when the minutes slip away faster and faster and the time we have together is coming to an end.

Either way, my body reacts to his words and I grow wetter. Flynn groans, and with a final thrust, is all the way inside me, that fucking piercing of his hitting precisely the right spot that will quickly have me coming.

"Drenched," he murmurs, and my head falls back against the wall. "Ready, *mon soleil*?"

"God yes," I breathe. "Fuck me hard, Flynn."

That's exactly what he does. No teasing, no leisure, and not gentle. He gives me what I need in his pace, his thrusts, the way his fingers grip my hip like he'll never release me. My head falls into the curve of his shoulder, crying through the building pressure. Between being stretched and his piercing brushing the sensitive spot inside me, it won't take long.

Even if I don't want it to. I don't want to come. I don't want him to come. Because then he leaves this room and the future is unknown. While he's here, it's on pause.

My back rubs against the wall and I'm sure it'll be red in the morning, but it doesn't matter. It'll be a memory of this moment.

His hands move from my hips to my ass, and he grips each cheek, taking the skin in a hold that should be painful. That *is* painful but I love it. Love his touch. Always have.

He meets my eyes, our conversation silent besides the breathy pants, the struggle I'm having in keeping eye contact when they just want to shut and let go. My nails scrape violently at his skin, aiming to mark him the same way he's marked me over the days.

My own claim on him.

Then one of his hands shifts and he reaches between us, gathering wetness before replacing his hand on my ass. This time, at a different spot, and his finger pushes against the tight ring of muscle back there, making me tense. No one's touched that part of me before, but it feels right that Flynn would. He's gotten all my other firsts.

"Relax," he whispers, and I do. Just like that because Flynn won't hurt me. Not past the point I can accept, not past the point I enjoy.

Slowly, slower than I've ever been able to believe his man capable of, he pushes his digit inside me. I hiss, the feeling unfamiliar, and my eyes slam shut, my head falling into his neck again. He lets me and it's the scent of him I cling to, my nails digging back into his skin again.

"Breathe. If it hurts, tell me."

It doesn't; it's simply different.

He's stopped thrusting his cock though, and I'm thankful for that so my body can focus on one sensation at a time. He reaches the first knuckle and my body instinctively tries to push him out. Instead, my motions help him gain another inch, to the next knuckle.

"Does it hurt?"

I shake my head, so he can feel my response against his chest. Without the pain, my nails unhook from his skin, but something slippery soon follows.

"You made me bleed," he says with an amused tone. "You marked my skin, bad girl. You'll pay for that." With his final word, he thrusts again, and I feel Flynn *everywhere.*

His finger in my ass, his cock buried to the hilt inside me, his piercing hitting the sensitive parts of me again.

His breath painting my skin.

His heart thumping against mine.

His blood beneath my nails.

His soul fused with mine.

"If this is me paying, then the price isn't that high." The breathy taunt is out before I realize how bad of an idea it is to entice him when he's already on edge.

Blinding pleasure and complete and utter ecstasy consume me.

He takes my mouth, his tongue battling mine, and he's officially filled every one of my holes.

We're everything as Flynn fucks me.

Light.

Darkness.

Messy.

And absolutely fucking right.

I come at the same time he does, a heated rope of cum shooting to the very deepest parts of me. My pussy clenches around his thick cock, my ass squeezing his finger, keeping him inside me, my moan swallowed by his.

Until my exhausted body stops fighting what we both know as he claims me.

All of me.

The future is unknown. My life is in the balance. If the Corsettis release me, I'll be leaving.

But my soul will remain.

His finger slides out of me, the same time his sated cock does, and he releases my mouth. There's not enough breath in the world to cool the fire in my veins. Every muscle in my body is tense, ready to go again, preparing to never let him go.

And yet...

Flynn readjusts me in his arms until I'm cradled to his chest and he backs away from the wall, heading for the bed nearby. He rests me on my back, my head on the pillow, and even tugs the blanket over me. This sense of care from him is strange compared to every one of our other interactions, but I revel in it. His fingers linger on my throat, and then my cheek, his gaze saying what he isn't allowing himself to. My body is in desperate need of a shower after what we did, and he knows this, but for now, I let him care for me.

Because Flynn's aftercare means everything.

"I'm gonna find your father, Rozelyn, and he'll pay for what he did to you. I promise."

Then he leaves, shutting the door behind him, with no signal of when or if I'll see him again.

## 27
### FLYNN

The scent of Rozelyn is all over me and I fucking hate it—hate how much I love it. My dislike is made worse when the solider posted outside Rozelyn's new cage, who must have arrived while we were inside, smirks and shoots me a knowing look, which I ignore.

I head for Nico's office, finding only him and Rosen there, speaking low to one another.

"Rafael left too?" If Nico's making a plan of action, Rafael, as Capo, would typically be here for it.

Nico shares an amused look with Rosen. "He's heading to Toronto for a doctor's appointment. Something regarding Isabelle."

"Got it."

Nico gestures for the open chair beside Rosen, but I don't take it, instead positioning myself behind it. "Rozelyn in her new room?"

"Yeah."

"She say anything further?"

The truth isn't all mine, so I leave the details at a minimum.

"Just why she's working against him. Guess he's been abusing her for years." Why tell Nico at all? Maybe he'll have further compassion for her actions and it'll guarantee her life after this because I'm dying to know what's in my underboss's head.

Nico's brows lift and even Rosen glances toward me, his low whistle filling the air. "So she's a woman scorned," he says. "That's why she's so frightened we'd fuck this up."

I nod as Nico curses, lightly banging his fist on the desk. "How many people can a single man fucking traumatize during his lifetime? Well, Stefano is now our focus." He reaches for a glass to his right, sliding it in front of him but doesn't drink, only stares at the amber liquid. "If anyone told me a year ago, I'd be dealing with bullshit about a hidden society, I would have laughed, but here we are." His attention flashes to me. "Return here tomorrow morning at nine. I want you in on the meeting. You're dismissed, Flynn."

Grateful to be finished, I push off the chair and spin on my heel, only to be stopped by my underboss again with a single word.

"Thanks." He pauses. "I know dealing with Rozelyn might not have been easy on you, but you did what was necessary. You have my respect."

For the first time ever, I don't feel worthy of his respect, with Rozelyn still on my fingers, my dick. Her marks, half-moons that have stopped bleeding, imprinted into my shoulders start burning beneath Nico's watchful gaze, like an invisible signal admitting my wrongdoings.

"Thanks, sir," I manage before rushing away.

~

I wake from a dream in the middle of the night. A nightmare.

The first ending of Rozelyn and me, and it's no coincidence the memory has slipped into my head on the very same day I might have just unknowingly said goodbye to her.

*At the school's front doors, I step off to the side, where I kiss Rozelyn goodbye every day. Through the glass doors, parked by the curb, is the black car that drops her off and picks her up each day. I both love and hate that vehicle. In the front seat, there's the usual outline of a man, who she confirmed is not her father.*

*The sky seems darker than normal, the grey overhead clouds threatening a thunderstorm, so I'd like her to get inside the car before she gets soaked, but I also don't want to release her yet.*

*Rozelyn might believe I'm oblivious, but I'm not. She wears designer labels, gets dropped off and picked up each day by a driver, and carries a backpack with her that would feed a family for months with its value. Rozelyn comes from money—real money.*

*My arm snakes her waist and I pull her against my chest, and the rest of the world falls away. The other students rushing around, some out the front door, others away, toward the sports field for their after-school activities, have no effect on us. It's always like this with her; so easy to tune the chaos around us. She eases the noise in my head, my frazzled thoughts become focused when they're attuned to her.*

*Rozelyn doesn't meet my eyes and she's staring off to the side, her lips curled down, her teeth scraping her bottom lip. She's been off all day and no matter how many times I bother her, she won't tell me what's wrong. I know something is because I can easily read her. It became especially apparent earlier when I pulled her into the dressing room.*

*"Hey," I prompt her attention with a thumb to her bottom lip, freeing it from her teeth, "what's in your head?"*

*Her frown shifts the opposite way, but the smile doesn't meet her eyes. She shrugs, still studying the school around us.*

*"Hey," I repeat, this time in a firmer tone. Grabbing her jaw, I force her eyes onto me, and it's then I notice the water edging them. Shit. "What's wrong,* mon soleil*?"*

*"I…" She blinks, and a single tear slides down her cheek, landing on the back of my hand. It's cool, branding me with her emotions, which I fight to understand. "I…"*

*Her partial sentences have me shifting, bringing her even nearer as I back us into the corner for more privacy.*

*"Rozelyn—"*

*She lifts onto her toes and smashes her lips to mine. Her lips taste like tears, rather than the ocean. Like desperation as her hands claw at my shoulders. She kisses me with a feral intensity and more tears slip between our cheeks, joining in the kiss.*

*Weight fills my stomach. Something's wrong. She needs to explain soon before I go insane. Fisting my free hand ensures I don't end up shaking sense into her. She'll tell me on her own terms, but that better be now.*

*After a long kiss that's both the best and worst one she's ever given me, she pulls back, shuts her eyes, and whispers, "I-I'm sorry, Flynn."*

*Finally, her eyes open again and she studies me. I do the same, greedily drinking in the curve of her lips, the shape of her eyes, the specks of darker blue amongst the light colour. Her waterfall of hair I adore.*

*Why do I get the sense I need to commit her to memory?*

*"I-I have to go."*

*"Home." Even though I know, deep down, she means longer than just for the day.*

*She shakes her head, revealing what I've already assumed. "I'm leaving the school, Flynn. My father's making me return to my old one."*

*Considering she's never let me near her house, or told me anything about her family, somehow, I know my argument will fall on deaf ears. "School's gonna fuckin' suck without you here, but we'll meet up every evening, if you want."*

*She cups my cheek, her skin cooler than normal. Her heat, her brightness, it's fading right in front of my eyes. My sunlight is covering with clouds as dark as the ones outside.*

*"We're over, Flynn, I'm...I'm s-sorry. You and I...we can't be."*

*She releases me and backs away, but I allow her no more than a single step before I'm clutching onto the edge of her dress, grabbing her hand, and hauling her to the wall at my back, pinning her there with my body. Uncaring that her fancy driver is awaiting her or that students and teachers are all around us, I kiss her.*

*I kiss her. I steal her. I imprint myself on her.*

*It's with that kiss I tell her everything I have yet to. That I love her. That she's been healing me in ways I never believed possible. That walking up to her at the smoke bench was single-handedly the best decision of my life. That she makes me feel wanted so when my father reminds me how much I'm not, I replay all my interactions with her.*

*"Flynn," she whispers, shaking her head and shattering our connection. "I have to go. They're waiting on me."*

*"No." I kiss her harder. She can't go.*

*She tilts her head, breaking it again. "Flynn, I'm sorry."*

*"Why?" I meet her eyes, demanding the truth. "Why now? Why is your father suddenly demanding this?"*

*Her lips press together. She squeezes her eyes and another tear falls. When she opens them, there's a flash of an apology and then...nothing. An expression blanker than I've ever seen from her. A deadness that chills me to my core.*

*"I had a deadline to be here, and it's come. I made a deal, which I now need to follow through on my end."*

*"Bullshit." That sounds entirely made up. I grab onto her upper arms, no muscle, nerve, or organ inside my body willing to release her. Now, or ever. Not until she gives me a valid reason. "Tell me the truth."*

*"It is the truth," she emphasizes every word. "Look, I wanted to do this nicely to spare you but seems you're not being easy about this. This," with a pinkie and a thumb, she indicates the both of us, "was a game. It was fun. Attend the same private school your entire life, with the same people, the same expectations, you get bored. My friend and I made a bet that I wouldn't be able to live a regular high school life."*

*A bet.*

*My fingers begin lifting from her skin, one by one. The urge to hold her remains, but confusion mingles too. Her words sound like a lie, but apparently, all this girl's done is present herself as false, so this is likely the truth.*

*"A bet to have a regular high school life," I recount her claim as I scan her. The dress made from fine material, meanwhile my faded jeans are torn with age and wear. Her hair, shiny and silky, while mine remains dull from cheap shampoo. Everything about this girl screams money, which made her a bright light amidst a school of desolation.*

*My bright light.*

*But apparently a light that was manufactured for her own twisted games.*

*"Then where did I fit into it?"*

*Her lips lift in a cruel smirk that seems entirely wrong on her. "Part of the high school experience and all that. Once we met, my friend added to the bet that I wouldn't be able to get one of you," she gestures around the school, "to fall in love with me. But look at that—I did it. Trust me, Flynn, my life has no place for you. You're not good enough for me."*

*Not good enough for her. Every word is a punch to the gut. A fact that makes me want to hit something if she wasn't correct. I've never been wanted by anyone, never been good enough for anyone...except her.*

*But I suppose that was a lie too.*

*The white scar on my palm burns. She has a matching one. She played the game well apparently. Made her lies really damn realistic.*

*While my insides are shattering, there's something keeping me together. Something that allows me to stand upright through her emotional onslaught. My gaze drops from her nasty expression to her wrists, to her shoulders covered by the dress. I've seen the bruises numerous times. The fear. That couldn't be false.*

*More so, I've felt her love.*

*Or was all of that fake?*

*My head throbs, confused, conflicted, and crumbling with every word she speaks, uncertain the difference between reality and illusions.*

*Taking my stony silence as a goodbye, she steps away from me entirely, backing up a step, and then two. And another.*

*Everything falls away, except one thing. Her. We might be done. I might have been a game, or I was the realist fucking thing she's had, but either way, I am not finished with this conversation and she doesn't get to escape yet.*

*Shoving someone who steps between us out of the way, I reach her, looping my arm around her waist and yank her back to my body with a low gasp and panicked eyes. Her fingers lace with my shirt, making my heart thump a bit faster because her instincts are to hold onto me, not push me away.*

*"If we're never gonna see each other again—" My throat burns. "If we're done and I was all some sort of game—fine. Never good enough for anyone so it makes complete fuckin' sense."*

*She flinches. "Flynn—"*

*"No," I cut her off, not wanting her pointless explanation*

*because it won't change her decision. Her time for talking is finished. "I'm not done. You're about to walk out those front doors and get into that fancy car, with a driver you refuse to name, who'll return you to a home I cannot find and I'll probably never see you again. But before you do, I want one more fuckin' thing from you."*

*Wariness flickers in her light eyes. "What?"*

*"When you're feeling lost and afraid, isolated and miserable, think of me." Emphasizing my words, I reach for her palm, pressing my thumb over the mark.*

*"I doubt I'll ever forget you."*

*"Good. And when you're feeling low and all those other emotions, just know, I'm feeling the fuckin' same. Because when you walk out those doors, you'll take my reason for coming to this hellhole every day with you."*

*Her jaw clenches and unclenches before she speaks. "Be mad, Flynn. I told you, you were a bet. I won."*

*Except I don't totally believe her, even if her declaration rips me apart. Not good enough when she's the only one who made me feel like I am. Proficient actress.*

*"Yeah, I'm mad," I agree, finally releasing her entirely to create space between us. With every step away, more and more of the air clears; sense and rationality return, unhindered by the girl who's my everything. "Goodbye, Rozelyn. Return to your golden tower in your castle. Have a good life."*

*I turn and walk away. Every step demands I peek back, but I don't. Instead, pieces of my heart crumble, leaving a connecting trail from me to her. A trail that won't ever go away; it'll be invisible until the day I get over this and her.*

*I will get over her.*

*I duck around the corner until she leaves, watching as she exits the front doors. She pauses at her vehicle and peeks behind her, staring straight at me, but I know with distance and shadows, it's impossible she sees me watching her. A flash of wistfulness passes over her expression before she shuts down and climbs into the back seat.*

*Gone is my Rozelyn. In her place, whatever princess personality she's come from.*

*The moment her door is shut, I emerge from my hiding spot and tread toward the front entrance again. The car drives off school property, down the road, and out of view.*

*Then the dark, grey clouds break open and a heavy downpour falls from the sky, officially ridding the day of sunlight.*

*And I hope I never see her again.*

# 28

## ROZELYN

The day after Flynn dropped me off in my prettier cage, I wake, use the bathroom, and return right back to bed to stare at the ceiling. If not the ceiling, my second option is out the window and over the massive land the Corsetti mansion rests on. In some ways, this is worse than the basement. At least down there, Flynn joined me, and the uncertainty of my day always made it stimulating.

This is...what the fuck is this anyway? Boring.

I inhale a large gulp of air and blow it out through pursed lips. And again. By the third time, I'm doing it simply for fun; the sound breaking up the tense silence.

I stare at the door. By now, I'm assuming there's someone on the other side. I'd check, on the chance there isn't, but what's the point? Escape is futile when I have nowhere to go. Until the Corsettis retrieve Dad, I'm stuck.

*Knock, knock.*

Well, this got more exciting. More so, whoever's on the other side is knocking, which implies requesting entry. Who the hell here would *ask* to see me?

I open the door, and my ex-stepsister stares back at me, her hair up, a mess compared to her pretty, blue sundress. In her hands is a tray of food, which my stomach greets with a grumble, the overpowering scent activating hunger.

"Can I come in?"

I step aside, catching the eye of a very angry looking guy on the other side of the doorway. He's clearly throwing me a warning as his future mafia queen enters enemy territory alone.

I slam the door shut, my smirk a goodbye.

"What brought you to my humble abode?" I ask, turning in time to catch Della resting the tray of food on the nightstand. The lack of furniture in here doesn't leave many options, which I'm sure was their plan.

"Wanted to check on you." She smiles, but it doesn't meet her eyes. She's distracted.

"Well. Thanks." Words evade me. After yesterday, I was certain my future would consist of soldiers, Nico, and perhaps his father when they decide my fate.

"What you did is appreciated. I'm sorry you went through all that. I never knew."

And she still doesn't know it all. "That was the point, Della." I cross my arms, scanning her, studying her expensive dress, so different than the cheap clothing she once entered this life in, until my father showered her and her family with riches. "Remember when I dressed you for the party to get you into this place?

"Vividly."

"Worked out for you."

"Say what you want to, Rozelyn." She lifts her chin a fraction, her jaw clenching. "You're not jealous of my place here, because that's not who you are. What are you getting at?"

"Nothing," I tell her the truth. "Stating a fact, that's all.

Imagine if Dad didn't have his insane plans. You'd never have met Nico."

"That's how I prefer to look at it," she replies, her tone with slightly less bite than earlier. "Despite the darkness of our pasts, there's always a light fighting to emerge. It's what Nico is for me. What he can even be for you. You gave us what we needed, Rozelyn. Once he finds your father, this is over."

I scoff. "Being over and gaining freedom are two different things."

Della tips her head to the side, her lips pursed thoughtfully. "Nico won't kill you."

"He tell you that?"

"No, but he doesn't have to. He didn't kill me when I literally handed him over to his enemy, and that was before he loved me. He didn't kill the solider assigned to protect his baby sister when learning they were having a secret affair. For all Nico's claims, he sees the larger picture."

I scoff again, shaking my head at her examples. Non-examples, if anything, because I don't fall into any of those categories. Nico didn't kill her because he was obsessed with her. Aurora's bodyguard-turned-lover, based on Dad's reports, is one of Nico's friends and highly trusted soldiers. I'm simply his enemy's daughter.

"Is that why you've come?" I shift the conversation slightly. "To reassure me with fake promises you don't even have the power to keep."

"I came to see if you're okay after yesterday. Betraying your father probably wasn't easy, and despite your motives, he still raised you. That means something."

My heart pangs. She's right. But sometimes the negatives outweigh the positives and with Dad alive, he brings too much harm.

"I'm fine," I tell her. Anything to end her sympathy tour.

"Go report to your husband I still don't regret anything and I expect him to uphold his end of the deal."

"He will."

When she doesn't budge, I demand, "There's more to your visit, Della. Get it out. You always sucked at lying." It's shocking she managed to dupe Corsetti at all.

With a heavy sigh, she looks away, finding the window behind us, with the curtain I drew open earlier, so I could stare at the grassy land and the forest in the distance. "You all must think I'm oblivious. Nico and Ariella included. My sister once mentioned something about protecting me and I couldn't figure out what she meant. Then you detailed your whole story, explaining how your father had so much mapped out, including meeting my mother. A single woman with two daughters. It's like he was duplicating his own family." Her eyes shift to me, the hint of a deep pink lining her eyes—tears forming. "He did it, didn't he? He's the reason she's no longer here. He married my mother because of Ariella and me, and then when he had us in his grip, he had no further need for her."

*Fuck.* Regardless of everything between us, *this* I want to grant her the decency of being able to say. Of being able to have peace, aware her mother's murderer will soon pay for his crimes.

A lie would be more beneficial because between every second of passing silence, her heart visibly cracks. She swallows rapidly, unblinking, and her brows lower with the emotional anguish. No one deserves to hear about and re-live their mother's murder.

"Rozelyn..." she pleads, breaking me down with every heartbroken word, "please."

*Dad stands at the window, gazing out at the front of the property. His head is tipped in the direction of the driveway.*

*"She's getting into the car now. Mhm. Yes."*

I didn't stick around after that, not thinking much of his

conversation until the call from the police came later. I hid in my bathroom and threw up everything I'd eaten that day, somehow knowing.

"I didn't hear him give the order, so I can't be certain, but...yeah. I think he is, Della, and I'm so sorry. I overheard him on the phone that day, mentioning how she was getting into a car. I put it together once the police came to deliver the news."

Her shoulders lower as she decompresses with heartbreak. "Why didn't you say anything?"

*Because I was an asshole.*

*Because I couldn't be certain.*

*Because I would have paid the price.*

*Because I saved you from the abuse.* Who knows what Dad would have done if he thought Della knew the truth?

"I was a bitch at her funeral for not supporting you when the truth was, I was guilty. I *wanted* to tell you, but Dad would have—I was protecting myself."

For a long second, I think she didn't hear me. She stares at the floor, her mouth slipping open slowly. Her arms loose by her side. Muscles going lax until her shoulders droop. She looks...lost. Broken.

And I'm stuck. Feet glued to the floor, unable to go to her. Uncertain if I *need* to go to her. I glance at the door, wondering if now would be a good time to get that guard.

But then Della utters a single word: "Thanks."

She passes me, her shoulder brushing mine, and gets to the door. It opens and I reach for her. Not sure why, but I do. Needing to apologize for hiding it. For her to understand why I did. To...I don't know? Embrace her.

But she's gone and my hand clutches onto nothing, and the guard is right there in the doorway, blocking my view and demanding, "What the fuck did you do?"

"Told her something she shouldn't have heard. I didn't physically harm her, so back off."

He lets out a growly noise, which strikes me how different it is from the ones Flynn makes. The ones that make my thighs clench. This one rolls his eyes and slams the door shut in my face, clearly deeming me unworthy of his time.

Whatever.

I head for the nightstand where Della laid the food tray holding fresh pancakes but now I'm no longer hungry.

I feel empty.

My gaze finds the door again.

Guilty.

It's less than an hour later when I hear something on the other side of the door. A scuffle, a growl, and a demanding, "Fuckin' get outta my way!"

Flynn.

I roll to my feet, preparing for his entrance. After yesterday, he made it seem like he wasn't going to return, so why is he? I should send him away.

Regardless of what happened, our goals are different. The situation with my father tore us apart once, but life kept us apart. And will continue keeping us apart. I'll be searching for Yasmine and he'll be continuing his enforcer job.

"Don't give me reason to punch you, man."

"Don't give me reason to stab you." That was Flynn.

I approach the door, my hand going for the wrought-iron knob, ready to open it. If only to determine why he's returned.

To *see* him again.

Because my stupid heart beats faster just hearing his voice.

Another growl.

And silence.

Two minutes later, it's still quiet and I return to bed.

Nico's sitting on the edge of his desk, his parents on one side of him, talking quietly amongst themselves. To his right, Rosen stands with his hand in Aurora's. Ariella lingers nearby, silently fiddling with her fingers.

I take up a position by the door and wait for Nico to begin the meeting. There's two people missing, and I assume he's waiting on them. His wife and his brother.

"Where's Rafael?" Caterina asks.

"I told him I'd catch him up later," Nico answers, looking up from his phone. "He's with Isabelle. She's demanding to leave and he's having a last day with her or something."

"She's not needed any longer," Enzo cuts in, his tone cold. Lorenzo is never a fan of people outside the Corsetti organization, and I get the sense the daughter of a traitor isn't falling onto his list of favourite people. "He should return her home and come back, to do his job."

Nico's eyes cut to his father's, sharper than even Enzo's tone. "Something tells me Rafael won't like that plan. He didn't exactly leave much room for an argument this morning. We'll leave them alone and I'll catch him up later. As for Della," Nico finds me across the room, "she's delivering food to Rozelyn. We'll begin when she's back."

Jealousy burns down my spine. I should be the one delivering her food. I'm the enforcer here, which means she's *my* captive.

Mine.

Has been since the moment at the bench.

As if being called on, the door flies open, breaking my glare with Nico as a bundle of blonde hair and energy rushes into the room, heading right for her sister. The entire room falls silent, all previous conversation ending instantly as all attention falls on the argument Della creates.

"You knew! You fucking *knew*, Ariella, and you didn't tell me. *Me!* And don't lie because you've already alluded to it."

Nico slides from his desk, rushing to his wife's side, who's placed herself in Ariella's personal space. He grabs for Della.

"*Petite souris*, what is going on?" Before he can touch her, she whirls, stabbing her nail into the middle of his chest.

"Did you know too? I bet you fucking did because how could you not? What I don't get is why no one told me!"

The strain in Nico's expression is one I've seen many times before, and while I'm positive he will not harm Della, his next movements are jerky, snatching her wrist away from him and commanding control again.

"What the fuck are you talking about?"

"My mother!" She rips from his hold, facing her sister again, and in that movement, anger morphs into heartbreak, tears filling her eyes. "*He* killed our mother. Rozelyn basically confirmed it." Della grabs her sister's shoulders, and Rosen moves, reaching to separate the women, but Nico holds up a hand, stopping him. "You knew, Ariella, and you didn't say anything." Her voice cracks at the end, indicating the yelling is finished.

Silence falls through the room. Della's heavy breathing. Nico's tenseness. No one moves, waiting for the mute woman to talk. Even if we'll be waiting a while for such a thing.

*I'm sorry,* she finally mouths.

"Everyone out," Nico commands.

Not even a beat passes before I'm yanking open the door and getting out of there. Drama, I don't do. Hate it. Nico can deal with the arguing sisters while I return to my silence. Behind me and murmuring to themselves, I hear Rosen, Aurora, and the elder Corsettis exit the office too.

I head for the staircase toward the guest wing.

Why? I wish I fucking knew.

To punish her for hurting Della? To check on her? Clearly, they had a conversation that left Della low, but what was the effect on Rozelyn?

So many options, but none of them seem quite right. Quite certain.

The guard stationed outside Rozelyn's door is Vlad, a newer soldier, only inducted two years prior. The moment he spots me approaching, he pushes off the wall and erects himself in front of the doorway, as though to block me from entering but that'd be stupid on his part.

"Go away, Flynn."

His command goes ignored and I certainly don't care as a swell of anger quickens my pace. My height puts me a couple inches taller than him and my bulk will be an advantage to show him I'm not playing around, but he shoves into my chest.

Glaring, I yell, "Fuckin' get outta my way!"

Vlad shakes his head. "Sorry, orders."

*Orders.* Only three select people would have the power to do so. Rafael, who isn't here, Lorenzo, who's stepped back almost entirely, and Nico, who's been in charge of dealing with the De Falco situation. The person responsible is obvious.

"Move."

He crosses his arms, which pushes against my chest. "Don't give me reason to punch you, man."

I reach for the knife I keep stored in my boot for such an occasion. "Don't give me reason to stab you."

With two palms, he shoves me away, and I arch my arm up to stab him, only to lose balance with a sudden punch to the stomach. It wasn't hard enough to harm me but it makes a point. Vlad straightens, staring meaningfully at me, waiting for me to make the next move.

It's not really him keeping me from her, so Vlad isn't who my issue is with. Stabbing him won't do any good. A comrade will fall and another will take his place. Which means, getting to the top.

Spinning on my heel, I leave with a growl and head straight for Nico's office, uncaring if he's still dealing with his wife and sister-in-law. I find him alone, seated on the edge of his desk, and he looks up at his phone at my entry, no surprise in his expression at my reappearance.

"Vlad texted."

"What the fuck? You keepin' me from her?"

"That's precisely what I'm doing. For this very reason." He gestures two fingers up and down the length of my body. "This isn't you, Flynn. Whatever that girl's done to your senses, I refuse to lose you. You're too good a soldier and an enforcer. She's not worth it."

*She's worth everything.*

"Sir—"

"Vlad isn't standing guard to ensure she remains inside."

"He's there to keep me out," I piece together what he hasn't said. "She's *my* captive."

A muscle ticks in Nico's jaw as he crosses his arms and his legs at the ankle; a look of ease in an otherwise tense situation. "She's not your anything and I need your head on straight. We'll find De Falco, but you can't be wrapped up in his daughter. Consider this for *your* protection."

An animalistic growl works at my lungs and I can't breathe. I've never thought of tearing any Corsetti apart, but I fucking crave it now. Not sure why or how or when it changed. When Rozelyn showed up in my life, she was secondary to my vows, but now...

"I just want to see her." Even I hear the pathetic brokenness in my tone.

"Did you know, my father mentioned you rambling about her whenever you get drunk?"

"Which times?" Getting drunk is something I do so infrequently.

"Precisely my point. You will stay away from that door, Flynn, and that's a direct order. Any anger you're feeling toward me, redirect to De Falco. This is all I will say on this matter. If I learn of you attempting to see her again..." He trails off, his threat unfinished for me to fill in the gaps.

*She's not worth my death.*

Another notion slips into my mind. One more rational. One more true. One that brings air to my lungs.

*She's worth everything.*

Which idea is right? Contradictory of one another, neither making sense.

"I'm sorry, sir." Not sure how much I mean the apology, but I give it.

Nico shoves off his desk and strides toward me, slapping a palm on each of my shoulders as he catches my eye. "I meant what I said yesterday, man, I get it's hard. But you have a job to do. She might be on our side, but we truly don't know what's in her head. She's not safe for you."

*Like Della wasn't for you.*

His phone ringing cuts through the tense silence and he glances at the screen. "I have to take this." With a final slap to my upper arm, Nico walks away, answering the call.

And leaving me directionless.

### *2 Days Later*

Turns out, the call Nico answered was serious. A call from Hawke, Nico's eldest brother who left the organization when he was twelve, turned into Rosen and Nico babysitting a passed-out Rafael who drank himself to near-death in misery over the Dupont girl leaving.

Babysitting him turned into a whole battle with De Falco's hired mercenaries. News only spread after it went down, and they've been by his bedside, nursing a wounded Rafael back to health.

In the past two days, I've obeyed my boss and avoided Rozelyn's door. Vlad works on rotation with another soldier, and I know this because even if I've remained away, it doesn't mean I've stopped paying attention.

To pass the time, I've basically moved into the gym. Working out gives my mind and body something to focus on. Fills my days since being an enforcer has little purpose with no enemies around.

I wake early, eat breakfast, and go for a jog around the property. Then I take my bike for a detoured drive on my way to the gym, which is where I hang out for many hours until my exhausted body only craves one thing—sleep. This is how it'll go until Rafael is back on his feet and Nico calls another meeting to hunt De Falco.

It's the only way to avoid temptation.

The only way to avoid *thinking* about her. About the past, or even days ago. Thinking about her makes my dick hard and my heart soft and my brain tempted with the idea of betraying my underboss's orders, therefore tiring my body is the healthier option.

Earbuds in, I see him before I hear him. Lorenzo Corsetti approaches and leans against the leg press machine. He's not here often anymore, age catching up with him, so seeing him in the gym is a much less common occurrence.

Not wanting to speak with him, but knowing him well enough I won't have an option, I tug both AirPods out of my ears, which ends my music instantly.

"Yes?" I grit, pushing my legs against the weight bearing down on them. He's gained enough of my attention I removed my headphones, but not to end my reps.

"Heard you've been here almost all day for the past couple," he comments, tapping his fingers against the machine. "You're going to injure yourself if you don't take a day off."

*That's the point.* "And?"

"This is how you always run away from your problems, Flynn."

*Slam!* His words rob my focus for a moment and the weight bears down on my legs before I can push them in the opposite direction. Not bothering to find my pace again, I stand and head for the far side of the gym, to the mats and the punching bags hanging from the ceiling.

He trails like an annoying shadow. "Flynn, you forget who found you. Who trained you. Who got you drunk because it was the only way you'd open up."

He cuts in front of me, blocking my path to the nearest

punching bag so, with a glare, I head for one toward my right, but he hops in front again. Despite his age, he's always been a quick fucker on his feet.

With a huff, I stop walking, cross my arms, and stare at him. Clearly, he won't give up until this is hashed out. "Where you goin' with this?"

"You're pissed because Nico is keeping you away from Rozelyn."

*No. Yes.* I open my mouth to agree—to deny—I don't know. Instead, I grunt.

"Exactly." He smirks. "In your attempt to avoid the mansion, you're hiding here. You're running away from your problems."

"How'd you know this is where I've been?"

He gestures over his shoulder to the single staff member at the front counter. Her eyes widen when she catches my death glare and becomes suddenly busy on the computer.

"Fucking Christ. Nothing's sacred anymore."

"No. And you're returning to your old habits. When things get tough, you hide. The very reason we found you on the streets in the first place."

His words—the truth—slices my nerves. They shouldn't be fucking correct, but they are, and I hate him for pointing it out.

"Does it matter? Mansion or here, until De Falco's in hand, my skills aren't needed."

"True. And with Rafael healing, Nico's waiting. Any passing time merely brings De Falco back here to our turf. Instead of running away, Flynn, we can talk."

I stare at my boss, waiting for the punchline of his comment. He wants to...talk? To talk. The Boss of the Corsetti crime family wants to *talk* about my emotions.

"Talking's stupid." I step aside, heading for another

punching bag to end this conversation. "Working it out through physical energy is best for me."

"If that's true," his voice sounds further now, having not followed me, "then you wouldn't be feeling what you are now. You would have worked through all of these emotions a decade ago."

With that final statement, he walks away, his steps seeming so fucking loud. He heads toward the opposite end of the gym and claims an open treadmill, tugging his own headphones from the pocket of his shorts. With a final head tip at me, he starts up the machine and begins his run.

I turn back to the nearest punching bag, stretching a hand out to steady it, even if it's not moving. More so, I use it to steady myself.

From the truths.

From the lies.

From *her*.

# 30
## ROZELYN

The only interaction with people I've had over the past couple days are with the same two guards, which tells me they're working on rotational shifts when they deliver food and fresh clothing. This bedroom has become my gilded cage; prettier and more comfortable than my last but no different.

No less freeing, or boring. I may not be tied to a chair or chained to a pole but down there, I at least had the element of never knowing what would happen in my day. It became an open battlefield for my mind to wander over all of my father's victims—me, Mom, Yasmine, Della, Ariella, their mother, the Haynes, and even the Corsettis. All people affected by Dad's choices.

My thoughts were always in limbo. Life, death, and freedom were common themes.

In the past two days, Della hasn't returned, or any Corsetti. Certainly not Flynn. Whatever random visitation he attempted the other day seems to have been the final one. He's given up, not that I really blame him. He has his life here and it seems much happier and more suited for him than the one he existed in as a teenager.

Which makes me content.

I reflect on the present frequently and ask myself stuff like *what happens next?* while considering all the possible outcomes. Maybe Dad brings an army bigger than the Corsettis expect and they die on their own lands, and then I'm really fucked. Stuck, chained for the rest of my life with a monster.

For now, my present consists of...I study the elegant room... this.

*Bang!*

Hands in the mattress, I hoist myself up and watch the door. Normally the soldiers enter without asking permission.

*Bang!*

That noise isn't coming from the door...

*Bang!*

I follow the trajectory of it, sliding off the bed and heading toward the large window to my right. The dark curtains cover the window are thick and heavy, daylight proof, and with a firm grip, I slide one panel to the right.

Through the glass, Flynn stares back, his knuckles white where they're gripping onto the brick ledge. His face is flushed red, strained, and his arms are corded.

"Open the fuckin' window, Rozelyn." It's muted through the glass, but I still hear him well enough.

These open? I assumed they were panes of glass that were sealed to the building. Feeling the edge, I find a latch, and with effort indicating these windows don't get opened often, I manage to slide it to the side.

Flynn immediately shifts his hands to the window's edge and lifts himself into the air, through the window, and rolling to his feet with a light thud that has us both pausing, glancing at the door.

Nothing.

Flynn straightens from his crouch, more agile than I imagined a man his size could be. He stumbles, swaying, and reaches out for the bed post to steady himself. I suppose climbing a house would fuck with someone's equilibrium.

*Wait...* "What the hell, Flynn?" We're easily three stories high. "You climbed *that*?"

"Shh," he hisses, attention darting to the door again. "If you're gonna yell, don't do it so fuckin' loud. If you pay attention, the mansion wasn't built with a completely flat siding. Bricks pop out for aesthetic or whatever shit. That's how."

There's a slight slur to his words, which I note, first glancing out the window. The low sun casting a glow over the land makes it difficult to see the details of the mansion's brick siding, so I shut the window and slide the curtain into place.

"That's how you got in here. *Why* have you come?"

Stony silence.

I drag my gaze to him, actually *looking*. Behind low, measured breaths from his climb, Flynn's a mess. His eyes are bloodshot, like he hasn't slept in days, and a light purple-black rings the base of each eye. His hair is frazzled, like he's ran his fingers through it too many times. His cheeks are more shallow than usual.

He looks exhausted.

"I don't know. 'Cause you won't get out of my head."

My heart hammers, urging me forward, but I make my feet into bricks, determined to remain in spot. "And you think seeing me will help?"

"No." He growls. "Yes." Fingers skate through his hair, frustrated. "I don't fuckin' know, *mon soleil*."

My thighs clench. My hands weave together in front of me. Flynn's never caused my nerves to react, even from the moment he's had a knife to my neck, so I don't know how to handle this.

"Sneaking in was the only way I could see you. Nico ordered me away from you."

He snuck in here against orders. Living with Dad taught me how dangerous disobeying a mafia boss's order can be. My resolve cracks slightly, and I approach, reaching for him.

I haven't gotten close enough to make contact when I catch the whiff of what I had missed with his entry. He didn't only stumble because he climbed a mansion; he stumbled because he wreaks of alcohol.

"Are you drunk?"

The hollow eyes, the messy hair; it's not exhaustion. It's lowered inhibitions, which also explains his subtle slurring.

He grins messily, reminding me of the younger version from my memories.

"You got drunk and climbed a mansion."

"For you."

"Maybe you should sit." Even though he *shouldn't* be here, I urge him toward the bed.

He follows my suggestion but quicker than I catch, his arm snakes around my waist and tugs me over his lap. The movement has me shoving my hands against his shoulder, keeping myself righted, but as fast as I manage to, his mouth claims mine in a heated kiss.

I fall into it for a second, long enough for a cloud of lust to begin claiming me, when rationality takes over and I pull my head away, pushing into his shoulders at the same time to make my point.

We both know he could fight my denial if he wanted to, but he lets me go with a groan and instead grips the back of my neck, holding me steady as drunken, blurred eyes—*how did I not notice before?*—stare at me so intently, I feel them throughout my entire body.

"I spent *years* trying to forget you. After all, we were *eigh-*

*teen.* Children," he sneers the word. "Teenage love isn't the real, lifelong thing. Your words hurt so fuckin' bad, even when a part of me felt, deep down, the bet you claimed to have made was a damn lie. Tell that to me back then though. When you left, when the Corsettis found me, it was another two years before I stopped thinkin' about you all the time. No—not only thinkin' about you. *Worrying* about you. You fed me some bullshit lie, which I wanted to believe." One hand cups my face, his touch tender. "I wondered if you were safe. If you were still in the city. There wasn't a place I went that I didn't look for you. And then...time fades. Wounds heal. I ended up with a different life."

I press my palm over his heart, knowing what's there. The sign of that different life he speaks of.

"At least I thought it did. I thought I moved on. But then you fuckin' showed up here," his fingers grip my neck tighter, "and everything went to hell. I've never debated breaking my vows, but here I fuckin' am." His tone is harsh, despite his whisper. "Being in this very room goes against a direct order and if Nico found out, my ass would be on the line. The family who took me in. The family that found me. That *made* me."

"Are you blaming me?" I jerk away, shoving into his chest only for the hold on my neck to get heavier. "Asshole. I didn't invite you in here."

"But you fuckin' did." He drops my face, my neck, and with both arms, winds my waist, locking me to his chest. No amount of fighting will free me now. Alcohol breath blows over my face, but I realize, with it, he's being more open than ever. "You did when you batted your fuckin' eyelashes at me on the bench that day."

"You said so yourself, that was so many years ago. I'm not accountable for my actions."

He barks out a single laugh. "God, how was I so stupid back then not to see it? You even *sound* like a damn princess. You talk so refined, even then." His laughter fades into a single huff before he goes on, "You invited me in here the moment you chose *this* family to target. Until you ended up in *my* chains." He undoes one hand around my neck to trace my collarbone to the space between my breasts.

My breath stalls and I watch and wait for his next move. His fingers dip beneath my bra and find my nipples, pointed and betraying my every logical desire—to get away from him. For my own safety, whatever he's trying to offer me, I can't take. And for his safety, he needs to get away from here.

He pinches the pointed nub, causing my teeth to press into my bottom lip, hiding my desire from him and those that could hear us beyond the door.

"This skin." He emphasizes his words with another pinch. "Your blood, so fucking lovely. My own *petit soleil*," little sun, "orbiting all for me. When you were in my chains, I know how much you secretly enjoyed it." He leans forward and his next and final statement is whispered in my ear. "You like the loss of control."

His lips trail my shoulder as his hand slides away from my breast. The relief doesn't last for long because then he's pulling my shirt over my head, unsnapping my bra, and taking both breasts, one in each hand, thumb and forefinger playing with my nipples respectively.

"Fuck." My head falls back. "Flynn, we shouldn't—"

"No," he chuckles darkly against my skin, "we shouldn't. We *really* fuckin' shouldn't but you forget, you're my personal sun. You burn away sensibility, leaving only heat and destruction in your path. You ended up in my basement, opened your pretty little mouth, and I fell right back to where I was in high school."

My mind is still catching up, trying to decipher his latest statement when he stands, flips me over on my back, and crouches over me in a flash quicker than a drunk person should be able to. His hands by my head press into the mattress, holding him up, his knees on either side of my hips. When he rocks into me, his erection becomes obvious through his jeans.

"You took and took and fucking *took*, Rozelyn. And now it's my turn."

It might be his devious grin, or his ominous words, or the fact that he gets off the bed and unsnaps his jeans, but finally, meaning registers.

And I only have one word as a response: *No.*

But it doesn't come out. My numb lips don't do anything but form the word without making the sound to accompany it. Maybe because I don't want to deny him but also...I don't know what I want.

With both hands, he grabs hold of the leggings the Corsettis have given me and pulls them off me. With that movement though, I crab walk away from him, making it only a foot before he's yanking me back into position and climbing atop me again.

"Running away?" He tilts his head, grinning down with an expression partially menacing and partially sexy. "Thought you liked this, Rozelyn. You enjoy it rough. You enjoy pretending to fight. You certainly weren't complaining when you climbed in my bed and I sliced up your pussy."

I do, but not like this. Not while he's drunk and obviously erratic. Making decisions that'll cost him his life. Coming in here, luring me in with a false sense of security with his recollection of his feelings for me all to get me on my back.

This is revenge.

"No, Flynn, stop. You need to go."

With my next kick, he grabs my ankle and lowers it to the side, staring down with remorseless, meaningful eyes as a finger swipes between my folds and my betraying body reacts with a low moan.

"There she is. Don't be too loud now."

Ignoring him, I do make noise. With a grunt, I kick my other leg out, which he captures too, with the hand he was petting me with.

"You're out of hands." I smirk. "Gotta try better than that."

He releases both of my legs to glide his hands up the insides of my thighs, pausing right at my core. His fingers lightly brush my folds, teasing his next move.

"And if you really wanted me gone, you'd yell. One loud shout, and he'll come running. I'll get in trouble for being here."

"Maybe that's why I'm not. Because you'll get in trouble." A partial lie because he's right. I don't *not* want this...and one loud shout would get him out of here.

He makes a sound in the back of his throat, and with his eyes locked to mine, his thumbs stroke me, one on either side of my clit. A low moan works at my throat and I bite down on my lip as he passes over my swollen clit.

"Fuck."

"Fuck is right. You're so wet for someone not wanting this."

"I can run," I taunt. "One kick to your face and I'll be across the room instantly."

"So do it. Please. I beg you to so when I fuck you, it'll be against the wall and you'll understand exactly how you've fucked up."

I almost want to call his bluff but then he slides his finger inside me. One single thrust, before he pulls back and adds another and my thighs drop to the side, spreading as wide as I can for him.

"The old you would have had more fight. Shame."

"You wouldn't be fucking the old me for revenge," I

counter, finding a defence amidst the bliss. "If we were playing, it'd be different, but you didn't come here to play, did you?"

"Nope." With the word, he jams his fingers roughly inside me, curling them on the button he's always been able to find. He does it again and again, not letting up, not allowing me to breathe, as every thrust steals more air from my lungs. He's on the verge of hurting my insides, but the hurt is so damn good I can't complain.

A whimper, so I shove a fist into my mouth, biting down on the skin before I make too much noise and alert the soldier outside. When his thumb brushes my sensitive, swollen clit, my back arches, my teeth slamming into my skin, and I'm positive I'm about to break skin.

He doesn't let up. The pain and pleasure mingle. My insides clench around his fingers, gratification consuming my mind, body, and fucking soul. My bite gets deeper as I fight to remain as quiet as I can through my orgasm. My cum is dripping down between his hand and down my ass—*Did I squirt?*

He makes an appreciative noise and pulls his fingers from my pussy, abandoning me before I was ready for him to be. He grins, holding his fingers up for me to see my body's betrayal.

Then he sucks them deeply into his mouth, licking my cum from his fingers, and I swear, it's the fucking hottest thing. But it doesn't mean he's in his right mind, and what just happened is an example. The old Flynn would have stopped when I said to.

But this time, he didn't even hesitate.

I roll, getting to my knees and off the bed on the opposite side, remaining there with only my dignity left.

"Decided now to remember your own claims?" His brow lifts. "Too bad your body didn't get the message."

"You're drunk, Flynn, and you're making stupid decisions. Leave. Come back when you're sober."

He barks out a rough laugh. "Granting permission now? That's cute, considering you're the fuckin' captive here."

My arms cross, fingers digging into my sides, reminding me the physical pain I bring my body isn't less than the emotional one Flynn is trying to elicit.

"You're angry because you blame me for the years you couldn't let me go. You came here with plans to punish. Go away before you're found and then you'll find more ways to blame me."

*And I'm not sure how much more of your hatred I can take.*

Light flickers through his soulful eyes, his responding slow smile making my stomach flip. "Only if you tell me one thing."

"What?" He could ask for anything and I'm not sure if I'll be able to respond to all the possible questions.

"Do you actually want me to go or you just sayin' that?"

*I'm saying it because this isn't you.* This isn't even the Flynn from the basement. At least that one had a purpose in hating me.

"I actually want you to go."

"Fuckin' liar. Always were one, and nothing's ever gonna change, is it?"

In a flash, he lunges over the bed to my side and before I manage a step, one hand's slapped over my mouth, the other shoving into my back, forcing my chest to the bed. He releases my mouth, seeing as we both know I won't shout, and grasps both my wrists, pinning them behind me.

The cloth of his shirt rubs against my bare back as he bends over, his lips softly trailing the skin at the top of my spine. I shiver, the tingles he creates doing ungodly things to my core. Everything else in the world is so easily ignorable when he's touching me.

I push out my hips, but all that does is rub my bare ass against him. He groans, and with his free hand, strokes the skin and mumbles, "Careful now. One would think you're asking for it."

"Fuck you." I wiggle, trying to break his impossible grip..

"No, fuck *you, mon soliel.*"

Turns out, that was his warning, because two fingers slam right back into my pussy. My scream muffles into the blanket, my hips undulating for more. My stupid legs inch farther apart, welcoming his roughness.

*This* is the old Flynn. Unforgiving and unyielding because that's what I preferred, even then. I never enjoyed tender and calm. I wanted *this*. Animalistic. Rough.

His thumb passes over my clit and I moan again.

"Fighting so hard, aren't you. Fighting as well as any slut does."

"Fuck off. Go away, Flynn." It's breathless and without an ounce of menace behind the words, making the entire command useless and pathetic.

"Go away?" he repeats, phrasing it as a question. "Why would I do that when your wet, tight pussy continues to disrupt my life? Maybe if I fuck you hard enough, you'll get the hint to leave me the hell alone."

"One last fuck and then we're done." I manage to turn my head enough to catch his hateful, shadowy gaze. "Is that what ends this?"

No answer. His teeth bare and I hate how my pussy clenches around his fingers with the sight.

"So tired of your mouth, Rozelyn. One more word and I'll find another use for it."

*Try me.* That *almost* gets said aloud. *Almost.*

He removes his fingers, leaving me empty and needy, my core clenching around nothing. He stops holding me entirely and finishes removing his clothing. I'm freed from his grasp, which means escape just got easier.

But he still has a tight, firm grip on me.

On my useless heart.

So I don't move an inch.

He doesn't comment, but we're both aware I could have used the moment to escape.

The head of his cock replaces where his fingers were and he strokes himself against me, transferring my cum over his length.

"You fight so hard, Rozelyn. So pathetically hard, all to end up with your legs spread and your pussy ready to take my cock." He pauses speaking *and* stroking, and his next words aren't spoken with a drunken slur or even a malicious darkness. "One final chance, *mon soleil*. One brief second to crawl across this bed and escape and I will let you go. Or remain right where you are."

He's giving me an out. A reprieve from his vengeance. Maybe the alcohol's begun wearing off and he's emerging from the drunken fog.

I don't move.

He thrusts inside me.

Our cries mingle, each of us shutting up when remembering how easy it'd be to get caught. He reaches between us and strums my sensitive clit, and grabs my wrists again in one hand, pinning them until I have no further control. I'm his to fuck, to claim, to do whatever he wants to me.

With my next moan, I shove my face into the bed to muffle the noise.

"Let me hear you, Rozelyn."

Is this supposed to be a test of restraint? I turn my head, so I'm still partially muffled by the bed.

His cock glides through my wet core easily, his piercing hitting the end. His finger against my clit moves faster. There's so much happening to my body at this second, so much for my erratic mind to make sense of, except all I feel is him. His length claiming me—*re*-claiming me, since he already owned me once, still, and again.

"I'm going to come, Flynn." It won't be much longer, not like this.

His thrusts quicken and the second my pussy tightens, he releases my wrists, leans over my back, and grasps my chin, angling my head back to him, to take my lips. He kisses me roughly, swallowing my cries as the orgasm eradicates my body. His own groan is imprinted upon my lips, a sound I'll feel and taste forever.

When he comes, it's with a single statement. *"Mon soleil. Ma raison d'être."*

My sun. My reason for being.

After the gym, I ended up at one of the Corsetti-owned bars and based on the looks the bartenders continuously sent my way, everyone knew something was wrong. The last time I stepped foot into one of these places was... almost never. Probably long before any of them were hired. I'm a horrible drinker, unable to stop at one, so I avoid the habit altogether.

I retained enough sense to stop after a few since passed out at a bar isn't my ideal night. The drive home on my bike was slower and blurrier than I'd prefer, but I managed, although I don't recall parking it in the garage.

Fuck, all I remember is standing beneath Rozelyn's window, calculating the climb. The only reason I managed it was because it wasn't a first-time thing. When I moved in eleven-years-ago, I'd often climb the mansion and would sit on the roof, until Lorenzo commanded I stop.

The alcohol was meant to clear my mind, but all it did was bring me to her. Despite my presence directly disobeying Nico's orders, I don't regret coming. Even if sleep evades me most of the night, leaving me upright beside a sleeping Rozelyn. Her long hair drapes the pillow and covers her shoulders, and she looks so at peace, it pains me.

*Fucking Christ.* I rub a hand down my face. The little bit of sleep I got cleared the alcohol from my head, resulting in a slight throb. But the more I remain beside her, the quicker the headache disperses.

When sunlight begins to peep between the curtains, my time is up. I should leave before I'm discovered. Climb down the side of the house and return to my room before food is delivered to her.

Instead, I stand from the bed, check my phone for any messages demanding immediate attention, and when finding none, head for the attached bathroom. Since Rozelyn was put up in one of the guest rooms, the bathroom is the size of my entire room.

I pass the glass-walled shower and head for the oversized bathtub in the far corner. Switching the taps on, I test the water until finding the ideal temperature between hot without being scalding, and wait for it to fill.

When the tub's full, I twist the knob, cutting off the water, and then return to the bedroom, finding Rozelyn in the same position I left her in. I stop by the end of the bed to study her. How will I watch her walk away again?

Life's brought us here, which means the cards we each hold now is our only play.

What happened today—last night—will be the final time. That's the vow I make to myself. It *must* be because it's impossible for me to stay away from Rozelyn, but defying my bosses fills my throat with bile.

A streak of sunlight falls between the wall and the curtain, creating a glowing band over her skin. *Mon soleil* in her literal form.

Watching her sleep will become my favourite pastime, so before it has a chance to fully resonate in my head, I stride toward the bed and pull the comforter off her. She makes a noise in her sleep when the room's temperature brushes her otherwise tepid skin. With one arm beneath her legs and the other under her shoulders, I lift her from the bed. Her head lolls, and she remains asleep.

Back in the bathroom, I carefully lower us both into the tub, turning her in my arms as we go down, my back to the tub, and her between my legs.

She wakens at the water's heat, blinking sleepily up at me. Her lips curl into a genuine, soothing smile, which I look away from. It's times like this that remind me so much of the past, and that's not what I need. One bath, and then it's goodbye.

"What are you doing?" she mumbles, her voice leaden with sleep.

Without responding, I reach for the wrapped soap bar on the side table, equipped with brand-new items for any visiting guest. After unwrapping it, I dip the bar into the water, wetting it and creating suds before stroking it over where her neck and shoulder connect.

"You're cleaning me," she states. "I don't think you've ever cared for me like this."

Because every other time was in a dank basement smelling of blood and torture.

"First time for everything." I don't meet her inquisitive gaze. I can't. Her emotions are too strong for me to be able to walk away from.

"Thank you." She sighs and her eyes flutter shut again, her body limp. She's the ideal little victim, so trusting in her captor's arms.

Except Rozelyn is everything but a victim.

The soap bar glides over her shoulders, her neck, her breasts.

I avoid her nipples, and then dip the bar beneath the water. It makes the soap useless, but it doesn't stop me from washing her regardless. Passing over her thighs, the healed stab mark from Rosen, and to the space between her legs.

She opens them wider for me and sighs when I wash her. "This feels really nice, Flynn. Like we're in our own little world. One moon, one sun, together."

*I wish we were.*

Instead, we're two souls bound by pain and acceptance, constantly separated by circumstance.

"I want to wash you too."

"No."

It's not meant to come out as cold as it does, but when her lips curve into a frown, I'm tortured with the fragile line of right and wrong. Despising me means her walking away will be easier on us both. Neither of us will live our lives waiting for a third chance that isn't coming.

But granting her request, for both my desires and hers, has every nerve wanting to suck the word back in.

Rozelyn tips her head up to see me. She rolls, knocking my hands away until she's kneeling between my bent legs. Slowly, she lifts a thigh over each of mine, placing her pussy right over my cock, and then grabs the soap bar in my hand.

When I should be fighting to maintain my ownership of the soap, I release it to her. With a pleased grin that makes everything worth it, Rozelyn washes my neck, my shoulders, my chest, pausing over my tattoo. She wipes it intently for a second, shakes her head of whatever thoughts she had, and then dips the bar down my abs, which are more tender than usual after the rigorous workout during the past two days.

"You're quiet."

"Just thinking," I answer.

"About?"

"Nothing."

She rests the soap on the tub's side and cups my neck, leaning closer until her lips are a breath apart from mine.

"I think this is the gentlest we've ever been to one another. The aftercare is almost as good as last night."

My chest burns. My muscles urge me to get the hell out of here. I've never cared enough about another woman to do this for them. She's my first.

"It's meant to be," I murmur, moving her hair from her shoulder. Her skin is tinged pink from the water's heat but she doesn't seem to be complaining. "Did last night hurt?"

*I almost went too far.*

"Not even remotely close. Not the kind of pain that would hurt me, anyway."

*Of course, it didn't. Because you were made for me.*

"This is nice." With a heavy sigh, she lowers her head to my chest, right over my heart. My hands clasp the tub's siding; better it than her, to resist from hugging her to my chest as she curls up. Her restful, paced breaths blow over my wet skin, right over my tattoo, reminding me, yet again, of every reason I shouldn't be in here.

Everything good ever existing in my life—the very little there has been—always seems to come to an end.

Which is why I should have predicted what's next.

The door to the room crashes open and a holler of "Breakfast!" comes through the space, making us both tense.

"Fuck," she curses, shifting onto her knees to stand.

Fuck is right.

I grab her wrist, keeping her still to avoid making the water slosh and potential noise drift toward Vlad. The bathroom door is still open but if he leaves her food by the door and goes, we'll be good.

"De Falco?" A tone tinged with inquiry and stress.

*Fuck.* Of course. Because she's probably been visible for every visit, and the one time she isn't, he'll raise alarms.

I slide from beneath her, reaching over unhurriedly for a towel on a nearby rack. I hand it to her and reach for another. Once she's standing, I nudge my head for her to carefully get out of the tub and toward the doorway. If he sees her in a towel, he'll realize what he's interrupting and will leave.

Before either of us take another step, Vlad approaches the bathroom's entrance, spotting us immediately. First her, a towel partially wrapped around her body, and me, standing just on the outside of the tub, water dripping onto the shiny, white tile, holding a towel.

"Oh, fuck," he breathes, gaze darting between us, widening with every pass. "Flynn, what did you do?"

"Vlad." I lunge across the bathroom, tossing my towel to the side, needing him to understand before he correctly assumes.

He whirls, and with a speed trained into him, he has his Glock cocked and pointed at me. Somehow, when I came here last night, I felt it'd end with me staring into a barrel, but I didn't believe it'd be his.

"You betrayed orders."

I had, but it doesn't stop me from fighting back. My arm swings out and knocks his gun out of his hand. It flies a couple feet away, but our attention is on one another in a standoff.

Until Rozelyn steps between us. "Hey, he didn't—"

He lunges for me in that precise second, his fist swinging out to throw a punch my way, but with Rozelyn's last-minute interruption, he hits her instead, knocking her upside the head. She takes the sudden fall, the hand gripping her towel releasing it to catch herself.

Once again, everything good in my life always seems to have a deadline.

The first time, when Rozelyn walked away in high school.

Then when her captivity in the basement finished.

Last night turned morning coming to an end.

And now, my employment with the Corsetti organization.

Because a rage consumes me. I *feel* death—*his* death. And pain—*her* pain from where she lies on the ground, her towel half unwrapped, her free hand cupping her cheek as she wearily examines the scene.

Vlad realizes the exact moment he fucked up when he has to block my incoming punch. I leap on him, throwing a fist in his face, the satisfying crunch of his nose sealing my betrayal to Lorenzo and Nico. Vlad rolls to the side, lunging back, but not to attack; on the defense. His hands come up for my shoulders, blocking my next lunge, but I only have one focus.

"Flynn!" he yells. "Stop! Fucking stop, this isn't you."

This isn't me because I've only ever been a loyal soldier.

Through the noise in my head, Vlad's shouts, my growls, Rozelyn's whisper rises above it all, imbedding into my head. A single word. My name.

"Flynn."

For a moment, she wins. I pause, glancing at her, seeing the red mark blooming across her cheek and there's nothing in this world that can stop me now, not even her.

I throw myself at Vlad again, shoving a fist toward him. This time, he blocks it.

Between the yelling or the fighting, we garnered attention and the door flies opens. I don't bother checking; the snarl from my throat should be warning enough for whoever enters. Instead, two arms wrap around mine, wrenching me away from Vlad.

"Call Corsetti."

Whoever's voice that was—too lost in my head, I can't determine who it is—it does its very intention.

I stop.

Stop fighting.

Stop betraying.

My gaze finds Rozelyn on the ground, the towel slipping up her leg as she gapes, watching the group of soldiers fighting for dominance in her room. The bath we took seems so far away, as does last night.

I glance at Vlad, crouching nearby, rubbing at his face. He doesn't look mad, and that's the worst fucking part. They should all despise me.

My muscles go lax against whoever's holding me. They don't release me, but another puts his cell on speakerphone as he makes the call.

Nico's voice comes through right away, a slice to an already precarious moment. "Corsetti here."

"You might want to come to Rozelyn's room. There's an issue."

# 32
## ROZELYN

Thirty minutes later, I find myself dressed and seated in one of two chairs in Nico Corsetti's office. Surprisingly, not in cuffs or anything of the entrapment variety, but it doesn't make me feel any freer, given the weight of Nico's glare as he leans against his desk, opposite of me. If math serves correctly, I'm a year older than Nico, but with the situation and his influential glower, he makes me feel like a child.

Somewhere behind me, Flynn is standing farthest away from Nico. It's there where Nico's eyes flick to. "I gave you precise orders, Flynn, and you fucking betrayed them *for her*."

"I know."

No fight. No argument. Merely an agreement in a detached tone.

Nico sighs, rubbing his face. "I've called Rafael, Rosen, and my parents. We're finishing this *now*." His gaze returns to me. "Once we have your father, you will be free to go. Find your sister and do whatever the hell it is you want, as long as it's not anywhere near my territory. You will leave Flynn alone and we can all move past this. I won't lose my man to *you*." He spits the final word, clearly solely blaming me.

I take it with shoulders held high because Nico Corsetti will say whatever he needs to, to rationalize his own actions, and it's not worth fighting a losing battle over.

But the fact that Flynn remains silent cracks my heart. It's tempting to turn around and look toward him, but I don't. Directing dislike toward Nico makes hiding my shattering heart easier.

The tense silence in the room is itchy, uncomfortable, and when the office doors open, I've never been more excited to see the Corsettis. Della first, who walks to Nico's side, and then his parents who position themselves by the far wall, Lorenzo glaring daggers toward me.

"Why is she here?"

"There was a situation," Nico responds carefully. "Besides, after everything, don't you think it's fair she hears our plans to bring down her father?"

"Is that safe?" his father asks, tone sharp.

"She's not going anywhere." As Nico talks, he stares at me, his cocky grin making my dislike for him grow. "Nor does she want to. She's better off here than out there. Step a foot off this land and her father's disciples will find her."

*Maybe.* I can't begin to guess my father's plans anymore.

The door opens again, and this time, the youngest Corsetti male and the organization's capo, Rafael limps in. He has one hand holding his side and the other wrapped around Isabelle's hand, who follows him in with no less than a terrified expression. "What, Nico? You realize what you interrupted, right?"

Isabelle's cheeks flash red, indicating the meaning behind Rafael's statement.

"What happened?" Rafael continues in a more serious tone

as he takes up a stance to the side. His attention finds Flynn in the corner and then me, so it's clear Nico hinted toward us being at the centre of the drama.

Instead of Nico answering, the door opens yet again and three more people enter. Ariella heads to her sister's side, while Rosen and Aurora move close to Flynn, everyone staring expectantly at Nico.

His eyes take a sweep around the room, finishing with me, and then he kicks off the desk's edge. "With Rafael back in the land of the living—"

"Fuck you," the younger Corsetti grumbles.

"—we can return to planning for De Falco's takedown. The time spent taking out his mercenaries means he might be nearly here, if Rozelyn's timeline is any indication. Or maybe, he's not, and he's waiting for us. The fact is, the unknowns are too great and I will *not* risk any of our lives for that fucker's. Not now." His voice lowers, his attention shifting first to Aurora, and then to Della. "Not while we all have too much to live for. Which means insurance. A guarantee. We will hunt him down and attack first, regardless of whether or not he's in B.C., surrounded by the Seven, or not."

"You will lose," I state matter-of-factly in the exact moment Lorenzo approaches his son, a hand landing on his shoulder.

"I think we should buckle down and wait for them to come to us. His daughter had one thing correct at least; attacking on enemy territory is too great a risk. You talk of not wanting to take any, but your plan indicates otherwise."

Nico shoulders off his father and paces away from me and approaches his sister, who only narrows her eyes. The new focus allows me to also peek at Flynn, who isn't watching his boss, but rather glowering at me.

My neck prickles, my face feels hotter, and I hate this reaction. He's barely looked at me since Nico showed up at the bedroom they assigned me and dragged us here.

When Nico starts talking again, I send a silent thanks for the reprieve he brings. "As I've said, the unknowns are too great. I will not risk this family, but I also will not jeopardize our chance at revenge. Therefore, I've requested the support of the Rossi family. Erico Rossi and I have had a long conversation, and he's agreed, as a show of good faith for the pending union. He is presently travelling here with his men. His flight lands in a few hours."

Silence.

Tense silence.

There's a new meaning to the word *discomfort* because my belief that being locked to a chair was it, is incorrect. *This* moment is pure discomfort as he mentions the person Aurora is supposed to marry. I only know the name due to my time at the garden and all the conversations we shared. A simpler time, that while was a part of a larger plot, I kind of miss.

Somehow, Aurora gets taller, her nail jamming right into her brother's chest. "*No*. We had a deal, Nico. Call him off. Do not bring him here."

At her side, Rosen only looks wary, but his attention is more toward Aurora's behaviour than Nico's statement. Considering his girlfriend's supposed-to-be fiancé is on his way here, I'd think he'd be a bit more pissed off, but perhaps he was pre-warned.

Nico slides his arm between them and breaks her connection. "At some point, we need to face him. While I've agreed to end your engagement, he still believes it's happening in three weeks."

*Huh. That was quicker than I'd last heard from Aurora.*

"Therefore," Nico continues, voice level and calm, "we will utilize that to our advantage."

Lorenzo crosses the room, getting in his son's face again. "This sounds like a horrendous situation. It'll be one thing to break the engagement, but to do so right after they help us... there is no worse betrayal."

"Better than slaughtering their heir in cold blood." Nico throws his father a meaningful look, but they're losing me in this conversation. "Either way, the Rossis will be pissed at us, and rightfully so. My way, we get their assistance. The *Famiglia*'s forces are greater than ours. We use them, and then I'll deal with the fallout with Erico personally."

Aurora's shaking her head through his entire rationalization while Rosen stares calculatingly at his boss. It's clear he's thinking as Nico is, and not as Aurora is.

"I don't want to see him." Aurora pouts.

"Easy," Nico shrugs a shoulder, "stay away from the mansion then. In fact, you both should." He shifts his attention to Rosen. "Don't want him getting too pissed off and trying to take you out. Then I'll have Aurora's cranky ass to deal with."

Aurora huffs and tosses out a weak punch to her brother's arm, while Rafael barks out a round of laughter. The rest of the family's expressions range from concern to slight amusement at the siblings' showdown.

I'm not amused at all. I'm...jealous. Most of my life, Dad's made this family out to be the villains, when it was him all along. Deep down, I was aware, even before the abuse began. No family meeting between my parents, Yasmine, and me ever went like this. Fuck, there was no family meeting—period.

Even amidst the danger, the plotting, these people share such a deep connection with one another, they find the time to show it in the little ways. The humour, the looks.

Flynn's eyes burn into my face, telling me he's watching me, but I don't look at him. I can't. Somehow, he'd know what's in my head because that's how he operates. Able to read me, understand my misery before I've put words to it.

Rolling my lips together, I inhale a deep breath, and with my exhale, I put my walls back up and I shut my emotions off and return to observing the Corsettis.

"I do not approve of this plan, Nico," Lorenzo states, glowering at his son. "I expected better from you. We've already spoken about what'll happen after De Falco's takedown, but now I'm wondering—"

"Do you have a better idea?" Nico cuts his father off with his sharp tone. "If you forget, Father, you said yourself that this would be *my* responsibility. I won't fuck this up."

"Call him off, like Aurora said."

"I'll still have to break the news to him eventually and deal with the fallout. Which will have to be soon. Besides, isn't there a long-distant relative we can use? Swap Aurora for someone else."

Lorenzo snaps his finger and he wanders away, switching from doubtful to thoughtful as he wanders toward the windows behind us, Caterina closely on his trail. Clearly, he's taken Nico's suggestion seriously and I half expect him to start sketching out a family tree.

What amazes me most about this meeting, I think, scanning the room, is how they're *all* invited. Dad wouldn't dare breathe about anything criminal where Mom could overhear, but Nico and his father aren't keeping this as a male-only meeting. Hell, even their enemy's here.

Nico's phone vibrates then, cutting through the silent room. He lifts it, reading the notification, his eyes widening with every word. He glances up, seemingly at nothing, then his phone again, and then up again, turning with his question. His gaze locks on—me? No, not me. My left.

"You don't mean that."

Not even Della saw Ariella take her phone out, probably too busy watching her husband and sister-in-law battle it out, but with Nico's attention solely on the redhead, Della follows his gaze, leaning closer to read whatever Ariella typed into her phone.

In a blink, she snatches the device out of her sister's hand, placing it much too close to her face to read out the message again herself. "No! Fuck no, Ariella." She tosses the phone onto Nico's desk, like the small technology burned her. "You are fucking insane if you think I'll allow you to offer yourself up like that."

*Offer herself up—whoa.* Silent Ariella has some guts. Based on the wordless battle the sisters place themselves in, and Della's recent comments, I put it together.

Ariella offered to wed Erico Rossi.

Nico heads away from his sister to step beside his wife. "Della's right, Ariella. You don't need to do this. Admirable, nonetheless, but it's my job to fix this. Aurora's broken engagement isn't your concern, so don't think it is."

Before Ariella has the chance to reply, Della's yanking on her wrist and dragging her across the room and out of the office, presumably to fight in peace. If Ariella's the same as she was before my father had her locked away, she'll only speak to Della.

When the door slams shut and all is silent again, Rafael's question cuts through. "Did she just offer to wed Rossi?"

Nico glances at the message again. "That's precisely what she did."

Rafael whistles low, nodding appreciatively, and even I agree with his statement. "Badass."

Caterina walks away from Lorenzo and heads for the door, only to be stopped by Nico's hand slicing through the air. "Don't, Mother. I know you're trying to help, but since she only talks to Della, going out there will end their conversation."

Despite Nico's warning to their mother, Aurora breaks away from Rosen. "I should see her. She wouldn't be offering if it wasn't for the decisions I've made."

"When they've finished," Nico agrees. "Either way, Rossi is coming here. We'll deal with the engagement details another time. First," his attention slides to me for the first time in a while, "we go to B.C."

This is the exact reason I dislike people. They bring along drama and emotions I loathe facing. The complications of family and love, versus the simplicity of pain and torture. Of everything having a place in the simple hierarchy.

My gaze drifts to Rozelyn for the millionth time since we entered this room. Yes, love is too complicated. Looking at her is the reminder of what happened less than an hour ago, and the way ignoring Nico's orders makes me want to throw up. Love is too much to deal with.

Take the drama unfolding in front of me, which makes my head pound trying to follow it.

Aurora's soon-to-be ex-fiancé, since she adamantly refuses to wed anyone but Rosen, who also happens to be the under-boss of the New York *Famiglia*, is travelling here to assist what he believes will be his future in-laws. It's a precarious move on my underboss's part.

My one and only dealing with Ariella was when she visited

Rozelyn in the basement the other day. But based on everyone's reactions, and Della's mini freak out, her offer to take Aurora's place is out of character for her.

I do wonder what would compel the silent woman to *want* to be married off to a stranger. It'd mean leaving her sister and moving to New York to be with another organization. More so, she'd become the equivalent of Della—an underboss' wife.

As the yelling concludes and Nico commands his mother and sister to remain in the room for now, my attention finds Rozelyn again, who watches on, almost like she has a place here. It'd be easy to see her involved with everyone else here. She might have looked like a princess from the moment I met her, but she certainly isn't one. Corsettis don't do gentle women; everyone here is strong in their own way, and Rozelyn fits in.

*What am I saying?*

After addressing Aurora's request to follow Ariella and Della, Nico says, "Either way, Rossi is coming here. We'll deal with the engagement details another time. First," he turns to Rozelyn, announcing to her directly, "we go to B.C."

And then we capture her father.

And then she's free.

And I am too.

He's barely finished speaking when his phone rings again, this time with a call he answers immediately. After a beat, white flashes over his face in what I'd almost believe is fear, except I know Nico well enough that few things make him scared.

"I'll be right there," he manages after a minute, his voice lower than normal.

His thumb taps the red button to hang up as he lowers the phone back to his side. He glances right to me, tipping his head toward the door in a silent command for support. My hands brush over the weapons in my holster, reassuring me for whatever I'm about to follow him into. Nico exits his office first, followed by me, Rosen, Rafael, who jogs to catch up, and Lorenzo, who takes up the rear.

"Gonna explain what this is about?" Rafael calls out.

Nico leads us down the hallway and toward the front entrance. "Thirty seconds and you'll see for yourself." Over his shoulder, he commands to Rosen, "Get every soldier you can here on standby."

Rosen immediately takes out his phone, and my own *pings* a moment later with the call-out he places.

By the front entrance, the double doors are already open, a line of four of our own blocking the entrance with rifles positioned at a fifth's face. The fifth in question is merely gazing through them, his expression bored, only getting brighter when spotting Nico's approach.

Behind him, parked in front of the mansion, is a black car, with a single man leaning against the side door, gazing on. He's wearing sunglasses and his arms are by his sides to appear non-threatening.

Two against all of us, but still, I pull the gun from my holster and cock it, angling it toward the ground, ready to be utilized if needed. Beside me, Rosen does the same as the four lining the door step aside, parting for Nico.

The stranger watches on, patient, with no sign of fear in his cold, dark gaze. He's poised, dressed in a suit, much like the Corsettis around me, with his hands shoved into his front pockets, a relaxing guise despite being surrounded by many who'll drop him with a single hand gesture from Nico.

"Nico Corsetti. We share a mutual friend." The stranger's voice is oddly poetic, meant to be soothing, and immediately, I hate him for it. People who speak like that are proficient at playing others.

"Which is who?" Nico questions carefully.

When the man gestures something, everyone seems to shift at once, watching Nico for a command, which he doesn't give. Instead, the man snaps his fingers toward his driver, who turns to open the back passenger seat of the car.

When Nico tilts his head a fraction, two of the four soldiers surrounding us move outside, their weapons pointed toward the car and driver. The stranger in the entranceway even shifts to the side, allowing them quicker passage by him. Obviously, he's not stressed about having weapons pointed at his man.

The driver reaches inside the vehicle, ignoring the numerous threats behind him, and drags out a large sack of something.

A body.

A limp body who he drops to the cement driveway and rolls the person to his back, even angling the man's face toward us.

Even though we all clearly see him, even though Rafael curses at my side and Rosen takes a step closer, the stranger declares, "Stefano De Falco."

*What the fuck?* I share a look with Rosen and then Rafael, who both seem worried and confused. Rafael inches closer, his hands folding and unfolding twice.

"Then I presume you're the Seven," Nico states. Anyone who knows him well enough will catch the slight hitch in his tone. The exclamation of stress.

The man's lips purse and he narrows his eyes. "Hm. You knowing who I am before I'm even able to introduce myself bothers me, but yes, I am *one* of the Seven. It's in the name, you see. Seven of us. Seven factions."

"Which stands for what?"

He tsks, shaking his head. "That information is not important. What is, is him." He crooks two fingers toward his driver, who lifts De Falco's limp body, tossing him over his shoulders like a sack, and strides right through the wall of our soldiers, who shift out of the way to allow him by them. He drops De Falco unceremoniously at Nico's feet, causing me to wonder if he's already dead or if he'll wake up with a few bruises from the rough treatment.

I study his body, from what I can see of it, given how he's half curled up, searching for stab wounds or bullet holes, blood or anything indicating injury.

"Is he dead?" Rafael voices my own question.

The strangers gaze shifts from Nico to Rafael with a small smirk. "Rafael Corsetti, Capo." It's not a greeting; it's a threat. A suggestion of exactly how much this person—how much the Seven—knows. "He's still alive. For now. Figured you'd want the honour yourself. You...or Rose Haynes, in revenge. Although, I suppose she goes by Isabelle Dupont now, correct?"

The comment, his smirk, perhaps both, has Rafael breaking rank and lunging, only to be blocked by Nico, who throws his arm out to the right, turning on his brother with a firm warning to back down. Rafael shoves against his brother.

"Nic, let me go. They *know* about her."

While the brothers battle it out, the stranger waves his hand toward them. "She is in no danger from us at this point. Recently, we were made aware she was still alive. That De Falco," he turns his glare toward the passed-out man at his feet, "disobeyed our orders in capturing them and had their deaths faked, to lead us astray. And you as well. We will not touch her. Consider it another sign of good faith."

Good faith from this group seems unlikely.

Rafael, probably thinking the same, pulls from Nico's hold and glances past us all. All the women are still in Nico's office and then the realization hits—what if these two aren't alone? Rafael's face blanches white and he takes off toward the office.

Once he's around the corner, Nico treads closer, stopping only two feet away from the stranger. "You continue to mention 'good faith' but what is your definition of that?"

Instead of answering, he scans the guns trained on him, and then me, and finally Rosen beside me. "Think this conversation can be more private?"

"We're fine here. You can also start with your name."

With a slight shrug and palms open in submission, the stranger starts, "Elijah Reyes. As stated, head of one of the factions and this bastard here," he kicks out at Stefano's body, "was by my side at one point. When we realized that Quebec's crime scene has gone unmanaged, and therefore taken up by another group," his attention goes to Lorenzo, who was in charge at the time Elijah speaks of, "we wanted it back and had De Falco move to Montreal. With some influence, he slipped right into the city and started battling you. It was supposed to be a quick takeover, but he dragged it out too long. Understanding plans don't necessarily come to pass swiftly, we left him be. Even helped his growing plots and fostered a union between him and an Italian mob family—an organization we already had ties to and was more than happy to support."

That would have been the wedding to Rozelyn's mother.

"With them aligned with Stefano, we figured you'd be willing to talk business then. No one was more surprised than him when she announced a child out of wedlock and asked for his help to locate the girl."

Which would be Rozelyn. Born before her mother's marriage to Stefano, from a father unknown to anyone other than the mind and heart of a deceased woman.

"We could have located her easily, but Stefano decided to use this as a means to break through with you. In return for finding the daughter, you agreed to a wedding between her and your eldest son. Everything was in play, and De Falco was on his way to moving up the ranks. We'd gain control of the underground crime here in the province, all while you simply believed you aligned with another mob family. The Seven would remain unknown to you, and all would be well. But then, fate took a turn. You broke off the engagement and some years later, his wife died. That's when it got messy.

"We called him back, told him he had his chance, but he went rogue. Was determined to make his mark, his point, whatever. He was too sloppy and we nearly took him out ourselves, but after a vote, we decided to wait it out and see how he played it. Worst case, you'd kill him, in which," Elijah shrugs, uncaring, "the issue would be handled.

"Next thing we know, he's marrying another woman—a complete outsider—which was not approved. His decision-making was erratic. He started raving about finishing the task even if he had to slaughter you one-by-one to do it. With his new stepdaughters, he sent one to capture you." He stares at Nico, smirking. "Well, you know the outcome. Beautiful wedding, by the way."

Nico growls and Rosen glances at me again. It's disturbing how much Elijah truly knows.

"After that fiasco, De Falco returned to us very apologetic and blubbering about how badly he fucked up. He had, but now, we cut him off. As mentioned, years prior, we decided to be done with him and gave him his final chance, but when he came crawling back to us, expecting us to fix his mistakes—no. But we waited you out. I'll admit, we were disappointed you haven't come hunting for him yet."

So many uses of *we*, it's becoming obvious, Elijah isn't a single man part of an organization. He *is* the organization. He is them and they are him. The Seven functions as one. Elijah is merely the messenger.

"We were leaving soon," Nico says, responding to Elijah's latest point.

"I've saved you the trip." Tapping his shoe against Stefano, he declares, "I'm here to strike a deal. You get him after a single agreement."

A beat of silence. Nico's jaw moves. He rolls his shoulders. Finally: "Which is?"

"Be available when we need you."

Another break of silence.

"No profits?"

Elijah tucks his hands back into his pockets, his shoulders lowering in a lazy manner, the opposite disposition one making a business deal would have. "We have money, and a lot of it. We've accepted that owning the underground crime in Quebec will not be happening as we are aware of a union soon-to-be finalized between your sister and the New York *Famiglia*. Even we have our limits; therefore, we've amended terms. Why, before you ask— what was supposed to be a few years' plan has taken over two decades. Stefano De Falco royally fucked up and ruined a lot of people's lives. Even those standing in this room. And," his eyes flick to the hall at our backs, "those who aren't here. Therefore, we want nothing more to do with him, which makes him your problem. In exchange, be available. No money, no control, but a partnership. If we require something from you, something on this side of the country, something you maintain control of, you will do it."

My back prickles with discomfort. Elijah's words might sound pleasant, but they're tainted with a lie.

Nico crosses his arms, becoming bigger. "Those terms aren't defined enough."

Elijah, with a slight tip of his head, reaches toward the

driver still standing by the doorway, who grabs something from the inner pocket of his coat. Elijah takes the rolled-up sheet of paper and hands it over to Nico.

"Our terms," he explains, "in a more defined manner."

A moment passes of absolute silence. Of Lorenzo reading the document from over Nico's shoulder. Of Rosen shifting on the balls of his feet, bounding with an energy I'm also feeling. The uncomfortable prickle grows as we all wait for Nico's decision.

"Deal."

Elijah smiles.

With Nico's verdict, the driver bends and lifts De Falco again, stepping right by Nico and through the mansion's doorway, without requesting permission. He drops him by my feet and strides back to the car.

Elijah holds out his hand for Nico to take. "I'm pleased you walked the correct path and look forward to working with you. We'd appreciate if the Seven remained out of your mouths as well." He gestures to the paper in Nico's grip. "We don't exist. Until we do."

With those final, parting words, Elijah spins on his heel and strides toward the black car, not breaking pace as the driver opens the back door for him to enter. No one moves until the black car is pulling away.

"Follow them," Nico commands the four soldiers still standing there. "Ensure they make it to the Ontario border before returning." They move as one toward the side of the house to retrieve a vehicle.

"What now?" Lorenzo asks, staring down the road as the black car exits Corsetti property.

"They're no longer our concern. Not right now." Nico turns away from the open doorway, scanning us all and then to the limp man at our feet. A sick smile spreads on his face, and one I appreciate all too much. A grin of a winner. "Flynn, bring him to the ballroom. Tie him up.

I lean down to lift De Falco's limp body and Rosen trails closely behind, readying to help, as Lorenzo questions, "The ballroom?"

"The basement isn't required," Nico answers, his tone flat. "The bastard won't be living past today. But first, a father-daughter reunion needs to happen."

# 34
## ROZELYN

Turns out, for all the boredom I've ever experienced during captivity, in both the basement and the bedroom, it was better than being immersed with everyone's outwardly cautious and hostile stares.

After the men left, Isabelle remained across the room, staring at me like she wasn't sure if she should lump me in the same category as my father or not. After a moment, Aurora sat beside her, throwing cautious looks my way, like she's uncertain what to feel about me. Caterina spared me no extra glances as she paced the room up and down the length of the carpet to the point I nearly begged her to stop. Della and Ariella eventually returned, not commenting on their likely heated conversation regarding Ariella's offer.

"Where's everyone?" Della had asked, scanning the room, noticing the clear lack of testosterone.

Meanwhile, I've made a home on the edge of Nico's desk. No one's asked me to leave. No one's spoken to me. So here I am, waiting and drumming my fingers on the edge in tandem with Caterina's pacing.

Less than ten minutes after everyone left, the door opens again, but only one person enters. One person whose attention immediately goes to where he last stood—to Isabelle seated on the floor. He goes to her, scooping her into his arms, his head buried in her neck.

It's...sweet. In some ways, it reminds me of only hours ago, to when Flynn was caring for me in the hot bath he ran. Only hours ago, but it feels like a lifetime ago.

"What's happening out there?" Della treads across the office to Rafael's side.

He looks away from Isabelle briefly to answer, "I, um...I won't say yet. Let's wait it out."

Della huffs but returns to her sister's side, glaring at the door, clearly waiting for her own husband to enter with answers.

Another ten minutes pass, and this time, when the door opens, it's Lorenzo who enters first and heads for Caterina. Behind him, Nico, and Della runs into his arms with her immediate demand.

"What's going on?"

He shares a glance with his brother, and then of all people to look at, it's me. I push off his desk, suddenly feeling like I'll need to stand for whatever he's going to say. It *must* have to do with my father because, deep down, my gut says so.

Which makes his announcement of, "Your father is here," slightly less surprising. Of course, it's about him.

But wait—here. Nico said *here*. As in...he's back? With forces? But Nico wouldn't be standing in his office, hugging his wife after only leaving for ten minutes if Dad's arrived with an army.

"H-here? How?" I tread toward him and Della, needing to be closer, to ensure I heard him correctly. My legs feel heavy, my attention sliding from Nico to the door at his back. I hadn't considered this part of my plan. Handing over Dad's location—fine. But *seeing*—

"The Seven. Guess they were tired of his shit too and they brought him here."

Della opens her mouth, likely with a million questions, but he rests a finger against her parted lips, shaking his head. He'll probably wait till they're alone to say more. Or at the very least, until I'm gone.

"Come." He tips his head toward the door, and when I step by him, so does Della. "Not you," he tells her. "You don't need to see what's next."

"You told me I wouldn't be shielded."

"You don't need to see a man's death," he argues, that statement lodging in my chest.

I know Dad's dying today. Hell, I *want* it to happen—made it happen. But hearing his blatant fact is...I don't know. Striking. Makes my stomach ache with the unknown, my heart beat differently as reality comes crashing around me.

"In case you've forgotten," Della continues, stepping by her husband and toward me, "I've already seen death when I hopped in front of it *for you*." She meets my eyes, nods, and somehow, some fucking how, we're united. "I'm getting answers from the bastard, whether you like it or not, Nico Corsetti."

With a final grumble, she loops her arm through mine, making me jolt with her touch. The comradeship is unexpected but welcome and she pulls me toward the door, only pausing to glance back at her sister, who shakes her head.

"Stay here, 'kay," Rafael murmurs to Isabelle. "He'll pay for what he's done to you and your family."

"I'll sit with her," Aurora offers. "Tell Rosen I'm here."

While the three of them remain behind, Nico takes the lead with Della and me behind him. Lorenzo and Caterina follow us, with Rafael beside them. No one talks as I'm led through the various hallways and toward a room I haven't seen yet. A literal ballroom.

But it's not the grand room that draws my awe, but the grim vision in the centre of it. Amidst the shiny flooring, the expensive art hanging on the walls, and the arched entranceways, there's a blot of black in the centre.

Death.

Or, soon to be, anyway.

Dad is tied to a chair in the centre of the room, his wrists bound to the armrests, and his ankles to the chair's legs. His head is slumped forward, clearly passed out. He looks sicker than I've ever seen him, like he's lost twenty pounds. His cheeks hollowed in, dark marks beneath his eyes.

Rosen is standing behind him, glaring, while Flynn's positioned in front. He glances up at our entry, his eyes immediately finding me, and I spot an apology there.

Nico stops beside Flynn as his parents head to the other side and Della leads me closer to Dad.

"Start," Nico commands, and Flynn lifts a bucket of water I didn't previously notice. Water spills from the edges with his jerky movements, but he quickly angles it and tosses the pail's worth of water onto Dad. His body jolts, but he doesn't waken, and water flows off him, creating a large puddle at our feet. The edges greet my toes, but I don't shy away, my attention on the scene.

Flynn walks through the water and bends slightly, tapping his palm against Dad's wet cheek. Once, twice. "Wake up." Three times, and then Dad's lashes flutter.

My breath rattles through my lungs. Holding it in until he woke, and now that he has...

"Thanks, Flynn." Nico's words must hold a different

meaning because Flynn nods and paces away, his eyes immediately finding mine, that apology still there.

I want to go to him, but I don't budge from Della's side. I want his arms around me. Why, for what reason...I don't know. But I do. To feel a partnership through this.

But then Della squeezes my hand and it's enough of a band-aid for the moment.

Dad coughs and slowly lifts his head, blinking rapidly to wake himself quicker than what's natural. "What the fuck?" His voice is hoarse, and I wonder what was done to him to get him across the country in this state. He scans the room, an awareness settling in with every person he spots.

Lorenzo—shock. His throat moves in a rough swallow.

Rafael—fear. His face whitens.

Nico—acceptance. He rolls his neck and meets Nico's glare head-on.

When he finds me beside Della—anger. The paleness of his fear flushes a deep red of rage. His teeth press together and he jerks in the impossible binds that prevent him from moving.

"You fucking traitorous bitch. I should have known you'd turn on me."

Somehow, regardless of the previous instances of physical abuse, that comment hurts the most. Like a small part of me *wanted* him to beg, to apologize, to explain his evilness. Instead, he lashes out.

Della's hand strokes over mine comfortingly, which Dad notices. He chuckles without humour. "I can see it all worked out for both of you. Two stepdaughters. Two disappointments."

My heart curdles. *That* really pains me. Dad's never referred to me as his stepdaughter. As a child, he treated me no differently than Yasmine, but it's in his statement, he lumps me with Della.

Flynn meets my eyes, and Dad follows the trail, his own widening. "Oh, this is too good. Flynn Rhodes." His cruel smirk finds me again. "Is *he* why you betrayed your family? Once a slut, always a slut. You spread your legs for him in high school, and I should have had him killed then."

Flynn makes a noise and my peripheral vision catches Lorenzo gripping his shoulder, keeping him back, but I'm too busy staring at the same man who used to care for me when I fell down as a kid, the one who hugged me before Mom tucked me in.

The same one who hit me time and time again.

Who threatened Flynn.

Who married and murdered an innocent woman.

Who changed too many lives with a single accident.

"Enough," Nico orders. He sheds his suit's outer coat and tosses it to the side then rolls up his sleeves. Rosen reaches over to hand Nico a large knife, who takes it and re-angles it toward Dad's chest. "You've caused a lot of pain to everyone in this room."

My own heart pounds. Fear? Shock? Happiness? All of the above?

"Go for it," Dad mutters, grinning his regular cocky smirk. "What else do I have left? My own daughter betrayed me."

Nico looks pleased, like he was waiting for Dad to make that very statement. "For your own knowledge, she might have told us where you were, what you're doing in Montreal, and who truly owns you, but it was the Seven themselves who delivered you to our doorstep. When you piss off the wrong people, this is the outcome."

Dad's brows drop, his gaze going past everyone. "I...I have no memory of that. I was in a—"

In a flash, I nearly don't catch, Nico shoves the blade into Dad's upper thigh, similar to where I was stabbed, earning a blood-curdling scream from Dad that latches itself right into my head. I can't look away, even when I long to.

"That stays there for now, or else you'll bleed out much too soon and we can't have that. Now, fucking shut up." He straightens, looking to Della. "Still want to do this?"

Della releases me and stands beside Nico, who touches her cheek briefly, his anger shifting into a momentary hint of love, evidence of what Dad's actions have brought to the people around him.

"Answer her questions," Nico demands of Dad with no further threat.

Della glances at me, rolling her lips together, and then toward the direction we came. She must be thinking of her sister because the look in her expression is only one that matches the love and loyalty within a sibling bond. With a dark look I've never known her to be capable of, she crosses her arms.

"Did you kill my mother?"

"A…" He sucks in a deep breath, gritting his teeth through the pain in his thigh. "A-a car took her out."

"Did you order the accident?"

"Does it matter if I did?"

She flinches. "You confirm it then."

"Your mother did what I needed her to. She would have been in the way."

In that instant, Della defies every notion that women don't belong in the gritty aspects of mafia life and proves she'll be a queen worth following one day. She has no concern of ruining her nails or injuring herself when, in a flash, her arm cocks back and with force from her entire body, she lands a punch straight to his nose, immediately hissing and yanking her fist to her chest. Nico grabs her instantly, probing over her knuckles.

Dad moves his jaw around, the punch to his nose just hard enough that a small trickle of blood emerges. He glares at Della as Rafael barks out laughter, moving up in front of them, closer to my father.

"If you're done, Della..."

"I am." Still rubbing her hand, she mutters, "Make his death hurt. I need Ariella." She leaves, Nico watching her until she's out of sight, and the second she's gone, all signs of his love for her goes too as he shifts right back to a person capable of extracting death.

Rafael reaches into his pocket and pulls out a knife. "I really like how blades drag the pain out. In fact, just the other day, I had a certain doctor in a similar position as you. He gave Isabelle her scars, so I marked some of my own." For the little I know about the easy-going Corsetti, this side of him surprises me. I hadn't known Rafael was capable of such a psychopathic grin. "You had Isabelle's father killed."

Despite the pain Rafael's a breath away from inflicting, Dad stupidly rolls his eyes. "Fucking good-for-nothing mercenaries. They were supposed to take out both Haynes."

Clearly not the wisest for Dad to say, because Rafael slices a line down Dad's cheek, making him flinch. Then Rafael does it to his other cheek, before repositioning the blade to the centre of his chest.

My stomach lurches, bile rising to the top of my throat.

"I promised *ma belle* you'd pay for her father's death. And this is me keeping that promise." He continues sliding the knife toward Dad's arm, over his wrist, and pauses right where his fingers curl around the armrests' edges.

"No." Dad curls his fingers tighter, stretching his skin. "Please."

"*Please,*" Rafael repeats in an icy tone. "Please only gets you so far. Uncurl your fingers or I'll do it for you."

Dad doesn't listen. Not right away. He looks to me as one finger unfolds, and then another, and slowly another, his throat moving with a heavy swallow. "Is this what you wanted, Roz? *This* is what you signed up for?"

I look to the floor as the guilt makes my chest tighter.

*Slice.*

Dad's scream is a sound I'll hear in my nightmares. I force air through my lungs, but all I smell is blood and panic.

*He deserves this. He deserves this. He deserves—*

*Slice.* Another finger. The body part falls to the floor, seeming louder than it is.

I don't look at him. I barely even hear him since the blood rushing through my ears masks everything else. But I feel him. Flynn moves beside me, his very being drawing my attention up again. His hand brushes the back of mine, a question in his touch.

*Are you okay?*

I'm not sure I can answer that. Dad deserves all of this. Hell, wanting to witness his punishment, his death, is how I'm still managing to remain in this room. But it doesn't make this any less painful.

*Slice.*

*Slice.*

*Slice.*

By the time Dad is out of fingers, he's gasping. It's so different from Rafael's paced breaths, and especially the slight *drip drip drip* of blood.

Despite Rafael's obvious presence, Dad's focus remains on me. His head still upright, his teeth clamped together as he fights through the pain.

"I'm done," Rafael announces, passing the blooded knife to Rosen, who comes around to the front of Dad. "Your turn, man."

"This will be quick. For drugging Aurora, you bastard." Rosen pulls his arm back and sends a firm punch to Dad's face that has a loud *crack* filling the room. Della's hit was nothing compared to the effect of this one. Dad's head snaps back, his eyes fluttering shut. The drip of blood from his nose that Della activated is made worse and more gushes between his lips. But Rosen's right there, slapping Dad back to consciousness. "No escape for you. Not yet."

Once Dad's focused again, though barely, through heavy pants and unfocused eyes, Rosen steps away.

No one else moves. Nico glares down at Dad, and Dad manages to centre his gaze upwards, breaths heavy and deep.

"Noth...nothin' to say, Corsetti?"

"No. Because I have so much to say to you, but I'm fucking done. There's been too much pain, too much death, and I'm done wasting my time on you."

From his side, Nico pulls a gun. He cocks it, angles it right at Dad's forehead.

*No!*

*No...not yet.*

"Goodbye, De Falco."

Before I think about it, I break away from Flynn and right into the path of the gun's barrel.

"Wait."

# 35

## FLYNN

When Rozelyn leaps in front of Nico's gun, a nightmare is born. A vision I never want to see again. An emotion lodges itself in my heart, and it's one I've felt so infrequently in my life. The latest time also involving her; when I found her passed out in my shower.

Fear.

"Wait."

"Rozelyn—"

"I want to speak with him," she cuts Nico off, reaching up to lay her hand over the barrel and slowly lowers his gun. "You all got a chance to say what you needed to."

"You think to try *anything*—"

"Relax."

The two end up in a standoff until Nico backs down with a tilt of his head. He lowers his gun, but not all the way, remaining at the ready to attack if he needs to. If for any reason, Rozelyn decides to switch sides, they won't make it far anyway, based on De Falco's injuries.

His next location will be a grave.

Rozelyn faces her father and the energy in the room alters. No longer angry or vengeful, but rather, a discerning sensation. Every Corsetti waits and watches to see what the captive will do to her own father.

Even through the pain, De Falco smiles cruelly. His teeth are red from the blood that's dripped into his mouth and the entire thing looks sickeningly wrong. "Fucking bitch."

She shows no sign of hearing him and instead demands, "Did you ever love Mom?"

"Of course I did. It wasn't in the cards, certainly. Losing her was the worst pain I've ever felt."

"Did you love Della and Ariella's mother?"

"Never."

It might not be her mother he's speaking about, but Rozelyn flinches regardless, proving to us all that she's not heartless.

"Where's Yasmine?"

"Safe."

I glance at Nico because amidst everything, I'd nearly forgotten about the final De Falco somewhere in this world. Rozelyn believes her sister is innocent.

"In B.C.," she presumes. "Is she truly safe with the people who handed you in?"

"They promised me she would be."

"You always loved her most."

"She's my only daughter."

Rafael sucks in a sharp breath, sharing a wide-eyed look with me. Rozelyn, though, shows no sign of his words having an effect, except she does to anyone who truly knows her. Right in the base of her eye, a single tear forms.

"I'm from there, therefore so is she. She's amongst her own people again," he explains. "She always belonged there."

"She has Mom's blood too," Rozelyn counters. "Therefore,

my blood. She's more mine than theirs. I'll find her and bring her home."

"Good luck." De Falco shrugs a shoulder. "She has a new family now. Why would she want to return to the death and destruction here?"

Rozelyn falls silent. She stares at her father for a long ten seconds with her jaw working over the soundless words she's readying to dish out. It takes so long that Nico shifts, and like that noise woke her, she peeks toward me, more pain in her expression than I've ever seen, even when locking her downstairs.

Then she faces her father again and asks, in a broken whisper, "Why do you hate me, Dad? You pretended to love me, and then..."

"For your mother. You were never mine."

"Blood doesn't mean shit," she spits, the edge returning to her tone as she gestures to the people around her. "You think *any* of these people care about blood relations? Do you know what you truly did here, in your search for power? You handed your own enemy," she hooks a thumb toward Nico, "a wife. She and her sister have found a new family since we were so fucking shitty to them. Blood doesn't mean jack shit, so fuck you. Fuck. You. Try again." She advances a single step, bending to look him in the face. "Why did you abuse me?"

De Falco parts his bloodied, cracked lips to respond, but apparently, she's not done.

"You hit Mom too. I cried so fucking hard that day. Then...you hit me, and you never stopped." Another step, and she's leaning down, her hand gripping the hilt of the knife in his thigh. That action garners everyone's attention, in case she yanks it out. Instead, she presses her weight down until he lets out a pained moan. "There is *nothing* you can say that'll be a good enough reason for the abuse, you fucking asshole." She spits, a wad landing right on his chin, sliding down his neck.

"Look at you, growing up."

*"Growing up,"* she repeats, her back stiffening. "You *forced* me to grow up sooner than I wanted to. You think I wanted to drug Aurora? Do you know what I found in her? A genuinely good person. You know what I've found here, even when I was their captive because *you* abandoned me. A *good* group of people. A family who fights for one another."

With that statement, her walls crumble. Tears fill her eyes and I shift closer, to provide her a semblance of comfort. We only have two feet between us now, and it's in the short space, I feel my breath even out.

"Do you know what I've witnessed in my time here?" she continues, her tone a fraction quieter. "A woman whose trauma is owed to *you*, who offered herself up for a wedding for this family." Ariella. "Another woman, protected by one, who *became* them when you failed in having her killed." Isabelle. "A women who's going to be the best fucking mafia queen there ever was." Della. "Even better than Mom because Mom was no queen. She was simply one of your captives. I've found a man who should have killed me the moment he saw me. Yet, he didn't."

Pressing down on the knife again, she meets my eyes. Her final statement continues to roll through my head.

"I don't need to grow up, *Dad*. I simply needed a better fucking family than the one I was handed."

"I saved you," he spits, finally breaking his silence amidst her rant. "If I never asked them," he jerks his chin toward Caterina and Lorenzo standing off to the side, "to find you, who knows where you'd be. In a fucking whorehouse possibly."

"Or with a family who didn't use me because that's all you've done. You used me when you were frustrated. Used me when Mom wasn't here any longer to take your anger out on. Used me to drug an innocent girl. You're using me now, pleading to me like I'll save you." She straightens, nudging her hair off her shoulder as she shoots the final blow. "You're not going to be saved. Not by me and not by anyone in this room. You'll be six feet under before the end of the day and I *will* find Yasmine."

Finished, she straightens and a look of peace falls over her. The tenseness in her shoulders is gone and she turns, giving him her back, only to stop with his next words.

"You won't find her. I lied when I said she was safe. They're furious with me and took it out on her. Your sister is their new plaything, so good fucking luck getting through their stronghold. My advice, *daughter*, give up. Give up trying to save everyone else and worry only about yourself."

"That's all you've done, isn't it?" she sneers over her shoulder.

"I'm the only one who matters, Rozelyn. Not you, not your mother, not your sister. No one more than me."

Somewhere within that statement, Rozelyn moves again, but it's not to turn to face him. She also doesn't rush away. She runs toward me—toward the gun in my hand. And maybe I see her coming, maybe I don't, maybe I simply don't fight when she yanks the gun from me.

Despite the crowd of Corsettis who move as one, with a loud cry, she whirls around and pulls the trigger.

*Bang!*

Red seeps from the centre of his chest. His eyes bulge and then the colour fades from them. His head falls to the side. He shudders his final breath.

Stefano De Falco is dead.

Murdered by his own daughter.

With a cry that'll echo in my nightmares, she tosses the gun to the side and drops to the floor, her arms wrapping over her head. I fall too, cradling her into my arms as her disturbed, heartbroken scream latches onto my heart, my mind, my soul and is only penetrated by one thing: Nico's command, and one I'll obey.

"Fuck. Get her out of here, Flynn!"

Wrapping my arms around her, I lift her bridle-style and she buries her head into my chest and I feel, rather hear, her mumbling.

*He's dead.*

She repeats it over and over, for the entire trip to my room. The one she was given is larger, and where I should take her, but a deep-sated desire to hold her in my bed controls everything else. I vow to hold onto her as the grief slams into her with every breath she takes, to be there with every tear she sheds.

"He's dead," she verbally utters, as I enter my room and immediately get her tucked into my bed, sliding in beside her. My hand strokes over her hair, clearing strands that have fallen into her face, which she doesn't seem to notice.

"He is dead."

"I killed him."

When I shift from her hair to her arm, to stroke the skin there, it hits me that I don't know how to care for another person like this. How does one manage to console grief when I barely ever managed my own?

"Regret it?"

She lifts her head from my chest and what I see on her expression, I'll relive for many years to come. A look of complete and utter brokenness.

The first kill is always the most difficult. Guilt will continue to be there—maybe forever. Every person manages it differently, but given who she killed, I doubt she'll be forgetting this anytime soon.

"No. And I think that's the worst part, Flynn. I did it and," she sucks in a deep inhale I feel against my neck, "I'm free. I feel *free.*"

*Free and ready to shine, mon soleil.*

I don't say it out loud because I'm not sure I'm able to. Instead, cupping the back of her head, I draw her back to my chest and simply hold her.

With her father gone, Rozelyn's truly free. Free from his hold and free from our captivity. It's only a matter of time before Nico sends her away, so while I still have her, I grip her tighter, imprinting her to the shape of my body, breathing in her floral and rainfall scent, vowing to relive this moment forever.

I hold her for all day and night.

I hold her and pretend this is what we can be.

# 36
## ROZELYN

I wake alone, the large, comforting body of Flynn no longer keeping me grounded. No idea when he left—maybe when he gave up being my Kleenex. For a person who claims to be fine, I cried a lot yesterday and into the night.

Yesterday was an experience. One that didn't feel real. Like it wasn't me who grabbed the gun from Flynn or who pulled the trigger.

But I don't regret being the one to do it either.

Rubbing my eyes, I push to a sitting position and scan Flynn's small bedroom, catching sight of the person leaning by the door.

Flynn? *Wait.* I blink more sleep away, not sure how to feel.

Nico Corsetti leans against the shut door, his arms crossed, staring as I throw my legs over the side of the bed to stand. He's expressionless, but his brows lift a fraction at my scowl.

"This isn't creepy at all."

"It's my house." Shrugging, he pushes off the wall. "How are you?"

"Do you care?"

"My wife does. And killing people is heavy, especially one's parent. Little badass, you are. Didn't see that coming when you asked to speak with him."

*Neither did I.*

"Where's Flynn?"

"Out."

"Out where?"

"Do you care?" he tosses my own words back at me. "Not here. That's all you need to know."

He's avoiding me. After holding me all night, he knew what morning would bring. Nico already declared my freedom after my father's death and now that it's happened, Flynn made himself scarce not to be around when Nico sends me off.

*Coward.*

Not a coward, I think, as rationalism slips in. He's finished with me. When he snuck into my room, we both knew it was to say goodbye. Neither of us saw this as the next stage, so last night was merely a bonus. That's two goodbyes now.

I push to my feet. "Why are you here?"

"Upholding my end of the agreement. But first," he reaches into his pocket and pulls out three thin chains, which he hands over to me, "wanted to give you these."

Necklaces? The silver strings dangle from my hands with a single pendant at the end. A tiny, glass bottle with grey powder inside.

"Your father," Nico explains. "Well, his ashes. I had this overnight expressed. For all the hell he's brought to your later years, you did have positive ones when you were younger and one day, you might regret not having a piece of him around. One for you, one for Yasmine, and one for your mother's burial site. For better or worse, at some point, you all loved him, even your mother."

He...he made necklaces. Of Dad's ashes. Of his own enemy,

to give to a woman he hates. This isn't the Nico Corsetti I grew up hearing about.

"If you give me the location of your mother, I'll see to it personally that one gets buried with her. Or you can toss them away and never think of him again, but this way, you have the choice. My advice, choose well, Rozelyn." He pauses, rolling his lips together. "It was Flynn's idea. I was perfectly happy with dumping his body elsewhere, but Flynn had the idea to get him cremated and have this done for you."

Of course, it was Flynn. No matter what I do to that man, a piece of his heart will always reveal itself, regardless of how hard he tries to hide it. No matter the curse words, the protective behaviours, the hateful actions, *ma lune* always encompasses more than he even comprehends.

My hand tightens around the chains and I lower them to my lap. Now isn't the time to make a decision on these, and he's right. The thought of *any* part of that abuser in my life makes me sick, but one day...five years from now...I might think differently. Yasmine might feel differently, because the numerous versions of her status he told yesterday, I don't know which one is true at this time.

I rub at my face, trying to remain in the present and not fall into my emotions, while Nico watches on with a slight tilt to his head.

"Well," he says after a moment of silence, "Della left clean clothes for you in the bathroom. Shower. I'll return in thirty minutes."

Then he turns to open the door, but I stop him with, "Return for what?"

"You're free, Rozelyn. A promise is a promise."

He leaves, and not wanting to waste a minute of the thirty he's given to me, I strip and rush into the bathroom. Into

*Flynn's* bathroom, but I fight to ignore that fact and treat it exactly how I did my temporary, pretty cage upstairs.

I pour a healthy amount of shampoo into my hand and wash my hair until it smells like his. Wash my body until I leave here coated in his scent.

*Pathetic.* Wanting to smell like a man who's not even here to say goodbye. Couldn't care less about me leaving.

The notion has me scowling beneath the water that suddenly feels cooler so I quicken and get out. Dry myself with his towel and exit the bathroom, not wanting to touch anything more than I must. At the end of Flynn's bed, the necklaces of Dad's ashes wait, so I dress in the jeans, shirt, and cardigan Della left, and shove them into the front pocket.

Exactly thirty minutes later, Nico returns with a quick knock at the door and then throws it open, despite me not giving permission.

He scans me from head to toe before turning around and commanding, "Come."

At the doorway, I pause, glancing around the small space, recalling every single memory spent here. The first time he brought me here when he believed I was trying to seduce him, but I was so wrapped up in the memories. To the latest time, last night, with him soothing me as I cried out wave after wave of heartbreak, grief, and contentment.

The bed where we first had sex after eleven years of heartbreak. Of each of us pretending to be over one another. Of me shutting it all off with the fear Dad would hunt him down. Of him believing me to be a villain and closing his heart off from the world. Both of us stuck in our spiral, only an hour's drive away from one another.

This feels worse than the first time I said goodbye. That was to protect him. This feels...empty. Like I have a second chance, which I'm throwing away. Is it truly a second chance though?

It's one neither of us planned for. One neither of us explicitly stated wanting. Everything occurring in my captivity wasn't from our hearts, but rather our need to clear the air. To start at ground zero and we did precisely that.

Eleven years ago, I walked away from him. Today, he walked away from me.

So I walk too.

I follow Nico to my left, out the side entrance I've never paid attention to, but it's there. Just a few feet from Flynn's bedroom, an exit this entire time. Nico opens the door and steps outside, pausing by the black sports car parked there. He heads right for the driver's side.

I glance behind me at the shut door. That was the last time I'd be inside that mansion, but it feels...lackluster. No one, not even Della, came to say goodbye. I was useful for a time, but I've run my course. Della said what she needed to, Aurora heard the truth, and the rest of them got answers.

Like Dad, they all used me too.

Flynn's lumped into them as well. He used me to clear his own conscience. To get the vengeance he's dreamed of. To get answers for years prior.

"Wow." I force my voice to be high and perky, to hide the thick lining in my throat that has me wanting to cry. "Getting driven by the underboss himself. What did I do to deserve this?"

No response.

Nico starts the car and drives to the front of the house, and then away, down the road. In the rear-view mirror, I watch. Wait. Silently plead with the universe to see him one more time. For him to step outside and watch me be driven away. To *show* some sort of emotion to our second ending.

But maybe I'm hopeful.

Because why would he hold me all night if he didn't care at all? There's something in that black heart of his...isn't there?

Unless...

My eyes cut to the mobster beside me. "What did you do to him?"

"Nothing," he replies, not missing a beat, knowing exactly who I speak of. "He's completing a task for me."

*Does he know I'm leaving?* I want to ask, but it won't make much of a difference at this point. Even if he doesn't, he will soon. Asking Nico to turn around means nothing because he won't, and I know this. It's purposeful he's driving me himself.

So I remain silent as Nico expertly maneuvers the expensive car through late morning traffic, and my wonder of where we're headed finally gets answered when he parallel parks in front of the Greyhound Bus Station.

He switches off the car and his arms fall into his lap, but he doesn't stop staring through the front windshield. "In the trunk, there's a bag of clothes and other supplies. We found your IDs too. I suggest you take it. And here." He holds up a hand, still without looking at me. Clamped between two fingers are two one-hundred-dollar bills. "Money for a bus ticket. Leave, Rozelyn."

Before he removes his offer, I snatch the money, folding it into my palm as my confused and rattled heart thumps harder. "This isn't a trick? You're actually letting me go?"

"I am. Find your sister. Move on from all this. Be a normal woman and search for your happiness. It's all anyone deserves." Pause. "You did good, Rozelyn."

If I didn't know any better, I'd say he was almost genuine.

"Apologize to Aurora, would you? Tell her I really did enjoy gardening with her. When I was there, it was easier to forget about all the shit Dad was doing."

Green expressionless eyes blink in agreement.

"And Della and Ariella. Tell them I'm sorry I was such a

bitch. I had my reasons back then. Not great ones, but I was protecting my own heart."

"They know already."

"Tell them anyway. Please." I'm not above begging. With my hand on the door, I turn to leave, almost freed from the Corsettis entirely, but I can't with the weight on my chest demanding I send Nico back with one more message. "And tell Flynn..."

*Tell him I'm sorry for high school.*

*Tell him I'm sorry for the present.*

*Tell him I'm pleased he found people who deserve him.*

*Tell him I*—no, even I can't admit that to myself.

A complete ten tense seconds pass.

Nico finally glances at me. "Yes?"

"Nothing."

I get out of the car and retrieve the bag Nico mentioned from the popped trunk. It's a backpack with quite a bit of weight to it, which is positive. Means I'm not completely without things to my name.

Once it's nestled between my shoulder blades, I tighten the straps to the ideal location and return to the passenger side, leaning down to peek inside again. "Bye, Corsetti. I'd say it was nice knowing you, but, well, it wasn't."

With a two-fingered salute, he says, "Right back at you."

Once I back away from the curb, he leaves, clearly not bothering to ensure I go inside. Hell, I half-expected him to remain until I got onto a bus and out of his city, but they care so little about my life now, nothing matters.

One thing does: Yasmine.

I turn for the bus station. With the money he gave me, I have no idea if I'll get to B.C., let alone even halfway there, but we'll see. I'll use the money to get as far as I'm able to and then I'll figure it out.

How? Not sure. Haven't thought that far ahead.

Fuck, I haven't thought of anything yet. An hour ago, I was sleeping. Now I'm completely free. Free from them, from my father's plots, free to find Yasmine.

Downtown, at a bus station with dozens upon dozens of people milling around, moving every which way, cars honking and other city noises, I don't feel as free as I am though. My feet become bricks and I don't even want to head inside and buy a bus ticket.

I feel alone.

Stuck.

Lost.

Adrift with multiple paths: the right one and the one I want. The one my heart and mind wishes me to take.

But then there's the guilt, regarding the one I *should* be taking.

Once again, stuck. Wedged between my choices.

I sigh.

# 37
## FLYNN

"Dude, slow down."

Rosen clutches the car's dash, despite wearing a seat belt, as I zoom the vehicle through the streets and back to the Corsetti property. Yes, my foot's a bit heavier than normal on the gas pedal, but I have a good fucking reason.

"Relax, I won't get us killed."

He scoffs. "Now I get why you were so determined to drive."

Meaning, when he headed for the driver's seat, I pushed him out of the way and took it instead. The speed of the vehicle is healthy for me. Gives me something to focus on—remaining alive while driving at max speeds—and matches the energy coursing through me. If I allowed him to take the wheel, he'd drive slower than I need him to, making me an anxious mess.

At the next corner, I barely slow as I take a sharp turn and he curses. "Fuck, man, careful! She'll be there when you get back. *If* we get back. Don't kill us. In case you've forgotten, I also have someone to live for now."

"Yeah, yeah," I grumble, but instead of slowing, my foot presses heavier on the gas pedal. Disposing of Stefano De Falco's ashes took longer than I wanted it to, which means every passing minute is one less by her side. And I have an undetermined length of time with her left.

After holding her for the remainder of yesterday and into the night, Nico messaged very early this morning, which forced me away. After she remained up half the night sobbing, she barely had any rest, so I left, assuming she'll be asleep half the day anyway. By that math, she could be awake by now, but I really want to be by her side when she does wake up.

*Finally,* back at the mansion, I park on the side of the house, by the soldiers' entrance and exit the vehicle, still leaving it running with Rosen inside.

"Hey!" he hollers.

"Mind putting that in the garage?" His answer is lost as I enter the mansion, passing the bedroom he's recently moved out of, and finding mine.

Keeping my steps light, I slowly turn the knob, to avoid making any noise that might wake her. If she's still passed out, I'd like to keep it like that. The door opens an inch, then a foot, and finally enough for me to slip inside, eager to find her sprawled in *my* bed. Her hair draping my pillow. Buried beneath my blankets.

Empty.

My stomach drops.

"No."

She better be in the shower...even if I don't hear the shower running. And through the open door, I see it's empty.

Empty except a few specific things.

The clothing she wore all night is left in a mess on the floor. A damp towel showing signs of recent use hanging on the hook.

The shower itself is wet. She showered, dressed in new clothing...and left.

She fucking *left* without saying goodbye?

At least in high school, she gave me that much.

I pace back into to the bedroom, feeling...livid? A rage like none before. A feeling that has the room blurring with the need to destroy. With a bellow, I attack the nearest thing—my bed. The reminder of holding her last night, of the memories of when I first had her in here too much to handle.

After everything, she left without a damn goodbye. One fucking word. Less than twenty-four hours after she killed her own father, she decided to be finished. Up and left, taking the first chance for freedom, without even a second to consider what this means now. Wanting to leave—fine, but after all that has gone down in the couple weeks of her captivity, she can't find it in that black heart of hers to have a final conversation?

This is even worse than high school. At least then, Stefano forced her away from me. This time, this is entirely her doing.

Since the moment Rosen dragged her into the basement, my heart started to work again for the first time in eleven years. My breath returned. My life was back. For all my appreciation for the Corsettis and what Lorenzo and Caterina have done for me, there was always a small piece of my heart missing. One they never owned because she's always held it. With her back, I feel complete.

*Felt* complete.

I stare at the comforter at my feet, trying to calm my breathing, to unclench my tight jaw from the pain. She was asleep beneath it when I left, and now I wonder if she was faking. Waiting until I left so she could make her escape.

*This isn't Rozelyn.*

Rozelyn wouldn't leave without reason. This doesn't feel

like her. She'd want a formal goodbye as much as I would, if all our previous interactions were anything to go on.

But who...

Nico.

Fucking Nico.

I tear out of the room and down the hallways until I'm outside his office. No composure goes into my knock. My crash. My fist slamming into the wood, threatening to push it from its hinges until I hear him grant me entry.

"Where is she?" I demand the moment I'm over the threshold, my eyes only then registering who else is in the room.

I've seen this man once, from afar, the night of Nico's engagement party when I was walking the perimeter of the mansion. Erico Rossi, underboss of the New York *Famiglia*, sits opposite of Nico. He turns with a poised composure, a single brow hiking in slight amusement being his only indication of having emotions.

"Excuse me," Nico murmurs to Erico.

"No, please, continue. This is amusing." The New Yorker gestures, as though granting me permission and I continue forward.

My steps are heavy, my breaths heavier as I fight to maintain control in front of Rossi. My hands press into the wood of Nico's desk when I lean on it. "Where is she?"

He doesn't bother pretending not to know who I'm speaking of. Leaning back and positioning his elbows on each of his desk chair's arms, he props his chin on a fist. "Gone. I drove her away earlier."

"*You* did."

"Yes, I do know how to drive a vehicle," he replies dryly, enticing a chuckle from Erico. "She has another purpose, Flynn. She's searching for her sister. And your place is here."

*It is, but her place is with me too.*

"You didn't give me a chance to say goodbye."

"Isn't it better like this?"

Better than having a piece of your heart ripped away with no ability to fix it?

No.

So many words course through my head. Everything I want to shout at him. A few curse words. But I'm left speechless, our audience the only reminder to rein it in until later.

"Where did you take her?" I push out when I feel more in control of the ire moving through my body.

"Downtown bus station. She might be gone by now."

Half-surprised he gave me the answer, I shove off the desk and walk away. "Then I'll take a bus 'til I find her."

*You're not leaving yet, mon soliel. Not until you face me one more time.*

# 38
## ROZELYN

It's been hours. Two of them to be precise. After thirty minutes of standing on the sidewalk, staring at the bus station and getting bumped into a handful of different times as people go about their days, uncaring about the ghost of a woman standing in the middle of their walkway, I moved to lean against the building instead.

There's a huge possibility one of the dozen of buses I've seen come and go in the past hour is the one I've needed to begin my cross-country trip to Yasmine, and that missing it means waiting hours, or even until tomorrow for the next one out.

But that consideration still hasn't made me budge from my spot.

Neither has my growling stomach.

Not even the dark cloud that took over the sun about an hour ago. People walking by mentioned the weather forecasters predicting rain today, which means soon, I could get soaked.

And still, I remain. Feet stuck to the cement, heart to the city. Or more so, to one particular man.

Going inside means obeying Nico. It means finding Yasmine—possibly. Or dying, because who knows what I'm about to walk into. Going inside begins this next chapter.

Am I even through the previous chapter?

My entire life has been decided by other people. Dad controlled everything, right down to me breaking Flynn's heart eleven-years-ago. If I ever had a friend, it was Aurora, and he ruined that too. Hell, *I* fucked that one up in my determination to keep myself safe.

Guess Dad is right about one thing: keeping myself safe is most important.

But, is it really? In some ways, it's all I've done. Shut the emotions off to protect my heart, my sanity, as my life changed around me. Mom, Flynn—people taken from me. Della, Ariella—people I wasn't allowed to get close to.

Walking away from Flynn the first time was to save him. But this time, there is no reason.

I stare between two high rises, in what I think is the direction of the Corsetti property, but I'm so turned around, I can't be certain. Whatever job Nico gave him, is Flynn home now? Has he noticed me gone yet? Does he even care?

That wonder burns the edges of my heart.

He could very well be done with me. This might be the clean break we both need. No conversation. No goodbye. The first time I had the chance to say goodbye and the agony was excruciating, so this is better.

Is it? Is that why my insides feel like they're ripping apart?

Besides, my feelings for Flynn don't matter when it's my sister's life on the line. I need to find her, make sure she's alive, and bring her home. Wherever we choose to call home. Montreal is all her and me have ever known. Plus, we still have our house here, but maybe starting anew would be safest.

Yet, it's not enough to drag me inside the bus station.

I'm aware of precisely what holds me back, even if I won't admit it to myself. Won't say the words I both know and feel. The statement regarding Flynn. To do so feels like I'd be choosing him over Yasmine, and I can't do that.

But as quick as the guilt starts to gnaw at me, when it has me pushing off the building and turning for the door, I stop again.

I *can't* leave. Not yet. Not until at least talking to him.

I'm not choosing him over Yasmine. I'm doing what I should have had the opportunity to always do. To say goodbye in a way we both deserve.

To admit—

He might very well push me out the door anyway. I'll go and say what I need to and the outcome will be in his palm. He can make the decision. I chose for us years ago, and it's now his turn. Our story feels unfinished. Eleven-years-ago, it was, and we were given a second opportunity. Getting on a bus now is throwing away that opportunity.

I deserve this.

So does he. Fynn *is* good enough and he must know that. It's up to him to decide if I'm good enough for him.

Instead of turning for the door, I head to the curb, prepared to hail one of the many cabs that continue to stop, dropping off and picking up bus travellers. As I wait for the next one, I turn my head up, catching the sun partially edging the dark cloud.

The sun is there, wanting to emerge. *I* want to emerge for *ma lune.*

The next cab to stop by the curb lets out a mother and two young children. I wait for them to unload and walk away from the car before I'm sliding into the back seat.

An older gentleman peeks over his shoulder to greet me, his newest passenger. "Where to?"

"Do you know where the Corsetti family lives?"

He snorts, wiping a hand across his forehead. "Yes, but I'm not driving uninvited onto their property and risking my life. Find someone else to take you."

"Close to the house then," I demand. "A block away. Two. Whatever you can do." Then, to sweeten the deal, I toss the two bills Nico gifted me over and into the passenger seat. I might have just given away my only source of funding if Flynn turns me away. "Will that be enough to cover it?"

It's more than enough, and it serves as too sweet of a deal for the driver to avoid. He snatches the money, studying the tan, plastic bills, like he's checking for forgery, before shrugging and slipping them into his console then pulling the car away from the bus station.

Within thirty minutes, he's parking in front of the Corsetti property, right at the end of the driveway-slash-road that leads to the mansion. "Good luck, miss."

"Thanks," I say because I think I'll need it.

Then I begin up the road, which is easily the length of three city blocks. I study the massive property around me, the grassy yards of no sign of life. At any point, soldiers can descend, so I keep my hands free by my sides, so they see I'm not a threat.

The mansion, while large in the distance, grows bigger with every tree I pass until finally reaching the circular driveway. The threat of rain may have cooled the temperatures by blocking the sun's rays but still, I'm breathing heavy by the time I arrive.

The moment I reach the bottom step of the front entrance-way, the door opens, and my stomach jumps to my throat. Stupid hope that it's Flynn coming out to meet me gets shattered when it's Nico who steps out instead.

He strides forward until stopping at the top stair, smirking at me. "Welcome back. The cameras by the front entrance picked you up." He nods toward the driveway I'd just walked up. "I'm not entirely surprised to find you on my steps but also, did I not just drop you off downtown, no less than three hours ago?"

"You did." Without asking for permission, I walk up the stairs until reaching his side. "But I've decided to give my message to Flynn directly."

"You mean, your message of nothing." He smirks again. "Well, if you think so, by all means, go on in." He gestures toward the door, and considering how shockingly easy that was, I take his offer immediately and head for the open door, only to stop with his next words. "But you won't find him here."

"What?" I turn. "Where is he?"

"Out looking for you."

Four words have never sounded better.

If he's searching for me...it means, he didn't want me to go. It means, my goodbye might mean something.

"Then he won't have to look far."

I turn away from Nico again and enter the Corsetti mansion, this time as a free woman. Not a captive, not my father's daughter, merely a woman who's come to address her feelings toward her past.

I could wait in his bedroom, so when he returns, it'll be like this morning hasn't happened. He'd find me tucked in his bed like I'd never left. Instead, I walk in a different direction. A place more appropriate for him and me. A place he feels most comfortable and where our re-connection truly began.

Where he unbinds himself and becomes my everything. My light, my darkness, *mine*. My moon to the sun. *Ma lune.*

For the first time ever, I enter the basement willingly. I flick the light on as I enter and close the door behind me, half-surprised Nico has granted me free rein around his home. I tread down the stairs as all the memories assault me.

When the bag got ripped off my head and I was met with a

room full of vengeful men. Back when I was a different person too, stuck in a façade, forced to be my father's puppet.

When the universe decided to either make my life a joke or to give me a reprieve by having Flynn Rhodes be the Corsettis' enforcer.

When he kissed me for the first time in years, and I felt like I could breathe again.

Every single touch, every kiss, every whispered word.

Every recollection of pain, every resurgence of hate, every reminder of the divide between us.

Then the facts that became evident as time passed. Our obsession with one another, made obvious by him sneaking into my bedroom and me not kicking him out. Flynn and I have been each other's best and worst decisions. The healthiest and unhealthiest choices we've ever made. It's our addiction that brings us together and makes us go through withdrawals.

There's one place down here that feels the most right for him to find me in, so after dropping my backpack by the post I was once chained to, I head for the chair I woke tied to the first night.

The metal is cool against my arms, but it warms quickly.

Now, to wait.

# 39
## FLYNN

"Fuck, fuck, fuck."

Parking my bike back in the garage seems like a fucking loss. After checking the bus station, where none of the staff claimed to know who I was asking about, even after tossing threats and later money at them, I wandered the surrounding streets because...why the fuck not? I drove to our hold high school in some weird hope to find her on the bench again, and it's then I realized how much I long to see her there again. A representation of a better time, rather than the chaos we've found ourselves in lately.

She could be literally anywhere. She might not want to be found.

But I won't accept it.

Tomorrow, I'll demand time off. I'll fly to B.C. if I have to, since presumably, that's where she's headed: to look for her sister. I refuse to let her go without seeing her again.

Without telling her...without just...my thoughts trail off, uncertain of themselves. Defeated but they won't admit what my heart knows. That if there's any person in this world worth living for, it's her. Loyalty aside, my appreciation for the family who took me in, there's a part of me she'll forever own and it's up to Rozelyn to decide to make me whole again or take it with her when she goes.

Which is why coming home feels like giving up.

Even temporarily.

With a heavy sigh, after putting away my bike, I head for the side entrance and my room. Going there feels like a kick to the gut, considering it was the last place I saw her. Perhaps, I'll get changed and I'll spend the evening at the gym. Anywhere but this mansion.

Leaning on the outside of my door, Nico waits, his attention on his phone, which he tucks in his slacks the moment I close the outside door.

"What'd I do to deserve this visit? Punishment for interrupting your meeting this morning?"

He pushes off the wall, with the hint of a smirk on his lips, and before turning away, commands the last thing I'd expected him to. "Go to the basement and clean your knives or something. Anything."

"What?"

"It's an order, Flynn, and one you should obey for once." There's slight amusement in his tone.

Then he's gone and I'm dumbfounded, staring at my door and then in the direction he's headed. Nico's never lead me astray, so doing as he says, I head for the basement, finding the light already on.

Someone new already?

But no, he would have said something about that. Nico looked too amused, like he was playing some sick game.

Every step down is filled with caution, with wonder, and dare I fucking think it—with hope. Pointless hope?

At the bottom of the stairs, I find my every fucking desire.

"Holy fuck."

*Mon soleil* is *here*.

"Rozelyn."

She's seated in the chair I once had her chained to. Her hair falls around her like a perfect damn curtain and her gaze is firm on me. Her lips showing the hint of a smile, but it's uncertain, cautious.

"Hi, Flynn." Throaty, quiet, so fucking perfect.

The first time I saw her, I thought how much she looked like a princess, and once again, if this is the final time, I think it again. Only, she's *my* princess now. Her throne amidst a room that's only known death and destruction.

A million things go through my head, so many things to say to her, but one no more pressing than the last. Finally, a single thought breaks through: "I thought you left without a goodbye."

She huffs a laugh that doesn't sound at all amused. Her eyes flick toward the stairs and back. "And I thought you allowed me to go, for a clean break."

No break between her and me will ever be clean. We're messy. We'll always *be* messy.

She's talking of goodbye, but I can't let her go again. Not even if she repeats her same damn speech from all those years ago...I can't. I'll return to the darkness I once waded through; only this time, it'll be unfathomable, gloomier—worse. Worse because I've felt the sun again only to lose it once more. The rays that have been so fucking warm over these most recent days.

I don't know when I realized this, but I had. Somewhere between scouring the city for her and finding her down here. I had every intention of having this final conversation with her but now the thought of anything being final sickens me.

She's still waiting on a response so I shake my head and manage, "No. Nico needed help with something and pulled me away. When I returned, you were gone."

She purses her lips. "Your boss is an ass. When I woke up, he said you left and that my time was up. He drove me to the Greyhound Bus Station."

"I know. I went there looking for you. I guess we just missed each other."

"Guess so. When I arrived back here, Nico met me at the door. He allowed me inside."

He took her away from me but allowed her back in, even urged me down to the basement, knowing where she was. Sometimes his methods confound me.

I manage a step, my heart pounding faster than I'd ever known possible. "Why did you come back?"

She stares for a beat before looking down at her lap. "I'm homeless, Flynn. Family-less. My sister is having who-knows-what happening to her because my father's claims aren't much to go on. She's either living the high life in the Seven's fancy academy or she's their prisoner. Either way, I need a way to contact her, and then I need to find her. With my father's death, everything I've been surviving through is over."

This is her goodbye. My legs threaten to buckle, but I remain firm, unmoving.

"I've spent years hiding my emotions." She lifts two fingers on each hand. "Turning it off, I'd call it. It was my protective barrier from Dad. It was why I was mean to my stepsisters because I didn't bother getting close to them, knowing they were only pawns in Dad's ploy for power. I've lived in this personality for *years*, Flynn, and I'm fucking tired." Her expression breaks, a slightly deranged smile mingled with a furrowed brow. She repeats herself, this time whispering, "So fucking tired. I feel like I haven't slept since Mom died. Since I was able to be in your arms, before hell consumed my existence. But the moment I was captured, I slept for the first time in years."

A metaphor certainly, as I reflect on the exhausted woman kept in chains, but the meaning I understand nonetheless.

"The girl you met in grade twelve was the real me. I think it was the last time I was able to be *me* and that was all because of you. Because you approached the new girl on a bench one day."

Which became the greatest and worst decision of my life.

"I fell for you so fucking hard back then, Flynn. *Ma lune.*" She smiles sadly, and I can't comprehend how she's smiling at all when my heart feels seconds from dropping from my chest. "For years, I convinced myself it was teenage love. Fleeting, childish, but how could it be when it felt like I was never whole again after losing you? And believe me," she snorts lightly, shaking her head, "after over a decade, if I was going to feel whole again, I had quite a few years to figure it out."

*I felt the same.* But the words stick to my throat, unable to interrupt her thoughts.

She stands, and I feel like I'm the one in chains with the hold she has on every part of me as I watch and wait for her next words and actions.

"Now, with my father gone, I'm free. I can find Yasmine and rebuild my family—what's left of us. But I'm far from whole and the thought of leaving is impossible. I stood outside that bus station with the two-hundred-dollars that Nico had given me for a ticket and couldn't bring myself to enter the building. By now, I'd probably be leaving Quebec and on my way to Ontario already."

"Yet, you're here. While your sister is waiting for you."

She nods, pressing her lips together. "Or maybe not. I have no idea what's up with Yasmine, but at this point, I also need to live for me." She takes a single step, watching my own feet to see if I move away. I don't. So she takes another. "For *me*, Flynn. There was one time I made my own decision, and that was when I begged Mom to get me away from the private school. But even that was controlled. I enrolled under a fake last name, lied to stay with you longer, and was forced away with a single threat. So how much was I truly in control? I need to find my sister, yes, but if I get on that bus, how long will it take? How many more years will be controlled by my father's insanity, since the only reason she's in B.C. is because of him. I *can't* do that to myself, not without one more thing."

Another step.

"Which is?"

She continues until there's only inches between us, and despite her nearness, she's never felt further away. She doesn't touch me, just tips her head back to catch my gaze, even though it's never left her since the second I came down here.

"I returned with the intention of saying goodbye."

"Intention?" I repeat when she doesn't expand. Intention means something she planned to do but isn't necessarily happening.

"But then I arrived with two messages. Two that you may choose to leave separate and we're finished here, or two that contradict each other, and you pick one."

The noise in my head grows louder and louder, a buzzing that fills my ears and blocks everything else out until she takes her next breath, and with her short inhale, it's gone. Zapped away—deleted.

Completely silent.

"My first message is to say goodbye and explain where I'm headed. That, despite all the fucked-up shit we'd gone through down here, thank you. For not truly harming me more than I deserved, for giving me a part of myself back. For letting me cling to the past, to my lightness in a moment of darkness. For allowing the moon to break from the clouds again."

My palms grow damp. Fucking *sweaty*. Have I ever felt a reaction like this before?

"And the second?" Can I handle another?

Her hand stretches toward my arm, but right before our skin makes contact, she drops it to her side. "That I didn't only love you in high school, *ma lune*. I love you now too. Hell, maybe I never *stopped* loving you. What I said that day was all a lie, and I know I've explained this before, but I hope you believe me now. The bet with friends never happened. You being a part of it—well, there was no bet for you to be included in. Being with you was because I fell for you then. You made me feel better. You made me realize there's more in the world than what my father's life promised. And our time together now reminded me of all of that, so thank you. If I walk out of this basement today, if you're done with me, just *thank you* for reminding me of who I am. And..." Her teeth scrape her bottom lip, making it red. "And you certainly are good enough. I know your father and everyone else in your life instilled this belief in you, but I've never believed it, not once. Not for one moment. You *are* good enough and you finally have people in your life who know it too." Her gaze breaks from me to sweep the area.

She looks to the chains hanging from the ceiling, the staircase, the sleeping bag still down here. The urge to speak grows strong, but I wait for her to be completely finished. To make her decision.

After two minutes of looking away, I tilt her chin up, demanding her attention. But her speech is over, and it's my time. She's said so as much—I send her away with this as our final meeting and we each get back to where our lives have taken us. Or I accept her and we figure it the fuck out.

There's many considerations for each option but only one certainty: the sun and the moon go together and I won't live another eleven years without her.

Grabbing the back of my neck, I haul her to my chest, tip her face up and bring mine down, giving her my answer.

# 40

## ROZELYN

The only reason I managed to get everything out as quick as I had was because I've spent the past hour rehearsing it while waiting for him to show up. That and I knew, this is it. After today, everything I don't tell him remains unsaid forever.

But if saying it all wasn't bad enough, the thick silence following is. He reaches for me and I become very still, worried if I flinch or show signs of movement, he'll stop. A finger tilts my face up and his dark eyes study me.

*Say something,* I beg him. Every second that passes creates a tighter and tighter knot in my stomach and at what point will I stop breathing?

The hand beneath my chin shifts, sliding over my skin and it takes real effort to keep my eyes open and not fall into the bliss his touch brings. With his hand on the back of my neck, he hauls my body to his, every inch of me pressing against him, my breath a gasp and then no more as he tilts my head again and smashes his lips to mine.

It's heated, hungry, and packed with a desperation I've

never felt in Flynn before. I get the sense that this is his own goodbye, but if this is it for us, I'm pleased it's at least ending like this. With passion and not hate.

He bends lightly, looping an arm beneath my ass and lifts until I wind my legs around his waist, keeping him tight to me. I think he's walking, but it could also be my head going light from the oxygen he's robbing my lungs of.

When a sharp brick hits my back, I realize we're at the wall. He releases me on the faith my legs will maintain the hold, and grips both my wrists, hauling them above our heads so high, my back arches and the kiss breaks. His fingers push into my palms, pressing right over my scar.

For the first time since I've known him, a fresh fear runs through his gaze. It's about to open his heart wide even before he takes his first breath.

"I'm not good at words, Rozelyn, and you know that. I never have been. I was recently told the line between love and hate is thin, and you're the living, breathing proof of that fact. *Mon soleil*, I hated you because it was the single emotion I clung to, to replace the love I had for you. I didn't feel it, even when you first walked away from me. Deep down, I fuckin' knew what you told me wasn't true. I shut myself off from the world again because it was the easiest thing to do, to avoid from being ripped open like you had done to me the first time. Finding you down here was both a dream and a nightmare. A nightmare because I knew I'd be facing what I've spent years running from —my feelings for you."

His thumb strokes over my pulse on my wrist, which has definitely sped up during his speech. He talks of old hate, not fresh ones. And hope makes breathing both easier and a challenge.

"But when I returned to my room earlier and you were gone, I had one focus: finding you. I couldn't let you leave again." His hold on my wrists get tighter, his eyes narrowing, slightly crazed. "Do you hear me, Rozelyn? It was never about a clean break. About saying goodbye so you can go. Your absence this morning made me realize what I've always known, and the absolute fuckin' fact of it being, I love you, *mon soleil*, and you will *not* leave me again." His lips curl in the corners, his gaze flicking to the side, indicating the room we're in. "Even if I have to chain you up again and make you my captive."

Joy. Disbelief. Pleasure. It all blends in my heart, making my mind a blank mess to sort through the various emotions and thoughts that hit me all at once.

Logically, he and I make little sense. He's the enforcer to the family who despises mine. Who, at the very least, has too much of a negative history to deal with me being around, and I won't allow him to leave the Corsettis for me. Not the people who took him in when I abandoned him, who made him into the man he is today.

But I'm whole again. With my single nod, he kisses me again, his tongue skirting my lips until I part for him. He makes me complete, and I can't go another eleven years without this. I have my sister to track down, but I also, for once, need to think about me. About *us* and what today can mean.

Like he was thinking the same, he drops his forehead to mine, his heavy breaths mingling with mine. "I have no idea how this will work, Rozelyn, but I'll fight anyone who tries to take you from me."

"We'll figure it out," I tell him, since I have no answers for this conundrum either. With his mouth on me, my brain has stopped functioning entirely. I jerk against his tight hold, making a point with my next words, "Fuck me, Flynn. Fuck me like you wanted to the moment you found me down here."

His pupils dilate and he drops my wrists, doing the exact opposite of what I want, but as quick as I'm about to complain,

I shut up as he grabs my ass again and walks us away from the wall.

His movements are quick and methodical when he lowers me to my feet and grabs my wrists again. It's then I finally glance around and notice where I am. The chains he once had me stuck in.

This time, there's no trepidation. Only a deep-seated craving as he binds my wrists with the cuffs. First my right, and then my left. Flynn backs away, his head tipping as he studies my form with a calculating grin.

"Do you remember," he speaks, turning around and heading toward the table in the corner, "when I visited in the middle of the night?"

"When you looked like you lost your mind? Vividly."

He grabs a small knife and holds it up to the light, inspecting it before turning back toward me. My thighs press together because, this time, I know he won't hurt me.

"I did lose my mind," he agrees. "I came down here with the intention of fucking you out of my head."

He stops only inches from me, and I tilt my head to look at him and ask, "Yeah, and how'd that work out for you?"

"It didn't," he replies dryly. The knife comes up and he traces the cool metal over my cheek and my face toward my neck, following the dip. "It didn't at all because something held me back. For all my desire to own your fear, I guess I didn't want it after all. I couldn't hurt you like that."

"Even when you hated me?"

"Did I ever truly hate you?"

Neither of us answers his question as he slips the knife between my shirt and skin and begins slicing downward, his other hand gripping the bottom of my shirt to hold it taut. The shirt, with minimal difficulty, gets cut to the halfway point. It must be too slow for him, though, because he clamps his teeth around the blade instead and grips the edges of my shirt with either hand and rips.

My core clenches. Something about that was so fucking hot. Maybe all of it. Ripping my shirt away like it's nothing, but also the sight of the weapon between his teeth.

He shoves my shirt to the side, leaving me in only the pants Della had left for me earlier. With the blade still between his teeth, he crouches, hooking both my shoes from my feet, and then grabbing my pants and sliding them down my legs. I help him rid me of them, lifting each foot in rotation.

Then he takes the blade from his mouth, and I cling to the vision still, missing it already, but he slices the edges of my panties, tossing those to the side, and baring me to his eyes.

"Goddamn." He groans. He strokes the knife over where my panties were a moment ago; it feels colder against my hot skin, so I jerk away. "Stay still, *mon soleil*. Don't want to hurt yourself."

The knife travels over my mound, in the slim space between my pussy and thighs, and then down my leg, stopping by my knee. He leans forward and his tongue flicks against my pussy, eliciting a small gasp from me.

A silent plea that he does more, but instead, I only gain the simple lick before he's straightening, bringing the knife back up my side, over my stomach, and right between my breasts when he grins.

"So pretty, Rozelyn, and all mine for the taking. Are you going to pretend to fight me or just be the good little slut we both know you enjoy being?"

I'm breathless from that question alone, and the chains rattle with my quick movements. Flynn's only ever been the one to speak to me like that because I'd hurt anyone else.

I shake my head, earning a small *tsk*. "Which one are you saying no to?"

"Fighting." Because there's no fighting this after we've both agreed. "I want you to fuck me hard and fast, Flynn. Pretend it's that night again and I'm your captive. Show me what you craved doing when you came down here."

The blade drops from his hand and I nearly beg him to use it again. Flynn and his knives go together, and when they're not enticing danger within the act, I realize how much I've come to associate his touch with them.

But then he backs away and his hands go to the button on his faded jeans and any thought of complaining disappears. Captivated, I watch as he undoes his jeans and peels his shirt over his head, revealing a body etched in tattoos, and then slides his jeans down his legs. His cock bounces free, half-erect already and he grasps himself.

And strokes himself. His gaze on me, and mine on his. I jerk against the chains, feeling left out as his hand strokes over his length, his head, the piercing and back down until he's completely erect and ready.

"Fuck."

"I could come like this alone," he tells me, his lips parting with every pass of his hand. "Seeing you bound up like that... you're my personal show."

"Don't you dare." I aim for threatening, but I think it comes out more breathless. "Besides, this isn't what you dreamed of doing when you came down that night."

His head drops to his side at the same speed his hand falls away from his cock. "No, you're right." He strides toward me. "This is."

In the next instant, my body is in his grip again, my ass cupped in his large, coarse hands, which inch closer to my core. His fingers brush my centre, finding me wet.

"Drenched. Now I have to wonder what got you so wet—the chains or watching me stroke myself?"

"Both."

He makes a noise in the back of his throat and shifts his hand to his cock, rubbing himself over me, lubricating himself. And then his head is inside me, and inch-by-inch, he's stretching me, barely taking time to prepare me.

My head falls back, my arms limp and only held by the chains. I feel so full, so wonderfully full in an instant. So out of control too. His to use. Not to submit to, but to *enjoy*.

"This is what I imagined," he pushes out between thrusts. "Filling your cunt, your mind, and then I'd leave when I was satisfied and you'd feel what I had—a lack of control."

Every word from him becomes more and more faded as my body's entire focus is on the orgasm he's pulling forth. The mindless battle inside me that I won't win or lose: I'll explode.

*"Ma lune."*

For the slightest second, his thrusts pause. And then they quicken with an unimaginable pace. His fingers painfully grip into my skin. Painful but oh so fucking right.

"You have no fuckin' idea how much I've missed you saying those words to me."

Then I'll say them over and over so he'll never experience the loss again.

He grips my neck with one hand, forcing my face on his. My eyes flutter shut, the effort to hold on growing less by the second. Between his pace, his piercing, his everything, holding on isn't an option and my body stiffens before releasing, my muscles becoming liquid all while my core clamps down on his cock.

My cry sounds louder in the echoey basement and I wonder if I can be heard from above, but then don't care if I can because the rattling of the chains as my arms strain to grip something, his own breaths, and the blood rushing through my ears are all I can hear.

"That was your only one," he announces suddenly.

My only orgasm?

His thumb beneath my chin controls my face again. My eyes open, about to question his words when he continues.

"The only one you'll close your eyes for. The next time you come, you will look at me."

*Oh.*

His thrusts pick up pace again, but I still haven't come down from the previous orgasm. My insides clamp again, everything so damn sensitive, nothing's making sense anymore. I think I come again. Or maybe it was simply a long continuous one.

My cries grow louder, my arms jerking against the restraints. While I crave touching him, I also wouldn't change this for anything in the world.

"*Ma lune,*" I repeat, knowing how much he enjoys it.

*Thrust.*

"*Ma lune.*"

*Thrust.*

"*Ma lune.*"

*Thrust.*

And—"*Mon soliel,* you're fucking mine and you're never leaving again."

Warmth floods my insides, his thrusts ending with a final jerk. His lips smash against mine, our moans combining within a heated kiss that sets my insides on fire once again.

Slowly, he pulls back from the kiss, his breaths coming out in short pants. He cups my cheek before stroking down my neck, my side, and holding onto my thigh.

"You okay?"

"That felt amazing, Flynn. I'm fantastic."

"Feet down," he commands at the same time he lowers me,

keeping one arm around my waist to steady me as he reaches up and undoes each cuff one at a time.

Freed, I stumble. The weightless feeling returns, but only because he catches me with a throaty chuckle.

"Guess I'm not as okay as I believed I am."

"That's fine." His arms come around me, and then in a movement so quick, it makes my head light, I'm cradled against his chest and he's carrying me to the sleeping bag I was once so happy to use.

I reach for him again, but he backs away to get dressed, before tossing me my clothes. I suppose, as much as I want to live in the moment, this isn't even his house and walking around naked isn't an option.

As he finishes dressing, his angle, the lighting, all of it hits precisely right.

"On your ribs. Is that a—"

"A sun?" He twists, smirking, until I'm able to see the tattoo in better light.

A galaxy almost. Starts and constellations swirling together on his ribs, the colours muted with age but brighter than some of his other tattoos, which makes me wonder how I've never noticed it before. He was always so good at angling himself just the right way I suppose, and never lifting his arm.

Amidst the stars, a moon. Brighter than the rest of the tattoo, and directly across from it, a sun, its deep colours bold.

"Flynn...this whole time."

He drops to a knee in front of me and hauls me to his chest, nearly bending me backwards in his jerky movements. "I've told you, you've never been a question for me, Rozelyn. Even when I hated you, I loved you, and I could never get you out of my mind. You're it for me and that's all there is to it."

I reach for his side, needing to stroke over the ink as I reply, "You freed me, Flynn. Then and now, and I'm forever grateful."

With a final, scorching kiss, he helps me dress and then leads me from the basement. The second we reach the top, we're stopped by a man leaning against the far wall, his arms crossed, glare centering right on us.

"Being creepy, Corsetti, and listening in?" Harassing Nico might not be the smartest plan but who hangs outside of a basement door?

He rolls his eyes from me to Flynn and speaks directly to him, ignoring my comment. "When you've cleaned up, come see me. We need to talk about," he flicks his hand in our direction, "whatever this is."

# 41
## FLYNN

Thirty minutes later, we're back in Nico's office and I'm struck with major déjà vu. Similar to when we were caught in her bedroom, I'm standing while Rozelyn's seated across from Nico, who sits behind his desk, his gaze flicking between us, a glass of liquor in his hands, his fingers drumming rhythmically along the edge.

What Nico will tell us is completely a guess. He might demand me to move out of the mansion if I choose Rozelyn. That'll be an easy agreement. He might kick me out of the organization because of her. That'll be—I don't know what that'll be. Choosing between my heart and my life is an impossible feat no one should need to go through.

I expected this though. The turmoil of choice. I hadn't expected Nico to demand it today. I've barely gotten Rozelyn back in my life and now I might have it ripped apart.

Nico starts with a heavy huff, his glare directed at Rozelyn. "I don't like you."

Straight to it. Blatant and factual.

Rozelyn lifts her chin, meeting his stare head-on. "Yeah, well, you're not my favourite either, buddy."

I approach her chair, stroking over the back of her neck in a gentle but warning manner. She needs to cool the attitude before Nico decides to be done with both of us. His last command was for her to leave the city, and she defied that by returning to me.

Nico's eyes narrow where my hand touches her skin, but I don't move away. "I don't like you," he repeats, "because you have my enforcer changing. Before you, he was focused. Loyal. Since you've come into his life again, he's hesitated in doing his job, betrayed orders, and walked in on a very important meeting. All behaviours unlike him."

Though he's speaking to her and not me, every mark against me is a slice to my heart. When listed, I really fucked up.

Beneath my hands, her shoulders move up and down, reminding me of why I did every item on the list—for her.

"Maybe you got the boring version of him," Rozelyn counters with a shrug. "And I returned the old version."

Nico presses his lips together and I know him well enough to catch the hint of a smirk. Barely there. Nothing Rozelyn would notice, but he's amused by her, which is a positive sign.

"Perhaps," he replies dryly. "Nonetheless, you're a pain in my ass, and allowing you into my home is quite chaotic, considering what your family has done to mine. But—" He pauses, glancing at me, and then the glass of amber in his grip. "But I respect you, Rozelyn."

Respect from the Corsetti underboss is always earned, never given.

"What?"

Dragging the glass closer, he stares into it as he talks. "You're tough as nails, and I understand why you did what you had. The word victim is a very strong term with many connotations, each one understood differently by every individual. I'm telling you this so you see I don't pity you or think you less in any means. You were a victim, but in my books, victims are the strongest there are. Certainly more than their oppressor because it's the victims who have to survive their actions and still act okay after it all."

He lifts his eyes from his drink, abandoning it altogether to lean back, lightly rocking on the chair. A look of calculating ease that has my nerves sharpening.

"Della and Ariella suffered at the hands of your father. They lost a mother, their freedom, themselves, and each other. Ariella got the brunt. Their mother was killed. My sister was caught in your father's plans. *Your* mother. Your sister...and you. Rozelyn, if I held you to standards any differently than I do my wife, you may as well brand me a hypocrite. What you did was to protect yourself. You played the long game and fucking survived. That was war, and you did what any one of us would have done. Therefore," he tips his head forward, "yes, you have my respect, Rozelyn, and for that, I will grant you entry into my home to be with Flynn."

Her shoulders slump lower. I hadn't realized she was clinging to his approval so much, but for some reason, that makes me love her more. The fact she understands my place within the organization, and where Nico is situated in the chain.

This time, he looks at me. "It's all on you, Flynn. If you're sure about her, then I'll keep silent on the matter."

Gathering her hair, I use it to twist her head until she can see me, so I'm responding to her rather than Nico. "This woman's owned my heart since the first moment I saw her in school. When she was a stuck-up princess hiding a lot of pain. I'm very sure about her, sir."

Her slow smile is everything right in the world and she reaches back to touch me.

Amused, Nico coughs, pulling both our attention back to the reason we're in his office. I release her hair.

"Touching," he says. "Well, I'm sure we'll all take it one day at a time, but for now, Rozelyn, my only warning to you is not to hurt him. Again." The final word is a punch, but in Nico's fucked-up manner, it's him showing genuine care.

"I won't," Rozelyn vows in a clear voice, her thumb stroking right over my knuckles.

"Dismissed then."

I back up, giving her space to stand from the chair as Nico lifts his phone and responds to the numerous notifications I see flash over his screen. Rozelyn stands, but she remains in front of his desk, hesitating until he feels her looking at him.

"Yes?" he asks, all without looking away from his phone.

"Can I ask for your help with something?"

"Presuming it has to do with your sister?" Finally, he lowers his phone again to give her his undivided attention.

I'm not surprised by her request, since Yasmine claims so much of her focus. Asking Nico so soon after he's agreed to let her stay is less of a good idea. I'd rather we have gone back to my room, talked about it. I've never met Yasmine obviously, but she's *mon soleil*'s sister; therefore, I'll do anything I can to find her if it'll make Rozelyn content.

"You said you'd—"

"I said I'd leave her alone," he cuts off. "I've never offered my support to find her."

She crosses her arms, her spine straightening. "Then I'll fly out there alone, as was the original plan."

Not without me. A tenseness flashes through me. But I can't leave Montreal without orders and abandon my post. Not to search in enemy territory—agreement or no agreement.

Nico glances at me, knowing the silent debate within her statement. "Flynn is to not go with you but I get the sense, he won't let you go alone either."

"You can't tell me Della wouldn't approve."

Della's heart is too large and when realizing the De Falco sisters' nastiness toward her was a façade, she'll fight him on it. Testy subject, but pride for Rozelyn's tenacity runs through me.

"There's approving and then there's allowing. You seem to all think *she* rules the organization," he grumbles. "The agreement I made with the Seven will not allow me to go in there and take who they've now deemed one of their own. We have no idea what happened when she and your father arrived in B.C."

Rozelyn falls forward onto the desk, leaning closer. I move toward her, to pull her away, but her tone stops me. She's not argumentative, but rather, hopeful. "Nico, *please*. She's my sister. The fact no one knows is exactly what's worrying me. If you made a deal with the Seven, ask them about her. If she's happy and alive, I'll be okay knowing that. But if she isn't...You compared me to Della. Della lied to you to protect her sister. I'm asking for the same chance you gave her."

Nico stares at her through slitted eyes that get tinier with the mention of his wife. Possibly a terse subject, but the pressing of his lips tells me she's won. His final huff following confirms it.

"I will not promise anything, Rozelyn. I understand you're stressed, but if they are harming her, I will not start war so soon after getting into an agreement with them. Not for you. I'm sorry. So I will inquire about Yasmine...but not yet. Erico Rossi agreed to the union, so let me get Ariella settled into New York and ensure that agreement passes without concern. Give me a bit of time. A month or so, and then I'll reach out to the Seven. That's my final offer."

Around the edge of the desk, her fingers curl. She's

balancing concern for Yasmine with acting rationally, and really, it could go south if she went poking around in B.C. alone, so Nico is her best chance. Even with the timeline.

After a minute, she releases the wood and straightens. "Fine. Thanks."

The corner of his mouth hikes in a half-smirk. "Now, if you're done here, I'll be getting back to my job." Without waiting for a response, he picks up the phone and continues what he was previously working on, so I grab her arm and begin pulling her from the room.

In the hallway, she falls against the wall with a heavy breath. I want to kiss her, to hold her, but she's probably thinking about the deal she just agreed to, and the annoyance of having to wait for answers.

She reaches for me and tugs on my wrist. I go easily, caging her in with my body, and when I duck my head for a kiss, she does too, placing hers into my chest instead, her arms tight around my middle in a hug.

A hug. Such a simple hold, but so powerful. Her heart against mine, my face in her hair, breathing in everything she is. Happy to once again be able to claim this woman as mine.

"Now what?" she mumbles into my chest.

"One day at a time?"

I feel her nod with her head rubbing against mine. "That works."

There's never been anything to look forward to in my life. I've been content to live in the mansion, work when I'm called upon, and find my family within the organization.

But for once, I have something to truly live for.

And she's in my arms.

~

Later that night, I'm called downtown for a meeting, so I leave Rozelyn in my room and take my bike down to The Elixir, a Corsetti-owned club. This meeting was without warning, so I have to wonder if something important is happening. It was a wide call-out though, so I know it's not only to me.

I park behind the club, switching off the bike between Rafael and Rosen's cars, and leave the helmet on the handlebars. Anyone with a brain cell knows not to go near any of the vehicles back here, so it'll be safe.

Inside, I find a gathering of half of the Corsetti soldiers, and a few more are entering through the front entrance by the time I slink my way to the side of the room, finding an ideal position, close enough to the front where Nico and Lorenzo stand, watching the crowd, but far enough back I'm away from as many as possible.

Over the loud buzz of conversation, clinking at the bar steals my attention, and there's Rafael lining up a few dozen shot glasses, pouring tequila into each one. He's bouncing to some imaginary tune in his head, looking already halfway drunk.

A body sidles closer to me and I find Rosen leaning on the wall beside me, crooking a leg up and crossing his arms. "So you're sticking with her then, huh?"

No definition of *her* needed. "Never shoulda gone without her. What's all this?" I nod to the crowd, using them to change the subject away from my relationship.

He grins. "You'll see." Because of Rosen's position, he gets to know a lot of the inner workings. More now probably since he'll eventually be Nico and Rafael's brother-in-law.

Once more people arrive, Lorenzo steps forward and with his single action, the room falls silent. All except Rafael's clanging in the background.

"Thank you for coming on short notice. This won't be long, but I have news to share." With a heavy slap to Nico's shoulder, who, if it was possible he could look nervous, does. At Rosen's expanding grin, the purpose of this meeting begins to hit me. "As you're all well aware of, when I made my son under-boss, I began stepping back and spending more time with Caterina. Watching from the sidelines as he continued to lead this organization forward. In a short amount of time, he's unearthed and taken down an enemy, healed and created new relations with the New York *Famiglia*, and found himself a wife. A strong woman who'll stand beside him in the same manner Caterina stood beside me all these years."

"Damn." Rosen whistles. "He's always had his dislike of Della, but fuck, she won him over."

"Nico's better with her."

Like I am with Rozelyn. Something about finding your other half heals a wounded soul.

"And soon," Lorenzo continues, "we're all hopeful for an heir. In time, of course, but I have faith it'll happen eventually."

Nico rolls his lips together and nods. He shifts a fraction, a sign of nerves only a room full of people trained to monitor behaviours would catch, and I'm half-surprised Nico would give anything away like that.

"He's worried about having a kid?"

"The pressure to ensure an heir, I think," Rosen answers. "It'll happen for them, I'm sure. Babies don't exactly come up in conversation between us."

I wonder if Rozelyn wants children one day.

I wonder if *I* want children one day. I've never had to think about it. Children and I live in opposite worlds and I couldn't even begin to presume what they'd need from me. How to be a father.

"Which makes me extremely happy to announce," Lorenzo's voice grows louder, "that I have complete faith the organization will be in good hands. Next week, after the arrangement with New York is finalized and completed"—*meaning when Ariella is wed to Rossi*— "I will be retiring early and Nico will be your new Boss."

If Lorenzo had more to say, he doesn't get the chance because the room breaks out in chaos as cheers and whoops fill the club. Lorenzo's held so much of their respect for decades; he's a wise leader, and he's trained Nico to follow so closely, the others are equally pleased to have him controlling things.

No cheer is louder than Rafael's from the back, who finally finishes pouring the shots.

With a single palm in the air, Lorenzo silences the room again. "With Nico's promotion, I'd like to also announce Rafael will be your new Underboss and Rosen, your new Capo."

If their respect for Nico came out in their cheers, their appreciation of Rafael and Rosen are also apparent in the fresh wave of exclamation. Rafael's liked by so many of them, and Rosen, they see as one of their own. Now, he'll be more of a leader than he already is.

"Congrats," I tell him loudly over the booming cheers.

"Thanks."

A swarm takes him away and Rafael starts handing out shots, hammering back his own in between handing them out. Somewhere in the pit, Nico is tugged in and congratulated over and over. He's grinning as he's shoved toward the bar and handed a few shots from his brother. The two of them toast and knock the glasses back. Nico's so rarely free and happy, it's a strange look on him.

From the silence, a voice calls out, "Who's the new Consigliere then?"

Everyone's cheers cut off, like a switch, and they wait for Nico's response. He looks nearly uncomfortable as he scans the room, his gaze settling on Rosen and Rafael before shrugging. "I have my trusted circle. I don't need a single person by my side."

And then, his eyes meet mine from across the room and he subtly jerks his chin, acknowledging me. Recognizing me as one of his inner circle without making a blatant announcement as such.

My feet shift, a fresh wave of anxiety making me restless, searching for escape. It's an honour to be included in Nico's trust, but it's also a lot to live up to.

A figure takes up Rosen's old spot beside me and without looking, I know it's Lorenzo. His presence grounds me, gives me something to focus on as the soldiers accept Nico's words and cheers fly up again.

"Retirement, huh?"

"It's time." He shifts until he's standing in front of me, blocking my view of the party breaking out all around me. In his palm, he holds up a silver key. "It's also your time."

"My time for what?"

Grabbing my other hand, he rests the key in my palm. It's small in my hand, a cool spot in the centre, right over the scar once placed there by Rozelyn. "To find your future. Caterina and I might have taken you from the streets, but we never saved you, Flynn. You've been lost for years, and Rozelyn was that missing piece. That's a key to a small house a few neighbourhoods away from the mansion. Move out of your room and make a future with her."

The key's demanding my focus, but I can't look away from him. "You bought us a house?"

"Nico's aware you'll be living off-site from now on. You can come to work when he needs you. The two of you shouldn't be camped out in your bedroom. I'll text you the address so you can check it out."

Finally, the pull of the metal brings my attention to my hand. "A house," I repeat. Lorenzo Corsetti got me a house. My own house. With my woman who'll live in it with me. *Mine.* Something I get to claim, to own.

"I never thanked you and Caterina for helping me." Emotion clogs my throat, not used to speaking so openly like this, to him.

"You did." He touches my shoulder, earning my attention again. "In every single day you've been by our side, you've thanked us. This is us saying you're welcome. You're a damn good enforcer, Flynn, but don't live the rest of your life in that basement heartbroken over the past. You can still do your job well and find happiness."

Sincerity shines in his gaze and I wonder when his dislike for Rozelyn switched over to whatever it is I'm now seeing.

With a parting smile, he turns for the crowd, getting pulled in by Rafael, whose glassy glaze tells me he's already headed for a hangover.

The crowd is a lot though. The noise, the cheers, the yelling. It makes the buzzing in my head loud again so with a final sweep of the room, I turn for the exit. Nico catches my eye and nods, knowing exactly what I'm doing.

I'm going to calm the buzz in my mind with the only person who's ever truly succeeded in doing that.

# 42
## ROZELYN

After a half-hour of gripping Flynn so tightly, I'd believe my nails were about to come out of my skin and imbed into his leather coat, everything stops moving. The wind dies. My heart slows to the point of near-death.

Or it's simply because Flynn finally stopped moving. More so, his bike.

He drops the kickstand and pulls off his helmet, but I don't budge. Can't move if I wanted to. My arms are a vise around him, my legs as tight as they can be with the bulging motorcycle between my legs. Everything feels numb.

His heavy palm strokes over my jeans and I feel his heat, so I'm not totally numb. Good to know. "As much as I love the feeling of your legs around me, you gotta let me go." He nods toward the black SUV pulling up beside us. "The rest are here."

"Next time, I'm riding with them." After everyone piled into the SUV, Flynn offered to drive me on his bike and since I've never been on one, and his hopeful expression was too much for me to deny, I figured why not.

Never. Again.

Flynn throws a leg over the bike and turns for me, taking the helmet off my head since my hands are useless, clinging to the bike's seat he abandoned. One by one, he grabs my hands, loosening my hold, and then reaches for my hips, lifting and turning me so I'm seated on the edge, my legs framing his hips.

He tilts my head up and pastes a blistering kiss there. "The fact that *you* fear something in this world has me ecstatic. You were safe. I wouldn't have let anything happen to you."

"I know," I tell him, believing his words. "It doesn't lessen the fact that we drove way too quickly on vehicle that provides no protection."

He chuckles and frames my face. Behind him, everyone has climbed out of the SUV and are watching us, but he doesn't seem bothered by the observations. "You're cute. But they're waiting on you."

"They" being Ariella, Della, Isabelle, and Aurora who stand by the SUV, talking quietly, watching us, as their male counterparts lean against the vehicle, waiting for Flynn and me to finish up.

Behind them, the community garden where I already hear the kids yelling behind the building, out of sight from us. My fear over the trip here is quickly replaced by doubt. Once, coming here was a ploy, which turned into genuine enjoyment. I've never been around little kids enough to understand the ways they see the world, but hanging out with them for the days I had provided a bit of happiness in my grim life.

But it was a part of my father's plots. My old life. Somehow, it's mingling with my new one again and I'm unsure how to feel about this.

"Why did I agree to this?" I whisper, hearing my own anxiety within my tone.

"Because, deep down, you want to." His lips brush over my forehead in a calming motion I hardly knew him capable of. "I'll be right here if it gets too much, but it won't be. You'll make it through, *mon soleil.*"

This morning, Aurora showed up at Flynn's door, looking completely out of place as she shifted foot-to-foot and announced she was vising the garden today and offered me to accompany her. This is her way of trying to heal a broken past she had no part in ruining and it'd be insulting to turn her down. More so, I didn't *want* to. Flynn's correct in that, even if the knots in my stomach suggest otherwise.

Then Della and Ariella joined in "to check it out," Della claimed. She has days left before her sister is married and shipped to New York since Erico Rossi accepted the deal, so I think Della's trying to spend a lifetime with Ariella within this week. Della's still not pleased to be losing her sister, but I guess Ariella wasn't having her mind changed. Isabelle joined in too since everyone else was and she had the day off of work.

I nod, but it's more to myself than him, and slide from the bike with his help. Once I'm standing, Aurora, followed by everyone else, walks forward and after a meaningful look, leads the way to the building to check in.

After they all enter, I glance behind me, spotting Rosen leaning against the hood of the car, talking to Nico and Rafael. Nico's standing beside him, looking entirely out of place in his tailored suit, and Rafael's somehow worse. Seated on the grass in a rumpled suit, he's leaning back on his arms as he peers up at his brother and friend. Standing on Rosen's right is Flynn, who's watching me. His leather jacket and jeans give him a dangerous air, as does the gleaming bike to his left.

They all look dangerous. Made Men completely out of their element, standing in the middle of a field. It's laughable.

"Rozelyn?" Aurora prompts.

Right.

I enter the building.

~

"R oz!"

"Oh my god, Roz, you're back!"

"Why did you leave us?"

That final question almost breaks me.

Kids swarm me, so many familiar faces, as well as some new ones. They all but ignore Aurora, who still visits frequently, and slam into my legs in a giant swarm that has everyone laughing. They're laughing, but I feel like I'm seconds from a breakdown.

Everything's the same. The garden. The peaceful vibe. The memory that while here, I pretended to be normal. I pretended to have been making a genuine friend.

The worst part was always knowing it *was* real, but I had to pretend it wasn't. Shut off the pleasant emotions before I lost my way.

When the kids notice Isabelle, Della, and Ariella, whom they've never met, their short attention spans quickly take them toward the three, who all take turns greeting and getting to know every child.

I wander toward a flower patch of Morning Glory I once tended to. My fingers stroke over the purple petals, soft and packed full of memories that bombard me. Instead of falling into them, I stare into the afternoon sun, using the bold rays to burn away the prickle of tears.

"Hey," a gentle voice approaches. Of course, it's her. Aurora touches my elbow. "You okay?"

"Truthfully," I slide my gaze from the sun to her, and the

punch of emotions returns, "I have no idea. Being here reminds me of all the shitty things I did."

"Why do you think I invited you?" She gives me a partial smile. "We got to start somewhere, Rozelyn, and once, I really enjoyed spending time with you. I want us to be that again."

"I want that too." I mean that statement. "I'm really sorry for what I did."

She shrugs a single shoulder, right as one of the children, Amy, approaches. "Consider it a lengthy nap. No harm. Honestly, I think Rosen and my brothers were more affected by the ordeal than I was."

Amy rushes at me, wrapping her tiny arms around my thighs. "Roz, I missed you so much! Can I show you the rose bush I've been growing?" Then she clutches my hand and with all the strength in her tiny form, pulls my arm, urging me to follow.

After a final smile toward Aurora, I do. Aurora meets my look before turning toward another child.

We'll be all right. In time.

~

Once everyone's piled into the SUV again, I take the second helmet from Flynn's bike and prepare to lower it over my head. He reaches over to help adjust the straps.

"Thought you were gonna take the car?"

"If I survived that," I tip my head to the garden, "then I can survive this death trap."

Instead of laughing, I get a serious, blistering look. "Good. Because I fuckin' love your legs around me, knowing you're on *my* bike."

"Possessive."

With a growl, he lifts me and places me on the back of his bike, fixing my legs for me. "Because I now have something to be possessive about."

Flynn climbs on and quickly gets himself ready. He lifts the kickstand with a foot, which I find incredibly hot, and reaches behind me, placing my hands around his centre, telling me how he wants me to hold him. I shuffle as close as I can as he twists the handle and the bike takes off down the road behind the SUV.

The speed blows my long hair behind me, whipping through the strands, and as terrifying as the pace we're driving at is, I'm coming to appreciate the weightless sensation.

At one point, Flynn leans to the right and I do too, as he's instructed me to, and turns onto a road away from where the SUV with everyone else is headed.

"Where are we going?" I yell, but the winds are too strong for him to probably hear me over, so I'm stuck waiting until we arrive—whenever and wherever that'll be.

He turns into a neighbourhood that I'm struck with an insane amount of familiarity over. But it can't be...even when he takes the same corner my driver once took countless times. The rowhouses I always studied before turning out of view. The short block before approaching the single, huge building surrounded by grass.

"Oh my god," I breathe as Flynn comes to a stop in front of our old high school. The bike's rumble ends and for once, I'm not numb from the ride but rather the onslaught of memories that bombard me all at once.

The largest one, the bench he parks in front.

*The* bench.

Flynn swings himself from the bike and reaches for me,

undoing the helmet, and lifts me from the bike. He has to, since no part of my body is functioning any longer.

"Flynn..."

The school looks so much the same, but signs of age are apparent. The mural on the side, more faded than the fresh paint it had when we attended. Even the grass field around it could use a trim, but since it's summertime and school is out, maintenance standards are less than normal.

"What are we doing here?"

Flynn answers my question by leading me to the bench. With his hands on my shoulders, he pushes me down into the seat but doesn't join me. Not before positioning my hair like a curtain around me, and I know what he's doing. He's recreating our first moment.

Then he stands back to study me. "As beautiful as you looked the first time I saw you."

So I study him back, right down to his ripped jeans and scuffed boots. "As dangerous as the first time I saw you."

Chuckling, he takes the seat beside me, his arm stretching over the back. He fingers my hair as his legs fall open, identical to that first meeting.

"If there's one thing, I never regret, it's that day."

"Me neither."

"Because," he continues like I hadn't spoken, "I now get to call you mine."

The strands of my hair he was petting get gripped by his hand as he yanks on a chunk of my hair and pulls my head back. He moves closer to me, almost over me, his lips brushing over mine as desire courses through my core, making my entire body tight.

"Gonna lock me in your tower then and never let me go?"

He blinks and his gaze goes far away for a moment. Something passes through his head that has him smirking, and with his free hand, he reaches into the pocket of his leather coat, coming out with something in his palm.

Bringing his hand between us, he opens it, revealing what he has.

A key.

"How about I lock you in a house and never let you go?"

# 43



"No! I'm sorry—s-s-sorry! I-I'll get you the money. I swear!"

His excuses slide from him, as slimy as the sweat plastering his hair to his forehead after the hour of begging. He's had his chances though and he pissed off Nico, so this is his price. This fucker thought that Nico taking over as Boss meant control would slip when, in fact, it's tightened.

"Too late. You had your shot. See you in hell."

Between his next scream and his plea, I slam my knife right into his heart. A clean, simple death because Nico didn't want this dragged out too long. Just enough the fucker understood what he did wrong and to send a message to his crew. Also why the kill needed to be clean, so when we drop off the body later, it'll be intact and not in unrecognizable pieces.

Small hands come around my arms, massaging my biceps. "I ever tell you how hot you make me feel when you're in your element."

I turn away from the dead body to haul *mon soleil* to my

chest. "A few times, but I like hearing it." I lower a hand between us, pressing two fingers over her, over her pants. "Or I can just feel it for myself."

After I deliver the news to her.

She grins cheekily and slides her hands up my arms until she's gripping the back of my neck, pulling me down to her height. It puts my face nearest my new favourite part of her body—her collarbone and the tattoo she had done last week. A black and white piece of a full moon, half shadowed by clouds. It was her first tattoo and she did really well through the process and even the healing stages she's still experiencing.

I kiss the inscription *Ma Lune,* which is beneath the moon, every time I have her naked. My favourite piece of artwork has become one not even on my body. It even encompasses the piece I had done for her many years ago, because *I'm* on *her.*

My only regret: not knowing how to tattoo because seeing her flinch when someone else put the needle to her skin had me ready to gut the fucker. Even if he's the same artist that did most of mine and I know it's all part of the process.

"Is it weird to say down here holds so many good memories for me?" She scans the space, pausing on the dead body behind me, barely blinking and that right there guarantees she's the woman for me.

Nico's been understanding to her presence and she's kind of become my partner down here. Of the five kills I've had, this is only her second she's witnessed because I won't allow her down here for any of the torture.

But taking her comment as an opportunity, I say, "Well, let's add another to your list of good memories."

Smiling, she presses herself to me and while my dick wants to take her greenlight, my hands push her away a few inches, disliking the look she gets.

"Soon, but Nico gave me news this morning. Someone's on his way to B.C. to search for your sister."

Her mouth drops open in an O. "Someone here?"

"Someone from the *Famiglia*."

Her forehead dips. "Why would New York care about Yasmine?"

"It was at Ariella's request." She jerks in surprise, answering my next curiosity. "Did you know Yasmine was visiting Ariella in the medical centre?"

Her arms slip from my body. "No. What the hell? When... what?" She shakes her head roughly and looks up again, more determined. "No, that doesn't even make sense. She barely spoke to Ariella, even before the accident."

It's what Nico reported and he too was confused, so I have no answers for her. "I don't know. One of Rossi's men gained Nico's permission to be in the country. They handed over all the information we have on the Seven, and he's on his way to get her out."

She whirls away and heads for the stairs, but before she manages a full three steps, I grab her waist and haul her back to me.

"Flynn," she shoves against me, her ass rubbing over my cock, "I have to go help."

"There's nothing you can do. The more people who show up in B.C., the more questions Nico will get. This is better. He's going undercover with all the information, which keeps the Corsettis' hands clean. This is a better deal than the one you made with Nico. I'd accept it."

Her squirming slows when my hold on her waist is too tight for her to fight and win. With a final huff, she agrees, "Fine. I get it. I guess I should be grateful."

Me too because while I'd never tell her, I've noticed her

growing more and more agitated as the days passed without Nico bringing Yasmine up again.

"We'll wait out the news, Rozelyn, and the moment I know something, you will too."

"Okay."

I bring my hand down the front of her body, pressing her back against my hips, showing her what her movements have done to me. "But if you need help getting your mind off it..."

Her hair whips me in the face as she grins at me and rubs her ass against me. "Here?"

Fucking Rozelyn down here after she came back to apologize wasn't the final time we've done something in the basement, but with the dead body behind us, even I have my limits. Besides, I've grown to really enjoy taking her in our house, which we moved into two weeks ago. Something about fucking her on *our* furniture, against every wall in *our* house, on every surface, speaks to a brutish side of me.

"Let me talk to Nico really quick and we'll go home. Then, *mon soleil*, I'll bend you over the nearest surface and plan to get your mind off everything but sating your pussy."

Her breath hikes and she shivers. "*Ma lune*, yes. I want you to show me all the ways I deserve your love."

Simple.

Accepting.

Because she's mine. We've freed one another from our pasts.

And discovered a balance between love and hate.

Thank you for reading! Continue the series with The Sound in Silence (Fractured Ever Afters #5), a Little Mermaid inspired arranged marriage romance between Ariella & Erico.

Go back to high school and experience Flynn and Rozelyn's growing relationship and first kiss in the FREE bonus scenes! Download on my website.

Shop signed books by scanning the code below:

Lives are spent, sometimes wasted, chasing a dream—a happily-ever-after—only to end up living in reality. Caterina Bellini knows, for a woman, life in the mafia means having her future picked out for her, but even on her wedding day, she continues to dream of a happy ending. Until *he* arrives and snatches her away, locking her inside his own gilded tower, making her a prisoner.

Lorenzo "Enzo" Corsetti is more than a villain though. He's a villain with a need to reclaim what was stolen from him. Driven by revenge and hate, Caterina's a pawn in taking back his empire. In the end, happily-ever-after is a façade and the bad guys always win.

# ALSO BY M.L. PHILPITT

## Fractured Ever Afters

*A 6-book (& 2 novellas) mafia romance series of interconnected standalones based on fairytales, featuring the Montreal mafia and the New York Famiglia.*

The Desire in Deception (Prequel Novella)

The Hunt in Elusion

The Craving in Slumber

The Beauty in Scars

The Freedom in Captivity

The Sound in Silencea

The Obscurity in Wishing

The Bonds in Christmas (Epilogue Novella)

## The Bratva's Elite

*A 4-book mafia series of interconnected standalones featuring the Russian Bratva.*

Merciless Queen

Deadly Knight

Defensive Rook

Violent Pawn

## Captive Writings

*A new adult suspenseful romance series that progressively gets darker with each book*

Ruthless Letters

Obsessive Messages

Vicious Texts

Burning Notes

**Twisted Holidays**

*A series of dark romance holiday novellas*

Silent Night

Egg Hunt

Fright Night

Be Mine

Midnight Kiss

Lucky Clover

**Black Magick**

*A 5-book paranormal romance series of interconnected standalones
featuring witches, vampires, shifters, mortals, and demons.*

Dark Flame

Dark Mist

Dark Storm

**Standalones**

A Vampire for Christmas

**Audiobooks**

Silent Night

# ACKNOWLEDGMENTS

First and foremost, thank you to YOU - my readers.

To my betas: Megan, Colleen, & Lee Jacquot - Thank you!

Thank you to my editor Rebecca Barney from Fairest Reviews Editing Services. Another book down!

To Megan, my PA, who keeps me on track.

Thank you to The Next Step PR. Colleen, Megan, Anna, and of course, Kiki - you're all amazing. Thank you for everything you do. You're the best team to have!

Thank you to Cat Imb of TRC Designs for the gorgeous cover even when I was a pain in the ass over it.

Thank you to Karina (@id_rather.be.the.moon) for double checking my French.

Thank you to all the bloggers, booktokers, and bookstagrammers who helped with the release of this book. Your help doesn't go unnoticed!

# ABOUT THE AUTHOR

USA Today Bestselling author M.L. Philpitt writes both dark romance and paranormal romance. When she's not writing made-up realities, she's reading them. She lives in Canada with her four pets and survives life with coffee and an obsession with fictional characters, especially the morally grey kind. By day, she masks as a therapist.

- Recollections of physical abuse
- Explicit sexual content
- Death
- Recollections of manipulation
- Mention of previous deaths
- Mention of terminal illness
- Depictions of trauma
- Blood play
- Captivity
- Emotional abuse
- Murder
- Knife play
- Dubious consent
- Orgasm denial
- Anal play
- Degregation
- Physical violence